T0248141

MURDER IN AN
ITALIAN
CAFÉ

Books by Michael Falco

MURDER IN AN ITALIAN VILLAGE

MURDER IN AN ITALIAN CAFÉ`

Published by Kensington Publishing Corp.

MURDER IN AN
ITALIAN
CAFÉ

MICHAEL FALCO

Kensington Publishing Corp.
www.kensingtonbooks.com

KENSINGTON BOOKS are published by

Kensington Publishing Corp.
900 Third Avenue
New York, NY 10022

All Kensington titles, imprints, and distributed lines are available at special quantity discounts for bulk purchases for sales promotion, premiums, fund-raising, educational, or institutional use.

Special book excerpts or customized printings can also be created to fit specific needs. For details, write or phone the office of the Kensington Special Sales Manager: Attn. Special Sales Department, Kensington Publishing Corp., 900 Third Avenue, New York, NY 10022. Phone: 1-800-221-2647.

KENSINGTON and the KENSINGTON COZIES teapot logo Reg. US Pat. & TM Off.

Library of Congress Card Catalogue Number: 2024936516

ISBN: 978-1-4967-4216-2
First Kensington Hardcover Edition: October 2024

ISBN: 978-1-4967-4218-6 (ebook)

10 9 8 7 6 5 4 3 2 1

Printed in the United States of America

This book is dedicated to my Italian ancestors who instilled in me my core belief that without family, friendship, and food you cannot survive.

And here's hoping that they don't hold my garlic allergy against me.

Thank you yet again to my agent, Evan Marshall, and the entire Kensington team—my editor, John Scognamiglio; my copy editor, Rosemary Silva; cover illustrator David Doran and cover designer Kristine Noble, who turn every single cover into a work of art; and Miss Publicity herself, Larissa Ackerman.

Thank you all for sharing my words with the world for more than a decade.

MURDER IN AN
ITALIAN
CAFÉ

CHAPTER 1

Late September in Positano was like the last moments of a dream. A fantasy that was so mesmerizing, it couldn't possibly be real. And yet it was.

In this village nestled on Italy's legendary Amalfi Coast, every sense was catered to and embraced, especially at this time of year. The breeze was heavy with sweet lavender and sea salt; the sky a swath of blue that resembled a wave of joy. The chirps and cries of the sparrows and gulls could be heard alongside the sighs and murmurs of the entranced tourists, whose sun-kissed skin felt almost as smooth and soft as the sand of Positano's famous beaches. And the pasta, the sauces, the vegetables, the desserts on the tables of every home and café were overflowing with mouthwatering flavors enhanced by that special ingredient Italians were famous for—love.

Positano was a world like no other. A world that Bria Bartolucci now called home. And Bella Bella—the bed-and-breakfast she owned and in which she lived—was quickly becoming almost as popular as the village itself.

"I'm giving Bella Bella four stars!" Even though the woman who shouted that declaration had a shrill New York accent, the words were still music to Bria's ears. They were validation. Bria's hard work was paying off.

"Harvey and I have traveled all over the world, but this place is like heaven on earth!" The woman reached out and grabbed Bria's hand. "And you—*bella signora*—have been like our very own angel."

"Grazie mille." Bria handed the woman a small bag with the Bella Bella logo on it—a graphic design of the bright pink B and B set against a clear blue sky and a golden sun. "This is for your trip home, Patsy. It's the *bomboloni* your husband likes so much. I made some fresh this morning."

"Oh my God!" Patsy snatched the bag from Bria's hands and held it close to her nose. She inhaled deeply and let out a sound that reminded Bria of a ship's foghorn. Only louder. "Harvey *loves* these! A doughnut stuffed with chocolate is like Christmas morning to a retired New York City police officer."

"It's a long trip home," Bria said. "I want you to take a little bit of Positano back with you."

"We're taking so much more with us." Patsy looked around the room, and tears started to form in her eyes. "Memories that will last a lifetime."

"Che meraviglia. Grazie." Bria swallowed hard to prevent tears from welling in *her* eyes. "You and Harvey have a safe trip back home."

Rivaling the passion that Anna Magnani exuded in her Academy Award–winning performance in *The Rose Tattoo*, Patsy gazed longingly at something just beyond Bria's left shoulder. "Arrivederci, Positano!" Grandly, Patsy turned and exited through the front door. Less than five seconds later, she returned with a half-eaten *bombolone* raised to the sky and a delirious grin on her face. Patsy looked like Anna Magnani right after she had *won* her Oscar. "Bria Bartolucci! You and Bella Bella just earned yourselves *five* stars!"

Bria laughed as she watched Patsy exit—just as grandly—a second time, but soon the tears she had tried to restrain sprang from her eyes. Quickly, she wiped them away and silently chastised herself for becoming so emotional. Patsy was simply happy to have dessert at eight a.m., before beginning her thirteen-hour journey back home, so there was no reason to react like a *stolta*. Yet Bria didn't feel foolish; she felt proud.

Running the bed-and-breakfast that her late husband, Carlo, had bought for them was no longer a dream. It was a dream come true. There had been times when Bria didn't think she would prevail, when she thought no matter how hard she tried, she wouldn't succeed without her husband by her side. There had been times when she wanted to sell the place, give up, and leave Positano for the safety and security of her parents' home. For many reasons, she stayed.

She wanted to show her son, Marco, that it was always better to confront a challenge than to cower from one. She wanted to honor her late husband's vision for their future. Mainly, she wanted to prove to herself what she had begun to question—that she had the strength to survive, and even flourish, in the aftermath of such devastating loss and pain.

When she received the news that Carlo had died in a plane crash only a few months after they had moved to Positano from Rome, Bria felt as if her world had died along with her husband. Every hope and wish she had for her future included Carlo and their son, Marco. Their little family had become a triangle, three connected souls that could exist only if all three remained intact. Without Carlo, Bria and Marco's life was suddenly adrift, missing a vital element, and Bria truly didn't know if they would survive. One look into her son's eyes and Bria knew she didn't have a choice.

Renewed, Bria was determined to turn Bella Bella into the dream Carlo had envisioned. A place where travelers from all over the world could gather to experience the almost surreal beauty that Positano had to offer, could share their journey with other like-minded visitors, and might ignite a passion in Marco about the world that lay outside the village's borders. Enlisting the help of family, friends, and her new neighbors, Bria accomplished her goal. There was no denying it. Bella Bella was a success.

It wasn't just Patsy who had told Bria that their stay had exceeded expectations, it was almost all her guests. Bria was grateful and humbled by their praise, of course, but Bria was also competitive. It didn't matter if she had entered her painting in an art contest, if she had to defend her collegiate fencing championship, or if she wanted to have a satisfied customer. Her motivation was the same: she wanted to win.

And win she did. Bria felt as if she had just won millions of euros in the once-a-year Lotteria Italia drawing after buying only one ticket. But she knew she had not done it all by herself. She'd had help.

Her parents, Fifetta and Franco, had given her not only moral support but also practical advice, since for several decades, they had run Mondo dei Sogni, a banquet hall in Ravello, the mountaintop village perched high above the town of Amalfi. The hall had become *the* destination for weddings on the Amalfi Coast, thanks in part to its name, which in English meant "Dreamland." Who wouldn't want to start off their married life in the land of dreams?

Her *migliore amica* from the time she was thirteen years old, Rosalie was Bria's sounding board, confidant, and crisis manager. If she needed to choose a paint color for the bedroom walls, if she needed to test out a new recipe, or if she simply needed a shoulder to cry on, Rosalie was the first person Bria called for help.

Whenever Bria doubted herself or felt overwhelmed, she simply needed to think of her son, Marco, and those emotions were washed away with a wave of unconditional love. As was the case for most Italian mothers, thoughts of her child made Bria forget any sorrow that clung to her heart. If any worry did remain, Bria just had to think of the king of Bella Bella, her dog, Bravo. The two-year-old Segugio Italiano with the lean tan body and the long floppy ears was as irresistible as the unnaturally scenic Positano landscape.

Then there was Giovanni Monteverdi. Her blond-haired guy Friday with the bulging muscles and man bun was much more than her employee: he had become an indispensable member of her family. He cooked, he cleaned, he repaired repairs Bria didn't know were in need of repair, and he had—without her prodding or requesting—taken on the role of Marco's fun uncle. He helped the young boy improve his soccer skills, showed him how to perfectly skewer a wiggling worm on a fishhook, and even taught him how to make his bed.

Bria was glad that she hadn't listened to the villagers who told her Giovanni was nothing more than a *ladruncolo* and not someone who could be trusted. It was true that Giovanni had a shady history, but it was also true that he had overcome his troubled past to become an upstanding Positanese. There were still some members of the village who questioned Giovanni's transformation, and Bria knew she wasn't going to change their minds with words. Instead, she made it known that she trusted Giovanni with her son's life. For an Italian, that should be enough proof.

So lost in thought was Bria that she didn't immediately hear the noise in the back of the house. She went into the kitchen to look out the window and saw that it was Giovanni replacing a tile that had broken, thanks to the overgrown roots of an overzealous lemon tree. Bravo was sitting in the shade, overseeing the project, his eyes half-closed, and his tongue falling out of his mouth and looking almost as long as his ears. This was no time for work, however; this was time for a celebration.

Bria pulled two small jelly glasses from the kitchen cupboard and grabbed the bottle of limoncello from the counter. It was a common brand sold locally in all the gift shops that dotted the village, but quite good. Bria wanted to create her own concoction and call it Bella Bella Limoncella, but she hadn't yet figured out the perfect special ingredient to add to the traditional recipe that would give it a unique taste. Until then, she'd drink like a tourist.

With the bottle in one hand and the two glasses in the other, Bria walked outside and then down the small alleyway to the right of the building to join Giovanni in the backyard. Before she was even visible, Bravo started barking. "It's just me, *angioletto*."

When Bria entered the backyard, she saw that while Giovanni was working, Bravo was still sitting in the shade. He hadn't barked to ward off any intruders, he had just said hello. Then again, who needed a guard dog when they had a handyman who looked like Giovanni?

"*'Giorno*, Bria."

"Morning, Vanni." Bria placed the glasses down on the small patio table, unscrewed the cap off the limoncello bottle, and started to pour the sweet yellow liquid into the glasses. "It's break time."

Giovanni wiped the sweat off his brow with the back of his forearm, and the golden hairs on his arm glistened in the early morning sun. "Isn't it a bit early for limoncello?"

"*Sciocchezza!*" Bria handed one glass to Giovanni and raised hers in the air. "*Brindiamo al nostro successo!*"

"Why are we drinking to success?" Giovanni asked.

"Because we're successful."

Giovanni furrowed his brow, making his green eyes squint, and with his free hand, he tucked a long strand of blond hair that had escaped the rubber band that held his man bun in place. "*Scusa*, that isn't true."

"*Che cosa*? How can you say that?" Bria gulped her glass of limoncello and resumed speaking before Vanni could answer her questions. "We've been booked solid since May, almost every guest steals the lemon-scented soaps from their bathrooms, and Patsy, the woman from New York who just left, is going to give us a five-star rating!"

"I know all of that," Vanni replied. "Except the part about Patsy, which is *fantastico*."

It was Bria's turn to furrow her brow. "Then how can you say we're not a success?"

"We're not a success." Giovanni smiled at Bria, his green eyes now sparkling instead of squinting. "You are."

Maybe it was because Italians talked so much and talked so quickly that the power of words could sometimes get lost. It was good to be reminded that what a person said had an impact. Which was why when Bria spoke, she maintained eye contact with Giovanni. She wanted to make sure he understood how sincere she was. "You, Giovanni Monteverdi, are one of the main reasons Bella Bella is so successful. I could not have done any of this without you."

Vanni swallowed hard and blushed. He tried to hold Bria's gaze but couldn't. He looked over at Bravo and smiled. "Looks like the limoncello's gone to your mamma's head."

"*Forse, ma è la verità.* You have been instrumental in turning this place into one of the most popular B and B's in the village." Bria sat at the table and poured herself another glass. "Should I list all the things that you've done since we've opened, not to mention everything you did leading up to opening day? Repairing the central cooling system, repainting all the rooms, creating new recipes for the menu, carrying luggage up and down the stairs . . ."

"*Va bene, basta!*" Vanni shook his head but couldn't completely hide the smile that was forming on his lips. He sat down across from Bria and raised his glass toward her. *"Al nostro successo!"*

Bria watched Giovanni drink to their shared success, and it filled her with joy. This time, however, she took only a sip of her drink. She had a full day ahead of her, and she knew that if she gulped down two glasses of Positano's favorite beverage, she wouldn't make it past noon.

"Un'altra cosa," Bria said. "Without you, I don't think Marco would ever get to school on time."

Giovanni could no longer hide his smile; in fact, it grew and was accompanied by a belly laugh. "When I dropped Marco off this morning, Sister Benedicta said she still wasn't used to him arriving before the morning school bell chimed."

Bria couldn't blame Marco's favorite teacher, whom most everyone called Sister B, for her comment, because Bria knew it was the truth. It was hard being a single mother as well as a small business owner, and so certain responsibilities and tasks were sometimes overlooked, which was why she was so thankful to have Giovanni in her life. Even when he was telling her things she didn't like to hear.

"Have you, by any chance, spoken to your mother?" he asked.

"This morning? No."

"What about your mother-in-law?"

"Imperia? Not for a few days." Sensing trouble, Bria leaned in closer. *"Perché?* Is something wrong?"

"That depends."

"On what?"

"If we can trust Annamaria."

"Uffa!" Bria grabbed her glass and downed the rest of the limoncello. Tipsy head or not, she was going to need it to hear the rest of what Giovanni had to say.

Annamaria Antonelli was affectionally known as *le chiac-*

chierona di Positano, a moniker she embraced because she couldn't argue the fact that she was the biggest gossip in the village. If something happened, Annamaria knew about it, which was why Bria was anxious to hear what she knew about her mother and her mother-in-law.

"What did she say about my mother and Imperia?"

"They've been squabbling."

"Squabbling?"

"Yes. Over Marco."

"*Non può essere vero*," Bria declared. "They both love Marco. They would never fight over him."

"It's not a fight about him," Vanni clarified. "More of a fight over his Holy Communion."

"*Vabbè*," Bria said. "That makes more sense."

Traditionally, Holy Communion ceremonies were held in May. Because May was the beginning of the major tourist season in Positano and the weather was quite hot during that time of year, Sister Eugenia, the Mother Superior at St. Cecilia's Grammar School, petitioned to move the ceremony to October. It was a bold request and one that the archdiocese did not initially grant. Sister Eugenia, however, was a persuasive and skilled debater and pointed out that World Communion Day was celebrated in October and the Communion ceremony could be promoted as part of the Church's global outreach program. Ultimately, Sister Eugenia got her way.

Since the announcement, both Fifetta and Imperia had been badgering Bria to make a decision about Marco's party. Her mother wanted to have it at their banquet hall in Ravello, and Imperia wanted to have it on her yacht, which was docked at the marina in Positano, near Rosalie's tour boat. The only thing both women agreed on was that Bria's initial suggestion to hold the party at Bella Bella was inappropriate. They felt the B and B was much too small to be the venue for such an important milestone.

Bria agreed with them and was also concerned about how she would throw a family party at the B and B and still cater to her paying guests, but she couldn't tell them that, because then she'd have to choose one of their solutions. Her choices were to betray her mother or suffer her mother-in-law's wrath. Instead, Bria decided to avoid the subject. She had time to deal with the situation later. It wasn't even October yet, Marco's Communion was weeks away.

"Do me a favor, Giovanni."

"*Certo. Cosa vuoi?*"

"If either my mother or Imperia calls for me," Bria said, "tell them I ran away with Bravo."

The sound of his name roused the dog from his state of semiconsciousness, and he stretched and then let out a loud yawn. Bria got up from her chair and patted her thigh. In an instant, Bravo was at her side.

"I don't want to dwell on any squabbling," Bria announced. "*Andiamo*, Bravo. Let's take a walk through our beautiful village."

Despite the growing suspicion that the minor family strife created by the uncharacteristic argument between Marco's grandmothers was going to develop into major turmoil, Bria allowed herself to bask in the warm September sunshine as she, with Bravo a few steps ahead, walked into the village. Viale Pasitea, the main street in Positano, which curved from top to bottom like a long, lazy snake, was less crowded this time of year than during the high season, but the narrow road was hardly empty even at this time in the morning. There were cars and delivery trucks moving in both directions; Vespas, scooters, and three-wheelers, whose drivers didn't always follow the rules of the road; and, of course, tourists beguiled by the sublime landscape. It was an obstacle course that Bria and Bravo luckily had experience navigating.

As she walked, Bria listened to the sparrows chirp an impromptu melody, their sounds punctuated by the crunch of the dirt underneath her espadrilles—which she considered her salvation and the only shoes she would ever wear when walking through the steep village. She let the smell of the orange trees and lavender bushes waft over her and felt the mixture of the cool wind from the sea and the warmer air from inland caress her face and bare arms. She looked out at the glorious beachfront below and still couldn't believe this was where she lived.

Even though the English translation of *Positano* was "a place to stay," most people just visited. Built into the side of the craggy prehistoric Lattari Mountains, Positano was a marvel of modern-day architecture. As inhospitable as it was inviting, as isolated as it was welcoming, and as mysterious as it was recognizable. Say the name Positano to anyone and images of paradise would fill their minds. It *was* paradise, but Bria had learned very quickly that it was so much more. It was home.

When they rounded the bend, they could see behind Enrico's store, Flowers by Enrico, and Bria smiled when she saw Enrico and Paolo playing bocce. She wasn't surprised that Enrico was taking advantage of some leisure time before he opened his store, but she didn't expect to find Paolo next to him, throwing his bright green bocce in an effort to hit the smaller white *pallino*. As the owner of the largest parking lot in the village, one that was open twenty-four hours a day, Paolo didn't have much leisure time.

"*Buongiorno, signori!*" Bria called out to the men as Bravo raced over to join them on the small patch of grass.

"*'Giorno*, Bria!" Enrico cried. "*Buongiorno*, Bravo, *mio amico.*"

Bravo lay down on the grass and rolled onto his back to give Enrico unrestricted access to his belly. Enrico didn't disappoint and dutifully rubbed Bravo's stomach, making the dog's tongue, once again, flop out of his mouth.

"*Buongiorno*, Bria," Paolo said.

"*'Giorno*," Bria replied. "Who's minding the parking lot?"

"My nephew, Michele, started working for me as a mechanic in the garage so he can watch the lot when it's slow." Paolo started to gather up the stray balls as it appeared they had ended a frame. "Now I have some free time to let Enrico beat me at bocce."

"For every game I let him win, he gives me a free day of parking," Enrico said.

"*Che carino*," Bria said. "*Però* I didn't realize you had family nearby, Paolo."

Before Paolo answered, Bria noticed that he glanced at Enrico, who nodded his head slightly before throwing a twig, which Bravo rambunctiously ran after to retrieve. It was as if Paolo was asking for permission to speak or seeking reassurance that Bria could be trusted. It was evident by his reply that Paolo was being cautious with what he was willing to share.

"*È complicato*," Paolo replied.

"Most things that have to do with family are complicated," Bria replied. "I just found out that my mother and Imperia may be getting ready to go to war with each other."

"My money's on Fifetta." Enrico picked up the twig Bravo had dropped from his mouth and threw it to the other side of the yard. "Imperia looks tough, but your mamma is *una donna forte*."

"*Conta le tue benedizioni*, Bria," Paolo said. "Not all mothers are strong."

Bria paused a moment before replying because she sensed Paolo wanted to expand on what he had said, but he remained silent. "I assume your nephew just moved here. Otherwise Annamaria would've told me all about him."

"*Le chiacchierona di Positano* hasn't even met him yet," Paolo said.

"*Dio mio!*" Bria cried. "You mean there's something that the village gossip doesn't know?"

"Annamaria hasn't been herself lately," Enrico said. "*Preoccupata* and making a lot of secret phone calls."

"*Veramente?*" Bria said. "I've been so busy I haven't noticed."

"Mimi tried to talk to her to find out if something was wrong, but for once, Annamaria kept her mouth shut." Enrico took the twig from Bravo again, but this time he held it in his hand rather than throwing it, causing Bravo to drop to the ground and sulk.

"There's a first time for everything," Bria said. "*Vieni qui*, Bravo. It's time to go."

Reluctantly, Bravo rose from his position to join Bria, who was already walking down the road. "*Addio*, Paolo. I look forward to meeting your nephew."

This time Bria expected Paolo to hesitate before he replied, and he didn't disappoint her. "*Certo*. I'll make sure to bring him around."

Even though Bria suspected Paolo was hiding something from her, she was more concerned about Annamaria. Not gossiping and making secret phone calls was not like Annamaria at all. The woman loved to talk and lived for gossip. Despite her chattiness, she was beloved, not only because she had a good heart but also because she made the best coffee and pastries on all of the Amalfi Coast.

Caffè Positano was the most popular café in town. It was cozy and inviting, every item on the menu was delicious, and it was a perfect place to relax with an iced cappuccino. Which was suddenly what Bria's body was craving, most likely to counter the effects of her early morning limoncello. When she tried to open the front door, she knew something was very wrong. The café wasn't open.

"This doesn't make sense, Bravo. Annamaria's café opens at seven a.m. every morning." Bria looked at her watch. "It's almost nine."

Bria had started to walk to the side of the café, thinking Annamaria might be on the back patio, when the front door suddenly burst open. She whipped around and saw Annamaria locking the door, her cheeks growing red and her ample bosom rising up and down with each breath. "Annamaria! What's wrong?"

When Annamaria saw Bria, she shrieked and ran toward her friend. "*Niente*, Bria. Everything is *perfetto*!"

"Why is the café locked?"

"Because I have to get ready for the filming tomorrow."

"What filming?"

"For the new cooking show!"

"Whose show?"

"Chef Lugo's!"

Annamaria didn't have to say another word; Bria understood exactly why her friend was so excited. Luigi Gordonato—or Chef Lugo for short—was a celebrity chef known for applying modern culinary touches to traditional southern Italian dishes. Bria had used some of his recipes for her own menu at Bella Bella. Now she might get to meet the chef in person.

"I just got off the phone with his manager. He's been calling me for the past week but swore me to secrecy!"

Now Annamaria's anxiety and secret phone calls, which Enrico had talked about, made sense. When the town gossip had the juiciest gossip in years but couldn't tell a soul, of course she'd be anxious.

"Massimo—he's the manager—told me that Chef Lugo has a new book coming out. *Amalfi Toast: Italian Family Recipes.*

And he's going to start his book tour right here in Positano," Annamaria explained.

"You don't sell books. Mimi does," Bria said. "Why isn't he starting his book tour at A Word from Positano?"

"He is, but first, he's going to turn Caffè Positano into a TV studio and film the first episode of his new series right here!"

"Che emozione!"

"Mark my words, Bria, this is going to be the most exciting thing that's happened in the village in years!"

Bria had no idea how right her friend was.

CHAPTER 2

When Bria got back to Bella Bella, there was more excitement waiting for her. As the owner of a B and B, Bria was used to having strangers in her home, but typically, those strangers had reservations. The three people who were standing in the dining area with luggage scattered around their feet looked like guests, and yet she knew that the online reservation portal that she and Giovanni had spent hours refining was empty. Bria would have addressed one of the three strangers directly if it weren't for the presence of her best friend, Rosalie, among the group.

"Rosalie, would you mind explaining what's going on?"

Bria waited for the response and expected her friend to relay some outrageous story of how her tour boat passengers had been stranded in Positano, but Rosalie didn't say a word. She wasn't trying to be obstinate; she simply couldn't speak. She gasped for breath and bent over, placing her hands on her knees.

"Use your inhaler," Bria said.

In response, Rosalie raised her right arm and opened her clenched fist to reveal her inhaler. A lifelong asthma sufferer, Rosalie never went anywhere without her inhaler, in case she suffered an asthma attack, like she appeared to be now. Bent over, her curly reddish-brown hair bobbing up and down with each labored breath, Rosalie took another hit from her inhaler and within moments was upright and breathing normally again. Her cheeks still matched the color of her hair, but otherwise Rosalie looked like her old self. When she spoke, she sounded like it, too.

"*Fammi un favore*, Bria. Build an escalator from the beach up to this place," Rosalie barked. "No human being should be expected to walk up four hundred steps."

"Why didn't you take your scooter?" Bria asked.

"Mariana took the Piaggio to Praiano to pick up some pickles," Rosalie explained. "A pickle manufacturer from Ireland reserved the boat for a party this weekend, and there's a deli in Praiano that marinates them in garlic, lemons, *quello che vuoi*. You know I like to make my guests feel at home when they tour with me."

Rosalie ran a tour boat company, and the tour boat, *La Vie en Rosalie*, also doubled as her home. She moved to Positano before Bria and was the one who told Carlo that the B and B he eventually bought was for sale. Having her best friend living only ten minutes away was a huge selling point for Bria and one of the reasons she immediately agreed to alter the course of her family's life and relocate. Having a best friend like Rosalie living nearby also made life relentlessly interesting.

"*Va bene*, but why did you walk up the stairs?" Bria asked. "You know it sets off your asthma."

"*Prego*, it's because of me."

Bria turned to face the young woman standing next to Rosalie. She looked to be in her early twenties, was petite, and had long black hair, which was pulled back into a ponytail. By her olive complexion, Roman nose, and accent, Bria was rather certain she was a native of Italy.

"This is Pippa," Rosalie said. "She needs a place to stay."

"*Certo*. For the first time in months, we're completely empty."

"Not entirely."

This time Bria turned to face the tall man standing on the opposite side of Rosalie. He was twice Pippa's size and at least three times her age. His hair, while thinning, was still blond, and his accent, while slight, was definitely not Italian. Bria had been exposed to many different nationalities in the short time Bella Bella had been open, and she easily detected that his native language was German.

"We made a reservation early this morning with Giovanni under the name Tobias Kruger." The man grabbed the hand of the woman standing next to him. "One room for me and my wife, Daisy."

"*Molto bene,*" Bria replied. "Vanni is my assistant."

Rosalie raised her eyebrows and muttered, "Is that what you're calling him these days?"

Bria glared at Rosalie but didn't lose her smile or her train of thought. "We have enough rooms for all of you, *nessun problema.*"

"*Grazie.*" While Daisy was roughly the same age as Tobias, her features and accent were similar to Pippa's. But Bria had never heard of an Italian woman named Daisy.

"*Perdonami.* Are you Italian?" Bria asked.

"*Sì.* I was born in Positano." Daisy looked up at her husband and smiled. "My name is Daisetta—*strano*, I know—but everyone's called me Daisy since I was a baby."

"*Come è divertente!*" Pippa cried. "My full name is Papina Elisabetta Maria Del Baglivio, but no one's ever called me anything but Pippa."

"Daisy, do you know Annamaria Antonelli or Enrico Taglieri?" Bria asked. "They're roughly your age, and they've both lived here all their lives."

"I don't know anyone," Daisy said. "My family left when I was very little."

"To my good fortune, she moved to Munich." Tobias put his arm around Daisy. "We met as children, but it took me twenty years to make her my wife."

"We've come back here for a second honeymoon, so I could show Tobias where I was born," Daisy said.

"If you planned a second honeymoon, why didn't you make hotel reservations?" Bria asked.

"We had reservations at Casa Violetta, but there was a mix-up, and it was canceled," Tobias explained.

"They were completely booked when we arrived, which is why we called here," Daisy added.

"*Sono così dispiaciuta*," Bria said. "I know Violetta, and I'm sure it was an honest mistake."

"*Tutto è bene quel che finisce bene*," Rosalie said.

"*Grazie Dio!*" Pippa put her hand over her heart almost as dramatically as Patsy had earlier. "I'm glad it all ended well, too. If I didn't find a room, Massimo would have killed me."

Massimo? Where did Bria just hear that name? *Yes! Chef Lugo's manager.*

"Are you working on Chef Lugo's new TV show?" Bria asked.

"How do you know about that already?" Rosalie asked. "I wanted it to be a surprise."

"I bumped into Annamaria earlier. She told me the whole thing," Bria said. "How did you find out?"

Rosalie lifted her chin and smiled smugly. "Massimo told me."

"How do you know Chef Lugo's manager?"

"He stopped by the marina this morning to book my boat to film some shots of the coast to use in his show," Rosalie explained. "Massimo Angelini isn't just Chef Lugo's manager. He's also the producer of his new series."

"*Che meraviglia!*" Bria squealed. "Your business will get so much publicity!"

"Massimo's also my boss," Pippa added. "I'm a production

assistant, and like Tobias said, most of the hotels were already booked."

"So I told Massimo about Bella Bella, and he said he'd book a room for Pippa," Rosalie said.

"*Scusate*, who's this Chef Lugo?" Daisy asked.

"Only the most famous chef in the world," Rosalie declared.

"He's not that famous . . . yet," Pippa said.

"He will be," Rosalie said. "If my boat has anything to say about it."

"Massimo hopes that this TV series and book tour will make Chef Lugo a household name," Pippa added. "The next Salvatore De Riso."

"To think it's all going to start right here in the village," Bria gushed. "They're going to film the show at Caffè Positano tomorrow morning."

"The real excitement starts tonight," Rosalie said. "Massimo is inviting almost everyone in town to Le Sirenuse for a kickoff party."

"*Uffa*! That's very generous of him," Bria said. "Le Sirenuse is beautiful, but *molto costoso*."

"It's a business strategy, his way of thanking the village for letting us film here," Pippa explained. "*Prego*, I really need to get to my room so I can start sending out those invitations. Massimo will kill me if no one shows up."

Just as Bria was going to shout for Giovanni, he emerged from one of the upstairs bedrooms. "*Ciao a tutti*. Your rooms are ready."

"Vanni will help you all settle in," Bria said. "In the meantime, I need to get ready for a party."

When four Neapolitan siblings turned their summer home into a hotel in 1951, they could never have imagined that over half a century later, it would still be the most luxurious spot in Positano. Le Sirenuse was the epitome of cosmopolitan flair, harking back to a bygone era when men wore tuxedos to dinner and women accessorized their Oleg Cassini bathing suits with expensive jewelry. Named after the mythological sirens who lured sailors with their irresistible singing, Le Sirenuse continued to be a tempting destination for tourists from all over the world.

When Bria first came to the village, Carlo promised that he'd take her to the hotel for a few days to celebrate the start of their new journey. However, once they began working on turning Bella Bella into their own B and B, renovations, paperwork, and marketing their new business took precedence over leisure. The *spaghetti alle vongole* prepared by master chef Gennaro Russo would have to wait.

After Carlo died, Bria put aside thoughts of dining at the cliffside restaurant, with its breathtaking views of Marina Grande Beach, in favor of creating new ways for Marco to eat his vegetables. Now the idea of attending a party at Franco's Bar, the outdoor lounge at the hotel, filled her with anticipation. She felt like a little girl playing dress-up for the first time. A little girl wearing a wedding band.

Bria looked at herself in the mirror and wasn't sure she knew the woman looking back at her. Who was Bria Bartolucci? Mother, business owner, artist . . . Yes, she was all of those, but she was also a single woman. Recently turned thirty-three and was still young, with decades of life ahead of her. Then why couldn't she start that new life by taking off the slim band of gold that encircled the ring finger on her left hand? She twisted the metal, and although it moved freely and could easily be pulled off, it felt like a vise etched into her flesh, a permanent reminder of the past.

"*Non ancora,*" she whispered to her reflection.

She wasn't ready to let go of her husband. Not yet.

How could she when the most important man in her life reminded her of Carlo every day? Marco stood in the doorway of

Bria's bedroom, barefoot, his hair mussed from playing with Bravo, and the juice from the peach he was eating smeared across his mouth and chin. He took Bria's breath away, and she had to sit on her bed for fear of falling to her knees. Everything that was important to her, everything that she cherished was standing before her, wearing a crooked smile and a Pinocchio T-shirt.

"Mamma," Marco said. *"Sei bellissima."*

"Grazie, bambino mio," Bria said.

"I'm a boy, Mamma. Not a baby."

Laughing, Bria got up—confident that she had regained her strength enough to walk—and knelt down in front of her son. "You will always be *mio bambino*, even when you're old and gray."

"Like Nonno Franco?"

"Yes, just like Nonno Franco."

Marco scrunched up his forehead, and Bria knew he was thinking over what she had said. *"Bene,* as long as you'll always be my mamma."

Marco's words struck Bria with a jumble of pain and pleasure. She felt like she'd been pierced by a knife and then placed on a feather-soft cloud. Motherhood could be complicated.

Shaking her head and trying to prevent her tears from ruining her make-up, Bria hugged her son tightly. He didn't squirm in her arms; he needed the hug as much as she did. Bria, however, didn't need peach juice rolling down her cheek and onto her dress. *"Scusami, amore mio."* She went into the bathroom, wet a hand towel under the faucet, and dabbed her face with the cloth. Juice free, she dropped the towel into the laundry basket next to the sink and left the room to follow the sound of Marco's voice.

"Marco, who are you talking to?" When Bria entered the main room, she had her answer. Though not the one she was expecting.

"I'm talking to your date," Marco said. "Luca."

Luca Vivaldi was Rosalie's older brother, the chief of police in Positano, and the first man Bria had looked at in the same way she once looked at Carlo. Luca was also the first man to look at Bria the way Carlo used to look at her. Up until now they had only looked at each other, maybe flirted a bit, but their relationship was strictly platonic. They were friends, nothing more.

"Marco!" Bria cried. "Luca isn't my date."

"But he's all dressed up, too," Marco said.

"That's good detective work, Marco," Luca said. "But it only means that your mamma and I are going to the same party."

"Don't forget the sister."

Bria always found it odd when Rosalie and Luca stood side by side, because they looked nothing alike. Luca had black hair, which he almost always slicked back, like he had it now, light brown eyes, olive skin, and a lean build. Rosalie had curly reddish-brown hair, black eyes, a lighter complexion, and a curvy body. They could have passed for distant cousins, but not necessarily siblings. Physical dissimilarities notwithstanding, they shared an unbreakable bond.

Luca was the older brother who treated Rosalie more like a daughter than a sister. While Rosalie, a free spirit, made fun of her brother's responsible nature, she greatly respected him. They were proud of each other, but like most brothers and sisters, they preferred to tease each other instead of expressing what was in their hearts. Marco did not have that problem.

"*Ciao*, Rosalie," Marco said. "I love your costume."

Before Bria could scold Marco for using what she considered to be an inappropriate word to describe a woman's outfit, Rosalie scooped Marco up off the floor and twirled him in circles. His word choice, however, wasn't that off the mark. Rosalie was wearing a sleeveless green jumpsuit that highlighted all her curves, and attached to the collar was a floor-length color-blocked silk cape in red, white, and green. When she twirled around with Marco in her arms, she looked like she was waving the Italian flag.

"Mamma, I want a cape," Marco declared.

"You can borrow mine after tonight," Rosalie said.

"*Freddo!*" Marco cried.

"Now, *il mio topolino*, it's time for bed," Bria said. "Giovanni will tuck you in."

"*Buona notte*," Marco said.

Rosalie and Luca took turns hugging and kissing Marco and watched him scamper off to his room. Bravo roused from his nap in a corner of Bria's bedroom and raced after him. When the three adults were left alone, there was a moment of awkward silence as Bria and Luca stared at each other. Rosalie, in her unique way, was able to break the silence and make things even more awkward.

"Did you two decide to dress as twins?"

Whereas Rosalie gravitated toward a more rule-breaking wardrobe, Luca tended to be a traditionalist, and now he wore a simple navy blue suit, a white dress shirt, and black loafers without socks. The only dash of color was the pink satin handkerchief that had been tucked, nonchalantly, into the breast pocket of his jacket. It was a classic look and one that mirrored Bria's.

She had chosen a navy satin sheath dress, cut above the knee, with three-quarter sleeves. Formfitting, yet elegant. What made the dress give the impression that she and Luca had gone shopping at a his and hers fancy party clothing store was the pink sash around her waist, the exact same color as Luca's pocket square. The choices seemed deliberate, and perhaps they were. Everyone knew Bria's favorite color was pink. Maybe Luca was trying to send Bria a subliminal message. Whatever he had or hadn't done, she noticed.

"I love your pocket square," Bria said.

"I love your belt," Luca replied.

"You both know how I love my shrimp cocktail." Rosalie glared. "If there isn't any because we showed up late to the party, I'll take Bria's belt and strangle you with it."

Luca raised his eyebrows. "You're going to strangle me and not Bria?"

Rosalie shrugged her shoulders. "I can't leave Marco an orphan."

Suddenly Bria felt claustrophobic. Rosalie hadn't mentioned Carlo's name, but her reference to him was enough to make Bria feel as if he was in the room. What would he think if he could see his wife all dressed up and ready to go out on the town with another man by her side? She avoided looking at Luca, but when he spoke, she knew he was thinking the same thing.

"*Ah bene*, I know when I'm defeated."

When they arrived at Franco's Bar, the alfresco lounge at Le Sirenuse, the party was in full swing. Named after one of the original owners of the hotel, the bar was a must-see for every kind of tourist. Franco Sersale had believed that the beauty of Positano should be experienced by everyone, not just the elite who could afford it. You didn't have to be a guest at Le Sirenuse to share in the luxury; you could just show up. How exciting it must have been to mingle with Frank Sinatra, Julie Christie, or Rudolf Nureyev—all frequent visitors to Positano over the decades—while sipping an Aperol spritz and gazing at the violet sunset.

On any other night of the year, no reservations were necessary, but if you didn't have an invitation tonight, you would be turned away. Massimo Angelini, the evening's orchestrator, liked to be in control. At six feet, five inches tall and about 225 pounds, Massimo didn't have to try very hard to stand out; it came naturally to him. As did giving orders and bossing people around, which, when you thought about it, was exactly what a TV producer did. He was working in a job that suited his personality perfectly.

"Bria Bartolucci!" Massimo extended his arms and held Bria's hands in his. "I've heard quite a bit about you."

Both of Bria's eyebrows rose as she glanced at Rosalie. Massimo let out a high-pitched belly laugh, a girlish sound that belied his more brutish appearance. "Don't blame Rosalie. I know your family."

As Massimo kissed Bria's hands, she tried to imagine how he could know her parents. They had no connection to the entertainment world, so she didn't think they could have crossed paths in business. Maybe he was a friend of theirs from before she was born? Before she could ask him to explain his comment, someone swooped in and took control of the conversation.

"Massimo!" Dante grabbed Massimo's shoulders and looked up at him. "Welcome to my little village of Positano." Dante hesitated, expecting Massimo to bend closer to him so they could kiss each other's cheeks. The producer wasn't so inclined, forcing Dante to greet Massimo with a much less affectionate air-kiss.

"Dante La Costa," Massimo said, a sneer attached to his smirk. "Positano belongs to the people."

"That it does," Dante said without missing a beat. "I'm proud to serve them as their mayor."

"Ever the politician." Massimo pivoted and turned his back to Dante. "Rosalie, I'm so glad you're going to work with us."

"I can't wait," Rosalie replied. "To think, my boat is going to be famous."

"We'll use the location shots as an online teaser before we jump into the weekly series," Massimo explained. "It'll give the world time to read Lugo's book and increase anticipation for the show."

"Ever the producer," Dante replied.

"Luca, may we speak privately about the security measures you're putting in place before tomorrow's filming?" Massimo said, ignoring Dante's jab. "I want to make sure we're covered for every possibility."

"What kind of possibilities are you concerned about?" Bria asked.

"It's my job to worry about any and all kinds," Massimo replied.

"Is there something specific?" Bria asked. "I mean, it's a television show. What could go wrong?"

Massimo's laugh was even louder and higher pitched than before. "When you're filming a live television show like we'll be doing, anything can happen. It's my job to make sure that we're prepared for any outcome."

"*Non preoccuparti*, Massimo. My team is prepared," Luca said. "We have a lot of experience handling live events in the village. They happen all the time."

"But never with a celebrity chef on the cusp of becoming the most famous culinary export Italy's ever seen," Dante said.

Considering the long legacy of famous Italian chefs and television personalities who had taught millions how to cook better and serve more gastronomically adventurous meals to their family, friends and, in some cases, the diners at their own restaurants, Dante's declaration was a bit of an overstatement. Yet there was an air of electricity circulating among the guests. Everyone knew they were about to witness something important, that Chef Lugo was going to give them something to remember.

Where was the chef? Bria knew what the man looked like from the back cover of his previous books and the few times she'd caught him as a guest on a talk show, but so far she hadn't spotted him in the crowd. Shouldn't he be working his audience, shaking hands and thanking everyone for allowing him to film in their village?

At that precise moment, Pippa ran up to Massimo, stood on her tiptoes, and whispered something into his ear. No one heard the woman, but whatever she said, it made all the color drain from Massimo's face. His complexion resembled the stark white railing that surrounded the bar.

"What do you mean, you can't find him?" he bellowed.

"*Proprio ciò che ho detto!*" Pippa cried. "I've looked everywhere, and Chef Lugo is nowhere to be found."

Massimo raised a clenched fist into the air. "*Questo è impossibile!*"

"Impossible or not," Pippa said, "the guest of honor has disappeared."

CHAPTER 3

Could there be a party to celebrate a celebrity if that celebrity wasn't celebrating at the party? That was the question bouncing around Bria's brain and the same one, she imagined, that was troubling Massimo's thoughts. Except, whereas Bria looked intrigued, Massimo looked incensed. Worse, Pippa looked terrified.

"Did you check his room?" Massimo asked.

"Yes," Pippa replied.

"Did you call his cell phone?"

"Twice." Before another word passed Massimo's lips, Pippa spoke again. "And I texted him four times."

Massimo clenched his fists and looked around the patio. Bria thought he looked like an animal locked in a cage that was slightly too small to allow it to flex its muscles fully. Suddenly Massimo lurched at Pippa, bending down so their faces were inches apart, causing the woman to crouch. "I cannot believe you allowed this to happen!"

Shock registered in Pippa's eyes. "It wasn't my turn to watch him."

Watch him? Bria thought. *Chef Lugo isn't a child.*

"*Dio aiutami*!" Massimo swatted the air above Pippa's head

and then rose up to his full height. "When I find him, he'll wish he really did disappear!"

"I texted Nunzi, and she confirmed that no incidents have been reported, and no one has been taken to the Red Cross," Luca announced.

"Can you be sure Nunzi gave you the right information?" Rosalie asked.

"*Non cominciare*, Rosa!" Luca cried. "Nunzi is a good cop."

Rosalie shrugged her shoulders and popped another shrimp into her mouth. "If you say so."

"I'm the chief of police, and I do say so," Luca said. "Massimo, the good news is that it doesn't seem Chef Lugo has been hurt. Nor has he been the victim of a crime."

"*Grazie*, Luca," Massimo said. "But that doesn't mean anything."

"It means he's probably nervous about tomorrow and is somewhere trying to calm down before coming to his party," Luca replied.

Bria watched Massimo's face and got the feeling that he was working very hard to maintain his composure. His eyes were staring right at Luca, unblinking, his lips were pressed tightly against each other, and he was breathing deeply through his nose. Bria wasn't sure if he was going to scream or propel himself through the roof like a rocket.

"*Scusami*, but you obviously don't know my Lugo very well," Massimo seethed. "Now, if you'll excuse me, I need to find my star, or there will be no TV show tomorrow."

The other guests were glancing in their direction instead of looking at the breathtaking view of the sea and were whispering clandestinely instead of chattering animatedly. These were telltale signs that they were aware something was wrong. Bria knew the party was in serious trouble of erupting into a full-blown disaster if someone didn't take action to divert their attention. She didn't want Annamaria's fifteen minutes of fame to be over before they started, and for some reason, she felt protective of Pippa and didn't want her to suffer any more of Massimo's fury. If someone needed to take action, why not her?

She stood in front of the huge gold fountain that was the centerpiece of Franco's Bar. Built by the famed Italian sculptor Giuseppe Ducrot, the neo-Baroque creation was both vulgar and refined. Ostentatious in its material, the fountain stood out from the rest of the plain white walls that encompassed the patio like a bejeweled queen on a soup line. Despite its audacious look, the exquisite craftsmanship of its design couldn't be dismissed. Neither could Bria.

"*Signore e signori, posso avere la vostra attenzione per favore?*"

Well, now that everyone's looking at you, Bria thought, *you'd better say something!*

Correction. Dante had better say something.

"I'd like to introduce the mayor of Positano," Bria cried. "Dante La Costa."

Of all the people Bria knew at the party, Dante had the biggest ego. He would never refuse an opportunity to speak to a crowd, even if he knew the crowd had not come to hear him speak. Bria didn't care, as long as he distracted the guests from noticing that the guest of honor had not yet arrived.

When Dante stood next to her in front of the fountain, he was smiling so naturally that Bria couldn't tell if he was angry with her for putting him on the spot or delighted that she had given him an opportunity to address an audience. As long as he kept the guests entertained and gave the search party time to find Chef Lugo, she didn't care.

"*Grazie*, Bria. Our little village has seen much excitement through the decades," Dante started. "We have welcomed dignitaries, movie stars, literary icons, the famed, and the infamous, but soon we will welcome a man who understands the one thing that makes Italy better than any country in the world."

Dante paused for effect, and Bria noticed that the age-old trick delivered. The crowd grew silent and leaned toward Dante, anxious for him to continue speaking. They had forgotten there had been an argument, they hadn't noticed Lugo was missing, and all they wanted was for Dante to tell them what made them the best.

"Our food!"

Roars of delight erupted from the crowd. Bria exhaled and let herself relax. Crisis averted for the time being, but the main problem remained: Chef Lugo was still nowhere to be seen.

Bria tugged on Rosalie's arm. *"Venga con me."*

"Where are we going?"

"To find Chef Lugo."

As they walked by Luca, Bria whispered, "You should see if you can find out where Massimo went to."

Luca leaned closer to Bria and whispered back, "Yes, signora."

She felt a tingle tickle her spine. Luca had responded in the perfect way to get a woman's attention—by softly pressing his unshaven chin against her earlobe. Unfortunately, another man needed her attention at the moment, so Bria couldn't dwell on the unexpected feelings created by the sensation of Luca's stubble brushing against her skin.

Franco's Bar wasn't large, so as the women walked to the exit, they could see everyone at the party. Bria saw Enrico holding a glass of wine, standing next to Mimi, who was holding a small bouquet of flowers, which Bria knew Enrico had given her. Bria smiled because she knew it was only a matter of time before the friends became a couple. Bria also saw Violetta standing next to Matteo, one of the cops who worked with Luca, and wondered if they were on a date. She then realized they couldn't date, because they were both born in Positano.

Local law prohibited someone on the police force from becoming romantically involved with anyone who was born in the village, because it could create bias if they found themselves on opposite ends of a crime. Bria felt an unexpected wave of relief that she wasn't born in Positano, and so if she ever wanted to date Luca, there wouldn't be any restrictions.

Uffa! Bria thought. *Concentrate and get on with the search.*

Shaking her head, Bria led Rosalie out of the bar and headed into the hotel itself. The interior design was almost as breathtaking as the magnificent views from the bar. In some ways, it was more impressive, because it was created by men and women and wasn't a product of nature.

They took about ten steps and found themselves in La Sponda, the domain of Gennaro Russo. A series of arched windows lined the walls and were highlighted by vines that looked like they had grown there naturally. The green marble tile resembled the Tyrrhenian Sea, allowing the patrons to imagine they could walk on water. Each table was adorned with a crisp white tablecloth, white china place settings, and sterling silver accessories. Soft music filled the room and fused with the sound of the distant waves to create a sultry soundtrack to the visual feast.

They continued to walk through the restaurant, looking everywhere, in the hopes of finding Chef Lugo hiding in a corner or seeking refuge behind one of the large potted plants. All they saw were couples sharing romantic dinners and groups of people relishing their good fortune to be at one of the most glamorous hotels in the world. Bria passed by two men sharing an appetizer of grilled octopus, one of the La Sponda's specialties, and she smelled a familiar fragrance. It was Versace's Eros cologne, which Carlo would often wear on formal occasions. The scent enveloped her as tightly as her wedding band encircled her finger.

Maybe the reason Bria was intent on finding Chef Lugo, a

man she had no personal ties to, was that it prevented her from having to deal with the other men in her life. If she could spend the entire night scouring the village for a wayward cook, she could avoid an intimate conversation with Luca or a sweet memory of Carlo.

"I found him," Rosalie said.

The night suddenly got a lot shorter.

"Where?" Bria asked.

When Rosalie pointed to a man standing near a window in a corner of the room, Bria knew her evening was far from over.

"That isn't Chef Lugo," Bria said.

"I know."

"Then who is it?"

"*Non lo so*, but I think you're looking at my next boyfriend."

Bria didn't recognize the man Rosalie wanted to date, but she did recognize him as Rosalie's type. He looked to be in his midthirties and had chin-length straight black hair, which he had tucked behind his ears. Bria did have to admit that he was handsome, with the bone structure, large nose, and lean body of a southern Italian. She also felt he was *losco*, a bit sketchy and rough around the edges.

He was wearing a black suit jacket over a white shirt, paired with a pair of jeans. The top button of the shirt was unbuttoned, making the skinny black tie that hung from his neck look like an abandoned noose. Either the man didn't like anything too tight around his throat or he rebelled against any type of restraint.

He leaned against the wall, slightly hunched over, and when Bria looked over, he was in the process of biting a fingernail. The stranger could be shy, or he could be planning to rob the place. If they had the time, Bria would have initiated a conversation with him to uncover more details, but they were on a mission. They needed to find one mystery man, not pick up another.

"Sorry, Rosalie, but we need to keep looking for Lugo," Bria said.

"Bene." Rosalie sighed and swung her cape from side to side. "I've lived this long without a husband, what's another decade? Or two?"

A feeling of sympathy engulfed Bria. She knew Rosalie was acting cavalier to hide deeper emotions—depression, fear, anger—which all had to do with the fact that Rosalie never emerged victorious from romantic entanglements. Her relationships were typically short-lived and left her questioning her choice in men or what she had done to cause the breakup. The women had spent many nights finishing many bottles of Chianti while talking about Rosalie's quest to find love, and they would have many more, but Bria knew that now wasn't the time or the place.

Bria smiled and gave Rosalie's hand a squeeze. "Why don't you go down to the lobby and check with the front desk to see if they saw Lugo go up to his room. I'll check out the bar near the beach."

Rosalie returned the smile and the squeeze. *"Buona idea.* I'll meet you back at Franco's in ten minutes."

The women parted ways, and just as Bria was about to take the stairs, she remembered Le Sirenuse had something very rare—an elevator that went down to the beach. It was the epitome of luxury and added to the hotel's magical quality. One short ride took you from Franco's Bar, overlooking the mountains and the Tyrrhenian Sea, to Marina Grande Beach.

The ride was short, and when the elevator doors opened, the view transformed from spectacular to sensational. In the distance, standing on the beach, was the missing chef. In the arms of a woman.

Bria hid behind a large lemon tree and watched as Chef Lugo kissed a woman she had never seen before. He pulled out of the kiss but still held her face in his hands. Whoever this woman was, Lugo was in love with her. Bria didn't need to see the desire in his eyes. She saw how tenderly he held her, how his thumb gently rubbed against her cheek, and how he maintained eye contact with the woman, as if he didn't dare turn away.

The woman was harder to read. She was undeniably beautiful, with sultry eyes that were almost almond shaped, full lips, and high cheekbones. Her mass of blond hair cascaded down to her shoulders in long waves and indicated that if she was Italian, she was probably from northern Italy. Wherever she came from, she was captivating. Bria couldn't tell, however, if she was captivated.

The woman was staring at Lugo with a blank expression. She looked interested but at the same time aloof. Until her lips moved and formed a snarl. She shook her head from side to side in the universal expression of disapproval and raised her arms in between Lugo's hands and flicked them to the sides to break any physical contact. Lugo staggered back and had to reach out to grab the gate at the edge of the walkway to steady himself. Instead of helping him, the woman ran off.

Slowly, Bria walked toward Lugo and knew he was in no condition to chase after the woman. Not by how he looked, but by how he smelled. The chef was drunk.

"Lugo." Bria waited for the chef to face her, but he made no attempt. Bria called out again, this time using his real name. "Luigi."

He turned to face Bria and tried to stand fully upright but only partially succeeded. He swayed a bit before speaking. "Who are you?"

"Bria," she replied. "Bria Bartolucci."

"*Oh certo*," Lugo said. "The café owner."

"No, that's Annamaria. She owns Caffè Positano." Bria waited a moment, hoping that Lugo would recognize the name. When the confused look didn't leave his face, Bria knew he was too drunk to remember. "Where you're filming your show tomorrow."

Finally, there was recollection in Lugo's eyes, but not excitement. He seemed completely disinterested in what was supposed to be a turning point in his life. Then again, that could be the very reason he was drunk: to forget that tomorrow was going to change his life forever. Bria remembered how nervous she was the night before the first guests were set to arrive at Bella Bella. If it weren't for the fact that she had had Marco with her, she might have had one too many glasses of limoncello to ward off the suffocating terror created by self-doubt.

Regardless of the reasons why, Lugo was drunk, and he had the look in his eye that told Bria he only wanted to get drunker. There was no one in her life who abused alcohol, but during her days at Rome University of Fine Arts, she had had many classmates who majored in getting drunk to avoid having to work hard to achieve their potential. If Lugo kept on drinking, the shoot might not go on tomorrow, not because the star was missing, but because the star would be unconscious. She had to get him back to the party so Massimo could look after him.

"A lot of people are looking for you," Bria said.

Lugo turned and looked off into the distance, in the direction where the woman had run. Bria waited for him to respond, but he just kept staring.

"Why don't you come upstairs with me and say hello to them," Bria said. "You're Positano's special guest star. Everyone's thrilled that you're here."

Lugo looked at Bria and it was as if he instantly turned sober. His bloodshot eyes became clear, his body straightened, and when he spoke his speech wasn't slurred. "Only because they don't know the truth."

"What do you mean?"

Lugo looked at Bria, and his hardened mask softened when he smiled this time. "You'll have to wait like the rest of them, but don't you worry, Bria. I'm going to confess everything."

Bria saw Massimo peering down at them from Franco's Bar. She knew it would take him less than a minute to join them on the beach. She also instinctively knew that once Lugo saw him, he wouldn't say another word. If Bria wanted to find out what Lugo was going to confess to, she was going to have to act quickly. She moved to the left so Lugo had to turn slightly to face her. He was now standing with his back to the elevator, so there was no chance he could see Massimo when the doors opened. "What are you going to confess?"

Lugo leaned in closer to Bria, and she could smell the sweet stench of alcohol on his breath. "I'm going to show them something that will change . . . *everything*."

The elevator doors opened, and Bria watched as Massimo stepped off and raced toward them.

"What's going to change everything?" Bria asked.

Before Lugo could respond, Massimo bellowed, "That's right, Luigi! You are on the cusp of unfathomable change."

Massimo looked the same but sounded different. When he spoke to Lugo, his normally deep voice transitioned into a basso profundo. It sounded theatrical, almost unnatural, but Bria realized it was a fitting tactic for a man who created things. A producer was like an impresario, someone who presented an act that was based on fiction, not fact.

"*Grazie molte*, Bria. I knew my Lugo wouldn't traipse off too far, not with such a big day ahead of us." Massimo put his hands underneath Lugo's armpits and lifted him until he was standing perfectly upright. He looked the man in the eyes and waited until Lugo returned the gaze. "Isn't that right, Lugo?"

The chef didn't respond verbally; he merely nodded his head. He looked defeated, and yet Bria could see a spark in his eyes. A flicker of defiance. Like that of a prisoner who believes he is mere moments from escape.

"Let's go up to your hotel room so you can get some sleep," Massimo said, putting his arm around Lugo's shoulders. "*Grazie ancora*, Bria."

"*Prego.*"

Massimo turned to face Bria. "This will be our secret, yes?"

The icy tone of Massimo's voice was in stark contrast to his smiling eyes. Without a doubt, Bria knew he was not requesting her compliance; he was threatening her to keep quiet about what she had witnessed. She wasn't afraid for herself, since she knew Massimo wouldn't retaliate in any physical way, but she was scared for Lugo.

"*Naturalmente*," Bria replied.

"*Bene.*"

Bria watched Massimo lead Lugo back to the elevator, and she blew out a deep breath. She couldn't wait for tomorrow. She didn't know what was going to happen, but she knew Lugo was right. Tomorrow was going to change everything.

CHAPTER 4

Domani era finalmente oggi.

It was something Fifetta had told Bria when she was a little girl. Whenever she had been waiting excitedly for a day to arrive so she could visit her grandmother, go on a school trip, or celebrate Christmas, her mother would wake her up by whispering in her ear that tomorrow was finally today. Bria had carried on the tradition with Marco on the first day of soccer practice, on Bravo's birthday, and on other special occasions as a way to honor the arrival of an expectation.

That was how Bria felt this morning. After her brief encounter with Chef Lugo last night, she wasn't sure if today would be the kind of day everyone was expecting, but it had finally arrived. If Pippa's actions were any indication, the day was going to be a bumpy ride.

"Has anyone seen my lucky barrette?" Pippa asked.

Her petite frame was practically vibrating with nervous energy as she sat at the table. Tobias and Daisy were sitting across from her, and Marco was to her left, with Bravo sprawled out on the floor next to his feet. They were all eating one of Giovanni's signature breakfasts: citrus croissants, polenta cakes, fresh fruit and yogurt, and *uova in purgatorio*. While the eggs were cooked in tomato sauce and were not actually languishing in purgatory, the name of the breakfast dish was proof that religion found its way into many aspects of an Italian's daily life. In fact, as Pippa waited for a response, her lips were moving as she softly recited a Hail Mary.

"You mean the pink butterfly that's in your hair?" Marco said, chomping on a piece of melon.

Pippa's hand fluttered up to her head, and when she felt the barrette, she let out a sigh. "*Scusatemi*, it's a very important day, and I guess I'm a little nervous."

"Did you study?" Marco asked.

"*Scusa?*" Pippa said.

"I think Marco means, are you prepared?" Tobias explained.

"*Sì, certo*," Pippa replied.

"When I have a test or a spelling bee, Mamma tells me I have nothing to worry about as long as I've studied," Marco said.

Pippa gulped down the rest of her espresso. "That might work in school, but not in the TV world. If something can go wrong, it will go wrong, and when something does go wrong, I'll get blamed for it since I'm the newest member of the crew."

Bria could see Marco thinking about what Pippa had said, and she knew by his expression that he didn't like what he'd heard. "That isn't fair."

"Massimo doesn't understand the word *fair*," Pippa said.

Before Bria could explain to her that she didn't have to be bullied by her boss, Pippa glanced at her watch and jumped out of her chair. "I have to go. *Grazie*, Giovanni! This breakfast was *delizioso*. *Ciao!*"

After the front door slammed, they all looked at each other and started to laugh.

"She certainly is a whirlwind," Daisy said.

"I don't think I've ever been that nervous on the job," Tobias said. "And I was an emergency room doctor."

"I think TV people take themselves much more seriously than doctors," Bria said. "Especially Massimo."

Suddenly the front door swung open, and Pippa burst back into the room.

"How was the shoot?" Tobias deadpanned.

"*La mia testa*!" Pippa shouted, slapping herself on the side of the head. "I forgot the fake croissants! We can't film a cooking show without fake food."

Pippa ran upstairs to her room, and the others looked at each other quizzically. Within a few seconds she was running back down the stairs with a large bag slung over her shoulder.

Marco asked the question they were all thinking about. "Isn't a cooking show supposed to be about cooking real food?"

Pippa dropped the bag, pulled out a croissant, and waved it in front of her. "Fake food looks better on camera."

Bria took the croissant Pippa was holding and inspected it. Even though it was rock hard, it looked like something that could be found in Annamaria's café. Golden brown, flaky, and as if it had been dipped in butter. "*Uffa*! This looks good enough to eat."

"Every show uses them, in case the real food doesn't cook or bake properly," Pippa said. "We're filming live, so we can't bake another batch if the first one is ruined. Instead, we use a prop. Some of them even split open like a real croissant." Pippa broke the fake pastry in half to prove her point.

"*Dio mio*!" Daisy cried. "It's hollow inside."

"The audience at home won't know the difference," Pippa said, shoving the fake croissant back into her bag.

"Are you going to film the whole series at Annamaria's café?" Marco asked. "Maybe if you shoot on Sundays, I can come watch, as long as you film it after church and soccer practice."

Daisy shook her head. "No, after today they're going to shoot in Tuscany."

Bria turned to face Daisy and wondered how the woman knew the show's future production location. Daisy lifted a copy of *La Vita Positano*, and Bria realized Aldo must have gotten another scoop. As the editor and sole reporter of the paper, Aldo Bombalino was sometimes known as the eyes and ears of the village.

"If something goes wrong today," Pippa said, "we may be out of a job before we get on the train to Tuscany."

Bria thought back to what Chef Lugo had said about today changing everything and realized Pippa's fears weren't unsubstantiated. There was the very real possibility that starting this afternoon, she'd need to look for a new job. But there was no reason to worry about that now.

"I'm sure everything will go smoothly," Bria said. "I'm looking forward to watching the filming in person."

"If I don't get going, I may miss it," Pippa said. *"Ciao!"*

Tobias tilted his head toward the front closet, where Bravo was sniffing a small box Pippa had left there earlier. "Aren't you forgetting something?"

"Bravo can't help himself when he smells food," Marco said.

"That box isn't filled with food," Pippa said, picking up the box. "Those are the chef's special towels. *Dio mio!* I can't believe I almost forgot them too."

"Bravo! *Smettila*!" Bria cried. "Come by Mamma."

Reluctantly, Bravo stopped pawing at the box and sulked over to Bria. But he wasn't the only one who was confused.

"You have a bag that contains croissants that aren't real croissants and don't smell," Giovanni observed. "And a box that contains towels that aren't real towels and smell like food."

"They're lavender scented," Pippa explained. "Lugo says they relax him before personal appearances and calm his nerves."

Pippa picked up the box and the bag and somehow managed to open the front door. *"Ciao!* And this time I mean it."

After the front door slammed, they all stared at it, expecting Pippa to burst back into the room. When it opened, they all thought she was making another entrance. It wasn't Pippa; it was Enrico.

At the sight of Enrico standing at the front door, Bravo jumped up and ran toward him. On his way he must have bumped into Daisy's leg, because she spilled her coffee on her blouse. Daisy jumped up from the table just as Bravo jumped up onto Enrico.

"*Prego, scusa!*" Bria said. "Bravo is usually such a good boy."

"Don't blame him. It was my fault," Daisy said. "I think Pippa's anxiety is contagious."

"It's my fault," Enrico declared. "I brought mozzarella for Bravo as a treat."

"I told you Bravo can't help himself when he smells food," Marco said.

"I should change my blouse," Daisy said before heading up the stairs.

"Luckily, my wife brought enough clothes for us to relocate instead of enjoy a two-week vacation," Tobias said.

"*Grazie*, Enrico, for taking Marco to school," Bria said.

"*Non dirlo neanche*," Enrico replied. "I love spending time with Marcolo."

"He loves spending time with you," Bria said. "But I am grateful. I need to get to Annamaria's, and Giovanni needs to stay here and be in charge while I'm gone."

"Giovanni, you promised to help me pick what I should bring for *mostra e racconta*," Marco said.

"*Una promessa è una promessa.*" Giovanni crouched down and Marco jumped onto his back. "Let's find something you can show and tell."

Bria watched Giovanni gallop into Marco's bedroom, with Marco pretending to be a cowboy. She had a flash of a memory of sitting with her father on their couch, watching old spaghetti westerns, when she was a young girl. It reminded her that the last time one of her guests was in Positano, she was roughly the same age.

"Enrico, you grew up here. Do you remember a girl named Daisy?" Bria asked. "She's Tobias's wife."

"Her full name is Daisetta," Tobias added.

Enrico shook his head. "No, I don't remember anyone by that name."

"Tobias, what was Daisy's maiden name?" Bria asked.

"If I can't remember Daisetta," Enrico said, "a last name won't help."

Marco came running out of his room, holding a small globe, with Giovanni right behind him. "I'm going to show my class all the places where our guests have come from."

"*Brillante*!" Bria cried. "My little boy is so smart."

"The only way to get smarter is to get to school," Enrico said.

Bria kissed Marco on both of his cheeks, and even though it was in front of Enrico and a virtual stranger, he didn't pull away. Marco might be receiving his first Holy Communion soon and then turning nine the following month, but luckily, he still acted like Bria's little boy. She knew the day would come when he recoiled from her embrace, but for now, she was holding on as tightly as she could.

"Be good for Sister Benedicta," Bria said.

"I'm always good, Mamma," Marco said. *"Ciao."*

Bria stared at the door for a few seconds after they left, lost in her thoughts. She wasn't the only one reminiscing. She turned around and saw that Daisy had entered the room, wearing a new blouse. When Daisy caught Bria looking at her, she smiled and said, "A boy's love for his mother is one of the purest things God ever created."

In agreement, Bria made the sign of the cross.

"Daisy, will you be going to the café to try to catch a glimpse of Chef Lugo?" Giovanni asked.

"We won't have time," she replied. "I want to show Tobias

where I used to live, and we might go up to Ravello to see the Duomo, the church my family used to belong to."

"My parents go to mass at the Duomo every Sunday," Bria said. "It's even more beautiful now, after all the refurbishments they've done the past few years."

"I'm sure we'll have a very eventful day," Tobias said. "But it sounds like you're going to be where all the action is."

When Bria arrived at Caffè Positano, there was definitely action, but it was not the good kind. She walked inside and expected to find a busy atmosphere, with lots of people running around, setting up cameras, and fiddling with cables, all the things you'd expect from a television film crew. What she didn't expect was to hear yelling and screaming, see Pippa near tears, holding an inedible croissant, and to have Rosalie race over to her the moment she entered the café.

"*Grazie Dio!*" Rosalie cried.

"What's going on?" Bria asked.

"Let me see . . . Where should I start?" Rosalie quipped. "Pippa's crying, Massimo is screaming, Chef Lugo's hiding in the back room, and Annamaria's nowhere to be found."

"Annamaria's not here?" Bria said. "All she's talked about is the filming. Where is she?"

"No one knows," Rosalie replied. "And without her, they can't start filming."

From across the café, Massimo saw Bria. He didn't bother to walk over to her. He shouted his question from where he was standing. "Where's Annamaria?"

"*Perdonami*, I don't know," Bria said.

She looked over at Pippa, who was unsuccessfully trying not to cry, and Bria knew exactly how she felt. She hardly knew Massimo, he wasn't her boss, he literally meant nothing to her, and yet he was making her feel as if she had failed him. Intellectually, Bria knew her feelings were without validation, yet emotionally she felt beaten. How could Pippa work like this every day? No wonder she was so tightly wound and nervous all the time. Could Massimo have treated Annamaria like this? Could he have made the normally gregarious café owner run from her first and probably only chance of appearing on television?

"Rosalie," Bria said, "do you have any idea where Annamaria is?"

"None," Rosalie replied. "I've called and texted her, but she hasn't responded."

"Did you call Mimi? Maybe she knows where she is."

"She was my first phone call."

"Your first?"

"Yes."

Bria looked at Rosalie as if she had just been slapped in the face. "Why would you call Mimi first and not me? I always call you first, even when my first call should be to the police. I can't believe you would betray me like this."

"*Ah per l'amor di Dio*!" Rosalie cried. "I didn't betray you! I would never do that."

"But you did! Why did you call Mimi and not me?"

"Because Chef Lugo is going to the bookstore right after the filming," Rosalie said. "I thought Annamaria might be there with Mimi to coordinate things, make sure there was a smooth transition from one place to the next."

For a moment Bria didn't respond. Then she shook her head and raised her arms, palms to the ceiling. "This is my fault."

"Annamaria not being here?"

"No, your betrayal."

"I didn't betray you! *Dio mio*! I explained why I called Mimi before I called you."

"I know, but the real reason is that I betrayed you first."

The chatter in the room was so loud, no one heard Rosalie

gasp. "Bria Nicoletta Faustina D'Abruzzo Bartolucci! *You* betrayed *me*?"

Bria closed her eyes and nodded. "*Mi dispiace*, but yes, I didn't tell you everything I saw last night."

"Yes you did. You told me you found Chef Lugo, and he couldn't have been drunker if Modigliani had got trapped in a wine cellar."

"There's more."

"More! What else could he have been doing if he was so drunk?"

"He was kissing a woman."

"A woman? Who?"

"I didn't recognize her. She looked Italian, but she was blond, so probably northern Italian. Not our people. But after they were kissing, she pushed Lugo away and stormed off."

"Who else have you told?"

"No one. You're the first."

"Bria! Then you really didn't betray me."

"Yes I did! I should've told you right away. I kept it to myself, and I'm sorry."

Rosalie held out her arms to Bria. "I forgive you, *mia amica*."

The women hugged tightly and didn't hear the front door open, but they did become aware of the hush that filled the café and then the collection of groans and sighs that quickly followed. They thought the crowd was reacting to them, but then they looked toward the front door. Unless Annamaria had grown five inches, lost about thirty-five pounds, and started wearing a police officer's uniform, the woman standing in front of the door wasn't her.

"'*Giorno*, Nunzi," Rosalie said. "Disappointing crowds wherever you go, I see."

"Nunzi, what are you doing here?" Bria asked.

"I'm here for the filming," Nunzi replied. "Like everybody else."

"There may not be a filming," Rosalie whispered.

"*Mio Dio*, why not?"

"Because the cohost is missing," Rosalie replied. "She's out running an errand and hasn't come back yet."

"Why would she go out to run an errand if she knew she was going to be rubbing elbows with the most famous, best-looking chef ever to pick up a frying pan?"

Bria and Rosalie watched as Nunzi attempted to control her breathing. The policewoman was normally unemotional, especially when she was in uniform. Now she was acting like an out-of-control fan.

"*Dio mio*! You have a crush on Chef Lugo," Rosalie said.

"I do not," Nunzi protested.

"Do too!" Rosalie cried. "You can't deny it."

"I think it's sweet," Bria said. "He is very handsome."

Nunzi's eyes lit up. "Isn't he? And he's single."

"Yes he is," Bria replied. "But from what I've heard, he's focusing on his career right now and isn't interested in having a girlfriend."

"He likes to play the field, Nunzi," Rosalie said. "With blondes."

Nunzi unconsciously tugged at her long brown hair.

"Do yourself a favor," Rosalie said. "Forget about Lugo and just keep spending Saturday night alone with Puttanesca."

"Who's Puttanesca?" Nunzi asked.

"Your cat."

Nunzi glared at Rosalie. "His name is Primavera."

Just when it looked like Rosalie and Nunzi might get into a literal catfight, Massimo made an announcement. "Bria, get into make-up. You're going to take Annamaria's place."

"*Solo un minuto*!" Bria cried. "I don't know anything about being on TV."

"Neither does Annamaria," Massimo said, handing Bria a script. "Smile, follow Lugo's lead, memorize your lines, and you'll be fine."

Bria heard Rosalie and Nunzi wish her good luck as Pippa whisked her to the kitchen, which had been transformed into a backstage area. The first thing she noticed out of place was Lugo, who was hunched over a table, with his head clasped in his hands. It was possible that he was meditating, but it was also possible that he was getting ready to bang his head against the table several times.

Pippa made Bria sit and then stepped back to examine her. "Green looks good on you, and your top has a nice clean neckline. The jeans are a bit too casual, but they'll be hidden behind the counter, so no one will see."

Bria was happy her outfit passed muster, since she hadn't dressed to be camera ready this morning. Her face was a different matter.

"I need to fix the bags under your eyes, though," Pippa said.

"*Che cosa*? I don't have bags under my eyes," Bria protested.

"TV lights are like critics. They're ruthless," Lugo said, still cradling his head in his hands. "The slightest imperfection is magnified. Even a beautiful woman like you, Bria, is going to need some help."

"*Grazie*," Bria said. "I think."

"Close your eyes." Pippa dabbed cream underneath Bria's eyes to conceal the slightly darkened pigment and almost imperceptible puffiness. She then swept the blush brush across Bria's cheeks, forehead, chin, and neck. "Lugo, what do you think?"

The chef lifted his head to look at Bria, and his eyebrows rose. If Lugo was surprised by Bria's appearance, she was stunned by his. The last time Bria saw Lugo—less than twelve hours ago—he looked like he hadn't slept in days. Now he looked like a star. A bit more rugged than glamorous, but captivating all the same. Bria thought he could serve those fake croissants and still make it as a celebrity chef based on his looks alone. It seemed that Lugo held similar thoughts about Bria.

"You're even more beautiful than I thought you were last night," Lugo said.

"You two have met?" Pippa asked.

"Yes, at the party," Bria said.

"I thought you skipped the party, Lugo," Pippa said.

"I did," Lugo said. Pippa waited for a further explanation, but none came. "I don't always agree with Massimo, but he's right, Bria. All you have to do is smile, look pretty, and follow my lead. I'll get us through this."

"*Grazie*," Bria said. "I'll do my best not to ruin anything."

"*Scusate*, I need to speak with my producer."

Pippa watched Lugo walk over to Massimo and waited until after they were both out of earshot to speak again. "We have a serious problem."

"I know. Annamaria has run off somewhere."

"She went to find a notary."

"A notary? Why?"

"To notarize the permit that's required for us to film here. Without it, this is an illegal shoot."

"Does Massimo know?"

"No, *grazie Dio*. I'm covering for Annamaria, because he'll kill her if he finds out we don't have the permit. But she left hours ago," Pippa said. "This village isn't that big. How long can it possibly take to find a notary?"

"Will the police really stop you from filming if you don't have the permit?"

"I know Luca is supportive, but he may not have a choice but to shut down production if he finds out," Pippa said. "I'm hoping that Annamaria will show up with it after we're done, and everything will be fine. I just pray that happens before Massimo finds out what's really going on."

In response, Bria laughed and clutched Pippa's hand. She

knew the young woman would be confused by her actions, but Bria wanted to stop Pippa from talking any further because she saw Massimo walking toward them, his arm wrapped around Lugo's shoulder. When Pippa noticed Massimo and Lugo had reentered the kitchen, she burst into laughter to join Bria. They must have sounded peculiar, but neither man seemed to notice. Massimo and Lugo were having their own private conversation.

"This is your moment, Luigi. It's what we've worked so hard to achieve," Massimo said. "In a few minutes your world is going to change forever."

"Both our worlds," Lugo said.

Lugo stared at Massimo intently, his black eyes like two onyx stones, conveying whatever message he didn't want to speak out loud. Bria looked away, not wanting to intrude, but she noticed Pippa did not. She was staring right at the men.

"I know how you like to drink your espresso chilled." Massimo pulled a cup of the espresso out of the refrigerator and handed it to Lugo. "I prepared some for you earlier."

"*Grazie di tutto,*" Lugo said.

Massimo pulled out a small bottle from his pants pocket and placed it next to the cup. "I know you like to add some flavor to your espresso." He then kissed Lugo on the cheek. His smile faded when he addressed Pippa. "It's time."

Pippa scurried out of the kitchen, and Bria wondered if she should follow, but Massimo had other plans. "Bria, stay here with Lugo. We'll call you when it's thirty seconds to roll."

"Isn't that cutting it close?" she asked.

"Thirty seconds on live TV is a lifetime," Massimo said. "You'll be fine."

Bria took a few deep, cleansing breaths after Massimo left, and tried to convince herself that Annamaria was going to show up at the last second to take her rightful place next to Lugo. She took a few more breaths, because if that didn't happen, she needed to trick herself into thinking she possessed the poise to speak in front of a global audience. She tried to read the script Massimo had given her, but the words looked like hieroglyphics.

Needing a distraction, she looked in her bag to see if she had some chocolate or hand cream and found something better— Carlo's old Polaroid camera. She remembered something Cesare Pavese, one of Italy's most famous writers, once said: *We do not remember days, we remember moments*. As unexpected as it was, this was a moment Bria wanted to remember.

She crouched down next to Lugo as he poured what looked like anisette into his espresso at the table, and held the Polaroid in front of them. "Smile." Before Lugo could protest, she clicked the shutter button on the camera and took a selfie the old-fashioned way. As the photo developed in Bria's hand, she saw that Lugo had posed for the camera but hadn't smiled. This was more than nerves. Something was wrong.

"You must be happy about all of this," Bria said.

"I am."

"Forgive me, but you don't look very happy."

"*Perdonami*. This is all a bit overwhelming."

"I can imagine. I'm overwhelmed, and I'm not even going to do anything. Massimo seems to have everything under control, though."

Lugo looked directly into Bria's eyes. "*Senti*, I should warn you."

"Warn me, about what?" Bria asked. "If we follow the script, we won't have a problem."

"I'm not going to follow it," Lugo confessed. "There are some things that I have to say that aren't Massimo approved and are not part of the official script."

Bria felt the warmth spread from her belly to her throat and then to her cheeks. Lugo was going to go rogue. On live TV.

"What exactly do you have to say?" Bria asked.

Lugo smiled, but looked even more nervous and apprehensive than he had just a few seconds ago. "Nothing for you to worry about, I just don't want you to be surprised."

There was a commotion in the front room, and Bria prayed Annamaria had finally returned and would take her place. She opened the kitchen door to look into the café and was not only disappointed but also confused as to why Mimi was waving a rolling pin in front of Massimo's face.

"Look at it closely," Mimi said as she handed the rolling pin to Massimo. "It has the logo of my store on it. It'll be good cross-promotion for the launch of the book tour."

"It won't make any sense to the viewers," Massimo replied. "They'll be watching Lugo in Caffè Positano and won't understand why the rolling pin says A WORD FROM POSITANO."

"Annamaria can mention the name of the bookstore on air," Mimi suggested.

"Lugo will mention the bookstore as planned, but we're not using the rolling pin," Massimo declared. *"Capisci?"*

Although Massimo managed to keep the tone of his voice conversational when he tossed the rolling pin onto the counter, it made a thud, and Mimi had to lunge across the counter to grab it before it rolled off the other side. Just as she caught it, Mimi saw Bria standing in the kitchen doorway.

"Where's Annamaria?" Mimi asked.

"No one seems to know," Bria replied. "That's why I'm taking her place."

"La poverina! She's going to be so upset that she missed this," Mimi said. *"Però,* this is your chance to be a star."

Bria hardly felt like a star; she felt like a witness. She had the growing suspicion that she was about to see an event unfold, something memorable, something Signor Pavese would deem worth remembering. Mimi hugged her and then said she had to go back to the bookstore to get ready for the signing. Before she could wish Lugo luck, Massimo's voice bellowed through the café as he shouted the one word that created both excitement and anxiety in everyone. "Places!"

It was so loud, Bria actually jumped, but Lugo remained calm. His face was buried in one of the lavender-scented towels Pippa had brought for him. They smelled heavenly, and Bria pondered if she should grab one and inhale deeply. It might just calm her nerves. As if reading her mind, Lugo lifted his head, still hidden behind the towel, and pointed to the box where the others were.

"Try one," Lugo said. "They work like a charm."

The lavender scent was alluring, and it did smell vaguely like candy. Bria reached for one of the rolled-up towels as Massimo's voice, once again, reverberated through the café, demanding that the on-air talent take their places. "I think Massimo has other plans."

Lugo took the towel off his face and smiled at Bria. The lavender worked, and Lugo radiated tranquility. He looked peaceful, and not a trace of anxiety clung to his skin. "Let's do this," he said.

Bria followed Lugo out into the café, and Massimo gave them their final instructions. They were to look into the camera whenever they were speaking to the audience, and they should keep one eye out for him and Pippa, who would be on either side of the camera, as they might wave their hands for them to get closer together or farther apart. Pippa informed Bria that the tray of food in front of her was edible, but the items on top of the counter and on the fancy plates were not. Biting into one of those would mean a trip to the dentist.

"I'm going to count down from ten, and then we're a go," Massimo said. "Bria, you know what you have to say, *corretto*?"

"Yes."

"Introduce Chef Lugo, and then he'll take over from there," Massimo said. "Ready? Ten, nine, eight . . ."

"Where's my rolling pin?" Lugo asked. "I put it right there."

Bria nodded to the kitchen utensil on the countertop. "It's right there."

"Five, four . . ."

"No, that isn't . . ."

Bria didn't hear anything else Lugo said. Her heart was racing too fast. Things had happened so quickly. Massimo had orchestrated the situation, and Bria felt like a pawn, a willing one, of course, because she didn't want to be the spoiler and ruin things for Lugo and, mainly, for the village. Positano basked in the sun quite literally almost every day of the year, but this was an opportunity to bask in the figurative sun, and she didn't want to be the reason that light was eclipsed. But Bria needed something, too. She needed to see her best friend.

The moment Bria found Rosalie's smile, she relaxed. They had been through so much together. Bria knew it didn't matter if she flubbed every line or lost a tooth trying to eat a prop pastry. When it was over, she and Rosalie would laugh about it. Like they laughed about almost everything.

"Three, two, one."

Bria smiled, took a beat, and then made her television debut.

"*Ciao*. I'm Bria Bartolucci at the famous Caffè Positano, one of the finest cafés on the Amalfi Coast. And today I'd like to introduce you to someone you may already know but after today you'll never forget. Italy's own Luigi Gordonato, more commonly known as Chef Lugo. He's here today to tell us all about his new book, *Amalfi Toast*, and his upcoming television series, which will bring the taste of Italy right into your kitchen. Please welcome Chef Lugo."

The people in the café didn't have to be told to start clapping. They did so automatically. Lugo, on the other hand, needed a bit of a push to do his part. Bria waited for him to speak, but when he didn't raise his gaze from the counter, she did what any cohost with an untalkative guest would do. She ad-libbed.

"You've waited for this day for quite a while. How does it feel for it to finally be here?"

Lugo remained silent. Bria fought the panic she felt creeping up her spine and remembered that Pippa had told her no one would see her pants, which meant no one would see her feet. With a smile plastered on her face, she stepped on Lugo's toes and pressed down firmly. Finally, it got him to react.

"It feels wonderful to be here."

There was another pause, and Bria could feel sweat start to trickle down the back of her neck. Lugo was right: the lights were unkind. She imagined if Annamaria were here, she wouldn't have a problem filling in the silence, because Annamaria talked nonstop. Bria racked her brain to think of something to say but couldn't come up with anything until she glanced down and saw all the food right in front of her. She didn't need to speak; she could just eat.

"I bet you're hungry for one of your own creations." Bria picked up a pastry, broke it in half, and put it in Lugo's hands. "I've been dying to try one of these. They smell delicious. Go on, take a bite."

Dutifully, Lugo bit into the pastry. Bria picked one up for herself, but before she could take a bite, Lugo started to choke. He spit most of the food out of his mouth and tried to talk, but Bria couldn't hear what he was saying, because he was gasping for breath. Bria desperately looked around for a glass of water or something that he could drink, but the only thing in front of her was food, real and otherwise.

Lugo grabbed Bria's hand, and their eyes connected. The rest of the world around them became silent, invisible. Bria couldn't hear or see anything other than what was right in front of her. And all she saw was the undeniable proof that Lugo was frightened. He was pleading with his eyes and his very soul for Bria to do something; he was begging for her to save his life.

Instantly, Bria thought of Carlo. Her body visibly shook as

she wondered if her husband's beautiful blue eyes had contained the same fear, the same terror when he realized he was going to die. She had thought of Carlo's final moments many times since his death, but never before had she felt them so intensely, with such brutal force. It was as if she were on the plane, sitting next to Carlo, holding his hand, fully aware that they had only seconds left to live.

As Bria screamed, Lugo clutched his throat and fell onto the counter. Bria stood back in horror as she realized Lugo had just died in front of her and, worse, in front of a live audience. She had known the man for less than a day, but now they would be connected for all eternity. Because the last thing Chef Lugo saw before he left this earth was Bria's face.

Chapter 5

"Bria, *amore mio*, I'm all right. There's nothing to cry about."

Bria was vaguely aware that there were people screaming around her. She couldn't decipher what they were saying; all she could hear was Carlo's voice. She didn't know if he was speaking to her from beyond the grave, from a part of the universe that could not be seen by human eyes, or if she was making up the words in her head. But it didn't matter, because it brought her comfort. Standing inches from Lugo's lifeless body, she could use all the comfort she could get.

Slowly, Lugo's body dematerialized until it was replaced with Carlo's. He looked like he had dozed off in front of the computer, like he had done so many times while he was alive. Slumped forward, his head resting on his arm, his eyes closed, but even then, a trace of a smile remained on his lips. Whether awake or asleep, Carlo found joy in something.

Bria felt the tears stream down her face as she wondered—for what was perhaps the millionth time—if he had been able to keep some joy in his heart once he knew the plane was going to crash. All this time she hadn't been able to grasp the concept that one second, he was alive, and the next, he was dead. But she had just borne witness to it. One second, Lugo was reaching out to her, begging for life, and the next, he was sprawled out on the café counter, his request denied.

"Now you know, my Bria. Now you know."

She shut her eyes tight, unable to bear the sight of her husband any longer, and when she opened them, Carlo was gone. Had he ever been there? She didn't know, but now it was clear that the person who was making everyone scream was Chef Lugo.

Completely aware of her surroundings now, Bria felt like she was in the center of a storm. She looked around and saw that the once happy crowd looked more like a chaotic mob. She felt panic start to overtake her body and looked out into the audience, searching for Rosalie or even Nunzi, someone she knew who would be an anchor, someone whose face represented life and not death. The first face she saw, however, was Massimo's.

"Cut!" Massimo shouted. "Stop filming now!"

It wasn't the friendly connection she had been searching for, but Massimo's command jolted Bria back to reality. She saw that the cameraman had dropped his camera to the side and pressed a button, presumably to stop filming. The small audience, while still wearing expressions of horror and fear, had for the moment stopped screaming in response to Massimo's order.

Massimo approached the counter, and Bria watched him stand for a moment over Lugo's unmoving body. His eyes were dry, and he looked at Lugo with disbelief. Bria stood as motionless as the body lying next to her as Massimo lifted Lugo's wrist and felt for a pulse. Everyone in the café held their breath. Massimo gently placed Lugo's hand back down on the counter and shook his head. "He's dead."

Bria immediately made the sign of the cross. To a cynic, it might appear that the action was nothing more than a reflex, the result of a parochial school education or a religious upbringing. But to Bria and so many others, it held much more significance. It was a way to honor something greater than themselves at a moment of crisis and a way to humbly request divine intervention.

She silently recited the Our Father and asked God to welcome Lugo's soul into heaven. A simple prayer for an extraordinary appeal and the stuff that faith was built on. At that moment Bria believed more in her faith than she did in her reality. How could any of this be real? How could she have heard Carlo's voice? How could a man on the verge of a life-changing event have another life-changing event that forever changed his life? She didn't understand anything, but sadly, she completely understood why Massimo was shouting.

"Stop taking pictures!"

Massimo whirled around and watched as several of the people in the crowd were taking photos of Lugo with their camera. A twenty-first-century reaction based on primal instinct. Disrespectful but, unfortunately, accepted by many, and one that Bria herself had succumbed to in the past.

"Pippa!" Massimo yelled. "Lock the front door."

Before anyone could leave or protest, Pippa ran to the front door and locked it.

"I want to see everyone's cell phones now." Massimo walked away from the counter and into the belly of the café, the crowd parting to give him free range. "Delete all the photos you've just taken, or I'll sue each and every one of you."

"Italy's a free country!" one man cried.

"Outside maybe," Massimo replied. "But not in here."

"Since when did you become dictator?" a woman asked.

Massimo stared at the woman and pointed to the front door. "Did you read the sign in the window before you came in here?"

"No," the woman said sheepishly.

"It informed you that by entering this café, you agreed to be filmed for television without getting paid, and not to take any photographs or videos while inside." Massimo dropped his arm but not his gaze. "Under penalty of a fine and prison time."

"*È ridicolo!*" the man cried.

"It's the law," Nunzi replied.

Once again, Bria was reminded how authoritative Nunzi could sound. And look. Nunzi had a swimmer's body, with broad shoulders that tapered to a small waist. In her form-fitting navy blue uniform, with its thick white belt, powder-blue stripe down the side of each trouser leg, and white cap, she looked formidable. When she spoke, her tone was devoid of emotion. She was giving an order, not asking you to like her.

"If you've taken any photos or videos while you've been in here," Nunzi announced, "I strongly suggest you delete them now."

"And because I don't trust anyone," Massimo added, "Pippa and Nunzi will inspect your phones."

"You can't do that!" someone cried.

"Yes we can." Again, Nunzi's voice wasn't loud, but it was commanding. In response, some people shook their head in objection, but the majority began to delete the photos they had taken before and after Lugo collapsed. "Everyone, please show your phones to me or Pippa. *Grazie.*"

The crowd formed two lines and held up their cameras to Pippa, who was guarding the door, or Nunzi, who now stood with her back against the shelving unit that displayed coffee mugs, water bottles, and other items for sale. When someone approached either woman, Lugo was behind them and out of their range of vision. The proof of Lugo's death might get deleted from cell phones, but thanks to the event being filmed live, it had still been witnessed by thousands of viewers.

Bria walked out from behind the counter and was greeted by Rosalie. As much as she needed to be in the presence of her best friend, Bria had more of a need to get closer to Massimo.

Bria clutched Rosalie's hand to make sure she didn't stray too far away, but she whispered Massimo's name. He was so deep in thought, he didn't hear her, and Bria had to touch his arm to get his attention. "*Scusi*, but what does it matter if people took photos? Lugo just died on live TV."

"No he didn't," he replied.

"What are you talking about?" Rosalie said. "Your cameraman captured everything."

"I put a three-minute delay on the taping," he explained.

Bria and Rosalie looked at each other, both confused and both apparently sharing the same thought.

"Why would you do that?" Rosalie asked.

"Wasn't the whole purpose to make this a live event?" Bria added.

Massimo stared at Bria and then at Rosalie and did his very best to maintain a blank expression on his face. Despite his attempt, Bria could tell that he was not used to having his actions or motives questioned. "When you've been in this business as long as I have, you understand the need to take precautions. I wouldn't expect either of you to understand what it's like to work on a project of this magnitude."

Bria could feel Rosalie's palms grow sweaty, and she knew her friend was insulted by Massimo's tone and the implication of his remark.

"I guess you've forgotten that both Bria and I are small business owners," Rosalie said.

One corner of Massimo's mouth lifted into an undeniable snarl. "No, I have not. But as you so wisely pointed out, your businesses are small."

Bria wanted to believe that Massimo was getting angry at them as a way to channel his fury that Lugo was dead. But she sensed his insolence was a natural instinct, and not a natural reaction to the extreme circumstances. He was, after all, a man.

"Our businesses might be small, but we run them ourselves, each of us only having one employee." Rosalie tilted her head toward Massimo's crew. "Not an entire team."

Massimo seethed. This time Bria knew that his anger was in direct response to Rosalie's comment and had nothing to do with the dead man a few feet away. "Producing a television show requires one leader—me—who must manage an entire team to prevent a million little things from going wrong."

"Despite your best efforts, there could still be one fatal mistake," Bria said.

Rosalie squeezed Bria's hand in triumph, and Massimo appeared ready to strike back in one final attempt to win their dispute. Before the argument could escalate any further, they heard banging on the front door. Immediately, Bria thought it might be Aldo Bombalino leading a gang of independent journalists anxious to get the scoop on Lugo's death. When she turned around, she was filled with relief that she was wrong.

"*Fammi entrare!*" Annamaria cried, loud enough to be heard through the locked door.

"*Finalmente!*" Bria cried. "Let them in."

Pippa unlocked the door, and Annamaria ran into the café, bosom heaving, cheeks reddened and glistening with sweat. She was followed by Luca, who looked much calmer, although that wasn't a hard task, because the second Pippa relocked the door, Annamaria started screaming.

"*Dio mio*! What happened?"

Annamaria took one look at Chef Lugo's corpse, and she didn't need anyone to explain to her what had transpired in her café in her absence. "He's dead! Right next to the *sfogliatelle* and panettone! *Caro Dio*! Chef Lugo's turned Caffè Positano into Caffè della Morte! How did this happen?"

Bria put her arms around Annamaria and turned her so she was no longer facing the man who was supposed to have been her costar. "We don't really know."

Massimo wasn't nearly as comforting when he addressed Annamaria. "What I want to know is, where the hell have you been?"

Annamaria waved a piece of paper frantically in the air. "Getting this notarized."

"Is that the document allowing the crew to film in your café?" Bria asked.

"Yes," Annamaria confirmed.

Massimo whipped around to face Pippa. "You told me that was taken care of!"

Pippa's neck and cheeks turned beet red, and she stuttered an unintelligible response.

Luckily, Annamaria came to her rescue. "It's my fault. Pippa reminded me, but I forgot until this morning, and then it took me forever to track down Dante."

"Dante's the mayor, not a notary," Bria stated.

"He's also a lawyer," Luca said.

"He's the mayor *and* a lawyer?" Rosalie asked.

"Yes," Luca replied. "And an Italian lawyer is also a notary."

Massimo walked toward Luca, and Bria was certain he deliberately made his heels sound louder on the blue-and-yellow porcelain tile with each step. "I assume you're here because Nunzi texted you about Lugo's death, and the news hasn't yet spread like wildfire throughout this gossip-hungry little village."

Bria noticed Luca flinch at Massimo's unflattering description of Positano, but he maintained his composure, as not only the chief of police but also an informal ambassador. His reaction was impressive, and Bria was reminded that he was the opposite of the stereotypical hotheaded Italian man.

Luca nodded at Massimo. "That is correct." He then went into action and addressed the crowd.

"May I have your attention, *per favore*. I need everyone except the television crew to exit the café, but remain in the sectioned-off area outside. My team will collect your contact information and take brief statements from all of you. *Grazie*."

Most of the crowd followed Nunzi, exiting quickly and without any further protests. Although Bria, Rosalie, and Annamaria weren't part of the crew, they remained behind. Whether he was allowing his personal feelings to overrule his professional orders or he believed they had important information to add, Luca allowed them to stay.

"Now," Luca said, "will someone tell me what happened?"

Bria and Massimo started to speak at the same time and stopped only when Luca raised his hand. "Massimo, why don't you go first."

"We had just started filming, and Luca appeared to be nervous."

"He was," Bria interjected.

Luca smiled patiently as Rosalie gave Bria's hand a hard squeeze. "*Prego*, let me hear from Massimo first, and then you can add to the story."

"*Certo. Perdonami,*" Bria said. "It's only that I was the one standing right next to him."

"Why were you standing next to him?" Annamaria asked. In an instant, she put the pieces together. "*Dio mio*! You took my place and were filming with Chef Lugo! Bria, I'm so sorry. I didn't mean to put you right next to death's door!"

Bria hugged Annamaria, and Rosalie patted her back for good measure. The woman had expected this morning to be filled with elation, not remorse. After a minute of crying, she pulled herself together and grabbed a napkin from one of the café tables. She wiped her eyes and tearstained cheeks, blew her nose, and crumpled up the napkin and tucked it into her cleavage. She looked directly at Bria and said, "Tell me exactly what happened."

"Lugo and I had just started filming," Bria said. "I recited the introduction Massimo had written and asked Lugo if he was excited to be here in Positano and the café. Like Massimo said, Lugo appeared to be nervous, so I tried to think of something to say to calm him down, but before I could, he started to choke."

"Did he drink or eat anything just before he started choking?" Luca asked.

"Yes, *scusa*, I picked up a pastry, split it in half, and gave it to him," Bria said. "He took a bite out of it and started to cough."

"Was it my *maritozzo*?" Annamaria cried. "It's stuffed with whipped cream. Maybe Lugo was lactose intolerant."

Luca turned to Massimo, but it took the producer a moment to realize Luca was seeking confirmation or denial regarding Annamaria's assumption. "No, Chef Lugo was not lactose intolerant or allergic to dairy."

"It wasn't the *maritozzo* or any of your pastries, Annamaria. It was a mini *presnitz* Lugo made this morning," Pippa said.

"How can you be so sure it was something Lugo baked himself?" Luca asked.

"Because I was the one who put the pastries on the tray Bria chose from," Pippa said. "Annamaria's pastries were on the shelves in the glass counters, out of Bria's reach."

"*Grazie Dio*!" Annamaria said. "I wouldn't want to be responsible for killing Chef Lugo."

"Nobody killed Lugo," Massimo said.

"You don't know that," Bria claimed.

"You think he was murdered?" Annamaria cried.

"It's possible," Bria said.

"That's ridiculous!" Massimo cried. "Obviously, he had a heart attack."

"*Chiedo scusa*, but there's nothing obvious about this," Bria said. "We have to investigate first to find out exactly how he died."

"*We?*" Luca asked.

"I mean, *we*, as in the police department, need to explore all possibilities that could have resulted in Chef Lugo's death," Bria said.

Rosalie tilted her head and whispered in Bria's ear, "Nice save."

"*Grazie*," Bria mumbled.

"Maybe he had an allergic reaction to something he baked," Annamaria suggested.

"Will you listen to this nonsense!" Massimo replied. "If Lugo baked the pastries, he would've chosen the ingredients."

"Someone could have added to the recipe," Bria said.

"You mean *tampered* with the recipe, right?" Rosalie asked.

"Bria was trying to be subtle," Luca said. "Take notes, *sorella*."

"Who else had access to the kitchen?" Bria asked.

"*That* was subtle?" Rosalie asked.

"We're getting ahead of ourselves," Luca said. "We need to wait until the medical examiner has a chance to examine the body and do an autopsy."

"Those things take forever, Luca, and you know that," Bria said.

"It's called due process, and it's how the police operates," Luca replied.

The rest of Positano operated in a different way.

"I was in the kitchen this morning, before I realized I hadn't gotten the document notarized and had to leave," Annamaria announced.

"I was there, too," Pippa said. "Along with the rest of the crew."

Massimo threw his hands up. "I went back to the kitchen several times to talk to Lugo, so you can add me to the suspect list."

"No one is a suspect," Luca said.

"*Anzi*! We're all suspects," Bria contradicted. "Any one of us in here could've killed Lugo."

"Basta! We don't know that he was killed!" Luca said. "Only the clues and the facts will tell us that, not your imagination."

"You say imagination," Bria said. "I say instinct."

"I say that we need to let the chief of police do his job," Massimo said. "Which is follow this investigation to wherever it leads. Starting right now."

Luca waited a moment before moving. Bria thought his hesitation was a way to make it look like he was carrying out his duty on his own timetable and not in response to Massimo's order. He pulled out latex gloves from his pants pocket and put them on as he walked over to Lugo's body. He took out a plastic bag from a compartment on his belt and filled it with the remnants of the pastry Lugo had been eating at the time of his death. He lifted the dead man's shoulder to get a better look at his face, and Bria saw that Lugo's mouth remained open, as if he was about to say something. Which was because right before he died, he had wanted to say something.

"I remembered something else," Bria announced. "When we were waiting in the back, Lugo told me he wanted to make an announcement."

"About what?" Massimo asked.

"I don't know, but it was off script," Bria said. "He warned me about it because he didn't want me to get nervous when he started ad-libbing."

"That is untrue!" Massimo cried. "Luigi and I went over that script for weeks, perfecting it. Anything he wanted to say was already in there."

"Bria, did he tell you what he was going to say?" Luca asked.

"No, only that it was something he had to confess," Bria said.

"Confess?" Massimo asked.

"Yes, that's the word he used," Bria said.

Luca ran a latex-clad finger alongside the bulging red splotches on Lugo's neck. "Tell us, Massimo, what would Chef Lugo have to confess?"

Massimo forced himself to laugh. "Why are you asking me such a question?"

"Because according to you, you were Chef Lugo's manager, producer, and scriptwriter," Luca said. "If Lugo wanted to change the script, he would have discussed it with you."

"Unless he didn't want Massimo to know what changes he wanted to make," Bria said.

Massimo scowled at Bria. When he realized every eye in the room was staring at him, he began to smile. "There were no secrets between me and Luigi. Whatever he wanted to say would not have been a surprise to me."

Bria knew Massimo was wrong. She knew it in her gut and because of what Lugo had told her at the party and before the filming. He was going to confess something that would change the course of his life. It was not something that anyone else knew about but him. Whatever Lugo had wanted to share with his TV audience died with him and, for now at least, would remain unspoken. The kitchen, however, was not nearly as quiet.

"What was that noise?" Annamaria asked.

"A mouse?" Rosalie queried.

"*Sei pazza*!" Annamaria shouted. "There has *never* been a mouse in my kitchen!"

They all turned toward the kitchen and remained silent until they heard the noise again. Luca entered the room first, followed by Bria and Annamaria, with the rest of the group close behind. They heard another noise and saw the closet door buckle. There was definitely something inside it, but when they heard a sneeze, they knew it wasn't a mouse. They all screamed and jumped back several feet when the door flew open and a man fell onto the floor at their feet.

"Bria, look!" Rosalie cried. "That's my boyfriend from Le Sirenuse!"

"No it isn't," Annamaria said.

"Then who is he?" Bria asked.

"He's Michele Vistigliano," Annamaria said. "Paolo's nephew."

CHAPTER 6

Michele rolled onto his back and looked up at the faces peering down at him. He looked stunned, his eyes moving from one person to the next, his mouth opening but emitting no sound. He clutched his forehead, and Bria could see the beginnings of a bump form on the spot that must have taken the brunt of the impact when he crashed into the floor. He'd have a welt for sure, although a minor bruise might be the least of his troubles.

When Bria saw Michele last night at Le Sirenuse, he'd reminded her of a *straccione*, a ragamuffin, based solely on his appearance and body language. Now, seeing him close up, her opinion changed, but only for the worse. Michele was wearing the same clothes, and from the odor emanating from his body and the oily condition of his hair, Bria was rather certain he hadn't showered this morning. He could be *pericoloso* or just *un'anima perduta*. Bria quickly corrected herself: he could be both—dangerous and a lost soul. And now that he'd been found hiding on the premises where Lugo had just died, Michele was definitely in a precarious situation.

"What the hell were you doing hiding in the closet?"

Michele twitched when Massimo bellowed. He covered his face with his hands in a juvenile attempt to disappear. When he finally accepted the fact that invisibility wasn't an option, Michele lowered his hands from his face and looked up at the group. Bria noticed that his eyes were a beautiful shade of brown, with unexpected flecks of amber and more than a little bit of fear. "I . . . I wasn't hiding."

"Then what were you doing in the closet?" Massimo asked. "Looking for a broom?"

"Massimo, *per favore*, let me handle this." Luca extended a hand to Michele, who, after a moment's hesitation, latched onto it. Luca pulled Michele up to a standing position, the movement such a jolt that Michele had to press himself into the closet door to steady himself.

Bria went to the kitchen sink and filled a cup with water. "Here. Drink this."

Michele took the cup from Bria and attempted to smile. *"Grazie."*

"Buon Dio!" Massimo cried. "Stop treating him like a guest, when he's obviously a criminal."

"I'm not a criminal!" Michele roared.

From the way Paolo had briefly talked about his nephew, Bria didn't think Michele's statement was entirely true. She suspected that his past had been marred by some kind of criminal behavior, whether it be petty or lethal, but he could have turned his life around like Giovanni had. He may no longer be a criminal, but he still needed to explain his actions.

"Why don't you tell us why you were hiding in the closet?" Bria asked.

"I told you, I wasn't hiding," Michele replied.

Massimo opened his mouth, but Luca was able to ask his question first. "Then what were you doing in there?"

Michele stared at Luca and then at Bria and then at the floor. "I . . . I guess I was hiding."

"Un bugiardo and a criminal!" Massimo shouted.

"I'm not lying!" Michele cried. "I just wanted to see Chef Lugo."

"Then why didn't you watch the filming like everyone else?" Bria asked. "Your uncle is friends with Annamaria. I'm sure he could have gotten you an invitation to sit inside with the rest of us."

"*Certo!*" Annamaria agreed. "I would do anything for Paolo."

"I didn't just want to see Chef Lugo," Michele said. "I wanted to talk to him."

"Talk to him about what?" Luca asked.

"About becoming a chef."

Bria glanced over at Luca and met his eyes. They were both thinking the same thing: Michele was, in fact, a liar.

"You just came to Positano to work with your uncle as a mechanic, and now you want to be a chef?" Bria asked.

Michele ran his hand through his oily hair and sighed heavily. "I'm a mechanic because I don't know how to earn money doing anything else, legitimately, anyway, but I want to be a chef."

"Paolo never mentioned anything to me about that," Annamaria said.

"He doesn't know," Michele replied. "He would think I'm *pazzo* and would tell me to focus on getting my life back on track and not go off to chase some idiotic dream."

"Wanting to be a chef isn't idiotic."

Michele's eyes lit up when Rosalie spoke. Bria didn't know if he had seen Rosalie at Le Sirenuse and was as attracted to her as she was to him, but it was evident by the way he looked at her that he was at least grateful for her understanding.

"But it is idiotic to hide in a closet in order to meet someone," Rosalie continued. "Did you ever think of going up to him and saying, '*Ciao*, Chef Lugo. I'd like to talk to you'?"

Then again, Rosalie wasn't always the understanding type.

"That's what I was going to do," Michele said.

"When?" Massimo asked. "Were you going to jump out during the filming and hijack his TV show?"

"No, of course not," Michele protested. "I was planning on staying hidden until after the filming and then try to get Chef Lugo alone to ask him for advice on how to become a chef or if there was any way I could maybe be a part of his show."

"Why didn't you ask him at the party?" Luca asked.

"By the time I worked up the nerve, I heard that he had already left," Michele replied.

Massimo stepped to the side and pointed to Chef Lugo in the other room. "Would you like to ask him now?" Lugo's body was in the same position it had been in since he died. The others had gotten used to seeing him slumped over and unmoving, but when Michele gasped, Bria realized the man didn't know what had transpired while he was behind a closed door.

"*Oh mio Dio!*" Michele cried. "What happened?"

"Why don't you tell us?" Massimo asked.

Luca placed his hand on Massimo's shoulder. As the chief of police as well as a local in the village, Luca often displayed two opposing sides of his personality, one being the authoritative commander and the other being the compassionate friend. Bria had witnessed both personas, sometimes during the same meeting, like now, but there was something about the way he touched Massimo that was different. Luca didn't appear commanding or compassionate; he appeared cautious.

Massimo was physically imposing when compared to Luca, even though Luca was in perfect shape and was almost fifteen years younger than the producer. Bria knew that Luca wanted to maintain control of the situation, but he didn't want to make Massimo feel that he was being confronted. The man had shown he had a temper; Luca was trying to keep him from showing that he could also be violent.

Thankfully, Luca's gesture helped Massimo maintain his composure. He glanced at Luca's hand, and for a second, Bria did think he was going to swipe it away, but instead he inhaled deeply and slowly let the air escape his nostrils. His shoulders relaxed, and he smiled when he returned Luca's gesture and placed his hand on the cop's shoulder.

"*Grazie*, Luca," Massimo said. "Perhaps you can ask Michele how he thinks Luigi wound up in this irreversible state."

"Who's Luigi?" Michele asked.

"Chef Lugo's real name is Luigi Gordonato," Bria informed him.

"I would like to know what you think, Michele," Luca said. "How do you suppose Lugo died?"

Hearing the truth about Lugo's condition transformed Michele back into a confused boy. He looked like he had when he had fallen onto the floor: his eyes were wide, and his mouth was open, but he was silent. He looked like he was searching for something. But what? The truth or a plausible alibi?

Michele looked at Bria and then at Luca. His voice was a whisper when he said, "I have no idea."

"You didn't see anything from the closet?" Luca asked.

"No. I hid in there before he arrived, and stayed there," Michele explained. "I could hear that the filming had started, and then there was some kind of commotion, but I couldn't hear what anyone said, because they were all in the other room."

"Weren't you afraid someone would open the closet and expose you?" Bria asked.

"There's hardly anything in there . . . some cleaning supplies and a mop," Michele replied. "As long as there wasn't a mess to clean up, I figured I was safe."

"How did you get into my café?" Annamaria asked. "I was here early with Pippa, and we never saw you."

"I climbed in through the back window," Michele said. "The two of you were arguing, and you never heard me come in."

"We weren't arguing!" Annamaria and Pippa shouted at the same time.

"I heard you both shouting about some document that Massimo needed," Michele said.

"The registration to film in Positano," Pippa explained.

"The one I forgot to get notarized," Annamaria confessed.

"And the one Pippa told me Massimo would kill you over, because if the document wasn't notarized, Luca could prevent the show from being filmed," Bria added. "Pippa, you don't really think Massimo would kill Annamaria, do you?"

Bria thought that Pippa's words had been an exaggeration and that Pippa hadn't truly believed Massimo would kill Annamaria, even if she caused the shoot to be delayed or canceled. The current circumstances, however, made it important to distinguish casual hyperbole from deliberate accusation. No one here knew Massimo better than Pippa—except Chef Lugo, who, unfortunately, could no longer vouch for the man's character—and maybe she knew something about the producer that needed to be shared. Like the fact that he possibly harbored homicidal tendencies.

"Had I known Annamaria's inability to carry out a simple task could have thwarted something we had planned for months and could make us look like fools to the industry, murder would not have been out of the question," Massimo fumed. "Luckily, I was unaware of the problem, because, ironically, Pippa did her job and didn't allow the issue to distract me from my singular goal."

"Which would be?" Luca asked.

"To bring Luigi's career to the next level," Massimo said.

"Along with your own," Bria added.

The producer stared at Bria, never losing the smirk that was now plastered on his face. "Last I heard, ambition wasn't a crime, even though the Italian Communist Party may disagree."

The sound of laughter made everyone turn to find the source. It was an unlikely one for sure. Nunzi stood in the doorway to the kitchen, with an expression that didn't look anything like the grim images on Communist propaganda posters.

"*Ti prego, perdonami,*" Nunzi said. "It's just that I've always found Communism to be very funny. Socialized medicine is an ethical goal, which we've achieved, but overthrowing all aspects of the government? I don't think so."

"Aren't you supposed to be guarding the café instead of giving us a boring history lesson?" Rosalie asked.

"I took everyone's contact information, and Matteo is collecting their statements," Nunzi replied. "I locked the front door and found what I heard to be very entertaining. I mean, even Palmiro Togliatti, one of Communism's biggest cheerleaders, gave up his Italian citizenship to become a Russian."

Rosalie shook her head and waved her hands wildly in front of her. "What has any of that got to do with Chef Lugo's death?"

Nunzi was done laughing, and a sadness clung to her eyes. A short while ago Nunzi had been gushing about Lugo, exposing her crush on the man, but now she was staring at his dead body. Witnessing such a terrible scene made people behave in many ways. "It means that Massimo's right. Italy doesn't criminalize ambition. Only murder."

Annamaria gasped. "You do think Chef Lugo was murdered!"

"I think it's a possibility," Nunzi replied.

"No one knows yet how Chef Lugo actually died," Luca stated.

Slowly, Michele walked from the kitchen into the café and stood in front of Chef Lugo's body. He looked at the corpse in awe, and Bria couldn't tell if it was because he had never seen a dead body before or because it was the body of his fallen idol. Either way, Michele was deeply affected by what he saw.

"I can't believe he's dead," Michele whispered.

"I can't believe someone may have murdered him," Annamaria added.

"Stop saying that!" Massimo cried. "No one would want to kill my Luigi."

"I hope that's true," Luca said. "But if it does turn out that Chef Lugo didn't die of natural causes, you, along with everyone else who was in this room, will be a suspect in his murder."

There was nothing like an accusation of homicide to quiet a room and smother it in a blanket of despair. Bria watched Luca look around the room at the potential suspects, and when his gaze landed on Massimo, she could have sworn his brown eyes started to twinkle.

"*Capite?*"

In response to Luca's question, every head nodded. Bria expected Massimo or Michele to argue or protest further, but they remained silent. If they had any second thoughts about their compliance, it was too late to respond, because the paramedics were knocking on the door. It was time to move the dead body from the café.

Nunzi unlocked the door, and Luca instructed everyone to stay inside as the paramedics prepared Chef Lugo's body to be transported to the morgue in Amalfi, where the medical examiner would perform the autopsy and determine the real cause of death. Regardless of the outcome, it was still a crime. A man in the prime of his life, on the verge of international success, had been extinguished. Either by his own body shutting down or by being shut down by another body.

Bria watched the paramedics wheel Chef Lugo out of the café. The white sheet that covered him from head to toe was meant to conceal the corpse, but all it did was broadcast that death had returned to Positano. The absence of his presence in the café, however, didn't change the fact that the deceased was still the primary topic of conversation.

"I can't believe that man died in my café!" Annamaria exclaimed. "Antonio will have to help me scrub this place from top to bottom."

"You can't do that, Annamaria," Bria said.

"*Perché no?*" Annamaria asked. "No one will want to eat here if they know I haven't cleaned."

"You can't clean until after my forensics team has completed their search for clues," Luca explained.

"Clues for what?" Annamaria asked.

"To be used to find the culprit, in case it turns out that Chef Lugo did die as a result of foul play," Bria said.

"Bria's right, Annamaria. I'm sorry," Luca said. "I'm going to need you to keep the café closed at least for the rest of the day and perhaps tomorrow so my team can sweep for fingerprints and look for any possible evidence."

Annamaria gasped and shook her head. "I can't believe this is happening here in my own café."

Bria knew exactly how her friend felt, having gone through a similar experience right before Bella Bella opened. She also knew that in a few days the excitement would wane and things would get back to normal. For most of the residents in the village, anyway.

"Nunzi, please take Michele back to the police station to get his formal statement," Luca ordered.

"*Davvero?*" Rosalie said. "Is that necessary?"

"If it wasn't necessary, the chief wouldn't have asked me to carry out his order," Nunzi replied.

"*Va bene*," Michele said. "I understand."

The shock of seeing Chef Lugo's dead body having worn off, and the realization that his dream of working alongside him would never come true having settled in, Michele had become transformed. He was no longer stuttering or scared; he was confident and almost a little cocky. Bria wasn't sure if he was being defiant in the face of police procedure or if he felt comfortable among law enforcement, having been in their company so many times before.

Michele raised his hands in front of him, wrists together, and smiled at Nunzi. "I know how these things work."

"Handcuffs aren't necessary," Nunzi replied. "But if you run, remember that I know the layout of this village better than the original architects who built it."

After Nunzi led Michele out of the café, Luca turned to the rest of the crowd. "Until we find out how Lugo died, I will need all of you to remain in the village."

Immediately the production crew started to complain and gripe, Massimo the loudest voice among them. "How long is it going to take to get an autopsy report in a little village like this that doesn't even have a real hospital?"

"I've asked the medical examiner in Amalfi to make this top priority, but it could still take a week or two to get a full report, including toxicology," Luca replied. "I know it's an inconvenience, but this is not a request."

"This is outrageous!" Massimo groused. "You're keeping us prisoner here!"

"I don't think anyone has ever considered an extended stay in Positano as a prison sentence," Luca replied. "But to answer your question, yes, no one is allowed to leave until I say so."

The producer had been fighting very hard to maintain his composure, but he suddenly erupted with the force of Vesuvius. His outburst wasn't entirely shocking, as the producer had already proven he was a hothead, *una testa calda*, but his explosion was terrifying, because it wasn't directed at the man in front of him but at the man who had been wheeled away.

"You're lucky you're dead, Luigi! If you were still alive, I'd strangle you to death with my bare hands!"

Bria felt the fire in her stomach ignite like an inferno. She was convinced that the man wasn't just letting off steam; she was convinced that Massimo Angelini was capable of murder.

CHAPTER 7

After the chaotic morning, Bria needed a moment of calm. She didn't need to look any further than into Bravo's eyes.

She had never wanted to get a dog. It had been Carlo's idea. Ever since he was a young boy, he had wanted a canine companion, but his parents—particularly Imperia—had refused to allow a pet of any kind into their home. When he finally had a house and a family of his own, he wanted to fulfill his childhood dream. At first, Bria wasn't entirely on board with the plan, but unexpected circumstances intervened, and ultimately, she changed her mind.

Two years after Marco was born, the couple actively tried to give him a sibling, but for whatever reason, Bria couldn't get pregnant again. Neither of them worried about it too much, and they believed if they were meant to have another child, they would. When Carlo suggested they get a dog as sort of a four-legged sibling, Bria took some convincing. It wasn't that she didn't like dogs. She simply hadn't grown up with them, and none of her close friends had had dogs, either. She hadn't experienced firsthand the kind of unconditional love and joyful turmoil a dog could bring to a family. The moment she laid eyes on Bravo's soulful expression and felt his gentle touch, all doubts faded, and she knew that her family had found its latest member.

"*Dimmelo, Bravo*," Bria said. "What do you make of all this?"

Bravo growled softly, more in response to Bria's fingers, which were rubbing the underside of his snout, than to her question. She had gotten away from the café, but it was hard to shake what she had recently witnessed. It felt good to be back home, but it was hard to stop seeing Chef's Lugo's frightened expression every time she closed her eyes.

After leaving Caffè Positano, Luca went directly to the police station to question the entire television crew, including Massimo and Pippa, while Rosalie had to get back to her boat for an afternoon tour. Mimi picked up Annamaria so they could commiserate together, Tobias and Daisy were still out sightseeing, and Marco didn't get out of school for another two hours. When Bria got home, she filled Giovanni in on what had happened, and he was naturally stunned by the news. Sensing how rattled Bria was, Vanni decided one way to help ease the unpleasant memory was to spend time in the kitchen and whip up a tantalizing dinner for her.

Sitting on her balcony with Bravo, Bria closed her eyes and inhaled the soothing aroma of a vegetable and rice casserole doused with lemon, herbs, and spices. Mingling with the aroma was the rich, meaty smell of grilled London broil. She also detected the faint scent of chocolate and remembered that Giovanni was making her mother's limoncello chocolate mousse for dessert. Bria knew that if Vanni's version was half as good as Fifetta's, everyone would be begging for seconds.

When Bravo scraped her knee with his paw several times, Bria laughed out loud. She pulled Bravo close and nuzzled her nose against his neck. "Someone's begging for attention." His action was universal dog language, and it meant "Take me for a walk." Bria had always been impressed with how insightful Bravo could be. After Carlo died, he wouldn't leave Marco's side, sensing that his friend needed constant comfort. Whenever she had felt overwhelmed and near the breaking point while fixing up Bella Bella, Bravo had pranced into the room from wherever he had been to distract Bria from her worries. Now he was giving her the remedy she needed. Instead of repeating the images of the morning in her head, she needed to fill her mind with happier sights and sounds. Nothing made Bria happier than strolling through the village.

Bria told Giovanni she was taking Bravo for a walk and on her way back she would pick up Marco from school. Bravo was waiting by the front door, his tail wagging like a metronome, and the moment Bria opened the door, he ran out into the sunshine. It was calming to live in a place where you could walk your dog without having him on a leash, where he could explore the world untethered. And if he got lost—which was a rarity, since Bravo knew every twist and turn of the village almost as well as Enrico and Nunzi, who had both grown up here—Bria knew that someone would recognize him and bring him home safe and sound. If only humans could be so lucky.

Try as she might to forget about the morning, Bria was still haunted by the look in Chef Lugo's eyes seconds before he died as she walked down the curved road of Viale Pasitea. At that moment, he wasn't safe and sound, and he knew it. His mind knew what was happening to him; he knew that very shortly he would cease to exist. Bria prayed that her presence in his final moments—even though she hadn't truly done anything—had given him some peace.

Basta! she cried to herself. *No more.*

Bria shook her head vigorously. She didn't want to dwell on Lugo's death. She had come out to be reminded that the world was still beautiful. And in Positano, no matter where you looked, the view was always beautiful.

The sun shone majestically in the center of a crisp blue sky that was unmarred except for a few puffy clouds that floated lazily above the horizon. The sea was a darker shade of blue and so tranquil, it appeared to be unmoving. The only thing that made it clear that it was water and not a frozen surface was the sailboat, with its gleaming white mainsail and jib, that was being propelled by the wind.

As Bria came around the bend, she could see a snippet of the iconic blue-and-white umbrellas that dotted Spiaggia Grande Beach. She knew blissful tourists were lounging underneath them, their bodies lathered in suntan lotion. Some, she was certain, were wearing racy bathing suits they wouldn't dare wear back home, wherever they lived, and sipping Aperol spritzes or, if they felt particularly decadent, a champagne cocktails. Positano did have a reputation for being a destination in which to explore the glamorous life. Every once in a while, like this morning, however, there was a reminder that life and death marched hand in hand with the sun and surf.

"*Uffa!*" Bria cried out loud. "Enough with thinking about a man I didn't even know."

Two Vespas sped by and came dangerously close to Bravo, who was intently watching a salamander slither over stones on the edge of the road. Bria had learned when she first moved here that it was useless to yell at the Vespas or the cars that sped down the road or at the people on bikes and electric scooters. They were all part of the complicated landscape that made up the village. The only way to deal with it all was to navigate carefully and, when possible, find refuge on a bench or in a café. Unfortunately, her favorite café was closed.

Bria knew that Caffè Positano wasn't going to be open for business, but she expected it to be occupied. She thought the forensics team would be working for several more hours, searching for clues and dusting for fingerprints, which in the most popular café in the village was an almost futile task. Peering through the front door, she saw that the lights were off and the café looked deserted. The team must have finished their work in record time.

Bria was about to turn away when she heard a scream.

It wasn't Annamaria's high, piercing cry, which Bria had heard the other day, when Annamaria had told her that the café would be the location for the first episode in Chef Lugo's new TV series. This sounded like someone was surprised or was crying for help. Bria knew that her imagination could be getting the best of her, but since she had witnessed one death already today, she wasn't going to take any chances. She did something very uncharacteristic: she texted the police instead of calling her best friend, Rosalie.

Come quick! I heard a scream from inside Annamaria's café.

Bria sent the text and immediately got a response from Luca.

On my way. Do not go in.

Bria obeyed Luca's command, but Bravo, who was otherwise very well trained, did not.

"Bravo, no!"

Ignoring Bria's command, as well, Bravo ran around the left side of the café and down the very narrow alleyway that separated the café from Vintage Positano, a consignment shop that was one of Bria and Rosalie's favorite stores and carried a large selection of mid-century modern clothes and home goods. Bria took one look at the narrow width separating the two stores and knew that she risked tearing her blouse or skin if she tried to take Bravo's route. Instead, she ran down the right side of the café, which was the path customers would take to get to the back patio. Once there, she saw Bravo slapping his paw against the door that led into the kitchen. When Bria stood behind him and looked through the small window in the center of the door, she understood why. He was trying to get Pippa's attention.

"Pippa!" Bria opened the door, which had been closed but not locked, and entered. She stepped into the front room and gasped. "What are you doing here?"

Pippa was standing over the pastries in the counter's glass display with her camera in her hand. Bria recognized her expression. She looked like Marco did whenever he got caught doing something he knew he shouldn't have been doing.

"Bria! *Ciao*. I can explain."

That was essentially what Marco always said, too.

Bria looked at the young woman and was filled with a sense of distrust. She didn't know Pippa very well, but she liked her. Her positive feelings for Pippa might have more to do with her immense dislike of Massimo, but regardless, there was absolutely no good reason for Pippa to be in Annamaria's closed café without Annamaria. Bria did her best to push judgment from her mind and listened.

"I came back after the police left and found that the back door had been left unlocked," Pippa started.

"That doesn't sound like something the police would do."

"Maybe they were in a rush and forgot—*non lo so*—but I was able to get in without tampering with the lock."

"I'll talk to Luca about that, but there's no way you would've noticed that the back door was unlocked if you hadn't deliberately come back here, hoping to sneak in. Why would you do that?"

"To take photos of the fake croissants I made."

Of all the things Bria expected Pippa to say, that was not one of them. It wasn't something Luca was expecting, either.

"You're going to need to explain things a bit further, Pippa."

Bria and Pippa turned around and saw Luca standing in the kitchen. Bravo was sprawled out on the floor next to him, belly up, waiting to be petted, but Luca was here on official business, and Bravo would have to wait.

Luca shrugged his shoulders. "I'm waiting."

"*Vi dirò tutto*. The croissants came out so good that I wanted to make sure I had photos of them to put in my portfolio," Pippa explained. "Now that the TV series is scrapped, I'm going to have to find another job."

Luca took a few steps closer, his eyes quickly surveying the counter and surrounding area to gauge if Pippa's explanation could be true. "Why didn't you ask for permission?"

"I was going to, which is why I came back here," Pippa said. "I thought I'd find you or Nunzi here, but the place was empty."

"The crew finished quickly," Luca replied. "And Annamaria said she'd keep the café closed as long as necessary, so another team will come back tonight to do a final search."

"Pippa said the back door was closed but unlocked, which is how she got in," Bria conveyed.

"*Veramente?*" Luca was as surprised to hear that news as Bria had been. "I'll have to speak to my people about that." He turned back to Pippa. "Is that all you were doing here?"

"Yes, I just wanted to take some photos."

Bria mulled over what Pippa had said, and she thought it sounded logical. Until she remembered why she had known there was someone in the café in the first place.

"Why did you scream?" Bria asked.

"Pippa screamed?" Luca asked.

"Yes," Bria replied. "That's how I knew there was someone inside."

Luca and Bria stared at each other for a moment, turned to Pippa, and then asked the same question in unison. "Why did you scream?"

"Because I found this inside one of the croissants."

Pippa was about to hand the piece of paper to Bria, but Luca stopped her. "Don't touch it."

"*Scusi,*" Pippa replied. "I already did."

"That's all right, but don't pick it up again."

Luca walked toward Pippa to make sure she followed his orders and to get a better look at what she had found. Bria and Luca stood on either side of Pippa behind the counter and saw a piece of paper lying on top of the fake croissants. They bent down and read the message: *Meet me at Le Sirenuse tonight.*

Mamma Rita. The message was straightforward, but it left them both confused.

"How did it get inside one of the croissants?" Luca asked.

"I don't know," Pippa said. "But anyone who was here could have done so without being noticed. Lots of people were handling the croissants, and some of them, like this one, snap open."

"They snap open?" Luca asked.

Pippa was about to pick up the croissant in which she'd found the note, but Luca reminded her again not to touch any potential evidence. She picked up one of the croissants at the far end of the tray and snapped it open, like she had when she'd previously shown Bria.

"*Stupefacente*," Luca murmured.

"I thought it was amazing, too," Bria said. "You're very talented, Pippa. I don't blame you for wanting to capture your work for your portfolio."

"But you shouldn't have just come in here without permission," Luca said.

"I know," Pippa replied. *"Mi dispiace."*

"So someone at some point put a note into a croissant presumably meant for Chef Lugo," Luca mused.

"Someone who calls themselves Mamma Rita," Bria said.

"Who's Mamma Rita?" Luca asked.

"I was hoping you'd know," Bria replied. "Pippa, do you have any idea who it could be?"

"No," Pippa said. "Lugo never mentioned her name."

Bria turned to Luca. "Could she be someone in the village?"

"If she is, I've never heard of her."

"There's only one way to find out who Mamma Rita is," Bria said.

"What's that?" Luca asked.

"Have a drink with me tonight at Le Sirenuse," Bria replied.

* * *

"Mamma!" Marco cried. *"Sei così bella."*

"Grazie, mi piccolino," Bria replied.

"Are you going to get dressed up every night?"

"No, *mi bello*, but it is becoming a habit, isn't it?"

She looked in the full-length mirror hanging on her bathroom door and was reminded of what Grand-mère Chantal, her French grandmother on her mother's side of the family, always said: *"Une femme sait quand elle est belle."* Chantal, like Fifetta, was rarely wrong. A woman did know when she was beautiful. Bria's wavy black hair had been tamed and pulled back into a loose bun. Curly tendrils fell against her cheekbones, but the upswept style accentuated Bria's slender neck, which was further highlighted by the low V-neck bodice of the green silk wrap dress she wore.

Soft make-up in shimmering shades of green to complement her eyes, diamond cluster teardrop earrings, and a simple diamond tennis bracelet were her only accessories. Although she really wanted to wear her espadrilles with the soft, cushiony soles, Bria knew they would clash with her outfit. Instead, she wore low-heeled tan mules she had had handmade at Rallo Antonio, one of the many family-owned shoe stores in the village.

"Do you have another date with Luca, Mamma?" Marco asked.

"No, angelo mio," Bria said. "Luca and I are friends."

"Mamma, you know that Luca is more than just your friend." Marco was sitting on her bed, eating a cherry Italian ice, Bravo at his feet, waiting for some of the fruity dessert to spill onto the floor. The picture of innocence.

If that was true, then why did Bria feel so guilty? She thought about it for a moment and then sighed. It was because her son was right. No matter how hard she tried to fight it, Luca was becoming much more than a friend. She didn't yet know what category he fell into, but if she was being honest, she couldn't label their relationship as completely platonic. At the moment, however, she didn't feel the need to be completely honest with her son.

"You're right, *mi lupo*," Bria said. "Luca is a very close family friend."

"Is he your *fidanzato*?" Marco asked.

"No, Luca is not my boyfriend," Bria said.

She then resorted to the only tactic that she knew would make Marco forget about his mother's romantic relationships. She tickled him. "You're the only boy in your mamma's life."

Marco held his cherry ice over his head as Bria tickled his stomach. He started giggling uncontrollably and teetered to the right, causing the ice in his hand to tilt and fall onto the floor. Bravo leapt at the dessert and lapped it up before Marco even noticed it had fallen. When he did, he started giggling louder, and Bria couldn't resist joining in. They stopped only when they were interrupted.

"You're dressed up for playtime."

Bria looked up and saw Giovanni standing in the doorway, causing several thoughts to ricochet through her brain at the same time. This was the closest Vanni had come to actually entering her bedroom, the blond hair on his tanned forearms looked like corn silk, and, most disconcerting, she had inadvertently copied his hairstyle. Except that his bun looked better.

"I love what you've done with your hair," Vanni said.

"*Grazie*, Vanni," Bria said. "I thought I'd try something different."

"For her date with Luca," Marco said.

"Marco, *smettila*. I told you already I'm not going on a date," Bria said.

"Are you sure?" Giovanni asked. "Because it looks like you're going on a date."

"*Uffa!*" Bria cried, throwing her hands up in the air. "Not you, too!"

"Whatever you're doing, you look beautiful."

Bria couldn't tell if Giovanni meant for his comment to be flirtatious. He was normally very straightforward in his speech, at least around Bria. In the company of others—especially the police—he was often guarded and secretive, but after working with Bria for nearly six months, he'd learned to speak to her with candor. Their relationship had been built on honesty and trust. Bria needed to play by the same rules.

"*Grazie*," Bria said. "I'm meeting Luca to discuss a business thing."

"About Bella Bella?" Giovanni asked.

"No," Bria replied. "A police business thing."

"Are you a *poliziotta* like Nunzi?" Marco asked.

"No, but Luca and I have some police business to discuss."

Giovanni smiled a bit devilishly. "I guess the *polizia stradale* got new uniforms."

Bria was still unsure if Giovanni was flirting. He could be teasing her like a younger brother. A very handsome, incredibly muscular younger brother. A younger brother who needed to be put in his place. "If you don't get back to work, I may have to arrest you."

"*Sì, signora*," Giovanni replied. "The guests are preparing for dinner, and the lasagna is being kept warm in the oven."

"*Bene*," Bria said. "I should be back by the time you serve dessert, so you won't have to stay late."

"That's all right," Vanni said. "I have to quiz Marco for his Communion test. Which reminds me . . . Imperia called twice for you."

"I didn't get any messages from her on my phone."

"She called my phone," Vanni said. "She said, and I quote, 'I know my daughter-in-law will ignore me. I hope she hasn't trained the help to treat me in the same way.'"

"Nonna Imperia makes me laugh," Marco said, giggling.

Bria and Giovanni looked at each other and soon joined in.

For a moment, Bria imagined the three of them as one unit, like a family. She just as quickly shook the thought from her mind. There was a man waiting for her at a bar, and she needed a nice long walk to clear her head.

By the time Bria sat down at the bar of Le Sirenuse, she thought her feet were going to fall off. She wasn't used to walking through the village with heels on. Oh, how she wished she was wearing her espadrilles. She prayed Mamma Rita would show herself quickly, so they could confront her and she could get home to soak her feet in hot water.

When she saw Luca walking through the crowd to join her at the bar, all hope for a short evening disappeared. He was wearing the same navy suit he had worn last night, but in a much more casual style. His white shirt was unbuttoned to the second button, so Bria could see that the gold crucifix he wore around his neck got lost amid his black chest hair. He didn't smile when he saw Bria. He examined her from toe to head. Bria felt a heat grow in her stomach, and it wasn't for the usual reason, that she suspected imminent danger, although she did suspect danger of a different kind.

"*Ciao*," Luca said.

"*Ciao*," she replied.

And then she couldn't think of anything else to say.

Luckily, as the chief of police and a bossy big brother to Rosalie, Luca was prepared to take charge. He ordered them two Aperol spritzes and quickly turned the conversation to the reason they were meeting. Mamma Rita.

"Have you thought any further about who she could be?" Luca asked.

"Yes, and it's possible that Mamma Rita could be a man."

"Someone posing as a woman?"

"No, more of an alias or a decoy," Bria said.

"What do you mean by that?"

"Mamma Rita could be real, but she might not be the person who left the note," Bria explained. "Someone could have been using Chef Lugo's relationship with this Mamma Rita to lure him into a trap."

Luca smiled, his eyebrows raised. "Impressive, as always."

"*Grazie*," Bria replied. "I thought of it only because of Michele."

"Do you think Paolo's nephew could be Mamma Rita?"

"He could be," Bria replied. "*Pensaci*. Michele had to have known there was the possibility that he'd get caught hiding in the closet and miss an opportunity to meet with Chef Lugo."

"I'm surprised someone didn't find him before the filming started," Luca said.

"*Di preciso*! So why not put a note in one of the fake croissants to secure a meeting later on?"

Their conversation was interrupted when the bartender, an older man who looked like he had lived his whole life behind the bar, placed their drinks in front of them. "For you capo and your *bellissima compagna*, these are on the house."

The two men looked at each other with deep respect. Bria didn't know if Luca personally knew the bartender or if the older man was simply a citizen thankful that his village was being protected by an honorable chief of police.

"*Grazie, amico mio*," Luca said, raising his glass. "From me and my *bellissima compagna*."

Bria felt a warmth spread across her cheeks as Luca winked at the bartender and then took a sip of his drink. He looked at Bria and smiled. "Isn't my *compagna* thirsty?"

Bria didn't know if she should flutter her eyelashes or throw her drink in Luca's face. She felt like she was on display as Luca's arm candy. Worse, she didn't hate the thought. It was nice to be on a date again. If this was really a date, of course. She hadn't entirely decided. What she did decide was to change the subject.

"Weren't we talking about using a plastic pastry as a way to anonymously invite someone to a secret meeting?" Bria asked.

"It's possible that was Michele's strategy," Luca replied. "But how could he be sure Lugo would open the croissant with the note in it?. Why take such a risk?"

"From what I know about Michele, he's had a checkered past. Maybe he thought if he asked Lugo to talk with him, someone would tell him to stay clear of the mechanic with the bad reputation."

"That's true, but let's not discount the obvious."

"Which is?"

"That Pippa could have easily planted the note and then acted surprised to take any suspicion off her."

"*Non possibile*," Bria said. "Pippa screamed when she found the note, and she was alone. She wasn't trying to convince anyone she had uncovered it."

"You got me there," Luca said. "Maybe you *should* be on the police force."

"Not you, too!" Bria cried. "Marco and Vanni said the same thing when I told them I was meeting you."

"Is that all Vanni said?" Luca asked, not trying to conceal his sly smile.

"Yes, because he was too busy getting ready to serve dinner to our guests," Bria said.

"That reminds me. I skipped lunch and could use some food while we stake out this place."

"Is that what we're doing?" Bria asked. "We're on a stakeout?"

"We can call it that if it makes you more comfortable." Luca stared at Bria and held his gaze for longer than was necessary. "*Mi scusa.* I need to get a menu."

Bria watched Luca walk to the end of the bar and be embraced by the maître d'. As the chief of police, Luca was known throughout the village, and thanks to his fairness and dedication, he had garnered an almost universally favorable reputation. He was, as her parents often reminded her, *un uomo buono*. Bria agreed that Luca was indeed a very good man.

But she wasn't sitting at a bar, sipping a cocktail, to get closer to a very good man; she was there to look for a very important woman. She swiveled on her barstool to look out onto the terrace and didn't notice the glorious orange and purple sunset. She didn't hear the lush, romantic sounds coming from the string quartet. All she saw was the woman sitting by herself on the balcony.

It was the same mystery woman Bria had seen Lugo kissing the night of his party.

CHAPTER 8

The woman was certainly old enough to be a mother, but Bria couldn't imagine any man calling her Mamma. *Bellissima* maybe, *mi amore* definitely, perhaps even *tesoro*. But it was hard to imagine that any man would confuse the woman Bria was staring at for his mother. Unless his mother was gorgeous, alluring, and looked like a movie star who had just jumped off the silver screen.

The epitome of *la moda Positano*, the woman looked like a starlet from the early seventies. Someone who would have been seen on the arm of Franco Nero one night, then Fabio Testi the next. A woman who never had to utter a word to make a man want to possess her.

Her blond hair fell just past her shoulders and cascaded in long, carefree waves, as if she had just gotten caught in a windstorm and couldn't be bothered to brush her hair. It didn't appear as if she had a stitch of make-up on, yet her cheeks glowed, and her lips shimmered. She wore a light blue crocheted jumpsuit with a halter top and flared pants. More striking than her outfit was her attitude—strong, sultry, and provocative. Whoever this woman was, Bria sensed she was in complete control at all times.

Bria still couldn't tell if the woman was Italian. She did have a long aquiline nose, thick eyebrows, and a strong jawline, which were traditional Italian features, but her blond hair and fair complexion made it possible that she was from another part of Europe, or even northern Italy, where the country bordered France, Switzerland, and Germany. She could be Polish, Irish, or some interesting ethnic combination.

The woman looked out at the stunning view with the awe of a tourist, but the casual way she lounged in her chair made it appear that she had been in these surroundings many times before. Then again, the woman could be one of those women who, no matter what they wore or what setting they were in, were so comfortable in their own skin that they appeared incredibly relaxed.

The only way to find out who she really was would be to talk to her.

Bria looked down to the end of the bar and saw that Luca was still talking to the maître d'—whoever said that Italian women talked a lot never met Italian men—and decided she couldn't wait for him any longer, as he could continue chatting for another ten minutes. By that time the woman—if she was the real Mamma Rita—might leave, thinking she had been stood up, and Bria would miss her chance to make contact. Bria stepped down from the barstool, but instead of walking to the terrace to confront a stranger, she bumped into a strange man.

"Dante," Bria gasped.

"The way you say my name, Bria, is music to my ears."

"I was hardly singing," she replied. "You surprised me."

"You surprised me last night, right in this very hotel, when you asked me to address an audience I didn't know I was going to address."

"And you did such a wonderful job on the spur of the moment," Bria said. "Dante, you truly have the gift of communication."

Dante clasped Bria's hand and smiled sweetly. "I know." He placed another hand on her shoulder, and his smile became not so sweet. "One good surprise deserves another, Bria, and I have so many surprises up my sleeve, I can hardly fit them all into this jacket."

Bria knew that Dante was attracted to her, and while she was always respectful in his presence, she made sure she never gave him any reason to think she returned his feelings. Quite the opposite, as the more she got to know him, the less she respected him. Since he was the mayor and a close friend of Imperia's, she couldn't risk having the man as an enemy, but she didn't want him to think they were anything more than acquaintances.

"I've had enough surprises for one day, Dante," Bria said. "I'm sure you heard about the incident this morning."

"I'm the mayor of Positano. Of course I've heard about it," Dante replied. "*Triste*, very, very sad. To die so suddenly in the prime of one's own life. That's why I say that every day you must *vivere, amare, e ridere.*"

Bria was certain she had seen that phrase—*live, love, and laugh*—written on a kitchen towel in La Casa Felice. Since the new owners took over, they'd filled the home goods store with new merchandise. If she brought this up, she'd have to continue the conversation when all she wanted to do was end it.

"We'll have to live and laugh another time, Dante."

"Don't forget the love."

"That's something you'll have to live without, Dante, because Bria and I are on a date."

Bria whirled around and, for the second time in one day, unexpectedly found Luca standing behind her. Either his shoes had the softest soles in Italy or he had learned how to sneak up on a person in the police academy. Either way, Bria found his sudden appearances disturbing. But not as much as Dante.

"A date?" Dante cried.

"Yes, a date," Luca said.

Dramatically, Dante stepped back and puffed out his barrel chest. "Signor Vivaldi, I accept your challenge. En garde."

Dante struck a pose that was neither challenging, threatening, nor alluring. His legs were spread apart, the right in front of the left; he was bent at the knees; his right arm was stretched out and limply pointing at Luca; and his left was bent at the elbow, with his hand curled underneath his chin. He looked like a statue that had started to melt.

"Do I need to remind you, Dante, that among the three of us, I'm the fencing champion?" Bria noted. "I won the southern Italian competition two years in a row while I was in university."

"How could I forget, Bria," Dante replied. "Your strength only enhances your beauty."

"Even with her face concealed by a fencing mask," Luca said, "Bria would still be a beautiful woman."

Unfortunately, the beautiful woman Bria had wanted to speak to was gone.

"Dammit!" Bria cried.

"What's wrong?" Luca asked.

Bria started to speak and then looked at Dante and quickly shut her mouth. "I'll explain later."

Dante stood back and bowed. "I understand that the chief of police has won this battle, but you both will soon find out that the mayor will win the war." He took Bria's hand, raised it to his lips, and kissed it. "Arrivederci, Bria."

As Dante walked away, Luca leaned in and whispered in Bria's ear, "Should my feelings be hurt that he didn't say goodbye to me?"

"No, but you'll be upset that we missed Mamma Rita," Bria replied.

"Mamma Rita was here?"

"I'm not sure if it was her, but the woman I saw kissing

Chef Lugo at the party last night was just here," Bria shared. "She was all dressed up and looked like she was waiting for someone."

"Why didn't you prevent her from leaving?"

"I was going over to her when I bumped into Dante and got delayed."

"*Aspetta un minuto!*" Luca said. "You didn't tell me you saw Chef Lugo kissing a woman at the party."

"*Scusa*. I didn't think it was important," Bria replied. "Now that I saw her again in the same hotel where someone named Mamma Rita wanted to meet Lugo, I guess it could be very important."

"Bria, what did I tell you about sharing information?"

Bria tried to stop herself from pouting but couldn't. "That I should share what I know and not keep it a secret."

"And what did you do?"

"I . . . kept information a secret."

"From now on, *per favore*, don't keep things to yourself that could help the police."

"So you admit it," Bria said.

"Admit what?"

"That I help the police."

Luca didn't look nearly as pleased as Bria was pleased with herself. Luca took a deep breath, exhaled, and shook his head at Bria. It had been quite a while since a man had looked at her with such exasperation. She really did enjoy being on a date.

"What did she look like?" Luca asked. "I can have Matteo and some other patrolmen look for her."

"If only I hadn't changed purses I could've taken a photo of her," Bria grumbled.

"That doesn't make any sense."

"Yes it does. My other purse is black, this one is tan."

"I still don't understand."

"*Uffa*! This one matches my shoes, Luca! You expect me to carry a black purse when I'm wearing tan shoes?"

"No, but I expect you to tell me what your purse has to do with not being able to take a photo of Mamma Rita!"

"This purse isn't as big as my black one, it's too small to carry my Polaroid."

Luca's jaw literally dropped and he stared at Bria for a few seconds with his mouth open. "You know you can take a photo with your cell phone, right?"

Bria tossed her head back and threw her arms in the air. "I always forget I can do that!"

Luca shook his head and tried not to laugh. "Just tell me what she looked like."

After Bria described the woman to Luca, he raised his left eyebrow, which was a tell of his. Whenever he did that, it meant that he didn't believe what he was being told. It wasn't the first time Bria had seen this happen while talking to Luca.

"You think I'm lying?"

"It sounds like the woman could have given Monica Vitti competition."

"If this woman had been an actress back then, Monica would've never made it on-screen."

"This woman was that beautiful?"

"If she is the woman who left the note for Lugo, all I can say is, 'Mamma mia, Mamma Rita is one sexy lady.'"

Luca shoved his hands into his pants pockets and tilted his head back, the cleft in his chin on prominent display. "She isn't the only one."

The next morning, as Bria walked behind Marco and Bravo on the way to St. Cecilia's, Bria couldn't stop thinking about what Luca had said to her last night. He thought she was a sexy lady. Remembering it now almost made her cry.

She looked down at her wedding band, a material object that still represented her bond to the man she had thought she'd live with for the rest of her life. She knew without a doubt that both of them would have honored their vows without hesitation had Carlo's life not been cut short. The plane accident had changed everything. Especially Bria's future.

Everything had been laid out so perfectly and properly, and now that fate had intervened, she wasn't sure what tomorrow would bring, let alone next year. Was she ready to enter into another intimate relationship when Carlo still took up so much real estate in her heart, the rest being occupied by Marco? She was also just beginning to spread her wings as a business-woman and enjoyed putting her energy into making Bella Bella the best B and B it could be.

Even though she had many personal and professional re-sponsibilities, she was free to do whatever she wanted with her life. Of course, her parents, her sister, and most definitely Ros-alie would offer their opinions regarding her choices, but for the first time in her adult life, Bria was on her own. The more she got used to it, the more she loved it.

When she was in college, she thought she'd travel the world, focus on her painting, experience things she had only dreamed about. Right before graduation she met Carlo, and she knew she wanted to marry him, be his wife, and settle down with him months before he asked her father for her hand in marriage. From the moment she said yes to his proposal, she never had any regrets, even though the life he offered her was the com-plete opposite of the life she had imagined.

She loved being married, but maybe that was because she was married to Carlo. Had she married someone else, perhaps it wouldn't have worked out. But there hadn't been anyone else. Until now.

Her feelings for Luca were complicated. He was a good friend, Rosalie's big brother, and a kind of colleague. Because he knew her whole family and they were both known by the entire village, entering into a relationship with Luca wasn't something that could be done casually. She couldn't just date him every now and then. There would be expectations. Despite Luca's spontaneous proclamation that they had gone out on a date, they both knew it couldn't officially be classified as that. Even still, there were already rumors in the village that they were a couple.

Then there was Giovanni. Her feelings for her employee were less complicated and stemmed from the fact that he was so good looking. She was physically attracted to him, as were many of the villagers, but there was also a vulnerability underneath the muscular surface, which Bria found enticing. And anyone who could make her son laugh as much as he could won her approval. But he was her employee. If they began a relationship that was anything more than friendly and it ended, how would that affect business? Selfishly, Bria wasn't yet ready to risk Bella Bella's future, even if it meant denying hers.

The most important piece of her future was right in front of her. She watched Marco and Bravo run toward St. Cecilia's front gate, like they did every morning, and like every morning, Sister Benedicta tried nonchalantly to give Bravo a treat. Some parts of life were delightfully uncomplicated.

"*Buongiorno*, Bria," Sister Benedicta said.

"*Buongiorno*, Sister," Bria replied.

"I see that you've walked to school again today," the nun said. "Always good to get exercise any way you can."

"What Sister B really wants to say is that lately, you haven't driven the car she loves so much," Marco added.

"Marco, *non lo sai*," Bria said.

"He's right," Sister B confessed. "I do miss seeing that car of yours."

Sister Benedicta was in love with Bria's bright yellow 1970 Fiat Dino convertible. Its original owner was Carlo's father, Guillermo, and it was the only thing Carlo had wanted of his father's when he died. Bria had kept the car in good shape with frequent trips to Paolo's garage, and her hope was that Marco would be able to drive it when he was old enough. Sister Benedicta came from a family of mechanics, and it was her dream to get behind the wheel a bit sooner than Marco's eighteenth birthday.

"Have you asked Mother Superior if you could go for a spin with me in the Fiat?" Bria asked.

"I asked if I could go to Ravello to pick up the ceramic angels they're giving to the students as Communion gifts," Sister B said. "I thought that if you were free, we could go together. In your car, of course."

"It's a date!" Bria squealed.

"Mamma, sisters aren't allowed to date," Marco said.

"These types of dates are allowed, Marco, don't worry," Sister B said. "I'll let you know when the angels are ready to be picked up."

"*Perfetto*!" Bria cried. "I'll even let you drive."

Sister Benedicta made the sign of the cross and smiled beatifically. It was good to know that someone's prayers had been answered.

When Bria got back home, she thought she may need to start praying. Nunzi was sitting at the dining room table, drinking an espresso, and Giovanni was sitting across from her. They seemed like they were involved in a very serious staring match.

"Nunzi's been waiting for you," Giovanni announced. "If you need me, I'll be in the back."

Bria could tell that Nunzi was not making a social call, because she was dressed in her uniform. Luca said he had asked the medical examiner to speed up the autopsy report, but it couldn't possibly be done so quickly. And if it was, why didn't Luca come over and tell her the results? Or call or text her? Was he embarrassed about his comment last night? Had he already realized he had made a mistake?

Shaking her head vigorously to clear it of all the extraneous thoughts she was having, Bria finally sat across from Nunzi and asked her what was going on.

"You know I don't like Rosalie," Nunzi said.

Nunzi did not need to make a special visit to inform Bria of that tidbit of information. It was a well-known fact in the village.

"I am aware that the two of you don't particularly get along," Bria replied.

"She dislikes me as much as I dislike her," Nunzi said. "But I still feel compelled to warn her."

"Warn her about what?"

"Not what. Who."

"Who does Rosalie need to be warned about?"

Bria silently answered her own question before Nunzi said Michele's name.

"*Oh, povera meo*," Bria said. "What did you find out?"

Nunzi leaned forward and lowered her voice, in case a certain handyman was eavesdropping. "Michele has a criminal record on par with Giovanni's."

That meant Michele had a history of being involved in multiple crimes as a young man, none of them violent, but taken as a whole, his past told the story of a man who wasn't as mild mannered as he appeared. Or pretended to be. Bria assumed Michele had been in trouble with the police, but Nunzi was offering proof.

"I could tell that Rosalie was interested in Michele, and I knew that if I brought this information to her, she'd think I was trying to end their relationship before it began," Nunzi explained. "I couldn't keep silent, so I thought it best to share it with you."

"*Grazie mille*, Nunzi. I really appreciate you telling me," Bria said. "But you know how I feel about Giovanni. He has overcome his past, so Michele could have done the same."

"It's possible, but if Giovanni has turned over his life, which

I'm still skeptical about, it's the exception to the rule," Nunzi said. "Most people who've been involved in as many crimes as he and Michele have don't change."

Bria looked directly into Nunzi's eyes. "Do you think Michele is dangerous?"

"Yes, I believe he could be."

"Could he have had something to do with Chef Lugo's death?"

"I think it's possible," Nunzi said. "But even if it turns out that Chef Lugo died of natural causes, I still don't trust Michele."

"I understand, but, Nunzi, what do you think I should tell Rosalie?"

"That if she acts on her feelings and gets close to this guy, her life could very well be in danger."

Chapter 9

When an afternoon limoncello spritz and leftover ravioli stuffed with broccoli rabe still couldn't make Bria feel better, she knew she had a problem. When the view from her balcony of Positano's rugged, nearly incomprehensible landscape and the sun-drenched sea, rippling lazily several hundred feet below, couldn't distract Bria from thinking about Michele's criminal past, she knew she was in serious trouble. When Luca arrived with the results of the autopsy report, she realized Nunzi hadn't been overreacting. Rosalie could very well be in danger.

"I was right," Bria said. "Chef Lugo was murdered."

"Yes," Luca replied. "He was poisoned."

Bria turned away from Luca and made the sign of the cross. Lugo's frightened face flashed in front of her once again, and she was filled with conflicting emotions. Compassion for the man, shame that she had been unable to help him, anger that someone had deliberately killed him. The man had been in Bria's life for less than twenty-four hours, and yet he had made a lasting impression.

Luca started to reach out to touch Bria but hesitated. "Are you all right?"

Bria wiped away the tears from her eyes, shook her head,

and exhaled. "*Dio mio*. The man was in the prime of his life and on the brink of major success."

"It's a tragedy," Luca said. "Despite the autopsy results, I'm still not convinced it was murder."

"Luca Vivaldi, how did you ever get to be the chief of police?"

Luca winced at Bria's accusation. "Because I worked hard, and I'm damn good at my job."

Bria saw the hurt in Luca's eyes, and she swallowed hard. She had more to say, but she needed to choose her words wisely. "*Prego, perdonami*. I just find it hard to believe that you can't see what's right in front of your eyes."

"I find it hard to believe that you still can't see what's right outside your imagination."

Unable to contain her emotions, Bria stopped caring about word choice and simply wanted to get her point across and through Luca's thick skull—if that was humanly possible. "*Uffa*! Enough with my wild imagination! Lugo was poisoned. It says so right there in the autopsy report. What more proof do you need that he didn't die from natural causes?"

"The autopsy report won't be complete until we get the lab results from toxicology!"

"When will that be?"

"I don't know!" Luca started to pace the room, and when he spoke, he was no longer shouting. "Maybe another two weeks. It's impossible to put a time frame on these things. But until we get the results, we won't have the full picture."

"Luca, I know that you have to follow the rules, but the toxicology report is only going to tell you what kind of poison Lugo died from. You don't need to know the type of poison to know that he was murdered."

Luca pulled out a chair from the dining room table and sat down. He was no longer angry. Bria didn't think he was amused, but he was smiling. "He could've been poisoned by accident, he could have had an allergic reaction to some non-poisonous chemical, or he could have poisoned himself, for all we know."

Bria made another sign of the cross as she sat down across from Luca. "You think he committed suicide?"

"I think that's highly unlikely, but I don't think it's impossible that he accidentally included a poisonous toxin in his recipe."

"You think an experienced chef could make a mistake like that?"

"You remember my *zio* Beppe?"

"Il pupazzo di neve!"

"Yes, everybody called him the snowman because he had white hair and was fat."

"Luca! He was chubby. Rosalie called him Chubby Beppe."

"He was five foot five and weighed three hundred pounds," Luca clarified. "The man was fat."

"Bene! Beppe was fat," Bria conceded. "What's your point?"

"Zio Beppe was a master electrician. He could fix anything," Luca said. "One night the fuse went out in his house, he climbed a ladder outside to fix it, but didn't lock the ladder in place. The ladder slipped out from under him, and he fell onto the sidewalk headfirst. Experts make mistakes, too."

"Che triste!" Bria cried. "I never knew that's how Chubby Beppe died."

"Unnecessarily," Luca replied. "Had he taken a moment to lock the ladder in place, he'd still be here. Well, maybe not."

"What do you mean?"

"He probably would have died from a heart attack. He had a terrible diet."

"Luca! *Non parlare male dei morti.*"

"I'm not speaking ill of the dead. I'm speaking the truth," Luca protested. "The problem with you, Bria—"

"I have a problem?" Bria interrupted.

"Yes, you most certainly do."

"Really? Tell me what my problem is. I'd love to hear it."

"I'll tell you."

"*Aspetta*! Should I get a pen to write this down?"

"*Molto divertente*. You want to know what your problem is?"

"I'm all ears."

"You jump to conclusions."

"*Falso*! I do not!"

"Yes you do! You're just like my sister!"

"That, Luca Vivaldi, was the best compliment you could ever pay me."

"No it wasn't! The two of you are always disregarding facts, ignoring possibilities, and jumping straight to whatever conclusion your crazy little minds think is the truth!"

Bria actually gasped. "How dare you call Rosalie crazy!"

Luca actually stomped his foot underneath the table. "I called both of you crazy!"

"I cannot believe that you would come into my house and call my best friend crazy!" Bria cried.

"I came here to share the autopsy results with you, and you immediately translate that into murder."

"Because Lugo was murdered, and you're not going to convince me otherwise," Bria said. "Have you tested the pastries?"

"*Che cosa?*"

"The pastries that Lugo prepared," Bria explained. "Have you tested them to see if they contain traces of the same poison found in Lugo's bloodstream?"

"Of course we're going to test the pastries," Luca replied.

"And what about his espresso?"

"What espresso?"

"The one he was drinking in the back room just before we started filming."

"We didn't find an espresso cup," Luca said. "Are you sure that isn't also a product of your imagination?"

Bria pushed back her chair with such force, it almost top-pled over. She grabbed her bag, which she had tossed on the sofa in the sitting room, and started pulling things out of it, all the while mumbling under her breath. Finally, she found what she was looking for and shoved it in front of Luca's face.

"What's this?"

"A photograph that I took with my Polaroid," Bria de-clared. "Look at what Lugo's holding in his hand."

Bria dropped the photo on the table and Luca leaned for-ward to get a better look at it. He picked up the photo and slowly stood up from the chair. Bria waited for him to respond, but he remained silent.

"Do you see what it is?"

"Yes, I see what it is."

"Do you mind sharing your findings with the court?"

"We're not in a court. We're in your B and B."

"Bella Bella is my court, and you're on trial!" Bria shouted. "What's Lugo holding?"

"An espresso cup," Luca conceded.

"Which could have contained some poison mixed in with his espresso."

Luca looked closer at the photo. "You may be right."

"Really?" Bria yanked the photo from Luca's hands to ex-amine it more thoroughly. After a moment her eyes widened, and her jaw dropped.

"I hadn't noticed that bottle before."

"Lugo probably mixed something into his espresso," Luca said. "It might not have been poison, but it looks like it was anisette."

"A bottle of anisette that Massimo brought him," Bria ex-plained.

"Are you sure?"

"Yes, I remember that Lugo was acting nervous. Massimo came in, and they chatted quietly. I couldn't hear what they were saying, but then I saw Massimo pull out a bottle from his pants pocket and place it next to Lugo's espresso," Bria explained. "I assumed Massimo was giving Lugo some anisette to, you know, calm his nerves."

"That's very possible," Luca said. "Or Massimo knew that Lugo liked the taste of licorice."

"My father does," Bria said. "He'd always say a little drop of anisette cuts the bitterness of the espresso."

"I'll head over to the station and see if the bottle is in the evidence room. I haven't had a chance to thoroughly review it," Luca announced. "In the meantime, don't be spreading rumors that Lugo was murdered."

"Only that he was poisoned."

"You should keep that to yourself, too," Luca said. "I shared that with you only because . . . well, you were right there when Lugo died."

"And because I've proven to be a helpful resource and an asset to the police department."

Dramatically, Luca shrugged his shoulders and extended his arms. "*Oh bene*, yes, in the past you have proven to be somewhat helpful. But you, Bria Bartolucci, have a tendency to hold back pieces of information." Luca stared at Bria. "You wouldn't be holding back something now, would you? Something that has convinced you Lugo was murdered."

Bria did her best to keep a straight face and not reveal the fact that Luca had essentially read her mind and uncovered that she was hiding an important fact. But she was keeping what she knew about Michele secret, for the moment, to protect two innocent lives. She was certain Nunzi had investigated Michele on her own, without a request or support from Luca, and she didn't want to get the cop in trouble with her boss. She also hadn't had a chance to tell Rosalie what she had learned about the guy she was clearly interested in. If she told Luca and he wasn't already aware of it, he'd reprimand Nunzi and warn Rosalie. Neither conversation would end with anyone feeling good, so Bria kept quiet.

"The only things that make me certain Lugo was murdered are the facts and my instinct," Bria declared. "I've learned to rely on both instead of taking the word of a man."

Less than an hour later, Bria had changed her mind and decided that she did need to rely on a man to get to the truth. She wasn't sure if it was a man she could trust, but she had to try. She filled up Bravo's bowl with fresh water, told him she'd be back soon, and ran out to the alley on the side of Bella Bella, where her Vespa was waiting.

She hopped onto the cycle, put the key in the ignition and turned it to the start position, pulled back the left brake handle, and pressed the START button. The motor purred as Bria grabbed the helmet that was hanging from the right handle and put it on. She hated wearing the helmet because it mussed her hair, but as Rosalie had once pointed out, a bad hair day was better than a severe brain injury.

Hardly a daredevil, Bria drove within the speed limit. Since Viale Pasitea was a serpentine road filled with cars, bike riders, scooters, and pedestrians going in both directions, it really was impossible to speed, and the road felt more like an obstacle course than a thoroughfare. Like most people who had grown up on the Amalfi Coast, or any place in Italy for that matter, Bria had been driving a Vespa since she was a teenager, which meant she knew how to handle the bike even in less than optimal circumstances. Still, when she arrived at Paolo's garage, she felt out of breath, though that probably had more to do with why she had made the trip than the trip itself.

"*Ciao*, Michele," Bria cried out.

Michele was working on a vintage baby blue Volkswagen Beetle. Kneeling on a cushion, he was hunched over the engine, which was in the back of the car, and held a wrench over the air regulator. As he started to unscrew the cap of the mal-functioning unit, Bria wheeled her Vespa into the garage and parked it next to him. Even if he wanted to focus on his work, there was no way he could ignore her presence.

"*Ciao*, Bria," Michele said. "Paolo is in the office."

"*Grazie*, but I didn't come here to see Paolo. I came here to see you."

Michele didn't look up to face Bria, but he did stop work-ing. He held his wrench, the regulator's cap caught within its teeth, and didn't move or speak. Bria waited for several sec-onds, and just when she thought she was going to have to carry on a one-sided conversation, Michele responded. But he still wouldn't look up to meet Bria's gaze.

"I would rather not talk about the other day," he said.

"*Buono*, because I'm not here to talk about that. I've been neglecting my Vespa, and it's in desperate need of a tune-up," Bria lied. "I thought I'd test the rumors and see if you're as good as people say you are."

Finally, Michele stood up. Because he was a few inches taller than Bria, he looked down at her, his brown eyes glistening with mystery. Bria wondered what lay just out of her reach.

"People say a lot of things about me," Michele said. "Only some of which are true."

"I'm sure what they say about your skill as a mechanic is true, which is why I'm here."

"No it isn't." The tone of Michele's voice had turned icy. His expression matched.

Bria suddenly felt like an idiot. She hadn't told anyone where she was going, and Bravo was the only one who knew she had left the house. While she was in the center of the village, the garage was behind the parking lot and at the moment, the lot was filled with cars but no drivers. The only inhabitants of the garage besides Bria and one angry mechanic were cars, motorcycles, and scooters. Paolo was less than one hundred feet away, but he was in his small office, with the blinds pulled down, most likely listening to the soccer game on the radio.

Bria crossed her arms and smiled, trying to adopt a stance of defiance with a dash of innocence. "Why else would I have come to a garage if it weren't to get my Vespa fixed?"

"You wanted to ask me more questions about why I was hiding out in the back room of the café."

"That isn't true," Bria said. "I leave those types of questions for the police to ask."

Bria felt good about not having to lie. She wasn't there to find out why he had snuck into Annamaria's café and hidden while they were taping Lugo's show. She was there to find out what he had to conceal about his past. The next thing she knew, Paolo was at her side, trying to prevent her from finding that out.

"Bria, what a nice surprise," Paolo said.

He grabbed Bria's hands, and kissed her on each cheek. He had never given Bria a more affectionate greeting. Startled, Bria returned the gesture but kept one eye on Michele. She didn't trust him, and she got the sense that Paolo didn't, either.

Paolo pointed to the other side of the garage. "Michele, could you please finish up on the Volvo Kombi?"

Michele looked over at the other side of the garage, and Bria followed his gaze until it landed on a dark green station wagon with two flat tires. He slammed down the hood of the Beetle and flipped the wrench in his hand. *"Certo, zio."* As he walked away, he turned to Bria with something vaguely resembling a smile on his lips. "Have a nice day."

"Anche tu," she replied.

When Michele was out of earshot, Paolo looked at Bria, his smile not looking much brighter than Michele's, and said, "Let's go have a cappuccino."

* * *

They sat at a small table outside Fiorello's Bakery, which was three doors down from the garage. Paolo knew the owner as well as the owner's parents and grandparents, which meant they got their beverages even faster than the normally quick service. Bria sipped her iced cappuccino while Paolo stared at his. She knew communication was not his forte, so Bria sat patiently until he was ready to speak.

"My nephew's had a troubled past. That's no secret," Paolo said. "But he's a good boy."

Bria responded to the urgency in Paolo's voice. "Are you trying to convince me of that or yourself?"

"I heard what happened yesterday."

"Did Michele tell you?"

"No, Annamaria," Paolo confessed. "She wanted me to know before it got around the village."

Bria smiled and patted Paolo's hand. "She, of all people, should know how quickly things travel through town."

Finally, Paolo looked at Bria, and her heart broke. His eyes were sad, filled with regret and shame. Bria didn't know if it was over things that he had done or Michele's past misdeeds. "He's cleaned up his past, thanks to my in-laws."

"Did Michele live with them before coming here?" Bria asked.

"He lived with them when he was much younger," Paolo replied. "I don't really like that side of the family, but they did the right thing and took Michele in."

"Why was it the right thing to do?" Bria asked. "What happened to his family?"

"My sister Lydia, Michele's mother, died when he was only five years old, and Vito, his father, well, *è un buono a nulla*," Paolo explained. "Vito wasn't interested in being a single father and left shortly after Lydia died—without Michele."

"*Oh mio Dio*," Bria said. "He left his little boy."

"With me," Paolo said. "I'm ashamed to admit that at that time in my life, I was no better than Vito. I wasn't fit to raise a dog, let alone a child."

"Paolo . . ."

"No, *è vero*," Paolo said. "You didn't know me then, and you wouldn't have wanted to, but like Michele, I've changed."

Maybe Luca was right. Maybe Bria did jump to conclusions. Just because Michele had a criminal past and a crime had been committed didn't mean that Michele was the culprit. Giovanni had overcome his past, and from what Paolo had just told her, so had he. If they could do it, why not Michele?

"The best thing I ever did was let my nephew stay with Teresina and her family," Paolo said.

"Who's Teresina?"

"Vito's sister."

"*Che bello*," Bria said. "Teresina must be a wonderful woman to take in a child like that."

Paolo tilted his head back and forth. "She was the one who took Michele in, but her sister was the one who raised him."

"Teresina's sister?"

"Yes, Margherita was like a mamma to Michele," Paolo said. "That's why he always called her Mamma Rita."

Bria made sure to keep her voice calm when she spoke. "*Interessante*. Please tell me more."

CHAPTER 10

As she walked home from the garage, Bria beamed. She smiled at tourists, waved to shop owners, and she even stopped to coo over a French poodle, whom she told was the cutest dog she had ever seen. Bria assumed the poodle didn't understand Italian and therefore wouldn't realize she was lying, because everyone knew that Bravo was the cutest dog in the world.

When Paolo had told her about Michele's link to Mamma Rita, the same person who left a note for Chef Lugo in one of the fake croissants, Bria hadn't blinked an eye. She hadn't appeared startled; she hadn't asked him to repeat himself. She'd simply let him continue talking uninterrupted. When he was done, she had learned everything she needed to know about Mamma Rita to take her investigation to the next level.

She stopped in her tracks right in front of Souvenir 'O Sarracino, one of the biggest souvenir shops in the village, and the woman behind her, who was pushing a baby carriage, had to swerve out of the way to avoid colliding with her. The woman said something to Bria that sounded like Turkish, but Bria knew less Turkish than the poodle knew Italian, so she wasn't insulted and hardly acknowledged the woman because she was so wrapped up in her own thoughts.

Not only was she surprised that she was investigating Lugo's murder, but she was also perplexed that she considered it to be *her* investigation. Although she and Rosalie joked around, Bria wasn't part of the police force and had no desire to be. She was a single mother and the owner of a bed-and-breakfast, and that was more than enough. Or was it?

Obviously, Bria felt connected to Lugo in an odd way, because hers was the last face he saw before he left this earth. That was a strong connection regardless of the fact that the two only knew of each other's existence for less than a full day. They would be inextricably tied for eternity. Bria viewed this not as a burden but rather as an honor. She felt an incredibly strong need to solve his murder and bring the killer to justice. She felt equally as strongly that she didn't have to ask Luca for permission or work with him and his police department in order to achieve her goal. She was overcome with a newfound feeling of independence, which washed over her like the scent of salt water and lavender that wafted in the air. Breathing it in made her feel revitalized, and she wasn't about to let the feeling go.

She was so invigorated, she decided to climb the 235 steps to Bella Bella. Had she been at the beach and thus faced with climbing the full 412 steps, she might have thought twice about it, but at roughly the halfway mark, she gladly started climbing. She kept a steady pace and was so preoccupied with going over the details Paolo had told her, she didn't even get out of breath.

After his mother died and his father abandoned him, Michele had lived with Paolo for a very short period of time. When Paolo quickly realized that he was not able to give Michele the secure home every child needed, and he didn't want to be burdened with a child, he reached out to his sisters-in-law, who had gladly welcomed Michele into their family. Without warning, Michele had moved to Frosinone to live with relatives he had never met.

Located about two and a half hours from Positano, Frosinone was situated southeast of Rome, in the region of Lazio. Settlers first called Frosinone home in the Bronze Age, and it was a thriving metropolis until the Second World War, when it was decimated and left in ruins, although traces of its auspicious history could be found, like the amphitheater near the river Cosa.

Over the years, the city was rebuilt, and today it was a nondescript suburb of Rome. Bria tried to think but couldn't remember ever visiting the city, despite having gone to RUFA, Rome University of Fine Arts. If it weren't for the fact that it held a clue to Chef Lugo's murder, Bria wouldn't be preparing to visit the city. And to convince Rosalie to come along for the ride.

Since Marco was still going to be in school for a few more hours, and things were quiet and in control back at Bella Bella, Bria went straight to the marina, where Rosalie lived in her houseboat. Aptly christened *La Vie en Rosalie*, the thirty-five-foot-long boat was white, with a navy blue cabin and brown wooden flooring. It sat up to fifteen people comfortably, but Rosalie usually hosted smaller tour groups, mostly private bookings of ten people or less.

It was in immaculate condition, thanks to Rosalie's constant maintenance, and Bria had enjoyed many a ride on the Tyrrhenian Sea and even the Mediterranean.. But when Bria got closer to the boat and saw who was standing on the dock, talking to Rosalie, she wanted to turn back toward the mainland. If she hadn't heard her name being yelled by not one person but by all three people, she would have sprinted the entire way home.

Walking as slow as she could in a pathetic attempt to delay the inevitable, Bria racked her brain to come up with a reason why Rosalie would be chatting with Massimo and Imperia. And why they would all be smiling. Imperia didn't like Rosalie, and Rosalie was afraid of Imperia, and based on Massimo's actions and his fondness for yelling, Bria didn't think that he liked anyone, but clearly, Bria was wrong. When she joined them in front of *La Vie en Rosalie*, all three were smiling, as if they were at a cocktail party.

"*Ciao a tutti*!" Bria cried, the volume of her voice overcompensating for her lack of sincerity.

"Bria, how nice to see you again," Massimo said. "This time under much more pleasant circumstances."

"*Ciao*, Bria," Imperia said. "I may be mistaken, though I very rarely am, but you don't look happy to see me."

Bria's mother-in-law, Imperia Bartolucci, lived two hours away in Rome but often made surprise visits to Positano. Typically, those visits involved a family matter or, more precisely, her desire to see her grandson, Marco. Even though her yacht was docked in the same marina as Rosalie's boat, they had never socialized before. If Bria had stumbled upon Imperia and Rosalie in the middle of friendly chitchat, that would have been an extraordinary occurrence. With Massimo as part of the group, it became an unprecedented event.

"*Scusa*, Imperia," Bria said. "I'm just surprised to see all three of you in the same company."

"Bria, I told you when I first met you that I know your family," Massimo said.

He did? Bria racked her brain, trying to remember. *Dio mio! Yes, he did!* she thought.

"When you said *family*, I thought you meant my parents, Franco and Fifetta D'Abruzzo," Bria said.

"Aren't I part of your family, too?" Imperia asked.

"Of course, *certo*. I just . . . didn't make the connection," Bria stuttered. "How exactly do the two of you know each other?"

"They just told me the whole story," Rosalie said. "Started when Massimo produced some commercials for Bartolucci Enterprises back in the early nineties."

"We've kept in touch through the years, and when I knew I

was going to be in Positano, I let Imperia know, hoping I could meet her in Rome," Massimo explained. "But *la mia incanta-trice* couldn't wait that long and rushed to see me."

When Bria turned to face Imperia, she saw a version of the woman she had never seen before. Not from before she and Carlo had got married, not when she had spied Imperia playing with Marco, not when she'd seen photographs of Imperia from when she was a young woman. The Imperia she saw now was acting like a lovesick teenager, a coquette, not a formidable businesswoman who ran her empire with an iron and well-manicured fist. Bria had never known Imperia to act as infatuated around her husband. Could it be possible that she was in love with Massimo?

Imperia gently patted Massimo on the chest and looked into his eyes, but only for a split second before lowering hers. "I didn't *rush*, Massimo, but I did tell my driver to disregard the speed limit." Imperia flashed a wicked grin, which immediately dissolved into a much more serious look. "Especially when I heard the terrible news."

Being in Imperia's presence was sometimes like experiencing whiplash, and today was no different. One moment she looked like she was going to burst into giggles with a new inamorato, and the next, she appeared solemn, reflecting on a young man's death. A young man's death that was still fresh in Bria's mind.

Imperia looked out at the horizon. "Is it true, Bria, that you witnessed Chef Lugo's death firsthand?"

Bria's gaze joined Imperia's, and soon she was watching the line where sea met sky. "Yes, I was standing right next to him when . . . it happened."

Despite the emotional distance between them, which could sometimes feel like an abyss, Bria and Imperia had a connection. Bria's husband and Imperia's son. His name didn't need to be spoken out loud for Bria to know Imperia was also thinking of Carlo.

"*Mi dispiace*. That couldn't have been easy."

"No, it wasn't."

Finally, Imperia turned to face Bria, her expression somewhere between blissful and solemn. "But now it's behind you, and you can think of more pleasant things, like Marco's Communion party."

That Communion party is going to be the death of me! Bria thought.

"I know I owe you an answer," Bria said. "*Lo prometto*, I'll talk to my mother, and we'll come up with a solution."

"I've already given you the solution." Imperia waved her hand to the right, toward the huge yacht in the marina that dwarfed all the other vessels, including Rosalie's. "I know you don't want to betray your mother, but you must admit that my yacht is the only place to have Marco's party."

"I promise that I'll talk to my mother soon," Bria replied. "But the yacht is definitely an option."

"The marina is quite the popular setting," Massimo said. "It's where I've found my new living arrangements."

Bria shot a glance at Rosalie and wondered if her friend had lost her mind. Could she possibly have invited Massimo to live on her houseboat? No, that didn't make any sense. The boat was perfect for one person, but there was only one cabin Rosalie used as her bedroom, so where would Massimo sleep? Bria knew that her best friend could be fickle when it came to romance, but not even she would jump from Michele to Massimo in less than a day. The only other option was almost as shocking.

"Now that Massimo and his crew can't leave town, there's no reason he should have to continue to pay for a room at Le Sirenuse," Imperia said. "He could afford it, *certo*, but the easiest way to become poor is to spend money frivolously. Wouldn't you agree, Rosalba?"

Who's Rosalba? Bria thought. She looked at Rosalie, and the truth dawned on them at the same time: Imperia had forgotten

Rosalie's name. Or she was deliberately calling Rosalie by the wrong name just to make it appear that she couldn't be bothered to remember her name. It was rude and juvenile, not entirely unfunny, and definitely a tactic Imperia would employ to keep her opponent off guard and to prove her superiority. Imperia didn't realize that Rosalie also loved being rude and juvenile. She was hardly offended; she played right along.

"Yes, Imperia, I do agree," Rosalie replied. *"Cento per cento."*

"Which is why I invited Massimo to stay on my yacht until this whole terrible ordeal is over," Imperia said.

Grazie Dio! Rosalie hadn't acquired a housemate; she'd gained a neighbor.

Massimo kissed Imperia's hand like he was bowing to a queen. *"Grazie infinite, amore mio."*

Visibly flustered, Imperia blushed like a courtesan.

"What about the rest of the crew?" Bria asked.

Quickly gaining her composure, Imperia replied, "What about them?"

"Are they going to stay on the yacht, too?"

"Heavens, no," Imperia said. "The yacht is my home, Bria, not a hotel."

"Don't you still have room for Pippa at your bed-and-breakfast?" Massimo asked.

"Yes, she can stay as long as she wants," Bria said. "And I'm not going to charge her for the extra days, since I know she isn't working."

"That's very gracious of you, Bria," Massimo said.

"It's nothing," Bria said. "I'm coming off the busy season, and I don't have any guests coming for a while."

"Perfetto," Imperia said. "I'm sure Pippa will be much more comfortable at your place than on a yacht."

"Yacht living isn't for everyone," Rosalie said.

"That is correct, Rosalba," Imperia said. "You have a very wise friend, Bria."

"*Grazie*," Bria replied. "I've always said that about . . . Rosalba."

"Now, if you would excuse us, I need to give Massimo a proper tour of his new living quarters, so he doesn't get lost," Imperia said.

"You may need a road map," Bria said. "It's even larger than it looks."

Massimo held out his arm, and Imperia slid hers into his. It was a lovely, romantic gesture, and if Imperia were taking the arm of any other man, it would make Bria happy to see her mother-in-law, who was usually so stoic and reserved, smile and emotionally connect with someone. But she didn't like Massimo. Worse, she didn't trust him.

"*Ciao*, Bria, Rosalba," Massimo said.

"*Ah, quasi dimenticavo*," Imperia said. "Tell Fifetta that I'm working on a menu for the Communion party, and I need the names of her side of the family for the invite list."

"I'm sure my mother will be delighted to hear that," Bria replied.

"She should be," Imperia said. "If it weren't for me, we'd be having the party in your tiny backyard. *Quella sarebbe una catastrofe*."

"I agree," Rosalie said. "An absolute catastrophe."

"*Stai zitta*, Rosalba," Bria said.

Watching Massimo and Imperia walk arm in arm down the dock toward Imperia's yacht, which had been christened simply *The Bartolucci*, Bria understood how Imperia had been crowned Miss Italia once upon another time. Decades later, Imperia still carried herself not like a beauty pageant contestant but like a winner. She was regal, beautiful, and now, thanks to Massimo, happy. Bria ignored the fire in her stomach that warned her Massimo couldn't be trusted. At some point she might have to destroy Imperia's happiness, but for now, she needed to focus on destroying Rosalie's.

"Do you have any wine?" Bria asked.

"That's like asking the Pope if he's hiding holy water underneath his vestments," Rosalie replied.

"Then crack open a bottle of red, Rosalba," Bria said. "You're going to need it."

A few minutes later they were sitting on the deck of Rosalie's boat, sipping glasses of Ornellaia 2020, a very expensive Italian wine one of Rosalie's guests had given her as a thank-you gift. The woman had thrown herself an impromptu bachelorette party the weekend of her wedding, and if Rosalie hadn't steered her boat away from the dock and into the cover of moonlight to hide the two male strippers the woman had smuggled on board, the marriage might have ended before it began. Rosalie could be trusted to do the right thing when it came to saving a relationship. Starting her own was a different story.

"I know you have feelings for Michele," Bria said.

"What kind of feelings?" Rosalie asked.

"Rosalie, I'm being serious," Bria said.

"*Scusami*, my name's Rosalba."

History had taught Bria that when Rosalie started making jokes and avoiding a subject, it meant that she was trying to hide her emotions and run from the truth. As hard as it would be to hear, Bria wasn't going to let that happen.

"Nunzi found out things about Michele," Bria shared. "Things that you should know."

"How can you trust anything Nunzi says where I'm concerned?" Rosalie said. "The woman hates me."

"She doesn't hate you."

"She doesn't like me."

"Not liking someone is different than hating them."

Rosalie took a long sip of wine and looked out at the horizon as the boat gently rocked in the sea. She closed her eyes for a moment and then looked up at the setting sun. Bria watched her friend and knew what was going on in her head, because they had had this kind of conversation many times before. The names changed, the details were different, but the end result was always the same: Rosalie wound up getting her heart broken.

"What did she find out?" Rosalie asked.

"He has a criminal record."

"A criminal record like Giovanni's or one that my brother wouldn't be able to ignore?"

"Somewhere in between."

Bria shared with Rosalie the information Nunzi had found out. Michele had spent time in jail, twice when he was a juvenile and again about ten years ago, when he was charged as an adult. Each time he got out early for good behavior, but each time he got picked up again for petty crimes that didn't put him back inside a jail cell but did make him face a judge. For the past four years, he had been clean and hadn't gotten into any trouble with the police. Either Paolo had described Michele accurately and he had changed his ways, or Michele had just learned how not to get caught.

"I sure can pick 'em, can't I?" Rosalie said.

She finished the rest of her wine with one gulp and quickly poured herself another glass. Chain drinking was an easy way to avoid talking about your feelings. Unless you had a best friend like Bria.

"You can get yourself drunk, but it won't change anything."

"Are you sure you can trust Nunzi?" Rosalie asked.

"I saw the report with my own eyes," Bria said.

"Why didn't she show it to me?"

"You might not like Nunzi, but you can't deny that she's smart and a good person," Bria said. "Nunzi knew that you wouldn't take anything she had to say seriously, and she wanted to make sure you were completely aware of Michele's past before starting anything up with him."

"We haven't started anything yet," Rosalie protested. "We've barely had a conversation."

"We both know it's only a matter of time before he's spending nights here with you on your boat."

Rosalie tilted her head back and forth. "That's true. I will say it shows Nunzi isn't all bad. But why do I get the feeling that this chat isn't just about preventing me from getting involved with a guy whose next home might be a prison cell? What aren't you telling me?"

"I think Michele is linked to Lugo's murder," Bria announced.

"Murder?"

"The autopsy report came back, and the cause of death was poison," Bria explained.

"How'd you find out what was in the autopsy report?"

"Luca came and told me."

"Luca paid you a special visit and told you?"

"Yes, he wanted me to know."

"I think you may want to pay attention to your own love life and not worry so much about mine."

"I don't have a love life!" Bria protested.

"And I'm not interested in a guy whose last date was a conjugal visit."

Bria and Rosalie looked at each other and proved once again that they had perfect timing. At exactly the same moment, they started cracking up and clinked their glasses together. The only difference was that Bria was able to swallow her mouthful of wine, while Rosalie spilled hers all over her white tunic.

"Another top ruined by an ill-fated romance."

"Don't throw the cards in without putting up a fight."

Rosalie blotted her blouse with a napkin. "You just told me Michele might be responsible for Lugo's death."

"I said he *might* be involved," Bria clarified. "Seriously, Rosalie, you have to learn to listen."

"You, Bria, need to learn how to communicate a bit more effectively," Rosalie countered. "How exactly is Michele involved in Lugo's murder?"

"Because of his connection to Mamma Rita."

"Who's Mamma Rita?"

"The woman who stuck a note in one of the fake croissants and tried to set up a meeting with Lugo for the night of the filming, but since he died in the morning, the meeting never took place."

"Do you think Mamma Rita and Michele are working together?" Rosalie asked.

"Possibly, but I'm not sure, because I never got a chance to ask her."

"What do you mean by that?"

"Luca and I went to Le Sirenuse, where the meeting was supposed to take place, in case the woman hadn't heard about Lugo's death and showed up, looking for him."

"What did you find?"

"The same mystery woman who was kissing Lugo the night of his party."

"The pretty one?"

"Yes, but I think she's too young to be Mamma Rita."

"You were a young mother."

"True, but I learned from Paolo that Mamma Rita is the woman who raised Michele as her own son after his mother died, which means she'd be at least my mother's age," Bria said. "The woman I saw was maybe a few years older than us."

"Sounds like Michele didn't have the greatest upbringing," Rosalie said.

"I'm not sure about that, but he definitely had a rough start in life," Bria replied. "From what Paolo said, Mamma Rita helped turn his life around."

"Do you have any idea where this Mamma Rita is?" Rosalie asked.

"No," Bria said. "But cancel all your plans for tomorrow, because we're going on a road trip to Frosinone."

"Why in the world are we going there?"

"Because if we can't find Mamma Rita, we need to pay a visit to Mamma Rita's sister."

CHAPTER 11

Like most mornings in Positano, it was an idyllic time for a road trip.

A quiet breeze wandered through the air, gently brushing against arms and legs, tickling the flesh. The sweet scent of the orange trees fused with the woodier aroma of black currants to produce a practically wild, primitive cologne, which, once inhaled, intoxicated the body. The turquoise sea, always present and always seductive, defied even the most apathetic eye not to glance in its direction. It was a nearly imaginary landscape, created to mimic perfection, and was the perfect backdrop for a jaunt out of town.

Bria sat in her bright yellow 1970 Fiat Dino convertible at the end of the marina and waited for Rosalie to arrive. As usual when she was going on a long drive, Bria looked like a movie star trying to escape the paparazzi. She was wearing her signature La Giardiniera black-and-white oval sunglasses, and her wavy hair, raven black and not yet disrupted by the strands of gray that would inevitably come, was pulled back and held in place with a thick white headband. A white man-tailored shirt, black capri pants, and bright pink mules—with a heel that was well-suited for driving, not walking—completed her outfit. If the mystery woman at Le Sirenuse evoked au naturel femininity of the 1970s, Bria channeled the more cosmopolitan flair of the 1960s. Imagine Audrey Hepburn going out for a spin around Rome after a night of chaste carousing with Cary Grant.

Rosalie, meanwhile, borrowed from several generations to curate a look that was all her own. Walking down the dock as if it were a runway in a site-specific Gucci fashion show, Rosalie wore a sleeveless maxi vest with royal-blue and white stripes from the seventies. Underneath, she wore a long-sleeved, safari-inspired white linen shirt from the eighties and baggy tan cargo pants from the nineties, cut off mid-shin to allow full exposure for her gladiator sandals, which had come back into the fashion spotlight at the turn of the century.

Wisely, she had let her reddish-brown hair dry naturally. Why spend time trying to tame her mass of curls and waves when, regardless of how much hair product she used, they would only get curlier and wavier after the drive in the convertible? Rosalie could have worn a scarf around her head or used a headband like Bria, but Rosalie's hair, like Rosalie herself, didn't like to be tied down. Bria's heart warmed when she saw that her friend's free spirit remained as alive as ever, despite the bad news she had received the previous day. That was what she loved most about Rosalie—well, after her raucous sense of humor, her unbridled devotion to adventure, and her firm understanding of loyalty—her ability to bounce back.

"Once again, you've outdone yourself," Bria remarked as Rosalie got into the Fiat.

"*Grazie.*" Rosalie put on a pair of black Ray-Ban sunglasses. "But let's get out of here before someone mistakes my vest for one of the umbrellas on Spiaggia Grande and tries to plant me in the sand."

Bria didn't need any further encouragement. She maneuvered the stick shift into position and sped out of the marina and onto the main road. All around them was the natural beauty of Positano; and between them, the beauty of friendship. For a few miles, they allowed the aura of the Amalfi Coast to envelope them and remind them that no matter where they roamed, home would always be waiting.

"Do you think Mamma Rita is still living in Frosinone?" Rosalie asked.

"I don't know," Bria replied. "Paolo only said that he gets a Christmas card from her sister Teresina. I didn't want to make him suspicious by quizzing him on his whole family tree."

"I'm surprised you got as much as you did out of him," Rosalie remarked. "He hardly ever says two words, unlike most men in the village, starting with Enrico and especially Fabrice. *Signore, abbi pietà*! That one never shuts up!"

Fabrice Belragasso was Bria's sister Lorenza's longtime boyfriend. Considered to be the most beautiful man anyone had ever met, he was also the chattiest. He was always smiling, always happy, and most importantly, he was deeply in love with Lorenza, so no one in Bria's family would ever tell him to stop talking. Most people simply stared at his insanely flawless features while he prattled on about whatever he was prattling on about.

"Technically, Fabrice doesn't live in the village, so he doesn't count," Bria said. "But you're right. He talks more than Sister Constantina."

"*Taci*," Rosalie said. "You might conjure her up if you say her name."

"*Dacci un taglio*!" Bria cried. "She's been dead for years."

"Which means she's desperate for conversation," Rosalie said. "If she suddenly appears on the side of the road, I blame you, Bria Bartolucci!"

"*Sei pazza!*" Bria laughed and looked over at her friend. "I'm glad to see that you haven't let the truth about Michele get you down."

"I finished the bottle of Ornellaia after you left, but then my pity party got pitiful even for me," Rosalie confessed. "If Michele has truly turned his life around, like you claim Giovanni has . . ."

"Vanni has changed! You've seen firsthand how much he helps me at Bella Bella, and Marco adores him."

"If I were an eight-year-old boy, I'd adore Giovanni, too," Rosalie said. "The guy plays soccer, makes dessert, and gets his fingernails dirty. What's not to love?"

"You like dirty fingernails?" Bria questioned.

"Not on me, but I don't mind if a man's hands look like a man's."

"A man's hands can look like a man's even if they're clean and manicured."

"Like Luca's hands?"

"Luca's? I haven't noticed his hands."

"*Bugiarda*!" Rosalie cried. "You are such a liar!"

"*Basta*! We're talking about you and Michele."

"That's just it. There is no me and Michele," Rosalie said. "If I find out that he's Vivaldi-worthy, I may revisit the issue, but until then, we need to figure out if I'm attracted to a murderer."

Rosalie's blunt summation of the situation made Bria's spine tingle. Her friend was right; Michele could have poisoned Lugo. If he was telling the truth and he had aspirations of becoming a chef, that implied that he had studied cooking, was aware of ingredients, and had some knowledge of chemistry. Good cooking was all based on how similar and disparate chemicals worked together and what tastes they created when combined. It was hardly a stretch to imagine that a curious culinary student would want to know which chemicals produced less than savory and possibly fatal results when united. If Chef Lugo was poisoned by something he ate, it could have been caused by a chemical reaction among two or more ingredients and not just by one specific toxin, like arsenic.

"*Francamente, sono sbalordita*! I thought Michele might lead us to the murderer," Bria declared. "I never thought that he could *be* the murderer."

"Because you're too trusting, Bria," Rosalie commented. "I've always said that."

"You've never said that before."

"What did I say when you agreed to fence Barbara Tuttuzi?"

Bria looked straight ahead at the road and wondered whether she could avoid answering Rosalie's question—which would be an admission that she had been wrong—if she took the E45 all the way to Norway—where the road ended. Concession was inevitable. "You told me I was too trusting."

"And what happened less than a minute after the match started?"

"Barbara's épée blade pierced my plastron."

"Because Signorina Tuttuzi allegedly forgot to put that little plastic thing on the tip of her blade."

"Those things are practically invisible," Bria replied. "Barbara thought it was on the blade. She made a mistake."

"*Allegedly!*"

"That's one time."

"Ricardo Pontiveste."

This time Bria briefly took her hands off the steering wheel and lifted them to the heavens, she was so enraged. "*Uffa!* Ricardo was a nice guy."

"Did he ever pay you back the three hundred euros you gave him to help out his friend, the Nigerian prince?"

"No, but the prince was able to buy another passport after his was stolen, so he could resume his studies at the University of Florence."

"Bria!" Rosalie turned in her seat so she was directly facing Bria, her hands moving as wildly as the wind. "How could a woman who's raising her son by herself while running her own business and who connected the dots so we're driving more than two hours to speak with a woman who may give us clues as to who poisoned a celebrity chef, not see that she was duped?"

"Sometimes I have blind spots in my personal life," Bria said. "I can pick up on hints of evidence when it's someone else's story, but not my own. It's like there's a blockade between me and the truth."

"Naïve, yet street smart," Rosalie said. "It's a powerful combination."

"Let's see if it works on Teresina," Bria said. "I have a feeling we're going to get more than we bargained for with her."

Frosinone was no Positano. The two towns had similarities, one being that they were both built into the face of a mountain range, the rugged exterior of the landscape coexisting with the modern enhancements made over the past century. But Positano was steps from the sea, glistening in the sunshine, and decorated with homes and businesses in pastel colors, whereas Frosinone was landlocked, cloudy, and drab. If the town was someone's first stop on a tour of Italy, it would appear fine, but once they got to witness the more breathtaking parts of the country, Frosinone would become nothing more than an afterthought.

Teresina Meloni lived in a small house on Via Parmenide, in the residential section of the town. To get there, you had to take Via Tiburtina and pass by a string of restaurants that would never be allowed anywhere on the Amalfi Coast—Burger King, McDonald's, and Glamour Food Station, whose name was a lie. Bria pulled up in front of the house and was happy to see that while it was small and nondescript, it was well maintained. Someone took pride in their home.

Bria and Rosalie hopped out of the Fiat and walked up to the front door. Just as Bria was going to knock, Rosalie grabbed her hand, preventing her from announcing their arrival.

"Who should we pretend to be?"

"How about Bria and Rosalie?" Bria replied.

"What if Teresina tells Michele that we showed up on her doorstep, and he gets mad that we're investigating him and decides to add to his body count?"

Bria stared at Rosalie for a moment. "*Dio mio*! Your mind goes to dark places very quickly."

"I am attracted to a man who has a criminal past and may have just committed the worst crime of his career," Rosalie said. "What do you expect?"

"*Senti*, let's be ourselves, friends of Michele's who are looking for Mamma Rita, which is the truth," Bria said. "The moment we get back home, we'll share all this with your brother. If Michele retaliates in any way, Luca will be ready and waiting."

"What if my brother's late and Michele kills us both?"

"At least he won't get away it," Bria said. "Now *basta*. Follow my lead."

"As long as you remember Mussolini."

"Why do I want to remember that horrible man?"

"Our safeword, Bria!" Rosalie cried. "In case Teresina is the real source of Michele's bad blood."

"We don't know how bad Michele's blood is just yet."

"With my luck," Rosalie said, "we'll be able to trace Michele's bloodline right back to Italy's most famous dictator himself."

Before Bria could raise her arm to knock on the door, it opened to reveal a woman wearing a floral housedress and holding a bag of garbage, and she looked just as surprised to see Bria and Rosalie as Bria and Rosalie looked to see her. All three gasped at the same time, and then they all laughed. Well, Bria and Rosalie laughed; the woman looked slightly terrified.

"*Ci scusi*," Bria said. "My name is Bria, and this is Rosalie. We're friends of Michele Vistigliano, and we came to see Mamma Rita."

This time when the woman gasped, she dropped the bag of garbage. On Rosalie's exposed toes. So much for making a fashion-forward statement.

"*Perdonatemi*. Wait here." The woman took the bag, walked outside, and disappeared around the side of the house. They heard some noises and assumed she was putting the bag in a garbage can. But then there was silence. Just when they thought that the woman had decided not to return, she was again standing at the front door, presumably having entered through the back of the house. "*Per favore*, come in."

"*Grazie*," Bria replied.

The inside of the house was the same as the outside. Simple, unadorned, but neat. Whoever lived here didn't have much, but they treasured what they had and understood the importance of keeping a clean home.

"My name is Teresina," the woman said. "But I suspect you already know that."

"Yes," Bria said. "Paolo Vistigliano told us about you."

Hearing Paolo's name caused the woman to chuckle. She tried to contain her laughter, but like a child who found something funny during mass, she was unsuccessful. "I'm sure that's not all he told you about me."

Bria contemplated sugarcoating things but decided that honesty would be the best tactic if she wanted to glean information from Teresina. "He did say that the two sides of the families didn't mix well together."

"*Così diplomatico*," Teresina replied. "Would you like some coffee, espresso?"

"*Grazie*," Bria said. "I'd love a coffee."

"Espresso for me please," Rosalie added. "*Prego*, with a lemon slice, and if you have some sambuca, feel free to pour in a drop or two. I'm not driving."

"You would've gotten along with my sister," Teresina said. "She loved a little sambuca in her espresso."

"Is that Rita?" Bria asked.

"Yes, Margherita, but everyone called her Rita from the time she was born because she was named after our mother."

Teresina entered the kitchen, and Rosalie grabbed Bria's arm, preventing her from leaving the living room. She turned to Bria, eyes wide open, and mouthed the words, "Their mother is Mamma Rita."

Bria thought about it but disagreed with Rosalie. It didn't add up.

Teresina was roughly the same age as Paolo, in her late sixties, which meant her mother was in her early eighties, possibly younger, since women of that time had babies much earlier in life than they did today. While it was very possible that Teresina's mother was still alive, it was doubtful that she would have been able to get to Positano and stuff a note into a fake piece of pastry without being noticed. Most of the young crew members and the other people who had been in Annamaria's café at the time of the filming were *locali* whom everyone knew. An unknown elderly woman would not have blended in. No, it made much more sense that Teresina's sister was Mamma Rita, just as Paolo had said.

They sat at the kitchen table, and Bria felt like she was sitting in her grandmother's kitchen. The starched tablecloth, with its grapevine design; the light pouring in through the window, which, despite the heavy clouds outside, was quite bright; and the tantalizing smells from whatever was being kept warm in the oven. Bria closed her eyes and inhaled deeply to savor the aroma.

"Would you like some *chiacchiere*?" Teresina asked.

Like a traditional Italian woman, when it came to food, Teresina didn't wait for a response. She couldn't fathom the thought of anyone not wanting to eat at any time of day. It was inconceivable that someone would say no to food. Bria and Rosalie weren't about to squash her belief.

As soon as Teresina placed a plate overflowing with *chicacchiere* in the center of the table, Bria grabbed one of the rectangular pastries and bit into the puffy dough, which had been generously dusted with powdered sugar. There was a reason *chiacchiere* were also known as angel wings: they tasted heavenly. Rosalie was so enraptured with the taste, she couldn't speak and made noises that were universally understood to mean she was utterly enjoying her food.

After her second piece of puffy goodness, Bria steered the conversation toward the reason they had driven over two hours to get here. She wasn't sure if it was going to be something Teresina would want to talk about, but there was only one way to find out. Teresina proved to be just as anxious to start talking.

"What has Michele done now?" she asked.

"Michele?"

"Yes. Isn't that why you're here?"

"Yes," Bria replied.

"Then tell me, what has he done this time?"

Teresina looked like a woman who was used to receiving bad news. The constant assault had left her weary and hard. Bria was thankful she didn't have to add to her misery, at least not yet.

"*Niente*," Bria said. "Nothing at all."

"Please don't think you have to lie to an old woman," Teresina replied. "I can handle whatever it is he's done. It won't be the first time."

"We promise you, Michele hasn't done anything," Rosalie said. "But something has happened back home, and it would be important to know a bit more about Michele."

"You mean what kind of boy he was," Teresina said.

"Yes," Rosalie replied. "The good and the bad."

"Unfortunately, with Michele, there's more bad than good," Teresina started. "It isn't entirely his fault. He never knew his mother, poor Lydia, God rest her soul, and his father, Vito . . . Well, he was not a good man."

"That's what Paolo said," Bria revealed.

"Paolo should know. Back then, he wasn't a very good man, either," Teresina said. *"Perdonatemi."*

"No need to be sorry," Bria replied. "Paolo described himself the same way. He said he's ashamed of the man he was."

"He should be," Teresina spat. "He was the one who should have raised Michele. The boy shouldn't have been carted off to strangers."

"You didn't want him to live with you?" Rosalie asked.

"Of course we wanted him! He was family! What kind of question is that?" Teresina said. "But Michele didn't know us. He had never seen us before. Paolo was the boy's uncle, and a boy needs a man in his life. Paolo should have raised Michele as if he was his own son."

"Isn't that what you did?" Bria asked.

Teresina took a deep breath, as if collecting strength to revisit the past. Her cheeks puffed up as she let the breath out, and then she took a sip of her espresso, one that, like Rosalie's, contained a healthy amount of sambuca. After she swallowed the elixir, she was ready to continue.

"When Michele arrived, I was pregnant with my third child and helping my Nico run our store," Teresina said. "My husband was a tailor, best in Frosinone. I sewed and made dresses. I was good, too. Not as good as Nico, but good. It was hard work, long hours, and once the baby came, my Ciara, I didn't have time to tend to a boy when I had a new baby."

"I'm sure you did the best that you could," Bria said.

Teresina rolled her eyes and shrugged her shoulders. "My sister, Rita, was the one who raised Michele. It was like God brought him here just for her."

"Why do you say that?"

"Rita is a few years older than me and got married when she was only seventeen. I waited until I was twenty, an old maid back then," Teresina explained. "She lost her only son to drugs when he was barely fourteen."

Teresina made the sign of the cross and remained silent for quite a while. Bria knew what she was doing: she was saying a Hail Mary for the boy's soul. Bria thought of Marco and how lucky she was that he was such a good son, but she knew that no matter how she raised him, outside influences and his own personality could lead him astray. She joined Teresina in silent prayer.

"Michele replaced Giancarlo and became the son Rita lost," Teresina said. "She needed to be someone's mother, and Michele didn't have parents. It was the perfect fit."

Bria was very moved by the story, but there was more she needed to know. When did Michele start to get into trouble, and how did Chef Lugo fit in? Once again, Teresina filled in the blanks.

"Things were going very well. Michele was thriving, and so was Rita," Teresina said. "Things got even better when Louis moved in."

"Who's Louis?" Rosalie asked.

"A teenager from America who was floundering," Teresina said. "He was backpacking through Europe, and he shoplifted from our store one day, when Rita was filling in for me because the baby was sick."

"He stole needles and thread?" Rosalie asked.

"No, we also sold some pastries that Rita made, cookies, *bomboloni*, whatever she felt like making to bring in some extra money," Teresina explained. "Rita didn't have the heart to call the police, so she invited him for dinner instead. That was Rita, always trying to be someone's mamma."

"She sounds like a wonderful woman," Bria said.

Teresina didn't respond; she only smiled and nodded her

head. "Louis had nowhere else to go and no money, so he wound up living with us for many years. He was a good influence on Michele, too, until he left."

"Where did he go?" Bria asked.

"We don't know," Teresina replied. "He left one day without saying good-bye and never came back."

"After all you did for him?" Rosalie asked.

"Rita was heartbroken. It was like losing her son all over again," Teresina said. "Because Louis was about the same age Giancarlo would have been, Rita felt like she was getting the chance to see her son grow up before her eyes, a chance she thought was taken from her when he died. We thought Louis felt the same way. He was the one who started calling her Mamma Rita. We all did after that. The sound of those words brought such light to her eyes, such light. When Louis left so abruptly, without any explanation, no good-bye, *nulla*, Rita was never the same."

Bria was afraid to ask her next question, because she thought she knew the answer, but she had to if she wanted to learn the truth. "What happened to Mamma Rita?"

Deeply moved, Teresina didn't turn away, and she didn't try to hide the tears that fell from her eyes. She shared them with her visitors. She was a simple woman, honest and straightforward. If she was going to tell a story, she'd even tell the part that broke her heart.

"After Louis left, Rita waited for him to return, but the days turned into weeks and then months, and it was obvious he was never coming back," Teresina said. "Without Louis, Rita forgot how to live. She was just existing, and I didn't help matters."

"What do you mean?" Rosalie asked.

Teresina closed her eyes and shook her head. "I blamed my sister for Louis leaving. I told her that it wasn't enough that she had pushed one son away, that she had had to push two."

Bria was stunned, but she understood. She and Lorenza

loved each other and would always have each other's back, but when you loved someone so deeply, you also possessed the power to hurt them just as profoundly. Bria wanted to believe that she and Lorenza would never say anything so vile and hurtful to each other, but she couldn't. She knew it was possible.

"I will never forgive myself for what I said, because I know it pushed Rita to do what she did," Teresina said. "My words helped convince my sister to take her own life."

Instinctively, Bria and Rosalie reached out to grab each other's hand. They needed to hold on to something good and pure after being told something so terrible and sad.

"Teresina, I am so sorry," Bria said.

"We had no idea," Rosalie added.

Teresina nodded and waved a hand in the air. "It's what happened. It needs to be spoken and shared. I'll carry the guilt and shame with me no matter who knows what I've done."

The women finally understood how and why Michele had started to make bad decisions. First, he had lost his parents, Paolo pushed him off to strangers, and then the stranger who became a mother to him killed herself because of another young man. How much could a boy take?

"Michele hated Louis and blamed him for Rita's death," Teresina said. "He desperately tried to find Louis because he wanted him to pay for killing Rita, but no matter how hard he looked, no matter how long he waited, he couldn't find him. Louis Gordon never came back."

Emotionally exhausted, Teresina was still a good hostess and asked her guests if they wanted more to drink or eat. They both said that they had already taken more than enough of her time and needed to drive back. They hugged, shed some more tears, and soon Teresina was waving good-bye as they drove off in Bria's car.

"What a story," Rosalie said. "It does give us insight into

Michele's past and his behavior, but if Mamma Rita's dead, the trip was kind of a waste of time."

"*Stai scherzando*!" Bria cried. "We learned more than I ever imagined."

"What are you talking about?"

"Doesn't the name Louis Gordon sound familiar?" Bria asked.

"No," Rosalie replied. "I've never heard it before."

"Yes you have," Bria assured her. "Give Louis Gordon an Italian makeover, and it becomes Luigi Gordonato."

It took a moment for the realization to settle into Rosalie's brain. When it did, she shrieked, "*Dio mio*! Louis Gordon grew up to become Chef Lugo!"

Chapter 12

Bria was dreaming. She was somewhere high up in the sky, looking down at Positano. From her vantage point, she saw the village from a completely different perspective, one she had never seen before. One that few people had seen before, unless they were in a helicopter or hanging on to the wings of a hawk.

She could see the roof of Bella Bella, painted the same hot pink as the rest of the exterior, and the over four hundred stairs that ran in a snakelike pattern from the B and B to the beach. She could see St. Cecilia's Grammar School, the dome of the Church of Santa Maria Assunta, the precarious trail known as the Path of the Gods that overlooked and presided over Positano and the sea. Although the landmarks were miles below, she could see them with perfect clarity. Even the people.

Chef Lugo was embracing the mysterious blond-haired woman, who was wearing a white string bikini, on the beach as the tide rushed in and swallowed their feet. They looked like they were floating on water. Not far from them, Bria saw Massimo staring, his fists clenched, angered by the scene. Behind him was Pippa, witnessing the same embrace but cowering. Bria could sense that the woman was afraid, but she couldn't tell if she was afraid of what she was seeing or its ramifications.

On the other side of the couple, Bria saw a man hiding behind a large umbrella. Michele was even angrier than Massimo, and he didn't have the self-restraint or the experience to hide his emotions. His rage was etched onto his face. Watching him was another woman, one Bria had never seen before, but instinctively, she knew it was Mamma Rita. Her eyes were filled with so much emotion, it made Bria weak, and she could feel herself descending.

Mamma Rita reached out to Michele, but she couldn't make contact. She stepped closer, but with each step, Michele was even farther away. Tears slid down the woman's face as she realized the separation was permanent. She and Michele would never see each other again, at least not in this lifetime.

The woman then turned to see Chef Lugo, who now stood alone in the center of a circle comprising Massimo, Pippa, Michele, Mamma Rita, and the blonde. All five of them were saying things to Lugo that Bria couldn't hear. She willed her body to move from the air to the ground, but it refused, and she remained perched high overhead, a seer, not a participant, when she felt a breeze.

A hawk flew past Bria, its wing brushing against her cheek like a cautious kiss. She twirled around as it encircled her, once, twice, until it stopped in front of her. The hawk, either uninterested in Bria or intimidated by her, shifted its gaze to the left, which allowed Bria to look deep into its eye. It was as if she was peering into a dying sun.

A shimmering golden circle, alive and vibrant, but with a black center that appeared cold and deadened. Life and death in one never-ending circle. Just like the people on the beach. In the center of that circle was Chef Lugo, the symbol of death, and surrounding him were the living, the people he had left behind. One of them had the stain of death on their hands.

Bria jolted out of sleep and for a few seconds still felt afloat. She clutched the covers and didn't let go until her breathing returned to normal and she knew she was safe. When she heard voices in the dining room, she knew she wasn't alone. A quick glance at her alarm clock revealed that she had overslept.

"*Uffa!*" Bria cried. "It's nine o'clock."

Usually, Bria was up at six. All her life she had been a morning person, so it was her routine to wake up early, but now that she was running Bella Bella, it was a requirement, especially if she wanted some quiet time by herself before the day began. Today it had begun without her, so she needed to catch up.

Quickly, she rose, got dressed, splashed water on her face, brushed her teeth, and pulled her thick mane of hair into a ponytail. She looked in the mirror and wasn't thrilled by her image, but she wasn't repulsed, either. Some mornings that was good enough. When she entered the dining room, she realized others didn't share her belief.

"Bria, what's wrong? Did you have a bad dream?"

"It must have been a nightmare, because you look horrible!"

Bria had not expected to find her mother and sister sitting around the dining room table, Daisy in between them. "What are you two doing here so early?" Bria gave her mother a kiss on both cheeks and started to lean over to Lorenza to do the same. When she saw Lorenza's eyes grow wide, she immediately knew they didn't stop over for a friendly visit. "What's going on? Is Papa all right?"

"Your father's fine." Fifetta made quite an effort of fixing the flowers that were in the vase on the dining room table. When she finished, they looked exactly the way they did before she started. "He sends his love."

"I don't believe you, but it's nice to see the two of you in my home," Bria gushed. "Makes me feel like a teenager again."

"You don't look like one, that's for sure." Lorenza munched on a flaky croissant and sipped her cappuccino. "Seriously, you looked like you just rolled out of bed."

"Because I did!" Bria shouted. "I slept right through my alarm."

"Bad dreams will do that," Fifetta said. "They lose their power if you wake up."

"Mamma, how did you know I had a bad dream?" Bria asked.

"Because you look horrible," Lorenza said.

"Renza, *basta*!" Fifetta cried. "Your sister is having a problem, and may I remind you that we have a guest?"

"Don't stop on my account." Daisy smiled and broke a muffin in two to expose its gooey blueberry center. "This reminds me of my family growing up. It's important to remember that love exposes itself in many different ways."

"Do me a favor." Bria looked at her sister and mother. "Love me less."

"Bria Nicoletta Faustina!" Fifetta cried.

"*Attenta*!" Lorenza exclaimed. "Mamma's using all three names."

"Don't ever ask your family to love you less than they do," Fifetta declared. "Without your family's love, you have nothing."

Fifetta's words were meant to sting, but Bria felt like she had been stabbed in the heart. She wasn't thinking about herself; she was thinking about Mamma Rita. When Lugo—or Louis, as he was called back then—left her, after her own son had left a few years earlier, she must have felt unloved. Having a husband or lover remove themselves from your life was hard to overcome, but when a family member voluntarily disappeared, especially a child, it was almost too painful to bear. It had made Mamma Rita give up and decide to disappear herself.

"*Mi dispiace, Mamma.*" Bria kissed Fifetta on the cheek. "It was a bad joke."

"Never joke about turning your back on your family," Fifetta said. "It isn't funny."

"Neither is this conversation," Lorenza said. "*Scusami*, Daisy, my family can be . . ."

"Like a family," Daisy remarked, finishing Fifetta's comment. "No need to apologize. I find it refreshing. So many families are broken and separated. Tobias likes to pretend we see our children all the time, but the truth is they only visit on holidays."

Fifetta nodded in agreement. "If my Gabrielo, *mio figlio*, showed up right now, I wouldn't recognize him."

"Mamma!" Bria cried. "He sends you photos all the time when he visits a new country."

"You just showed me a video of him riding a camel," Lorenza added.

"Your son's in Egypt?" Daisy asked.

"No, Belgium," Fifetta replied. "Where he's doing very important work."

"They have camels in Belgium?" Daisy asked.

"He was at the zoo," Lorenza explained. "After years of doing nothing, never having a job for more than a month at a time, our brother is suddenly a global citizen traveling the world."

"He's an interpreter," Bria explained. "His work takes him to some very exciting places, just like Lorenza."

"My daughter's a flight attendant," Fifetta said, not enthusiastically. "She gallivants all over the world."

"*Oh Dio mio!*" Lorenza exclaimed. "Gabi travels and that's important work, and I *gallivant*."

"*Tesoro*," Fifetta said, "you can't compare serving drinks on a plane to translating a conversation between two government officials."

"Mamma," Bria chided, "Lorenza has an important job. Don't belittle her."

"I know she has an important job," Fifetta said. "It's just not as important as Gabrielo's."

"Bravo!" Lorenza cried. "I think it's time you went for a walk."

At the sound of his name, Bravo came out from underneath

the dining room table, where he had been napping, and stood next to Lorenza. He extended his two front paws in front of him, lifted his rump high in the air, and stretched. When he was done, he gave his body a vigorous shake and then walked to the front door to wait for his escort.

"If you see Enrico, tell him I need more petunias," Bria said. *"Addio!"*

The moment the screen door closed and Lorenza and Bravo were out of sight, Bria turned to face her mother. "Mamma, *prego*. I want to show you something in the kitchen."

"I can see into the kitchen from right here," Fifetta replied. "Why do I have to get up?"

Daisy leaned forward, wearing a mischievous grin. "I think your daughter wants to yell at you in private."

That idea hadn't crossed Fifetta's mind until just then. "Bria, if you want to yell at me, you can do it in front of your guests. They're all Italian. They're used to yelling."

"Not all of us are Italian."

The women turned to see Tobias walking down the stairs. His tall, lean physique, thinning blond hair, and sharp features were undeniably German. As was his body language. Straight back, precise movements.

And although he was on vacation with his wife and they were actively playing the tourist, he never truly looked relaxed. Bria chalked it up to his background as an emergency room doctor and imagined that he had seen more trauma and horror than one person should in their lifetime. Despite his Germanic self-control, it was clear that he loved his wife.

Before he sat down, he grabbed Daisy's hand and kissed it. It was an old-fashioned, romantic gesture that Bria thought was lovely. He let his fingertips linger on Daisy's shoulder as he asked her if she wanted more coffee. She declined but agreed to put some fruit in her bag for their tour.

"Where are you going?" Fifetta asked.

"The Path of the Gods," Tobias replied.

"It's beautiful up there," Bria said. "You'll love it."

"*State attenti*," Fifetta added. "One wrong step and you could fall over the edge. God himself won't be able to save you."

"Mamma! Don't frighten them," Bria chastised.

"I'm warning them," Fifetta protested.

"Don't worry. I've already taken care of that."

The voice came from the staircase and this time when they turned around, it was Pippa who was running down the stairs. Bria thought the young woman looked different, and yet she couldn't put her finger on it. She was wearing her black hair loose, so it hung to her shoulders, and not pulled back into a tight ponytail, like she normally wore it. She was wearing a cute yellow sundress with a floral design that accentuated the few curves she had, instead of the baggy clothes she had been wearing up until then. But the change wasn't merely physical. Daisy said something to Pippa that Bria couldn't hear, but Pippa must have found humorous, because she started to chuckle. That was it: Pippa was happy.

Ever since she arrived on Bria's doorstep, like an orphan looking for a home, Pippa had been nervous and anxious, and she had always acted as if she was going to be reprimanded for something she had done. Which was accurate, because Massimo had done nothing but yell at her. Now that Chef Lugo was dead, she seemed like a new person. Could that be it? Could Pippa be happy that Lugo was dead?

"What a glorious morning," Pippa announced. "It really is the perfect day to be touring this beautiful village."

"Every day is the perfect time to explore Positano," Fifetta said. "Maybe I'll make some lasagna for your dinner."

"Oh, Mamma, would you?" Bria asked.

"Of course. It takes only a few minutes to prepare it," Fifetta replied.

"Only a true Italian woman would say it takes a few minutes to make a lasagna," Daisy said.

"Mamma's only half Italian," Bria said conspiratorially. "The other half is French."

"A wonderful combination," Tobias said. "Food is in your blood."

"Yes, it is," Fifetta said. "I could have been a famous chef if I had wanted to cook for more than just my family."

"The world just lost a celebrity chef. Here's your chance to make a name for yourself."

Bria looked around the room, and while no one laughed at Pippa's comment, no one seemed shocked, either. Maybe Bria was reading too much into Pippa's transformation. Lugo had defended her in front of everyone when Massimo had screamed at her, but maybe in Pippa's mind all the trauma and stress she had endured at Massimo's hands was a byproduct of her job working on Lugo's show. Maybe she was thrilled that Lugo was dead, because without a TV show to work on, there wouldn't be an opportunity for Massimo to bully her. Unemployment was much better than having an emotional breakdown.

"Is someone going on a tour?" Lorenza entered the house, with Bravo right behind her. "There's a van parked outside."

"That would be for us!" Pippa squealed. "Come on, everybody. The gods await."

Pippa shoved a banana into her fanny pack, put on a pair of tortoiseshell sunglasses, and ushered Tobias and Daisy out of the B and B.

"*Addio!*" Bria cried. "Have fun."

After they left, Bria was hoping she'd have some quiet time with her sister and mother, but they each had other ideas.

"I need to talk to you," they both said at the same time.

"About what?" Bria asked.

"It's private," they replied in unison.

"Is this some kind of joke?" Bria asked. "What's going on?"

Lorenza and Fifetta looked at each other with raised eyebrows, waiting for the other either to speak or to leave the room. They threw their hands in the air, like two mimes mimicking each other's movements.

"I want to talk to you about Marco's Communion," Fifetta said.

"I need to talk to you about Fabrice," Lorenza said.

"What about Fabrice?"

This time the two voices speaking in unison were Fifetta's and Bria's.

"Is he all right?" Bria asked.

"Did he finally dump you?" Fifetta asked.

"*Finally?*" Lorenza cried. "What's that supposed to mean? Do you expect Fabrice to dump me?"

Fifetta shrugged her shoulders. "You're not always very nice to him, *mi amore.*"

"You do boss him around a lot, Renza," Bria added.

"He loves to be bossed around!" Lorenza replied.

"No man likes to be bossed around by his girlfriend," Fifetta said. "Maybe if you were his wife, things would be different."

"Mamma! I'm not going to be Fabrice's wife," Lorenza said. "But I am going to be his roommate. We're moving in together."

"What?"

Bria was more surprised than Lorenza to realize she was the one who had spoken and not Fifetta, who was pale and appeared to be in shock. Bria ran to get her mother a glass of water, and Bravo, ever helpful, started licking Fifetta's fingers, which were dangling by her side.

"Mamma, stop it," Lorenza said. "Don't be so dramatic."

Bria offered Fifetta a glass of water. "Drink this, Mamma."

Instead of taking the water from Bria, Fifetta just stared into space. "Who are you?"

Lorenza and Bria looked at each other, alarm creeping into their bodies. Did Fifetta have a stroke? Had her memory been suddenly erased? Or was a strange woman standing next to the front door?

When Bria looked at the woman, she thought she was going to be the one to have a stroke. The woman she had seen kissing Chef Lugo and the woman she considered to be one of the suspects in his murder was standing less than ten feet away. The mysterious blonde had just arrived on Bria's doorstep.

CHAPTER 13

Bria wasn't sure if she loved the woman for showing up unexpectedly and putting an end to the search to find her or if she hated her because she looked so darn good this early in the morning. Bria believed in supporting all women, but there were limits.

Even with minimal make-up and a daytime wardrobe, and without the benefits of having her features softened by moonglow, the woman was still strikingly beautiful. She was roughly Bria's age, probably early thirties, but she carried herself with an elegant air, which made her look slightly more mature. She reminded Bria of her father Franco's favorite actress, Pier Angeli, who had made her screen debut in the film *Teresa* looking far older than the typical sixteen-year-old. While this woman didn't resemble Ms. Angeli, she shared that same elusive quality.

Now that Bria saw the woman close up, she noticed that she was taller than she had originally thought. Standing about five feet, ten inches, she was even taller than Rosalie. She possessed a dancer's body, with the slightest curve at the hips, broad shoulders, and a slender neck. A light blue halter top, tan capri pants, and ankle-high hiking boots in light brown suede complemented every inch. Her blond hair was held back by a navy blue kerchief, and in her hand, she held white-framed sunglasses. The only jewelry she wore was a gold watch that looked to be more functional than expensive.

Again, Bria felt certain that the woman wasn't 100 percent Italian. Her features were European, but her air, her aura was more grounded, more American. It was a combination that was startling, and she imagined that most men would find it hard to speak to her without a stutter. Bria herself had a difficult time finding her own voice in her presence. Bravo did not.

Channeling his inner guard dog, Bravo stood in front of Bria and assumed an aggressive stance. A slow growl seeped out of his throat that turned into a series of loud barks. He was protecting his family.

"Ciao." Bria smiled. "May I help you?"

Before the woman could speak, Bravo started barking again, and with each bark, he took a step, until he was right in front of the woman. She looked down at Bravo and smiled, as if she interpreted his gruff barks to be nothing more than a rough-sounding but happy greeting. Ignoring Bria's question, she bent down and started to rub Bravo under his chin, not at all worried that his growl was a warning of physical aggression. Naturally, the dog immediately transformed from a menacing watchdog into a playful pup.

"I'm so sorry. Bravo isn't usually aggressive."

"He probably smells my Genie," the woman replied.

"That's an odd name for a perfume," Fifetta remarked.

The woman let out a throaty laugh. "Genie is my dog, which is short for Eugene. She's a Segugio Italiano, just like your Bravo, except Genie is chocolate brown and not tan."

"What a coincidence," Lorenza said, unable to hide her sarcasm. "Is that why you barged in? To play with Bravo?"

"No," the woman replied. "May I please use your bathroom?"

That was not at all what Bria had expected her to say. A request to use the restroom was a far cry from "Hi. I'm Lugo's mystery girlfriend." Or "Please allow me to introduce myself. I'm Lugo's murderer."

"*Certo*. You can use the one through there." Bria pointed in the direction of her bedroom. "It's off to the right."

"Thank you so much." As the woman was about to go out of view, she turned back. *"Grazie!"*

When the woman disappeared down the hallway, Lorenza turned to Bria and asked, "Who is she?"

"I don't know," Bria replied.

"You're letting a strange woman use your bathroom?" Lorenza asked.

"Renza, I let strange people sleep in my beds," Bria said. "I own a bed-and-breakfast. That's the business model."

"*Così bella*," Fifetta said. "I think we may have finally found someone who's more beautiful than Fabrice."

"Mamma!" Lorenza cried. "Don't ever say anything like that out loud! Fabrice might hear you."

"How?" Fifetta asked. "He's probably flying a plane thousands of miles overhead."

"He's got friends all over. Nothing gets past that man!" Lorenza replied. "I once bought him a kilt on a layover in Scotland, and by the time I got home, he had waxed his legs."

"Your boyfriend waxes his legs?" Bria asked.

"He believes in being well groomed," Lorenza said. "Especially when wearing a skirt."

"I hope he believes in competition," Fifetta said. "Because whoever that woman is, she's going to give Fabrice a run for his money."

"Bria, we must find out who she is," Lorenza said. "My life depends on it."

The youngest member of the D'Abruzzo family had a tendency to exaggerate and extract drama out of the most mundane situation. Normally, Bria would roll her eyes and shake her head at such a hyperbolic comment. However, she thought Lorenza might have stated the obvious, but not for the reason that was obvious to Lorenza. If the woman currently in Bria's bathroom did, in fact, kill Lugo, who was to say she wouldn't kill again? Her sister was right; Bria needed to find out exactly who this woman was.

Pippa reappeared at the front door and came to Bria's rescue. "I'm sorry about Valentina."

Once again, Pippa looked more like the nervous woman Bria had first met, instead of the carefree version she had witnessed only minutes ago. Pippa stood in the doorway, with one hand on the doorjamb, as if she needed to keep herself from falling over. Although she looked to be in distress, Bria was grateful, because at least she now knew the mystery woman's first name.

"*Non essere sciocca*," Bria said. "It's perfectly fine for this woman—Valentina you said her name is—to use my bathroom."

"*Prego.*" Pippa let out a deep breath. "I thought it would be okay, but then I thought maybe I had overstepped. Massimo tells me I do that a lot. It's just that I want to prove that I can do a great job, so I can be producer one day."

"I'm sure you will," Fifetta said. "Work hard and you'll get results."

"Not always," Pippa replied. "I thought Lugo would let me be an associate producer on his show, but he said he needed someone with more experience."

"Experience takes time," Fifetta said.

"So does Valentina," Lorenza said. "Is she your friend?"

"No, she's our tour guide," Pippa said. "Valentina Travanti. She's doing the Path of the Gods tour, but she needed to use the toilet first, and I assumed it would be okay since you have so many bathrooms here."

"It's perfectly all right, Pippa," Bria said. "It's always nice to connect with another local businesswoman."

"That's what Valentina said!" Pippa replied. "She's new in town and doesn't know many people."

"If she didn't spend so much time in the bathroom, she could make some friends," Lorenza snapped.

Fifetta opened her mouth to scold her daughter, but Valentina kind of did that from the other room. They heard the toilet flush, which announced her imminent arrival. Bria wanted to make sure the subject was changed to something more innocuous than the tour guide's personal life.

"Thank you so much," Valentina said, entering the main room. "I think I had too much coffee this morning."

Bria smiled, though she disagreed. You could never have too much coffee, especially Lavazza's Qualità Rossa with steamed milk, her favorite. However, Bria wanted to make sure Valentina remained grateful in order for her plan to work. To do that, she needed to find a way to get closer to the woman.

"I better be going. I have a van full of tourists ready to walk with the gods," Valentina announced. *"Cin cin!"*

"Valentina, do you have room for one more?" Bria asked.

"As a matter of fact, I do," Valentina replied. "I had a last-minute cancellation."

"*Perfetto*!" Bria cried. "I haven't gone on the path since I first arrived here. It would be nice to see it again."

"This'll be so much fun!" Pippa squealed.

Bria wasn't sure if it would be fun, but it would hopefully be informative.

The good thing about always having your family around was that you always had your family around. Bria was able to make a spontaneous, yet calculated decision to join the tour because she knew Fifetta would be able to stay and pick up Marco from school if she got back late. She also knew there'd be a delicious tray of lasagna waiting for her and her guests when they returned. Bria felt guilty when she realized she had left Lorenza alone with Fifetta, who without a doubt was going to make Lorenza feel guilty for moving in with Fabrice without a wedding band on her ring finger. But then she realized her mother and sister would bicker regardless of Lorenza's living situation, it was just what they did. Italian families argued and shouted at each other because the bonds that held them together were indestructible. At least most Italian families.

Sitting in the bus next to Pippa, Bria wondered what Valentina's connection was to Chef Lugo. Had they just met? Was she an important part of his history? Did she know him when he was living with Mamma Rita? These were all questions she was determined to have answered, but first, she watched Valentina in action.

Standing at the front of the van, holding a microphone as nonchalantly as she might hold a boyfriend's hand, Valentina appeared completely comfortable being the center of the group's attention. She looked and sounded at ease, not as if she was reciting from a memorized script. Valentina sounded as if she was chatting with friends on a road trip. She was personable and funny, and she shared details about Positano that even Bria didn't know. She made a mental note to take Marco to the Vallone Porto ravine to see the hidden waterfalls.

Even the constant barrage of questions didn't jar Valentina. She really was like a poised performer who couldn't be thrown a curve, even if her scene partner forgot all their lines. She didn't get frazzled or miss a beat.

"Why are we leaving Positano?" one passenger asked. "I thought the path started here."

"Depending upon how you look at it, the path starts or ends in Positano," Valentina replied, speaking into her microphone.

"Then why aren't we starting here?" another passenger asked. "Seems like a waste of time to go so far out of our way."

"We could certainly start the path here, as long as you're ready to climb eighteen hundred stairs," Valentina said. "Raise your hand if you'd like to do that."

As expected, everyone kept their hands firmly in their laps.

"If we drive the two hours to Bomerano, we can start the hike there and climb down the eighteen hundred stairs instead of up," Valentina explained. "Which will make for a much more delightful tour."

She waited for the laughter to die down before continuing her monologue. She explained that locally the Path of the Gods was known as il Sentiero degli Dei and that it had gotten its name not because it was a terrifying trail that made travelers pray to a higher power to survive the hike, but because of the magnificent views of the Amalfi Coast that it provided. At an elevation of over sixteen hundred feet, the Path of the Gods truly made you feel like you were on the top of the world. The cliff-top trail offered unobstructed views of the world below, and the observer was temporarily bestowed the godlike power of the omniscient. Had Bria not already walked the path, she might have been skeptical of Valentina's description, but she knew everything she said was true.

During the ride to Bomerano—a mountainside village not unlike Positano in terms of its geography, but completely different in its visual appeal, since there were no pastel-colored houses dotting the landscape, no bustling town square and, most unfortunately, no beach access—Valentina pointed out some southern Italian highlights. There was the Hotel Piccolo Sant'Andrea in Praiano, which wasn't as well known as Le Sirenuse was but nearly as luxurious; and the dreamy Fiordo di Furore, a dramatic cove not far from Praiano.

Thanks to Valentina's banter and quick wit, the two-hour drive felt like a short trip down to Annamaria's café. Once they arrived, at the trailhead in Bomerano Bria started on her mission to get to know Valentina as a person and not just an exceptionally good tour guide. In order to do that, Bria needed to be an exceptionally good sleuth and to probe Valentina about her connection to Chef Lugo without her getting suspicious, which wouldn't be the easiest thing she had ever done, because the path was narrow and she needed to maneuver among the group of twelve tourists to get close enough to Valentina. Bria wished Rosalie was at her side, because it was times like these that she needed her best friend. If she was going to make any inroads in her investigation into the chef's death, she was going to have to do it on her own.

Pippa was still acting like an enthusiastic day-tripper and not a nervous Nellie, leading Bria to think that either the girl had a split personality or one of her personas was fake, which was something to dwell on later. For now, it was a lucky break. Not wanting to miss out on anything Valentina said, Pippa had quickened her step and sideswiped some slower members of the tour to position herself right behind Tobias and Daisy, who were at the head of the pack.

"How many times have you made this hike?" Tobias asked.

"I do this tour once a week, but I've only been with the company for a month," Valentina explained. "This is my fourth trip, but each time it's different."

"Where did you work before?" Bria asked.

Valentina turned to face Bria, and for the first time, it appeared that the veneer on her perfectly smooth face had started to crack. It could have been that she was surprised to hear her voice, since Bria had been toward the back of the group when they started walking, or it could have been that she was annoyed by the question, because it would force her to reveal something about her life. Whatever the reason, Bria didn't speak, hoping her silence would force Valentina to reply.

"I was working with a much smaller company back home," Valentina replied.

Bria opened her mouth to ask her next question, but Valentina proved to be a strong opponent and having already predicted Bria's response, she beat her to the punch. "I was living in America until recently."

I knew you weren't one hundred percent Italian, Bria thought.

"You have only the slightest of accents, though, unlike mine," Tobias said. "I'm sure you've deduced that I'm from Germany."

"From the Upper Rhine region?" Valentina asked, guessing.

"You have a very good ear," Tobias replied.

"You have the strong *t* sound, which is similar to the Pennsylvania Dutch back in the States," Valentina explained.

"Are you a linguist as well as a tour guide?" Pippa asked.

"Sometimes I feel like it." Valentina threw her head back and laughed. "I have to navigate so many different languages and dialects on each tour, it's like I work for the UN."

They came to a plateau, much wider than the path, that had a few benches placed around it for people to rest, catch their breath, and enjoy the sights. Valentina told the group they would take a five-minute break and then continue the hike. It was the perfect opportunity for Bria to swoop in and monopolize Valentina's time before someone else got her ear.

"Tell me, Valentina, how did an American ever wind up giving tours on the Amalfi Coast?" Bria asked, trying to sound as innocent as possible.

Valentina smiled, and the veneer was back in place, without a scratch on it.

"My father is Italian, from Parma, but my mother is American." Valentina took a drink from her water bottle. "They met while she was studying abroad during college, they instantly fell in love, he followed her back to America and never left. Thanks to my father, I have dual citizenship, so I can work in both countries."

"*Che affascinante*!" Bria cried. "What made you choose to work in Positano instead of Parma, where your father's from?"

"Papa lost touch with his relatives, so I never had a real connection to that part of Italy," Valentina explained. "After both my parents died, I felt in need of a change, and some sunshine."

"I'm so sorry to hear about your parents," Bria said.

"Thank you. I mean *grazie*," Valentina replied. "I'm bilingual but rusty. I haven't used my Italian in some time."

"I feel the same way," Daisy said, sitting next to Tobias on a bench. "I've lived in Germany for so long, I've almost forgotten which language is my native tongue."

"One is as good as the next," Tobias said. "Thankfully, she never forgot how to cook."

"Some of us never learned," Pippa said. "When I got hired to be on the show, I started cooking more, since I was going to have to work in a kitchen, but I quickly learned I'm not a very good cook."

"A television show?" Valentina asked.

"Yes." Pippa looked nervous again now that the topic of conversation had shifted to her occupation." "A cooking show with Chef Lugo."

"Who?" Valentina remarked.

Pippa stammered slightly as if formulating a reply, and Bria took advantage of her hesitancy to interrupt. "A celebrity chef. You must have heard of him."

Valentina took a sip of water from her water bottle and then shook her head. "No, I don't think so."

"Actually. Chef Lugo *was* a celebrity chef," Bria said. "He recently passed away."

"That's terrible. I'm so sorry to hear that." Valentina clicked her water bottle onto the hook on her belt. "Time to get back on the trail. Follow me."

Not only did Valentina look like an actress, she performed like one, too. Bria couldn't believe how easily she had lied about not knowing Chef Lugo. If she lied about her relationship with Lugo, what else was she concealing?

The path on this part of the hike was a bit wider, so there was more room to spread out and the group took advantage by stretching out and leaving more space between them. The side of the cliff also changed, becoming more jagged, and the drop to the next level of land increased by a few feet. If a hiker took a fall in this section of the path, it could easily be a deadly plunge.

"Be careful around this turn please." Valentina stood near a curve in the path where trees folded inward on both sides, creating a natural canopy. "There was some rain in the middle of the night, and it's made this section slippery, because it doesn't get much sun."

The group followed Valentina along the canopied curve of the path, and when Bria entered it, she slowed down to give her eyes a chance to adjust to the much dimmer light. It was hardly pitch black, but she was now walking in shadows instead of sunlight. Bria remembered from the last time she walked the path that this part was serpentine, similar to Viale Pasitea, but with much sharper bends that demanded the hiker's undivided attention. She slowed down her gait to keep from stepping too close to the edge. Unfortunately, her caution didn't prevent her from falling.

Bria felt something hit her ankle, possibly a rock protruding from the ground or a branch that had gotten stuck in the mud after the rain. She couldn't know for sure, because she couldn't see well in the dim light. Whatever the reason, she felt her legs slip out from underneath her, and in an instant her stomach slammed into the ground, and she felt herself slip to the left. She reached forward to clutch the ground and dug her fingers into the dirt to stabilize herself, but panic consumed her when her feet felt nothing but air. Now she felt pressure on her shoulder, and her body started to slip farther away from the path and over the side. She closed her eyes and saw Marco's face in front of her.

"Mamma, get up."

"Bria!"

She heard her name, but she didn't dare look up, in case the movement made her body slip farther over the side. She saw Marco's face more afraid now, and she knew that she had to fight. She picked up her hand and reached forward, hoping to grab on to a tree. She groped, her fingers searched, but found nothing they could hold on to.

"Tobias! Do something!"

She heard Daisy's voice and then felt Tobias's large, smooth hand, and she held on as tightly as she could. Tobias yanked Bria's arm, and in one swift movement, she was once again safely standing in the center of the trail. Her pants were ripped at the knees, espadrilles were stained with dirt, but she was safe and alive. Tears filled her eyes, and she embraced Tobias.

"Grazie, grazie mille."

"Oh my God, Bria. Are you okay?" Valentina called.

Valentina looked genuinely concerned, but only one thought filled Bria's mind: Valentina was a damn good actress. She looked as alarmed as the rest of the group members, who were now all clustered together, but Bria was not sure if Valentina was alarmed because Bria had almost fallen over the edge or because she hadn't.

"I'm fine. Don't worry." Bria brushed the dirt off her pants and wiped the tears from her eyes. "You were right. This path is slippery."

"Should we get you to a doctor?" Daisy asked.

"Maybe you should lie down for a bit," Pippa suggested.

"No, *grazie*. I'm fine, thanks to Tobias." Bria gave the former physician a hug and looked into his eyes. *"Grazie mille."*

"What happened?" Pippa asked.

"I don't know," Bria replied. "I was being careful, but suddenly I was on the ground and slipping off the side."

Several of the people on the tour gasped and made the sign

of the cross. They all understood how closely Bria had come to perishing or suffering a severe injury.

Bria knew it, too. She wasn't one to dwell on close calls, but the problem was Bria didn't know exactly what had happened. She didn't know if she had slipped on the path or if she had been pushed. All Bria knew was that Valentina might have tried to commit another murder: hers.

CHAPTER 14

The atmosphere on the ride home depended on where you sat.

In the front it felt like a ride home in a hearse from a cemetery. That group, which included Tobias and Daisy, appeared to be in mourning, not just for Lugo but also for Bria's near-death experience. They were mostly quiet and looked out the windows at the scenery, the beauty of which was amplified in the late afternoon sunshine. Riding in the back of the van was a rowdier experience, and it felt like driving home on a school bus after a field trip. Pippa and some of the others spent the ride talking about Chef Lugo and, more specifically, how he might have died. Bria was perfectly situated in the middle.

In this position she was able to observe and not participate in either group. She could remain respectful of the deceased and also act as if she was reflecting on her own accident, but at the same time she could eavesdrop on the gossip. She was loathe to admit it, but she found the action taking place behind her to be much more interesting than what was happening in the front of the van.

She overheard those in the back discussing every possible scenario they could dream up that might explain why and exactly how Lugo had died. From their comments, it was clear that many of them had read the article in *La Vita Positano* that Aldo had written in which he suggested the chef might not have died from natural causes. Luca was keeping the autopsy report from the public until the police had the results of the toxicology lab work. People could speculate that Lugo's death was the result of foul play, but no one had proof. Still, they might unwittingly share clues.

Bria listened to the chatter, hoping to pick up a hint of something she might have overlooked or acquire an idea of how Lugo had met such an untimely death. She fought the urge to join the discussion, so she could maintain her impartiality. At the front of the van, she saw Valentina sitting next to the window and every once in a while making a comment to the driver, but otherwise she remained quiet. Bria didn't know if Valentina was also eavesdropping on the conversation—the van wasn't very large so it was possible—but Bria didn't want to give the tour guide the impression that she was interested in what the others had to say about Chef Lugo.

Unfortunately, very little of what was said was helpful to Bria, except one comment a man inadvertently made about Massimo. A tourist from Australia found it interesting that there had been a tape delay on a show that was supposed to air live. He said that labeling a show as being live when technically it wasn't was a forgivable offense, but he felt that this made it appear that the producer knew something was going to go wrong.

When she heard that, Bria wanted to turn around and catch Pippa's expression. She already knew that Pippa didn't like Massimo, but Bria didn't know if Pippa shared her opinion that Massimo could have killed Lugo. Bria was curious to see how Pippa would react to the tourist's comment, but she thought it best to let the opportunity slip by. She'd have more chances to question Pippa on just what type of man she thought Massimo was and whether he was capable of murder.

Truthfully, Bria and the police force had to thank Massimo. Even if he was the one who had poisoned Lugo, he was also the one who had prevented Lugo's final moments from going viral on the Internet and turning the chef into an international obsession. Lugo's terrified face flashed before Bria's eyes, and she thanked God Lugo's demise hadn't been captured on video for all the world to see over and over again. Becoming fodder to entertain millions would have literally been a fate worse than death.

It was only a matter of time before the international press found out that Lugo had been murdered and hadn't died from a heart attack or stroke, as was currently being contemplated. Bria didn't know if Lugo was really famous enough for a horde of journalists and news crews to descend on the village, but she hoped they could uncover the murderer before that happened. Two of the people on her suspect list—Pippa and Valentina—were in the van with her. Bria had already figured out a lot about Pippa and, of course, knew where she lived, at least for the time being. It was time she got to know Valentina better.

When the van parked in front of Bella Bella, Bria made sure she was the last person to exit.

"Thank you for such a wonderful tour, Valentina."

"*Grazie*, Bria. That's very kind." Valentina's face suddenly took on a grave expression. "I'm so sorry it almost turned into a disaster. Nothing like that has ever happened before on any tour I've given. I feel horrible."

"This isn't your fault." Bria grabbed Valentina's hand and looked the woman in the eyes. "No matter how safe we try to be, no matter how many precautions we take, these things can happen. The most important thing is that the day didn't end in tragedy and I'm fine."

Valentina didn't try to pull away from Bria's touch; she seemed to embrace it. "You're very much like me, Bria Bartolucci, do you know that?"

"In what way?"

"I'm a 'glass half-full' girl myself." Valentina suddenly sounded much more American than Italian. "Whenever I'm faced with negativity or a bad day, I look at the bright side. You clearly do the same."

"I've learned that God takes away, but he also gives so much." Bria let go of Valentina's hand and suddenly laughed. "For instance, I thought I knew everything about the Path of the Gods, but I was wrong. Sort of makes up for almost falling to my death."

Bria replayed the words she had just uttered in her head, and realized they sounded much harsher than she had thought they would. She wanted to get closer to Valentina, not turn her away by making her feel uncomfortable or awkward with her comments. On the contrary, Valentina fully appreciated Bria's macabre humor.

"Maybe I should put that on my business cards! You might die, but you'll enjoy the tour."

Bria found herself laughing along with Valentina. But was she laughing along with a murderer? Or with someone who just had an interesting point of view about life and death?

"I really am glad you enjoyed the tour," Valentina said. "I love when I can share something new, especially with the locals, who, between you and me, think they know everything."

"I may be a local, but I've been in Positano for only a year," Bria said. "I know how intimidating it can be to build a life in a new place."

"Especially for us single girls," Valentina said. "We need to stick together."

Yes we do! Bria thought.

"Valentina, *per favore*, join us for dinner," Bria said. "I may be biased, but Mamma's lasagna really is the best you'll ever taste."

"*Grazie*," Valentina replied. "But I have to get home and take Genie for a walk."

There was no way Bria was going to be able to argue against that. As a dog owner, she knew canine companions were part of the family and always took precedence over homemade lasagna. One-on-one time with Valentina would have to wait.

"I completely understand," Bria said. "I'm sure we'll have leftovers."

"Leftover lasagna is always the best," Valentina replied. "I'll definitely take a rain check."

Bria watched the van drive down the road and disappear around the curve. The mysterious woman she had seen kissing Chef Lugo the night before he was killed was still a mystery. Hopefully, Bria would be able to unravel the details of her past very soon and discover the role Valentina might have played in Lugo's death, but at the moment the smell of lasagna wafting out of her house was making her incredibly hungry.

When she walked inside Bella Bella, it was as if she was transported to a Sunday afternoon of her childhood. The room was filled with loud voices, the heartwarming aroma of a home-cooked meal, and love. Love among family, friends, and even total strangers. Her mother, Lorenza, and Marco had been joined by Giovanni, and they were welcoming Pippa, Tobias, and Daisy to the table. Bria felt her eyes moisten and allowed herself a moment to be a mother, a daughter, and a friend. She could be an amateur investigator later; right now she needed to eat.

"Mamma!" Bria cried. "I just asked you to make a lasagna, not cook up a seven-course meal."

"*Oh andiamo!*" Fifetta cried, even louder. "How do you expect me to make one thing when I'm used to cooking for a banquet hall?"

"I tried to tell her you'd be upset." Giovanni placed a bowl of fried meatballs on the table. "But she said you'd be the first one to grab one of her meatballs."

Bria froze and held the meatball she had just taken from the bowl a few inches from her lips. Caught red-handed, she figured there was no way to dispute Giovanni's comment or her mother's claim, so she took a bite. It was like biting into the past. The meatball tasted the same as the one she'd bit into almost thirty-one years ago. Bria, like most two-year-olds, had been screaming, just because it was something new to do and the sound seemed to garner attention. When her mother shoved a meatball into her mouth, all thoughts of screaming had evaporated, and all she had wanted to do was savor the new taste forever. Thankfully, she had gotten her wish.

"*Deliziosa*," Bria said. "*Mangiate*, everyone. *Mangiate!*"

A mixture of emotions filled Bria's heart. Happiness, pride, humility, gratitude. She looked at the spread of food on the table, and while most others would think it took a team to produce such a feast, Bria knew that her mother had created the smorgasbord on her own. She also knew her sister, Lorenza, would disagree and swear that she had helped, when the most she ever did was slice up the mozzarella or toss the salad. But Bria was grateful for her sister, because whenever she doubted her own cooking skills, she remembered she'd never be as terrible a cook as Lorenza.

Two trays of lasagna were surrounded by the bowl of fried meatballs, a bowl of braciola, a split serving dish that was filled with broccoli rabe and steamed carrots, a plate of mozzarella and tomatoes cut into thick slices, and a plate filled with an assortment of olives. It was enough to feed her guests for the whole week, but Bria knew that her mother was questioning if she should have also made a tray of baked ziti. It was the Italian way. More food was always better than not enough.

Pippa, Tobias, and Daisy were filling up their plates with gusto, and Bria could tell they were trying to temper their enthusiasm in front of her. She was their host, after all, and although she knew the meals she and Giovanni prepared for them were scrumptious and garnered many raves, they paled in comparison to Fifetta's culinary creations. It didn't bother Bria in the least, but she knew her guests were unaware of that and didn't want to create an awkward scene between mother and daughter.

There was nothing they could do, however, to prevent an awkward scene between mother and her other daughter.

"Mamma, *seriamente*, are you going to pout all night long?" Lorenza asked.

"I'm not pouting!" Fifetta protested, clearly pouting. "I'm serving dinner."

"Giovanni's serving dinner," Lorenza replied. "You're pouting."

"Why should I pout?" Fifetta asked. "Is it because *mia bambina* refuses to make her parents happy?"

"Would you prefer I be a *bambocciona*?" Lorenza asked. "Live with you and Papa rent free and expect you to pay for everything?"

"No more pouting *or screaming* until we finish eating," Bria said.

"That probably won't happen." Marco turned to face Tobias. "Whenever family is around, someone starts screaming."

"That's because family loves each other so much, they feel comfortable enough to scream at each other," Tobias replied.

"I know," Marco said. "First, they yell, and then they hug."

"You're a very wise young man," Daisy said.

"*Grazie*," Marco replied. "Do you have a little boy?"

"No," Tobias said. "But I know a wise boy when I see one."

"Speaking of a wise boy," Bria interjected, "where are you and Fabrice going to live?"

First, Fifetta shot Bria a look that sliced into her like a hot knife slicing into a loaf of bread just pulled out of the oven. Then Lorenza tossed a smile in Bria's direction that lit up the room. Maintaining balance in a family was always a good thing.

"The lease on my apartment is up, and I was going to renew

it, but I thought, why am I wasting so much money when I'm hardly there?" Lorenza said. "I'm either flying on a plane or spending most nights at Fabrice's place."

The only interruption came in the form of Fifetta's heavy sigh and the elaborate sign of the cross she made before shaking her head slowly to make sure her actions were fully seen.

"We decided I would move into Fabrice's condo in Rome," Lorenza said. "Which I'll redecorate."

"You don't like your boyfriend's taste?" Pippa asked.

"*Oh Dio, no!*" Lorenza replied. "Fabrice has impeccable taste in everything. Clothes, art, furniture."

"Then why do you want to redecorate?" Pippa asked.

"To remind Fabrice who's boss," Bria answered.

"She's right," Lorenza agreed. "My boyfriend is a pilot, and when he's in the cockpit, he's completely in charge. Whatever he says goes. When it comes to his personal life, he prefers to let me take control, so he doesn't have to make all the decisions."

Bria hugged her sister. "I'm happy for you, Renza."

"*Grazie*, Bria."

Bria looked at her mother, who made a face, as if to convey that she had no idea what Bria wanted her to do. In response, Bria raised her eyebrows, tilted her head, and put her hands on her hips. There was no way Fifetta could misunderstand what Bria was trying to tell her. Which was to give Lorenza a hug, or succumb to Bria's constant nagging until she did.

"*Ah per l'amor di Dio!*" Fifetta cried. "I'm happy for you."

"Are you really happy, Mamma?" Lorenza asked. "Or are you just saying that because Bria has guests?"

"Don't push it, Renza," Bria chided. "Take the win."

"*Sinceramente*, I'm very happy for you and my Fabrice." Fifetta tried to hug Lorenza, but her daughter pulled away.

"*My* Fabrice?" Lorenza said. "Why didn't you say you were happy for Fabrice and *my bambina*?"

"*Oh Dio mio*!" Fifetta cried. "A mother can never win!"

"Isn't that the truth," Daisy remarked.

"Would anyone like seconds?" Giovanni asked.

"How about firsts?"

They all turned around and were surprised to see Luca standing in the doorway. Most everyone was happy to see their friend, except for Giovanni, who didn't see Luca, but rather the chief of police. And those two did not have a great relationship.

"I'll get another plate," Giovanni said before retreating into the kitchen.

Marco and Bravo jumped up to greet Luca, who bent down to hug them both and rub both of their heads. Marco seemed to like the roughhousing just as much as Bravo did, and Bria didn't have the heart to make them stop. Not because she felt bad about ending Marco's fun. She didn't want to ruin the cheerful sight.

Luca had never been married, he didn't have children, and yet, instinctively, Bria knew that he would make a wonderful husband and father. She stored that information in her head and then shook it, because she was thinking like a schoolgirl fantasizing about a potential boyfriend instead of a woman thinking about her friend. She needed to once again change her train of thought.

"Luca!" Bria cried. "What a surprise. Come eat with us."

"I'm unable to resist one of Fifetta's meals," Luca said.

"Wait a second," Bria said. "How do you know that my mother cooked?"

"I'm the chief of police," Luca said. "I get paid to pay attention to details."

After dinner, Fifetta took Marco and Bravo on a long walk into the village, with the promise of getting some gelato from the ice cream store next to Mimi's bookstore. Tobias and Daisy were resting in their room, and Pippa had said she wanted to buy some souvenirs for her parents. Giovanni and Lorenza were in the kitchen, making coffee, and he was teaching her how to make fresh whipped cream for the limoncello mousse they were going to have for dessert, which gave Bria the chance to be alone with Luca. Not as a woman or a friend, but as a colleague.

"I found out who our mystery woman is," Bria said.

"Who?" Luca asked.

"Valentina Travanti."

"I recognize that name. Who is she?"

"Positano's newest tour guide."

"How'd you find this out?"

"She needed to use my bathroom."

Based on the confused look on Luca's face, Bria knew she needed to explain the situation in a bit more detail. When she was finished, Luca still look confused.

"This still doesn't tell us how she's connected to Chef Lugo or Mamma Rita," Luca said.

"That's true, but at least we know who she is," Bria replied. "And that she's a liar."

"Who's a liar?" Lorenza asked. She placed the silver tray carrying four cups, an espresso decanter, and four small dishes of limoncello mousse topped with healthy dollops of fresh whipped cream on the small table in between where Bria and Luca were sitting on the couch in the sitting room. Lorenza sat in the empty chair next to them and starting pouring the espressos. "Are you talking about Nunzi?"

"No." Bria ran a lemon rind around the rim of her espresso cup. "Nunzi is very honest."

"Then it must be Rosalie," Lorenza said, passing a cup to Luca. "*Scusa*, I love her, but she can't always be trusted to tell the truth."

"Grazie." Luca took a sip of espresso. "As her brother, I cannot argue with that sentiment."

"I was talking about Valentina," Bria said.

"*Aspetta*, tour guides are known to embellish things to make mundane facts sound more exciting," Lorenza replied.

"From what I know of the village, she didn't exaggerate any of the facts, and she was entertaining," Bria said. "Still, she is a liar."

Giovanni tentatively sat on the wooden chair near the window. He was part of the group yet a safe distance from the chief of police. "What did she lie about?"

"Pippa mentioned Chef Lugo, and Valentina acted like she didn't know him." Bria shoved a spoonful of mousse in her mouth and closed her eyes. "Vanni, this is *delizioso. Grazie.*"

Giovanni smiled and may have blushed a little. *"Prego."*

"Did Valentina say she didn't know Lugo?" Luca asked. "Or just give the impression?"

"I didn't ask her directly if she knew him, but I explained who he was and that he had died," Bria relayed. "She did say it was terrible that he died, but then she quickly changed the subject."

"Maybe she was telling the truth," Lorenza said. "Not every woman's like Rosalie."

"I saw Valentina kissing Chef Lugo the night of his party," Bria explained. "At the time I didn't know who she was, but she definitely knew who Lugo was."

"If she knows Lugo and she's hiding it, can't the police bring her in for questioning?"

Luca turned to face Giovanni, and Bria could tell that Luca was considering Vanni's tone of voice. Bria hoped he wasn't challenging Luca's authority and was asking an innocent question. Since the two of them did not typically engage in friendly banter, there was the possibility Vanni was hoping to expose Luca's poor job performance.

"We could bring her in, but she wasn't anywhere near Annamaria's café the day of the filming, nor is she linked to the TV crew," Luca replied. "Even though Bria saw her and Lugo kissing, they could have just met. Since Valentina lives and works in Positano, there isn't any real threat of her leaving the village."

Giovanni nodded and faced Bria. "But you think she had something to do with Lugo's death, don't you?"

Bria opened her mouth and quickly shut it. She felt as if she needed to temper her enthusiasm. She didn't want Luca to think she was siding with Giovanni against him. But that was exactly what she was doing.

"I think Valentina and Lugo have some kind of connection," Bria said. "And that there's a very real possibility she knows how he died."

Unexpectedly, Giovanni clasped his hands together and smiled mischievously. "Then let's do a little online research."

Giovanni ran into the kitchen and came back with his laptop already booted up. As the others finished their mousse, he typed on the keyboard. His eyes moved back and forth as he read information on the screen, but he didn't look like a man who had just uncovered evidence.

"Did you find anything helpful?" Bria asked.

"Only that she's a tour guide with Positively Positano Tours and speaks fluent Italian, English, and Spanish," Vanni said. "There's a link to her Instagram account, but she's posted only twice. One is a photo of her and a dog, who looks just like Bravo, and a photo of the tour company's logo."

"She doesn't use social media much," Lorenza said. "Or she really wants to remain private."

"Vanni, do a search for Louis Gordon," Bria suggested.

"Who's Louis Gordon?" Luca asked.

"Chef Lugo," Bria replied.

"No, Chef Lugo's real name is Luigi Gordonato," Luca corrected.

"That's the name he made up to sound Italian," Bria said. "His real name is Louis Gordon."

"Do I even want to know how you found this out?" Luca asked.

"Rosalie and I paid a visit to Mamma Rita's family," Bria revealed.

"Neither you nor my sister bothered to tell me?" Luca asked.

"I told you your sister is a liar," Lorenza said.

"Your sister's no better," Luca countered.

"I never claimed she was," Lorenza retorted.

"*Basta!*" Bria shouted. "Vanni, did you find anything about Louis Gordon?"

"Yes, but again, there isn't much to tell."

"Let me see." Bria grabbed the laptop and turned it to face her. She only had to read the first two lines of his biography to gasp.

"I know that gasp! It means you uncovered something," Luca said. "What did you find out?"

"Confirmation that Valentina is a better liar than she is a tour guide," Bria said.

"You found evidence that she knew Chef Lugo?" Luca asked.

"According to this website, she did," Bria said.

She turned the laptop around again so the others could see the screen. Luca had a very different reaction after reading the text than Bria did. "How does a website for the University of Oregon link Valentina to Lugo?"

"Louis Gordon graduated from there," Bria said.

"And you think Louis Gordon changed his name to Luigi Gordonato?"

"I know he did," Bria said.

"*Bene*, but how does this information prove that Valentina and Chef Lugo knew each other?" Luca asked.

"Because the University of Oregon is in the town of Eugene," Bria declared.

"What's that supposed to mean?" Luca asked.

"The dog in the photo with Valentina is hers," Bria said. "And her dog's name just happens to be Eugene!"

CHAPTER 15

Sometimes coincidences happen. You decide to wear your sleeveless pink linen sheath dress to a party during senior year of college, and it's only after your arrival that you discover your best friend decided to wear the same exact dress. That's a coincidence. That a woman has named her dog after a town where a recently murdered man went to college is not. It's proof that the woman and the deceased are somehow connected. Proof to Bria at least. Luca still wasn't convinced it was enough to bring Valentina in for questioning. Which meant Bria would have to continue her investigation on her own. With a little help from Rosalie, of course.

Now that Caffè Positano had finally reopened, Bria and Rosalie decided to have their Sunday morning coffee at what had become the most notorious café in town. Annamaria's *pasticceria* had always been popular, but now that it could claim to be the place where a famous chef died, it had become one of Positano's hot spots. As the women sipped their cappuccinos and took bites of their *cornetti* filled with citrus marmalade, tourists and locals alike walked by and took photos of the café. Bria couldn't scold them for their behavior; she understood the fascination. The difference was that the onlookers simply wanted to gawk at what some of them had dubbed Caffè della

Morte, whereas Bria wanted to find out who had brought death to her friend's café.

"Do you know anything about Valentina?" Bria asked.

Rosalie wiped some crumbs from her vintage Diadora Bussani T-shirt. Rosalie felt a connection to the first woman who had tried to be admitted into the Italian Naval Academy in 1981. Her groundbreaking attempt was thwarted, but she did lead the way for female ship cadets. As the skipper of her own boat, Rosalie felt a kinship with Signora Bussani. She thought Valentina possessed some of the same qualities.

"From what I know of her, and it's really just the little bit I've heard from SBOOTAC . . ."

"That's the group you keep telling me join, *corretto*?"

"Yes. Small Business Owners on the Amalfi Coast," Rosalie replied. "SBOOTAC for short."

"That really isn't a great acronym," Bria said. "It sounds angry, like shop owners are yelling at rowdy customers."

"It's because you're saying it wrong," Rosalie replied.

"How else can you pronounce it?"

"You're putting the accent on the 'sboo' when you should be putting it on the 'tac,'" Rosalie instructed. "Try it."

"SBOO*TAC*," Bria said, trying to pronounce it with the accent on the correct syllable this time. "That doesn't sound right either. I think the group needs a new name."

"I think you need to focus on solving one problem at a time," Rosalie replied.

"*Bene.* So what do the SBOO*TAC* people have to say about Valentina?"

"First of all, everyone calls her Tina, and second, they seem to like her," Rosalie said. "She's experienced, funny, and Giorgio, the one who owns the leather goods store in Sorrento, said she's got the longest legs he's ever seen. He was part of the equestrian team at the two thousand ten world championships, so he should know."

"That's it?" Bria asked. "She's funny and has long legs?"

"And she has experience at being a tour guide."

"That doesn't help me connect her to Lugo," Bria said. "I need undeniable proof that they had some kind of relationship."

Rosalie shrugged a shoulder. "Bria, it's obvious they were college sweethearts."

"That's what I think," Bria replied. "But I need to find out for certain. Otherwise, it's just speculation."

"You sound like my brother," Rosalie said.

"Who do you think told me that?" Bria replied.

"*Madonna mia*!" Rosalie cried. "He will go to his grave playing by the rules. Has he not learned from me that sometimes you have to color outside the lines?"

"I think he's learned from you that when you color outside the lines, you sometimes wind up with a picture of life that isn't as pretty as you'd like it to be," Bria said.

"You know what else you've learned from my brother?" Rosalie asked.

"What's that?"

"The inability to be subtle."

Bria didn't respond. She simply took a long sip of her cappuccino and looked out at the constant parade of tourists who walked in both directions in front of the café, as if the street were a conveyor belt. It wasn't often that she could take advantage of the morning by having breakfast with her friend and basking in the sunshine. Usually, she had to make breakfast for her guests, clean up rooms, make beds, or pay bills. Fifetta had stayed the night and had taken Marco to school before returning home to Ravello. Fifetta had also made a quiche for breakfast while she was making last night's dinner, so Giovanni could also sleep in and take it easy this morning. Without having to solve problems at Bella Bella, Bria was free to wrestle with her own. And her friends.

"Have you seen Michele since he was questioned by the police?" Bria asked.

Rosalie didn't immediately make eye contact, which Bria translated as a yes. "Just once. I stopped by the garage to get some containers filled with petrol."

"You could do that at the marina."

"I like to give Paolo my business."

"Paolo doesn't need your business. He owns the best garage in the village."

"It's the only garage in the village where Michele works." Rosalie sighed and looked out at the crowd. "I know I can be my own worst enemy, but there is a chance he doesn't know Chef Lugo was the man he knew as Louis Gordon."

"That's true." Bria concentrated on her *cornetto* and avoided looking at Rosalie. "But it's an odd coincidence that they both showed up in Positano at roughly the same time."

"I know it is," Rosalie replied. "But he is handsome. You have to admit that."

Bria rolled her eyes. "Tread lightly."

"*Non preoccuparti*. I have no other plans to meet him until you solve this murder," Rosalie said.

"Hopefully, the police will solve it first," Bria said.

"I doubt that." Rosalie took one last gulp of her cappuccino. "Who else is on the list besides Michele?"

"Massimo, Pippa, Mamma Rita—well, she was a suspect, but she's dead—and Valentina."

A strong wind rushed past them, bringing with it the smell of the sea and the sound of barking. With it came a low-flying seagull that whipped past them and then careened to the left before flying down the street. A small gray terrier started barking frantically and leapt forward in an attempt to catch the gull, but its actions were futile. It did give Bria an idea. If you wanted to catch your prey, it was best to be on the same footing.

"Who are you calling?" Rosalie asked.

"*Ciao*, Valentina," Bria said.

"Valentina?" Rosalie whispered. "From Oregon Valentina?"

Bria swiped the air in front of Rosalie's face to get her to shut up so Valentina wouldn't hear her.

"*Ciao*, Bria," Valentina replied. "I'm sorry I missed your mother's lasagna last night. I'm sure it was beyond delicious."

"It was," Bria said. "I saved some for you, but that's not why I'm calling."

"Did you want to book another tour?"

"*In un certo senso*, I was about to take Bravo for a walk and wanted to know if you and Genie would like to join us."

"That is brilliant!" Rosalie whispered.

Bria nodded and mouthed the words "I know."

"We'd love to," Valentina said. "I don't have a tour until later this afternoon, and it would be good for my Genie to make a new friend."

"*Perfetto*!" Bria said. "Why don't we meet in front of Enrico's flower shop in a half hour."

"See you there! *Cin cin*!"

Forty minutes later, Bria and Bravo were still waiting outside of Flowers by Enrico for their double date to begin. Bria checked her cell phone a third time to see if she had missed a call or a text from Valentina, but the only texts she had received were from the other women in her life.

Rosalie had reminded her not to get distracted by Valentina's dog, no matter how super cute she might be, since Genie's *madre umana* could also be a murderer. Imperia had texted Bria to remind her to tell Fifetta that she needed the names and addresses of their family members to invite them to Marco's Communion party on her yacht, and Fifetta had texted Bria to remind her to tell Imperia that she needed to stop asking for names and addresses of their family members, because Marco's Communion party was going to be held at her banquet hall.

The whole issue surrounding where and how to celebrate Marco's religious milestone was not going away, like Bria wished it would. Fifetta and Imperia normally got along very well, and Bria couldn't remember any other time when they had argued. She prayed that this wasn't the start of a new chapter in their relationship and that they would find a suitable compromise. If the women remained stubborn and inflexible, Bria was going to have to make a very tough decision.

When her cell phone pinged again, indicating the arrival of yet another text, Bria was certain it was going to be from Valentina, telling her she was right around the corner or had been tied up unexpectedly and had to cancel. She was surprised to see that it was from Sister Benedicta. Bria immediately assumed something was wrong with Marco, that he was sick or had gotten hurt on the playground, but Sister B's text had nothing to do with Marco. Only with Marco's Communion.

Mother Superior has given me the okay to go with you to Ravello to pick up the ceramic angels, and she suggested that I drive!

Cavolo! Bria thought. *That's one progressive Mother Superior.*

She thinks it's wise that one of the sisters gets experience driving the local roads, in case there's ever an emergency.

Bria was thrilled that Sister B would get the chance to drive her Fiat and experience firsthand the joy of handling such a vehicle without having to defy Mother Superior's command. Having a clear conscience while driving was always a good thing, especially on the not so easy to navigate streets of Positano and the rest of the Amalfi Coast. Bria didn't want to invite God's wrath to come along for the ride.

Fantastico! **Tell me when you're ready and we'll make the trip!**

Sister B's response came in seconds.

Grazie mille!

"*Mille scuse!*"

Momentarily confused, Bria thought Sister Benedicta had sent a voice text, until she looked up and saw Valentina standing in front of her. Attached to the leash she was holding was an exact replica of Bravo, only in the chocolate-brown version. Valentina may have been beautiful, but her Genie was attracting all the attention. Especially from Bravo.

Since Bravo was the unofficial prince of Positano, he had learned he didn't need to expend any energy to receive attention. Walking around the village without a leash, Bravo was constantly greeted by locals and tourists alike, and he was given treats by the store owners, as well as by Sister B, whenever they saw him. Because of this special treatment, Bravo never considered other dogs competition. Bravo was a born leader, and whenever he came upon another dog while out for a walk, he was automatically the alpha. But Genie, perhaps because she was new to the village, had not yet received that memo. She appeared as aloof as her owner.

Despite her apology, Valentina didn't look like she had run to make up for lost time. In fact, she looked like she had been waiting for Bria to arrive. She wore a long-sleeved mint-green linen sweater that hung loosely over white shorts. With the accent on *short*. A green alligator belt and floral espadrilles finished her outfit. Once again, her blond hair fell freely against her cheekbones and shoulders, the wind making it flutter, giving Valentina a youthful glow.

It could have been another coincidence, but Bria thought the matching green collar Genie wore was a deliberate fashion statement. Valentina and Genie weren't just two girls out for a walk; they were out to be noticed. One glance over at Bravo confirmed that the duo was a success.

Instead of barking or turning away from Genie, Bravo did

something he rarely did: he sat motionless and stared. Had Valentina's dog been the same color as Bravo, Bria would have entertained the idea that Bravo thought he was looking at himself in a mirror. The two dogs were polar opposites. Bravo was staring at Genie because Genie wanted to be stared at. Valentina had taught her well.

"You are beautiful," Bria cooed.

She then realized that Valentina could have easily mistaken her compliment as being directed toward her, so Bria bent down and began to pet Genie under the chin. This action gave Bravo the chance to make contact. He got closer to Genie and started to sniff the air around her. While Genie—playing the aloof canine role to the hilt—didn't join in, she didn't push Bravo away, either.

"Genie isn't used to other dogs," Valentina said. "There weren't many in our old neighborhood, and I've been so busy with work, I haven't been able to take her out for long walks."

"Not a worry," Bria replied. "Bravo is very friendly, and I'm sure he'll win Genie over in a few minutes."

"If she isn't, it's my fault," Valentina said. "She's overheard me bad-mouthing men so much that she may have sworn them off like I have."

Bria knew an entrée to conversation when she heard one.

"Sounds like there's a story behind that statement," Bria said. "I'm all ears."

By the time they got to A Word from Positano, Mimi's bookstore, Valentina had filled Bria in on her romantic exploits. At least the ones she'd wanted to share. Bria had learned about Gino, her distant fourth cousin from Parma, who didn't quite understand the concept of a family tree; Roberto, who was a colleague with a girlfriend in every country in the European Union and even in countries the union refused to admit; and Steven, the shy restaurant manager from back home who could never work up the nerve to ask her out no matter how many times she dined solo in his establishment. Without any other prospects, Valentina had found no reason to keep her from leaving the States and starting a new journey.

"Do you miss America?" Bria asked.

"Some things, like the diners that stay open all night, the Broadway shows that would come through town," Valentina confessed. "Mainly, I miss college."

"Really?" Bria said, trying not to jump on the opportunity too quickly. "Where did you go to school?"

"A state college, very small," Valentina said, avoiding giving a specific answer. "But I loved living on campus, the camaraderie, learning new things, fencing."

"You fence?"

"I was on the fencing team all four years."

Could this be another coincidence involving Valentina?

"*Strano*! I was on the fencing team, too," Bria said. "For a short while, I thought I might try out for the Olympic team."

"You must have been good," Valentina said. "I enjoyed playing, but I wasn't the best on the team."

"I would love to start playing again, but I can never find anyone who fences or is willing to learn," Bria said. "We should play sometime."

"That would be fun, but I didn't bring any of my equipment with me," Valentina said. "I mean, what are the chances of meeting another former fencer?"

"I have enough for both of us," Bria said. "And access to a state-of-the-art gym."

"In Positano?"

"*Sì*. It's on my mother-in-law's yacht."

"Imperia Bartolucci has a gym on her yacht?" Valentina asked.

"Of course she does," Bria replied. "She also has a wine cellar, a tanning bed, and a panic room, you know, just in case."

"I can't believe you're related to Imperia," Valentina remarked. "She's one of the most famous women in Italy."

Bria knew Imperia was a successful businesswoman and a

former Miss Italia, but because she was also family, Bria didn't consider her to be famous. Was she wrong about that? Or had Valentina been doing some investigating of her own?

"My father was a politician in Parma, small time but very popular," Valentina explained. "Since the Miss Italia contest took place right in town, in Salsomaggiore Terme, he was invited to be a judge."

"What a small world," Bria said, with a measured hint of irony.

"He would always talk about sitting next to Vitto Scotti, Dino Risi, Ugo Tognazzi, all the famous actors and directors, and having his breath taken away by the contestants," Valentina said. "The most beautiful of all, according to my father, was Imperia Bartolucci, although he knew her as Imperia Stalazito."

Valentina knew Imperia's maiden name. Either she was telling the truth or she had really done her research. Even though Bria was getting closer to Valentina, the woman still remained a mystery.

"I'm sure Imperia would love to hear that she made such an impression on your father," Bria said. "And it looks like you may get the opportunity to tell her yourself."

They were so deep in conversation and had been so careful not to lose sight of the dogs, which were walking in front of them, that they almost walked by the couple sitting outside of Elisir di Positano, one of the more fashionable and expensive cafés in Positano. Whereas Annamaria's café was a place to go to relax, meet up with friends, and chat with strangers, Elisir was a place to go to be seen. The food was extraordinary, and the drinks were creative, but if you could afford to order off Elisir's menu, you had to be financially successful.

"*Ciao*," Massimo said. "If it isn't *due belle signore*."

Make that three. Although one of the pretty ladies was not acting very ladylike.

Genie's paws were on top of Massimo's thigh, and her head was tilted back to take full advantage of Massimo's petting. Her tongue was dangling out of the side of her mouth, and she was letting out moans of delight. Genie's detached personality had disappeared, and she was acting like a dog who was reuniting with a long-lost friend.

Valentina may have heard about Imperia through her father and read some more about her online, but there was no getting around the fact that she had a personal connection to Massimo.

Unlike tour guides, dogs never lied.

CHAPTER 16

Valentina tugged at Genie's collar and, after initial resistance, was able to pull her dog off Massimo. Even held tightly on her leash, the dog still yelped and lurched forward, trying to get back to the man she clearly knew, all the while ignoring everyone else around her, including Bravo. Bria caught Valentina's eye and saw that the woman wasn't upset that her dog wouldn't behave. She was upset that her dog had given her away.

"Looks like someone has made a new friend," Bria commented. She noticed Imperia peering at her from over her Bellini. "I'm referring to Genie, *certo*, not you, Imperia."

"*Ovviamente.*" Imperia set her drink on the table and placed her hand over Massimo's. "I'm sure Massimo knows the difference."

"Genie! *Basta, amore mio!*" Valentina cried.

"*Sono così dispiaciuta!*" Bria exclaimed. "This is Valentina Travanti, one of Positano's finest tour guides."

Bria watched Imperia take in Valentina's beauty and wasn't sure how her mother-in-law would respond. Few women rivaled Imperia's beauty no matter what their age, so Bria imagined it must be shocking to Imperia to be introduced to someone who looked like Valentina. The sight was so unexpected that it rendered Imperia speechless.

Imperia smiled and tilted her head toward Valentina. It was a classic piece of silent dialogue that spoke volumes without a sound being uttered. The mature beauty acknowledging a potential rival. For her part, Valentina understood her place and responded with respect in her voice.

"Signora Bartolucci, what a pleasure to meet you."

Imperia's violet eyes widened. "I'm flattered that you know who I am."

"I was just telling Bria that my father was a huge fan of yours," Valentina said. "He was a judge for the Miss Italia contest the year you won."

"*Grazie mille.*" Imperia ran one manicured finger down the length of her jet-black hair. "That was such an exciting part of my life, but it really does seem like a lifetime ago."

"I wish Papa was still alive," Valentina said. "If I told him I was in your company, he'd be on the first flight to join us no matter where he was."

"I'm sure your papa would be worthy competition." Massimo patted Imperia's hand and then extended his to Valentina. "*Ciao.* I'm Massimo Angelini."

Not only did Massimo prove to be an excellent behind-the-scenes producer, but based on his performance, Bria thought he could have a career in front of the camera, as well. He didn't give off a hint of familiarity and acted as if this was the first time he was in Valentina's or Genie's presence. His acting was so good that it appeared to Bria that even someone as naturally cynical and shrewd as Imperia didn't sense he wasn't telling the truth.

"Pleasure to meet you." Valentina shook hands with Massimo but had to cut the handshake short to use both hands to wrangle Genie back to a sitting position. "Genie loves meeting new people."

"She's a beautiful dog," Massimo said. "They both are."

"*Grazie,*" Valentina replied. "Bravo is proving he has much better manners than my Genie."

"Manners are highly overrated," Massimo said.

Imperia playfully slapped Massimo's hand and gasped. "They are not, unless, of course, you want to be labeled a barbarian."

Bria watched all three of them laugh, and she was once again befuddled by Imperia's gregarious mood. The only other times she had witnessed such behavior from her mother-in-law was when she was with Marco. Those occasions were rare, but they reminded Bria that Imperia was more than just a formidable businesswoman. She was also a woman who enjoyed to sit in an outdoor café with a powerful man.

"You must be the television producer," Valentina said. "Pippa told me about you, and I heard what happened to your chef. I'm so sorry for your loss."

"*Grazie*," Massimo replied. "We're all still in a state of shock."

In the company of two of the prime suspects, Bria felt she wouldn't get another chance like this to see how they responded to a new piece of information. She was convinced Massimo, Valentina, and Lugo were all connected, but exactly how, she wasn't sure. She did know of one way that might get her closer to the truth. By revealing the truth about Lugo's death.

"You all must be," Bria said. "Especially now that it's been confirmed that he was murdered."

"Murdered!"

Bria knew she had taken a risk. Luca was keeping the autopsy a secret until they had the complete report from the medical examiner. Her risk, however, paid off, because only one person reacted as if they were startled by the news—Imperia.

"What do you mean, he was murdered?" Imperia asked. "Aldo wrote that he died of natural causes."

"That was the original theory," Bria replied. "New evidence has emerged giving credence to the possibility of foul play."

"*Dio mio.*" Imperia made the sign of the cross and looked directly at Bria. "You witnessed it firsthand."

"You were there?" Valentina asked.

"Yes." Bria nodded. "I was standing right next to him."

"That must have been horrible," Valentina said. "First, you witness a murder, and then you almost die yourself."

"What?" Again, Imperia was the only one who spoke. "What are you talking about?"

"Nothing, Imperia, really," Bria replied, in as nonchalant a voice as possible. "I was on the Path of the Gods, and I fell. It sounds much worse than it was."

Imperia stared at Bria for quite some time, her eyes dancing, her eyelids flashing, and Bria realized her mother-in-law was trying not to cry.

"You must be careful when attempting to do foolish things," Imperia finally said.

"I know, but it really was nothing, and I'm fine," Bria said. "More than I can say about Lugo."

"I don't understand," Massimo said. "I was there, and I saw him collapse. He wasn't murdered."

"He was poisoned," Bria replied.

"That's ironic," Imperia remarked. "A chef dying from his own poisoned food."

"All the food was tested, and none of it was poisoned," Bria shared.

"Then how could this Chef Lugo have been poisoned?" Valentina asked.

"Possibly by something he drank."

Bria was only slightly surprised that Massimo had offered that alternative scenario. When she thought about it, she realized Massimo must have remembered that Bria was in the back room of the café when he gave Lugo the anisette to add to his espresso. Now that it had been determined that Lugo was poisoned in some way other than by consuming tainted food, the anisette was the likely culprit. By making the suggestion himself, Massimo probably felt it diverted attention away from him as a suspect. Bria wasn't going to make it so easy for him to feel victorious.

"That's one theory," Bria replied. "Of many."

"What are the other theories?" Valentina asked.

"I'm not at liberty to say," Bria said. "Luca swore me to secrecy."

"Since when does the chief of police confide in a woman who runs a guesthouse?" Imperia asked.

"I've been working with the police to help them with their investigation," Bria replied.

"Don't they have enough cops without employing civilians?" Massimo asked.

"I'm not employed by the police department," Bria corrected. "Since I was right next to Lugo when he died, and I was the last person to spend time with him backstage before we started filming, I have a certain insight into his death that others don't have."

"It must have been terrible to witness something like that," Valentina said.

"It was, but it's worse knowing that Lugo didn't die naturally," Bria replied. "That's why I want to help find his killer."

"When you find this person, Bria, you bring them to me, and I'll make them pay for what they did!" Massimo seethed, and it took him a moment to notice how loud his outburst was. "*Scusatemi*. Lugo was my friend as well as my colleague."

"He was lucky to have such a good friend as you," Valentina said. "Now, I better get going. A tour without a tour guide is no tour at all."

"We should go, too," Massimo announced.

"Yes, Paolo said he'd have your car ready by three," Imperia added.

It sounded logical, but Bria thought it was interesting that Massimo was getting his car fixed at the garage where Michele worked. "Paolo is fixing your car?"

"I needed new brakes, and I was told Paolo was the best in town," Massimo replied. "I won't trust just anyone with my Alfa Romeo Montreal."

"*Dio mio*! That must be as old as my Fiat Dino," Bria said. "It used to be my father-in-law's."

Massimo squeezed Imperia's hand. "Guillermo had excellent taste in cars, as well."

"You do realize that Michele is Paolo's nephew?" Bria said.

Luckily, there wasn't a wall nearby, because Massimo looked like he would have punched a hole in it. "I brought my car in when I first arrived. I found out Michele worked there only after we discovered him hiding in the closet at Caffè Positano."

"If it's any consolation," Bria said, "even if he is a murderer, I've heard Michele is an excellent mechanic."

Massimo looked at Bria and then at Imperia before he burst into laughter. "No wonder the two of you have such a close relationship. You both have a wicked sense of humor."

It had been an interesting day so far, but Bria wasn't ready to go home just yet. She and Bravo walked down to Spiaggia Grande Beach, and she watched as Bravo walked at the water's edge, curious but not fearless enough to walk farther into the ocean. She had raised Bravo the same way she was raising Marco, to be adventurous but cautious. If you weren't prepared to take a leap of faith, plant your two feet—or your four paws—firmly on the ground.

As Bria watched Bravo play in the sand, she thought about the three suspects she spoke with in the last twenty-four hours and wondered which one had all three prerequisites when it came to committing murder—means, motive, and opportunity. First, there was Michele, who had the opportunity, since he was hiding in the closet and was less than a foot from where Chef Lugo was sitting in the back room and about twenty feet from where he died. If Michele knew that Lugo was actually Louis Gordon, that would give him a motive, because he blamed Louis for Mamma Rita's suicide. The only thing missing was means. Did Michele have access to poison? Bria didn't have the answer to that question just yet.

So far it didn't look like Valentina had the means or the opportunity to kill Lugo, because she was nowhere near the café the morning he died. If she was romantically linked to him, she could have a motive. Maybe she felt that he was going to leave her when he got richer and more famous, and she wanted to prevent him from dumping her. The problem with that notion was that Valentina did not look like the jealous type. If anyone was doing the dumping, Bria felt certain it would be Valentina.

Which left Massimo. He definitely had the opportunity, since he was at the café with Lugo before the filming, and the means, since he gave the anisette to Lugo. But what was his motive? If Massimo and Lugo were business partners and Massimo's financial well-being hinged on the success of Lugo's television show, why would Massimo kill him? There could be many reasons, of course, but neither Bria nor Luca had discovered them.

When Bravo started to pick up speed and trot down the road, Bria thought he had discovered something more interesting than walking along the beach with his mamma.

"Bravo, stop!" Bria cried. "Come back here."

Bravo was being uncharacteristically disobedient and Bria thought she might have to limit his playdates with Genie. She didn't want her dog to act as uncontrollable as his new friend.

Bria raced after Bravo, who had now started to run. The dog knew his way around the village better than most of the locals, but he had rarely run from Bria before, and never when she was calling his name. The only person he listened to more intently was Marco.

Immediately, Bria felt adrenaline course through her veins. Could Bravo sense that Marco was in trouble? Often, a dog's intuition was much stronger than a human's and they could smell and hear things from a farther distance. Marco could be back at Bella Bella and be hurt or in trouble, and it was possible that Bravo had sensed it and was racing to him, knowing that Bria would be right behind.

Or Bravo had just heard Marco playing soccer and wanted to join in.

Bria turned the corner and saw Marco playing soccer with some boys on the field next to Hotel Positano. The boys, however, weren't the reason there was a group of teenage girls watching the game and giggling. The girls were there because Fabrice, Giovanni, and Luca were playing with the boys. While the kids had on their soccer uniforms, the men were running around with their shirts off. The sight of three adult men, all muscular and well defined, sweating and dirty, was almost too much for the teenagers to bear. It was almost too much for Bria.

"*Uffa*," Bria muttered. "*Igne, migne, magna, mo.*"

"You can't have *migne*. He's mine."

Bria turned around and saw her sister sitting on the ground, her back against a majestic maritime pine tree. The thick trunk curved slightly inward as it rose to nearly forty feet, its sloping branches providing ample shade from the late afternoon sunshine. Lorenza was reading one of Marco's comic books, *Tex*, a long-running series that followed the exploits of American cowboy Tex Willer. The epitome of rugged masculinity, Tex might even feel a bit insecure around the soccer-playing trio. Lorenza was more amused than impressed by the athletic exploits of her boyfriend and his friends.

"Men really are nothing more than little boys, aren't they?"

Bria sat down next to her sister. "*Molto vero.* The way Carlo used to roughhouse with Marco, sometimes I felt like I was the mother to twins."

Lorenza laid the comic on her lap and stared at her sister. "It's nice to see you smile again when you say his name."

Slightly perplexed, Bria turned to face Lorenza. "I always smile when I speak about my Marco."

"I was talking about Carlo." Lorenza took Bria's hand, a casual gesture representing the profound love the two sisters shared. "I know I play my role as the brassy little sister flying off to all parts of the world without a care in the world very well. Sometimes too well and most people think I'm just preoccupied with shiny objects."

"Renza, no one thinks that," Bria protested.

Lorenza laughed and kissed the back of Bria's hand. "Yes they do, and that's okay. I'm kind of like Rosalie. Neither of us really cares what the world thinks of us, which is why you love us so much."

"I do!" Bria kissed Lorenza's hand and held it next to her cheek, savoring the warmth. "You'll always be my little *mostriciattola*."

"Fabrice always tells me I'm a little monster!" Lorenza cried. "I'm also here for you if you ever need to talk."

"*Grazie*. I know that."

"I don't think you do, Bria," Lorenza said. "You think that you have to solve all my problems, which you always do, of course, but I've learned a lot from listening to you and Mamma. I can solve some problems, too."

Bria looked at her younger sister, a woman she loved with all her heart, but a woman she considered flighty and sometimes silly, and it was as if she was watching her grow up right before her eyes. "Renza, *grazie*, but don't worry about me. I don't have any problems."

"*Oh veramente?*" Lorenza looked out at the soccer field just as Luca kicked the ball in Giovanni's direction and Giovanni deflected it with his foot. "Two of them are out there right now."

Bria watched the men play for a few moments and then smiled. "Is it that obvious?"

"Probably not to them, but most people don't know you as well as I do."

Bria shook her head vigorously and patted Lorenza's hand. "It's nothing. I'm just . . ."

"Looking for love?" Lorenza asked. "There isn't anything wrong with that. *Senti*, no one is ever going to replace Carlo, not in your heart or the rest of the family's, but I want you to know that we all have room to love someone new. And so do you."

Ever since Bria could remember, Fifetta had told her two daughters that one of the greatest gifts God could ever give a girl was a sister. It meant that neither of them would ever be alone to face fear or celebrate joy. As the big sister with a family, Bria had lost sight of that. It was nice to know it was something Lorenza had never forgotten.

"I have been feeling lately that it's time to move on." Bria absentmindedly played with her wedding band, turning it around on her finger. "I'm not sure that I'm ready."

"There's no deadline for when you have to take your first step," Lorenza said. "Though some might say you've already taken it."

"Who's said that about me?"

"You know how Mamma and Papa talk."

"*Oh Dio mio*! I'm not a child."

"To them, you'll always be a child. We'll all be children to them until we're old and gray, which I personally will never be. You and Gabrielo, on the other hand, will take after Papa."

"*Zitta!*" Bria laughed. "*Ma seriamente, grazie*. I don't know what's happening, but lately I have been feeling . . . restless, wondering what life could be like with another man by my side."

"Or for just a night, maybe a long weekend."

"Renza!"

"It's your life and your heart. Carlo—God bless his soul—would approve, and he'd understand," Lorenza said. "He was a wonderful man, just like Luca and, surprisingly, Giovanni. With two good men like that, no wonder it's taking you so long to choose."

"Lorenza Babette D'Abruzzo, sometimes you go too far!" Bria shook her head in disbelief, then slowly started to smile. "*Ti amo*. I don't know if either man is the one for me and Marco, but thank you for your blessing."

The sisters hugged and held each other tightly. The embrace felt familiar and yet oddly new. It was like their roles had been reversed, for a brief time, anyway.

"Hey! Half-naked men!" Lorenza screamed. "When are you going to be done kicking that stupid ball?"

The men looked over and were surprised to see that Lorenza had company.

"Bria Bria!" Fabrice cried.

Bria shook her head and laughed. Fabrice always called her Bria Bria since the B and B was called Bella Bella. Like most of the things Fabrice said, he thought it was hilarious.

"Come join us!"

"*Ciao*, Fabrice!" Bria replied. "*Grazie*, but I'll stick to fencing. It's a much safer sport."

"If you're as good as your son is on the field, you won't have a problem." Fabrice ran in between two boys and kicked the ball to Giovanni. "Marco is going to be another Silvio Piola!"

Bria had no idea that Signor Piola was a legend in the sport and the all-time highest goal scorer in Serie A. She correctly assumed from the setting that Piola had something to do with Marco's favorite sport. If Marco wanted to be as good as Piola, he had large cleats to fill. If his rosy cheeks and beaming smile were any indication, he would enjoy every moment on the field as he tried to break Piola's record.

"Mamma!" Marco ran toward his mother, followed by a very sweaty Fabrice. "Fabrice taught us how to do the elastico!"

Again, Bria was at a loss and had no idea what she was being told.

"It's a soccer move, Bria Bria." Fabrice walked toward them, his chest glistening with sweat and his curly hair longer than Bria remembered. "Very difficult, but Marco's mastered it already."

Bria stood up, and Fabrice extended a hand to Lorenza to pull her up to a standing position. He leaned in to kiss Lorenza, but she pulled away.

"You're *puzzolente*!" she told him.

"It's just sweat, Zia Renza," Marco said. "I have to sweat if I want to be better than Tomaso."

For a second, Bria thought Marco was talking about another soccer player, but then she realized he was referring to his best friend and classmate at St. Cecilia's, Tomaso Ruggiero. Marco had to be turning into a skilled player, because Tomaso was about a foot taller than Marco already and was a natural athlete. Maybe Fabrice wasn't exaggerating, after all.

"That's all for today, boys." Giovanni ripped off the rubber band that held his hair in place and ran his hands through his long blond locks. "Remember what we learned, and I'll see you at practice on Saturday."

The boys started to leave the field, followed reluctantly by the teenage girls. Bria knew that Fabrice and Luca were friends, and that Fabrice and Giovanni knew each other and were on good terms, but she also knew that Luca and Giovanni didn't like each other. Why then were they playing soccer together?

"I saw Luca and Fabrice about to play racquetball and asked them to play soccer with us instead," Marco explained as if he'd read her mind.

"How could we refuse Marco and let the team down?" Luca said.

"Thank you for showing my son a good example of how people with different opinions can still get together and have fun," Bria said.

"That was not very subtle, Bria," Luca said.

"I wasn't trying to be subtle."

"You never do," Giovanni remarked as he walked up to the group, clearly having heard Bria's comment. "That was a good game. Thanks for showing the boys some new techniques."

Luca and Giovanni stared at each other, and for once, Bria didn't worry that they were going to get into an argument or a fight. "I don't want to be like Lorenza and speak for Fabrice, but it was our pleasure," Luca responded.

"Gentlemen, why don't you clean yourselves up and come back home," Bria said. "We need to talk."

The men had dried themselves off and put their shirts back on before they'd filed into the dining room and sat around the dining room table. Bria filled them in on the clues she'd uncovered and how she thought they linked Valentina to Massimo and Lugo. When Luca told her that he agreed with her assumption, she was filled with pride.

"I can't believe you agree with me," Bria said.

"Why would that surprise you?" Luca asked.

"Because you usually say that Bria's imagination has caused her to make assumptions that aren't based on fact, and that since you're the chief of police, you're always right," Giovanni interjected.

"I never pull the chief of police card," Luca said.

"Sometimes you do," Fabrice corrected.

"When?"

"When you're losing at racquetball, and suddenly you get a

text and have to get back to the station." Fabrice picked up an olive from the plate on the table and popped it into his mouth. "I know there's no text."

"There *are* texts, Fabrice," Luca insisted. "Sometimes."

"I guess the chief of police does break the rules every once in a while," Lorenza said.

"Why don't you tell me what else you know about Valentina," Luca said. "How long has she been a tour guide?"

"I'm not exactly sure," Bria said.

"Bria Bria, I can find that out." Fabrice pulled out his phone and started to type. "It'll take me one minute."

"How can you find that out?" Bria asked. "Do you know Valentina?"

"He better not," Lorenza said.

"No, but Kayla, one of the flight attendants, has a friend who works on the tourism board in Rome," Fabrice explained. "Allegrina—that's the friend—should be able to help."

"I don't like Allegrina," Lorenza said.

"Why not?" Bria asked.

"I'm not really sure, but I think it has something to do with her name."

"What's wrong with her name?" Giovanni asked.

Lorenza jabbed a fork into a slice of mozzarella. "The hard *g* annoys me."

"Fabrice has a hard *g* in his last name," Luca pointed out. "Belragasso."

"I like it on a man, not so much on a girl."

They all laughed at Lorenza's irrational rationale and stopped only when they heard the ping of Fabrice's cell phone.

"Is that from Allegrina?" Luca asked.

Fabrice looked at the cell phone. "Yes." He clicked on a link. "Valentina got her tour guide license a week ago."

"She lied!" Bria cried. "Valentina said that she'd been giving tours in Positano for a month, not a week."

210 / MICHAEL FALCO

"Which could mean that she came to town for only one reason," Luca said.

"To see Chef Lugo," Vanni answered.

"Fabrice, ask Allegrina to email the information to me so I can print it out," Bria said.

"Anything for you, Bria Bria," Fabrice replied.

He typed another note, and within seconds Bria received an email with Valentina's tour guide license attached. It was proper and official and perfectly in order. Still, when Bria read the document, it made her scream.

"What's wrong?" Fabrice asked.

"Valentina Travanti isn't a tour guide," Bria announced.

"She isn't?" Luca asked.

"No, Valentina *Gordonato* is!" Bria shouted.

"Gordonato is Luigi's last name!" Luca cried.

"Which means Valentina may not be Mamma Rita," Bria said. "but she is Chef Lugo's widow!"

CHAPTER 17

The mystery was less than a week old, and already it was beginning to unravel.

The next morning, after Bria had made sure her guests had another filling and healthy breakfast, once Fabrice and Lorenza were on their way to Ravello to spend time with her parents, and after Marco had been dropped off at school, she made her way to the police station, where she and Rosalie were planning to meet with Luca and go over all the clues they had found. Now that they had uncovered exactly who Valentina Travanti was, they agreed that it was time for them to share what they had found out about Michele Vistigliano. Once they were deep into conversation with Luca, they were surprised to discover they weren't sharing new news.

"You know about Michele?" Bria asked.

"Of course I do," Luca replied.

"How?" Rosalie questioned.

Luca leaned forward at his desk and stared at the women sitting in the two leather chairs opposite him. He smiled and shook his head, like a grandfather indulging his mischievous granddaughters. He pressed a button on the console of his phone and asked Nunzi to come into his office. Within seconds his trusted second-in-command was standing next to him, looking as formidable and surly as she always did when she was wearing her all-black *polizia municipale* uniform and her trademark scowl. Bria knew that Nunzi had a much softer side, but it was hard to remember that when she looked like an East German border guard.

Rosalie stood up and pointed a finger at Nunzi. "You told Luca about Michele?"

"*Certo*," Nunzi replied. "He's my boss, and Michele is a suspect in a murder case."

"But you told Bria you were sharing that information with her in confidence," Rosalie protested.

"Because the information wasn't public knowledge," Nunzi replied. "But I felt—and Luca agreed—that you should know about it since you have the hots for the mechanic."

"I do not have the hots for Michele!" Rosalie yelled

"Rosa, stop!" Luca cried. "You know you've always been attracted to the bad boy."

Rosalie opened her mouth to protest, but she caught Bria looking at her and wearing an expression that could be interpreted to state, "You know your brother's right, so you should stop talking now."

"There may be a modicum of truth to your statement," Rosalie conceded. "But Nunzi still lied."

"She was doing her job," Luca insisted.

"Which is to lie!" Rosalie cried.

"Which is to protect the people in this village," Luca said. "Technically, that includes you."

"What do you mean, *technically*?" Rosalie asked.

"You live on a houseboat, which is in the water," Bria explained. "*Technically*, you don't live in the village."

"Actually, you live in the Tyrrhenian Sea," Nunzi said. "Like a fish."

"I have a Positano address!" Rosalie cried.

"You have a Positano post office box," Bria corrected. "It isn't technically the same."

"I can't believe I'm just finding out about this now!" Rosalie cried.

"It's time you realize that details, Ms. Vivaldi, are not your forte."

Rosalie looked like she was going to slap the smirk off Nunzi's face for making that comment. Not wanting to have to call for the police in his own office, Luca walked around his desk to step in front of Nunzi. If Rosalie attacked, he'd act as a buffer.

"Regardless of your residence, Nunzi felt compelled to share the information she uncovered about Michele with you," Luca said. "She knew you wouldn't listen to her or to me, so she told Bria, the one person you trust implicitly."

"That was very thoughtful of you, Nunzi," Bria said. "Wasn't it, Rosalie?"

Rosalie glared at Bria and then spoke through gritted teeth. "I suppose so."

"It also led us to find out he and Chef Lugo share a connection to the deceased Mamma Rita," Bria shared. "Thank you for pushing us in the right direction, Nunzi."

"*Prego*," Nunzi replied. "Luca filled me in on Michele and Chef Lugo's connection, but when we spoke with Michele, he didn't mention anything of it."

"We're not sure Michele knows Louis Gordon grew up to become Chef Lugo," Bria explained. "Teresina, Mamma Rita's sister, gave no impression that she knew they were the same man, either."

"They all think that Louis Gordon just vanished one day and disappeared forever," Luca said.

"Causing Mamma Rita to commit suicide," Nunzi added.

"That's all true," Bria replied.

"What about Paolo?" Luca asked.

Bria looked confused. "What about him?"

"He's the one who sent Michele to live with Teresina and Mamma Rita, but he must have kept tabs on the boy, so he probably knew that Louis Gordon was living with them," Luca mused.

"I'm not sure he did check in on Michele," Bria said. "Paolo confessed that he wasn't in a good place in his life at that time. I got the impression that he had some demons to conquer, and he essentially ignored Michele's upbringing."

"Papa never had a nice thing to say about Paolo," Nunzi shared. "Obviously, the man has changed, but back then, he didn't have a very good reputation."

"Paolo has definitely made amends for his past transgressions," Luca said. "But he still could have known who Chef Lugo really was."

"Which means Paolo should be on the suspect list, too," Bria stated.

"Why would Paolo want revenge?" Rosalie asked.

"He might blame Lugo for Mamma Rita killing herself," Luca replied.

"Teresina does," Bria said. "At least she said her sister's suicide was a direct result of Louis disappearing from their lives. She couldn't bear losing another son."

"A person can have their heart broken only so many times before their spirit is broken, too," Nunzi commented.

"Why didn't this turn up in any of our investigations into Chef Lugo's past?" Luca asked.

Even though he was directing his question to Nunzi, Bria was the one who responded.

"When he lived with Mamma Rita, he went by his real name, Louis Gordon," Bria explained.

"Which he changed to Luigi Gordonato to sound more Italian," Luca added.

"You don't think Michele or Paolo could have figured out that Luigi Gordonato was the Italian version of Louis Gordon?" Nunzi asked.

"His real name was rarely used," Bria said. "The public really only knew him as Chef Lugo."

"I questioned Michele to find out how much he knew about Chef Lugo and Luigi Gordonato, but he admitted to knowing him only as a chef, not a person," Luca relayed.

"He could have been lying," Rosalie said. "His criminal history kind of implies that he'd be good at that."

Bria rubbed the small of Rosalie's back. She knew it wasn't easy for her friend to admit Nunzi could be right about Michele, especially in Nunzi's presence. Bria needed to support her friend by exposing another suspect.

"Michele isn't the only one with a motive," Bria said. "Valentina has one, too."

"The tour guide?" Nunzi asked.

"She also happens to be Chef Lugo's widow," Bria said.

"*Dio mio!*" Nunzi cried, showing surprising enthusiasm. "Is this true?"

"We think so," Luca said. "It hasn't been confirmed yet, but Valentina signed her tour guide license Valentina Gordonato."

"Which makes her Lugo's widow," Rosalie declared.

"Or his sister."

Nunzi really knew how to throw ice onto a fire with only a few words. None of them had considered that fact before, but it was a very real possibility. Valentina was from Oregon, which was where Louis Gordon had gone to college. Even though Gordonato was the Italian version of his last name, which he seemingly adopted after he left Italy and Mamma Rita's home, there was no reason that his sister couldn't have decided to share his reimagined surname. Especially if she wanted to highlight her Italian heritage as a tour guide in Positano.

"No, that doesn't make sense," Bria announced.

"Why not?" Nunzi asked.

"Because Travanti is already Italian," Bria said. "If Valentina is Lugo's sister, and her last name is Gordon, like Louis's, where'd the Travanti come from?"

"Maybe she made up Travanti and is using it now instead of Gordonato so people won't connect her to Chef Lugo," Luca said.

"Then why did she use Gordonato on her tour guide license?" Bria asked.

"She wouldn't have had a choice," Nunzi replied. "You have to show a current ID, such as a driver's license or a passport."

"Those pieces of identification would have her correct last name on them," Luca said. "Which seems to be Gordonato."

"Which makes Bria right and Nunzi wrong," Rosalie said. "Valentina is Lugo's widow and not his sister."

"Not only that, but she may also be his murderer," Bria added.

Fists on his hips, Luca paced his office, looking like a courtroom lawyer. "Why would she murder her husband when he was on the brink of major success?"

"He could have been cheating on her, and she was a disgruntled spouse," Nunzi said. "Men tend to do things like that."

"Then why was she kissing Lugo the night of his party?" Bria asked.

"*Il bacio della morte*!" Rosalie cried. "She was giving him the kiss of death! Like Michael Corleone gave Fredo in *The Godfather*!"

"Chief, you might want to remind your sister that *The Godfather* is a movie and this is reality," Nunzi said.

"Rosalie might not be wrong," Bria said.

"Which is not the same thing as being right," Nunzi countered.

"I saw the kiss, Nunzi, and Valentina was angry with Lugo, at least that's what it looked like," Bria said.

"She pushed him away, didn't she?" Rosalie questioned.

"Yes," Bria confirmed. "When I talked to Lugo right after Valentina stormed off, he was acting very strangely. I thought it was because he was drunk, but it could've been that he was scared."

"Scared that his wife had just kissed him?" Nunzi asked.

"Alleged wife," Luca corrected. "He could have been scared that he just found out his wife was going to kill him."

"Which might have been what he was going to announce live on TV," Bria suggested. "We still don't know why he was going to go off script or what he wanted to confess to."

"Valentina is nothing more than a real-life female version of Michael Corleone!" Rosalie cried.

"Rosa, *basta*," Luca said. "We need to find out what Tina's motive would be for killing Lugo."

"Tina?" Bria asked. "Since when do you call her Tina?"

"That's her name," Luca replied.

"No, her name's Valentina."

"Tina for short," Luca said. "Like Rosa for Rosalie."

"You call the tour guide by her nickname?" Bria asked.

"It saves time."

"I told you SBOOTAC calls her Tina," Rosalie added.

"*Uffa!*" Bria exclaimed. "Enough with this Tina. I know how we can find out *Valentina's* motive."

Rosalie and Luca looked at each other, then at Bria, then said the same word at the same time. "How?"

"Read Lugo's will."

"That's a brilliant idea, Bria!" Rosalie cried. "Don't you think so, Luca?"

"I do."

"Then why don't you look as excited as your sister?" Bria asked.

"Because we can't find the will," Luca said.

"You can't find it?" Rosalie asked. "What kind of a two-bit police station are you running here?"

"Rosalie!" Luca cried.

"Luca, Rosalie's right," Bria said. "Someone dies. There's a will. Why can't you find it?"

"It isn't that we can't find the will," Luca said. "We can't locate Lugo's lawyer."

"We've made phone calls and searched online, but nothing," Nunzi said.

"Because you've been looking for Luigi Gordonato's lawyer and not Louis Gordon's."

They thought Bria's suggestion would make a difference, but when Nunzi returned to Luca's office after doing some online research at her desk and making some phone calls to governmental agencies, she had no further information on who Luigi's lawyer was. Or even on Luigi Gordonato.

"If Louis Gordon officially changed his name to Luigi Gordonato while in the United States and had his will drawn up there, it'll be harder to get those documents," Nunzi explained. "I could spend weeks making phone calls and trying to get through American red tape or . . ."

"Or what?" Luca asked.

"I could fly to Oregon and talk to the local officials," Nunzi said. "I've never been to the States, and I think a high-profile murder case warrants a visit."

"I hate to ruin your travel plans, Nunzi," Bria announced, "but I have a better solution."

An hour later Bria and Luca were on Imperia's yacht, waiting for Massimo to come out on the deck to join them. If they weren't there to question a man about a murder, they could bask in the sunshine and gaze out at the horizon, with nothing more on their minds than trying to determine the exact shade of blue of the sky. Deep blue? Vivid blue? Summer blue? The

Italian sky could even sometimes be described as French blue. Color analysis would have to wait for another day; now they needed to figure out why Massimo was yelling. When Pippa emerged from belowdecks, they had their answer.

"What do you mean, you haven't started the insurance paperwork?" Massimo was still down below, but his voice was loud enough to drown out a lighthouse's foghorn.

"*Scusa*, but I've been very upset by Chef Lugo's death," Pippa yelled down the companionway. "I haven't been able to start the process."

That was a lie. Bria had been cavorting through Positano with Pippa on Valentina's tour the other day, and Pippa had been enthusiastic and filled with energy. Bria understood that the young woman needed to divert her attention away from the murder and focus on something that was filled with life. She also understood that Pippa couldn't openly share these things with such a hostile boss. But the fact of the matter remained, Pippa was a very convincing liar.

Massimo finally emerged on deck. His thick mane of jet-black hair with its touches of gray blew in the wind, looking as wild as his eyes. He was so focused on reprimanding Pippa that he didn't notice Bria and Luca standing near the starboard gunwale. He continued yelling, thinking he had an audience of one.

"We're all upset by Luigi's death. No one more than me!" Massimo cried. "But you're still on my payroll, which means you have a job to do!"

Pippa wasn't aware she had an audience, either, which allowed her to respond genuinely and not in any manufactured way. It gave those watching much better insight into her character. And made Bria realize Pippa was even more complicated than she had thought.

"Get off my back!" Pippa shouted. "Lugo's death means you no longer have a hold on me! *Capisci?*"

His shock over Pippa's outburst prevented Massimo from replying. He fiddled with a button on his double-breasted jacket but was otherwise motionless and silent.

Luca took the opportunity to translate. "Pippa asked you a question, Massimo. Do you understand?"

Employer and employee whipped around and were both surprised to see Luca and Bria staring at them.

Bria followed Luca's lead and used their silence to her advantage. "What kind of hold does Massimo have on you, Pippa?"

It was fascinating to watch Pippa shed her confrontational persona and retreat to the anxious, nervous girl Bria had first met. When the metamorphosis was complete, the spitfire was nowhere to be found. In her place was the scaredy cat. "I . . . I just meant that . . . that Massimo isn't my boss now that the show isn't happening."

"You signed a contract, and I still pay you," Massimo said. "Which makes me your boss."

"Writing her checks doesn't give you the right to keep harassing her," Bria said.

"I am not harassing anyone!" Massimo bellowed. "I simply want Pippa to do her job!"

"I'm sure that's all Pippa wants to do, as well." Luca's tone was much softer than Massimo's screams. "Witnessing a man die—*scusa,* be murdered—causes people to feel distracted, and they may find it hard to complete their duties."

"That's what I've been trying to explain to Massimo," Pippa said, with a quiver in her voice. "He won't listen to me."

"I don't have to listen to you!" Massimo seethed. "I don't have to listen to anyone. I'm the boss!"

Speaking of bosses, Bria wondered why Imperia hadn't joined the group. There was no way she couldn't hear Massimo's shouting. Unless, of course, she was in her oxygen chamber, undergoing rejuvenation therapy. Had Bria not seen the contraption before, she wouldn't believe that it existed.

"Where's Imperia?" Bria asked.

"She went to Rome this morning," Massimo said. "Now, there's a woman who understands the importance of maintaining a business despite undesirable circumstances."

Pippa looked at Bria and Luca. Her voice filled with accusation, she asked, "Why are you two here?"

"Isn't it obvious?" Massimo replied. "They came to visit Imperia."

"That would make sense if Bria had come alone, but you don't make a social visit with the chief of police tagging along," Pippa said. "Isn't that right?"

"You are right, Pippa," Luca replied. "We believe we've located Chef Lugo's next of kin."

"Really?" Pippa asked. "Who?"

"His wife," Bria replied.

Bria couldn't tell if the look of surprise that appeared on Massimo's face was sincere or simulated.

"Did either of you know that Lugo was married?" Luca asked.

"No," Pippa answered immediately. "He and I rarely spoke about anything other than camera shots and production details."

"Luigi and I were much closer, of course, but I have to admit that I'm thrown by this revelation," Massimo said. "Who is this woman?"

"We're not at liberty to say just yet," Bria said. "We need to contact Lugo's attorney to discuss his will. Can you help us find his lawyer?"

"I wish I could, but Luigi didn't talk about the personal side of his life," Massimo revealed. "He could be secretive about certain things."

Bria saw Pippa eyeing Massimo suspiciously. "Pippa, did you want to say anything else?"

"No," she replied unconvincingly. "Like Massimo said, I have work to finish. *Scusate.*"

Pippa wasn't even halfway down the companionway stairs when Massimo howled, "You two need to leave! I have been through enough, thanks to Luigi!"

"What do you mean by that?" Bria asked.

Massimo raised a clench fist in the air. "I gave that boy so much, and he wanted to throw it all away! Kiss his future good-bye!"

"In what way?" Luca asked.

For the first time since Bria had met the man, Massimo looked frightened. It took thirty seconds, but when he spoke again, he was in control. "Luigi was nervous about the tour and the new series. He threatened to quit several times, but I reminded him that he owed it to himself not to run from the amazing life that was about to be his."

"How did Lugo respond?" Bria asked. "By getting drunk and swearing he'd reveal all his secrets?"

Massimo glared at Bria and then let out a thunderous laugh. "Imperia was right about you, Bria. You really are very smart."

"Imperia said that about me?"

"Your mother-in-law has said many things about you," Massimo confirmed.

"What were you going to say about Chef Lugo?" Luca asked, hoping to get the conversation back on track.

"Luigi got drunk, slept it off, and then realized that I was right," Massimo said. "If he quit, he'd have nothing."

"Neither would you," Luca said.

"Momentarily perhaps," Massimo said.

"So the thought of Lugo betraying you didn't make you want to put him in his place," Luca commented. "You didn't have the urge to, let's say, put some poison in his coffee and watch him react to it on live TV. Oh wait, you were the only one who knew the feed had a three-minute delay. Any mistake that Lugo made could be deleted and erased forever, and Lugo would be more grateful than ever for your guidance and expertise."

Bria didn't watch Massimo's face; she was too busy looking at Luca. She hadn't even thought of that scenario, but Luca was right. Maybe the perpetrator only wanted to threaten Lugo, not kill him. Maybe Lugo's death was never meant to be a murder, merely a warning.

"I see that you're taking your detective work seriously, Luca, and I applaud you," Massimo said. "If Luigi had quit, I could have easily found someone else with the determination required to become an international sensation. Take Michele, for instance. He waited hours to meet with Luigi just to get advice on how to be a celebrity chef like him."

"We're aware of that," Luca said. "And all that Michele's actions imply."

"This so-called wife of Lugo's . . . ," Massimo said. "Are you aware of the implications if Lugo suddenly died?"

"Depending upon how his will was constructed, she could inherit his entire estate," Luca replied.

"So there you have it, two prime suspects," Massimo said. "The estranged wife and the eager wannabe chef. I think one of them will prove to be Luigi's murderer."

Bria fought to still every muscle in her body that wanted to jump up and down. She glanced over at Luca and couldn't believe how calm he looked after hearing what Massimo had just said. *Must be all his police training*, she thought. *You don't become chief of police without having self-control.*

"Now, if you'll excuse me, I need to check in with Pippa," Massimo said. "I think you can agree that she isn't the most reliable employee."

When Bria was sure Massimo was out of earshot, she grabbed

Luca's arm excitedly. He didn't share an ounce of Bria's enthusiasm. "Did you hear what Massimo said?"

"Yes, but it wasn't anything we don't already know."

"Luca!" Bria cried. "How can you say that?"

"Obviously, you heard something that I didn't," Luca replied. "What was it?"

"We never said anything about Lugo being *estranged* from
his wife."

CHAPTER 18

When Bria first realized Luca hadn't caught Massimo's slip of the tongue, she was surprised. A few seconds later she felt proud that she had recognized a clue when the chief of police hadn't. While they were walking back from the marina, she felt elated when she came up with an idea that might bring all the suspects together in one room.

"Valentina told me that she used to fence in college, like I used to," Bria said. "I told her that we should fence at Imperia's gym on her yacht."

Luca caught on much more quickly this time. "Where Massimo is staying."

"If I invite Rosalie to watch, she can use that as an excuse to bring along Michele as her date and all the activity will undoubtedly make Massimo curious and lure him into the gym," Bria continued. "Putting three of the suspects in Chef Lugo's death in one room."

"I don't like the idea of Michele being Rosalie's date," Luca remarked. "But it's a good idea."

"*Grazie*," Bria said. "I'll make some cannoli, maybe some tiramisu."

"Fifetta's recipe?"

"Is there any other kind?"

Luca smiled, exposing the slight wrinkles around his eyes. "Not as far as I'm concerned."

"I'll ask Pippa to bring them to the gym to make sure she's there, too."

"*Bene.* That one confuses me."

"I agree," Bria said. "I can't imagine why she'd want to kill Chef Lugo, but she's been acting strangely ever since his death. I suppose there could be a reason why she may have poisoned him."

"*Sfortunatamente*, anything is possible, but if we can get them all in one room, one of them may reveal another clue," Luca said. "This time, I promise to catch it!"

They were standing in front of Ristorante Pupetto, on Fornillo Beach, at the most tranquil time of the day. The sunset behind them, a blend of orange, purple, and red, looking like a gorgeous bruise; tourists, with their flowing linen and sunburnt faces, milling about; and soft music, laughter, and the wind created a soothing setting. Bria was barefoot in the sand, her espadrilles hanging from two fingers by her side. Luca looked out of place wearing his uniform, but only slightly, and as far as Bria was concerned, he was right where he should be.

"Would you like to get a drink?"

Luca appeared startled by the request and didn't reply.

"To celebrate the next phase of our investigation," Bria clarified.

"I can't. *Scusa.* I'm still on duty."

Bria looked at the darkening sky and raised an eyebrow. "At this hour?"

"I have to speak with the carabinieri to give them an update about Lugo's death," Luca explained. "I need all my wits about me, so I don't stutter. But thank you for the invitation."

Bria didn't feel awkward or disappointed that Luca declined her spontaneous invitation. That plan might not have worked out, but she had others to make.

* * *

Before Bria could ask Valentina for a fencing date, she first needed to secure the use of the gym on Imperia's yacht. She hated asking her mother-in-law for a favor, but she couldn't just show up in a fencing outfit, with an entourage in tow, and expect to use the gym. The yacht crew might be in the middle of a spin class. As much as she didn't want to, Bria needed to reserve gym time with the owner of the yacht.

"On one condition," Imperia said.

On the other end of the phone, Bria looked toward the heavens and raised a hand, silently asking God why he couldn't intervene and make Imperia more cooperative. "*Certo*. Anything."

"You help me plan Marco's Communion party."

Bria threw both hands up toward the heavens this time. She didn't know if she wanted to kill Imperia or her mother over the holy war surrounding Marco's Communion. Of course, she then had to make the sign of the cross and ask God for forgiveness for contemplating thoughts of homicide and comparing Marco's upcoming religious ceremony to a spiritual war. But that was what Imperia and Fifetta were turning the occasion into. Bria needed to make them both see reason and compromise, but for now, she simply agreed. "*Assolutamente*! As much time as you want."

After she ended the call, Bria felt like she had just betrayed her mother. Because that was exactly what she had done. She sighed heavily at the situation she had gotten herself into, and decided she would worry about the ramifications later. She made several more phone calls and was able to confirm that Valentina and the others would participate. There was only one more thing to do—find out if she could still fit into her college fencing uniform.

Bria couldn't see her face in the mirror, but she knew her satisfied smirk went well with her outfit. Despite giving birth and having a world-class cook like Fifetta for a mother, her youthful metabolism had not yet abandoned her. It was more than a minor victory, because the all-white fencing ensemble was not forgiving.

She had forgotten how much she enjoyed the snug fit, which she found to be both liberating and confining. The uniform was part straitjacket, part comfy sweater. It fit Bria perfectly.

Looking directly into the mirror, Bria held her sword, which was officially called an épée, in her gloved right hand and pointed it toward her image. Her left hand was raised over her head but behind her, bent at the wrist and pointing in the same direction as the épée. Her face was hidden by the metal mesh mask, so her smirk and the rest of her features couldn't be seen, but she could see clearly. During her competitive career, Bria had reveled in being able to be unseen. It had helped her dissolve into the character she needed to be in order to win a match. Hopefully it would help to solve a murder.

She pulled off her mask and let her hair spill past her shoulders. It was an action that Bria had sometimes exaggerated, knowing how sexy it looked and how unexpected the revelation when the audience saw it was a young woman under the mask. Although women had been fencing officially since the 1924 Olympics, it was only in 1981 that high schools and colleges added fencing to their girls' and women's athletic programs. As a result, spectators had often been surprised to see her jet-black hair flying in the air when she dramatically pulled off her mask at the end of a match, even if they knew they were watching two women compete. It was a mental trick: most people didn't consider women to be aggressive or able to handle a deadly weapon. Even if they knew a woman was lurking behind the mask of thin woven metal, when they were offered proof, it could be shocking.

That was how Carlo had fallen in love with Bria. He had assumed he was watching his friend spar with a male opponent, and he'd been impressed with the skill and the elegance the challenger possessed. After she'd easily beaten his friend, Bria took off her mask, and Carlo wanted to propose to her right then and there without even knowing her name. Had he asked, Bria would have accepted. She was as captivated by Carlo as Carlo was by her.

She allowed the memory to endure for only a few seconds before throwing the mask and the épée on her bed. That was then, and this was now. A large part of her wanted to move forward, and this fencing match might be the way to take that first giant step.

The next day, when Bria stood in the middle of the gym, she marveled that such a world-class facility could be housed in the bowels of Imperia's yacht. Roughly the size of the first floor of Bella Bella, the gym looked even larger thanks to the two mirrored walls that faced each other. A basketball court, four Fassi treadmills, two Panatta multipurpose exercise machines, and a rack of free weights composed most of the space. There was an empty area, typically used for yoga classes or filled with seats for spectators to watch a basketball game or another sporting event. Today's event, a fencing match.

Bria made sure she arrived early, so that she was dressed and waiting before Valentina showed up. Luca was waiting for her after she changed into her fencing ensemble, and Bria was happy to see that he was dressed not as a policeman, but as her friend. Unlike Nunzi, who stood in the middle of the gym, dressed in her cop's outfit and looking like she was going to raid the place.

"Nunzi, please don't take this the wrong way," Bria said. "What are you doing here?"

"I don't think there's any other way to take that comment but the wrong way," Nunzi replied.

"I asked her to come," Luca shared.

"Why?" Bria asked. "Do you want to give away our real intention? I'm surprised you don't have a sign that says, WILL CHEF LUGO'S REAL MURDERER PLEASE STAND UP!"

"I'm your referee."

"*Mizzia!*" Bria enthused "That's smart thinking, Nunzi."

"It was Luca's idea," Nunzi corrected. "You'll have to compliment him."

"*I miei complimenti.*" Bria bowed theatrically. "But no more surprises."

"I'm just going to watch you do your thing," Luca said.

"And watch Valentina, Massimo, Michele, and Pippa, I hope," Bria replied. "Or have you forgotten why we're here?"

"Why are we here, Bria?" came a voice from the other side of the gym.

Imperia sounded like her old self. Bossy, cold, and oh so imperious. Bria didn't have to turn around or look in the mirror to know that Massimo was nowhere near her. In his presence her comments may still be biting, but her voice was definitely softer. When Bria did turn around, she saw that Imperia's outfit was much softer than her typical attire.

Since she spent so much time as CEO of Bartolucci Enterprises, Imperia needed to present a strong presence. She did that by wearing tailored suits, power colors, and dramatic make-up. Her appearance in the gym was no less commanding, but for a completely different reason.

Imperia wore an organza floral dress cut just below the knee, with long flowing sleeves and a square-cut neckline. The red, yellow, and white design was both powerful and ethereal. She wore her trademark red lipstick, but instead of a matte finish, she had added some gloss to soften the look.

"*Ciao*, Imperia," Bria said. "Your dress is beautiful."

"It should be. It cost enough."

"It's almost as impressive as this gym," Bria observed.

"Everything on my yacht is impressive, but you failed to answer my question," Imperia replied. "What are we all doing here, and why have you brought the police?"

"We're not here in any official capacity," Luca replied. "I'm here to watch, and Nunzi to referee."

Imperia ignored Luca and examined Nunzi from boot to cap. "You certainly have the physique of a referee."

"*Grazie*," Nunzi said before blowing on her whistle for maximum impact.

"Why this sudden desire to fence again?" Imperia asked. "Carlo told me you hadn't touched a blade since you were married."

Once again, Imperia made Bria feel uneasy at the mention of Carlo. Imperia's comment inferred that the two women shared a personal intimacy, which simply didn't exist. Bria couldn't dwell on it; she needed to focus.

"I found a sparring partner," Bria said. "Valentina Travanti."

"Ah yes." Imperia raised her chin, tilted her head back, and dropped her voice. "The blonde."

Bria smiled. It was the perfect way to describe Valentina.

"She and I both expressed a desire to fence again, so I suggested we come here and make a little event out of it," Bria explained. "That's why we asked some people to come watch."

Imperia raised one beautifully arched eyebrow. "Personally, I've never found the need for applause from an audience to do my best."

"Your office in Rome is big enough if you want to install bleachers."

As expected, Imperia didn't laugh at Bria's joke. The awkward pause that followed was mercifully broken when Valentina strode into the gym. If she played half as good as she looked in her outfit, Bria thought she should contemplate forfeiting.

"You weren't exaggerating!" Valentina cried. "This gym is first class."

"Did you expect anything less from a Bartolucci?" Imperia asked.

"Not after all the stories Papa told me about you," Valentina replied. "But hearing about beauty and being in its presence are two different things."

All Bria heard come out of Valentina's mouth was blatant flattery. She prayed Imperia heard something less ingratiating.

"Your father raised a perceptive daughter," Imperia said.

Bria couldn't tell if Imperia's comment was sarcastic or genuine, but she didn't care, as long as Valentina and Imperia's verbal exchange didn't escalate into a heated argument. With all the different personalities that were set to gather, there would be enough tension. As if proving her point, Rosalie entered the gym, followed by Massimo and Michele. None of them looked happy.

"Did you already start the match?" Rosalie cried.

"No, we're still waiting for Pippa," Bria said.

"*Oh per favore*," Massimo said. "If we wait for that one, the match may never begin."

"I have a video meeting with Greece in an hour, and I'm sure the police need to get back to . . . policing." Imperia turned on her heel and faced Bria. "I strongly suggest you start this exhibition now."

Bria looked at Luca to gauge his opinion. He raised his eyebrows as discreetly as possible and shrugged his shoulders imperceptibly. Bria wasn't happy, but she knew he was right. They had no other choice but to start the match without Pippa. Three suspects instead of four would have to do. She looked at the crowd and shouted, "Let the games begin!"

As Massimo, Rosalie, Michele, Imperia, and Luca took their seats, Nunzi wheeled the equipment into the center of the gym, where Bria and Valentina waited. They put on their masks and fastened them to their neck bibs, then slipped padded gloves onto their sword hand and pulled their épées from the long cylindrical container in which they were housed. The women faced each other and nodded. Even though this was going to be a friendly match, there was no reason to skimp on formality.

Nunzi stood in between both women and faced the on-lookers. Valentina was to her right, and Bria to her left. Both women stood with their swords hanging at their sides, tips pointing to the gym floor, waiting to begin.

"En garde," Nunzi said.

At the sound of the command, Bria and Valentina took their fencing positions.

"*Prêtes.*"

Both women nodded their head to confirm that they were, indeed, ready.

"*Allez.*"

Although Nunzi gave them the command to go, neither woman moved. Perhaps they were both suddenly scared to get back in the game with an audience watching their every move. Perhaps they simply needed a push from a bystander.

"Are they going to do something, or is this a staring contest?" Imperia asked.

That was all Bria needed to hear to shock her back to reality. She was definitely nervous, but she had learned how to calm her nerves. She breathed in through her nose and let out a stream of air through slightly parted lips. She imagined she was standing on a long thin blade one hundred feet in the air. She was airborne yet grounded. Immediately, she felt her fencing legs coming back.

Bria thrust her épée forward, forcing Valentina to parry right and barely avoid getting touched by the tip of Bria's sword. Had Bria made contact with Valentina, she would have been awarded one point. Successfully avoiding being touched meant that the first bout could continue until the three minutes were up.

Standing in the general area of the fencers, but far enough

away that she wasn't part of the action, Nunzi kept one eye on the stopwatch and one eye on the audience. Massimo sat next to Imperia but couldn't keep his eyes off Valentina. Since she was fully covered, it wasn't as if he was admiring her beauty. He had to be interested in her for other reasons.

Sitting on the far right and on the opposite side of the producer, Luca positioned himself so he could look as if he was watching the match but when, in fact, he was staring at Michele and Massimo. Like Nunzi, he saw that Massimo couldn't take his eyes off Valentina, while Michele kept looking over at Massimo. It was as if an invisible string held all three of them together.

Valentina shifted back and forth and then suddenly lunged forward. At the last instant Bria jumped back, throwing her shoulders and feet forward as she bent at the waist to create as much distance between the tip of Valentina's blade and her stomach. The maneuver worked, and Valentina didn't make contact. Bria was about to regroup and make a defensive move when Nunzi hit the buzzer on her stopwatch, signaling the end of the first bout. Both women lifted their masks simultaneously and revealed that they were wearing matching grins.

"*È stato così divertente!*" Valentina cried.

It *was* fun, but Bria wasn't sure that it had yielded any reward just yet.

Nunzi channeled her inner referee and held the stopwatch overhead. "Three minutes rest."

Both women put their swords into the gear container, and Bria saw that Luca was holding a cup of water. She walked over to him and took the cup. As she drank, she made sure her back was to the rest of the group. "Anything?"

"Massimo can't stop staring at Valentina, and Michele can't stop staring at Massimo."

"They are connected."

"I think so, but it's all inconclusive. We don't have any details."

"Is Valentina talking to Massimo?" Bria asked.

"No, he's still sitting next to Imperia," Luca said. "Valentina's talking to Nunzi."

"Maybe Valentina will say something to her that we can use," Bria said. "Nunzi is still a police officer, even though she's not wearing a uniform, right?"

"Yes, we wear the badge whether or not we're wearing the badge," Luca replied.

They all stopped talking when they heard a door slam. They weren't frightened by the noise. They were hungry and happy to hear that Pippa had finally arrived bearing pastries. They were half right: dessert had arrived, but there was no Pippa.

"You're not Pippa!" Massimo shouted.

"No, I'm Tobias, and I come armed with the most delicious treats."

Bria felt her stomach tingle. It wasn't hunger pains; she was concerned. "Where's Pippa?"

"I don't know," Tobias replied. "Giovanni couldn't find her, so he asked me to make the delivery."

"*Dio mio!*" Massimo shouted. "That girl is the most unreliable employee I've ever had on my payroll!"

Imperia placed a hand on Massimo's arm and patted it several times. The gesture seemed to calm him down. Bria felt her stomach ignite. She did not begrudge Imperia's happiness, but she just knew that she wouldn't find it with Massimo, regardless of his role in Lugo's death.

"Please tell me that box contains Fifetta's cannoli," Rosalie said.

"I couldn't resist, and I ate one on the way over," Tobias said. "Giovanni sure knows his way around a kitchen."

Valentina reached into the box Tobias was carrying and

took out a freshly baked cannoli. She bit into the hard shell and tasted the creamy ricotta filling. Her knees buckled, she rolled her head to the side, and she started making sounds that were inappropriate for a gym. "*Delizioso*! Bria, I may need to convince Giovanni to give me his recipe."

"It's my mother's recipe," Bria replied.

"I think I'll have an easier time wrangling the recipe out of Giovanni than your mother," Valentina said. "Men are much easier to manipulate."

Valentina's comment elicited laughs from most everyone as they all gathered around the box to take a cannoli. Imperia handed a pastry to Massimo, who didn't accept it right away, because he was staring at Valentina as if he wanted to kill her. If Nunzi hadn't declared the start of the second round, Bria and Luca would not have been surprised if Massimo took one of the swords and attacked Valentina with it.

"Did you see that look Massimo gave Valentina?" Bria whispered to Luca.

"Yes, I did."

"Tell Rosalie to switch seats with Michele so he sits next to Massimo," Bria suggested. "Maybe they'll start talking."

"Good idea," Luca said. "And good luck. Or is saying that bad luck? Should I say, 'Break a leg'?"

Bria smiled at Luca's awkward banter. "Just go talk to your sister."

Luca was able to grab Rosalie, tell her to switch her seat with Michele, and get back to his own seat just before Bria and Valentina got into their positions for the start of the second bout. Nunzi once again counted them down. Within seconds the women were thrusting and parrying with even more skill than before.

Even though Bria knew the reason she was fencing was to see if they could uncover a clues to solve Chef Lugo's murder, she couldn't quell her competitive spirit. After the first shaky bout, she felt stronger, more in control of her body and her mind, and more assured of her ability to win. She routed her confidence into action and thrust forward, touched Valentina's left shoulder with the tip of her blade, exactly the spot she was aiming for.

"One point, Bria," Nunzi announced.

Far off in the distance Bria heard the smattering of applause, but like she used to do when in college, she pushed it from her mind. She focused only on her opponent. The only thing that mattered was Valentina. And then the blood.

At first, Bria felt a slight pinch in her chest, a small prick like a bumblebee's sting. She kept moving, even though Valentina stood immobile and Nunzi had rushed to her side. When she saw that they were staring at her chest, she looked down and watched the red spot grow.

"What's wrong?" Rosalie called.

Bria turned to answer Rosalie, but when her friend saw her bloodied uniform, she screamed. Then Massimo screamed, followed by Michele. Even Imperia let out a gasp.

Luca jumped out of his seat and rushed over to Bria. He was lowering Bria to the gym floor as Nunzi ran to the first aid counter in the corner of the gym. By the time she returned, Luca and Valentina had taken off Bria's jacket, so she was wearing only her white T-shirt on top now. Normally, Luca would have ripped the shirt completely open in such a situation, but since it was Bria, he hesitated. Tobias didn't.

The former emergency room physician took over and ripped Bria's T-shirt partially to show that her flesh had been pierced right under her left clavicle. Had Valentina made contact a few inches lower, the blade would have gone through Bria's heart. This was not how the match was supposed to end.

"It doesn't look to be a serious wound," Tobias announced. "You are a very lucky woman."

"Oh my God, Bria. I'm so sorry," Valentina cried. "I have no idea how this happened."

Valentina knelt beside Bria and held her hand. Tears were already filling her eyes. Bria wanted desperately to believe that Valentina was as shocked that their match had turned potentially deadly as she was, but she couldn't be swayed by a few tears. Valentina couldn't be trusted. Maybe she had tried to make up for not succeeding in pushing Bria to her death when they were on the Path of the Gods.

"Aren't those blades supposed to have rubber tips?" Rosalie asked, her voice shaking.

"They do," Bria confirmed. "One must have fallen off."

"Or someone deliberately removed it."

All heads turned to face Imperia. Bria was familiar with the look she saw on Imperia's face. It was one that she normally feared, but now she was grateful, because she knew that despite their differences, she could be assured that her mother-in-law would always be on her side. Someone had definitely removed the protective tip from the blade. Bria hadn't even thought to check for it, and she had almost paid for her mistake with her life.

"It's not a very deep wound, but we should still get you to the clinic and get you a tetanus shot," Tobias said.

Lucas put his hand on Tobias's shoulder. *"Grazie."*

"It must feel like you're back in the emergency room," Bria joked as she attempted to sit up.

"Sh," Tobias said. "Lie back and try not to move."

"Nunzi, please call for Matteo to come and help you collect the evidence," Luca ordered.

"Evidence?" Massimo cried. "What are you talking about?"

"This wasn't an accident," Rosalie said. "It was Barbara Tuttuzi all over again."

"Who?" Massimo asked.

Rosalie waved her hand in front of her face. "Never mind."

"I'm sure this was nothing more than an accident," Luca announced. "But I need to take precautions."

By the way everyone looked at Luca, it was clear that no one believed him. Because the culprit was almost certainly in the room, no one spoke. Bria knew the truth. She couldn't say it out loud, so she said it to herself.

Someone tried to kill me. Again.

CHAPTER 19

By the time Bria got back from the Red Cross, the entire village knew of her near demise. Unlike the last time, when she had almost slipped off the cliff while on the Path of the Gods, she couldn't chalk up her accident to clumsiness or a slippery landscape. Everyone knew what had happened, and it seemed like the entire village was now at Bella Bella. Instead of recuperating, she felt like she was the guest of honor at a surprise party.

"*La mia bambina!*"

"*Mio angioletto!*"

Bria's parents hugged her tightly, Fifetta on the left, Franco on the right. They didn't want to know what had happened. At the moment they didn't care; they only wanted to feel their eldest daughter and know that she was alive and breathing. That was all that mattered.

"When I heard the news, *Dio mio*, it was like time stood still," her father said. "I couldn't breathe. I couldn't speak. I could only think that I had to see my Bria."

"Papa, I'm right here, and you can see that I'm fine."

"I'll be at the Duomo tonight to give thanks," Franco said.

"I'll be kneeling right beside him."

Fifetta hugged Bria again and whispered in her ear. Bria

couldn't understand what her mother was saying, but she wasn't sure if she was meant to. It sounded as if Fifetta was thanking every angel and saint she could think of that her daughter didn't suffer a more serious injury.

When Bria whispered, she made sure her mother understood every word. "I'm *bene*, Mamma, *lo prometto*."

Reluctantly, Fifetta released Bria from her grip so another member of their family could take over. Seeing fear in her sister's eyes was too much for Bria, and she felt her own tears stream down her cheeks. A child watching their parents cry and worry over their children was normal; it's what parents did. Siblings, on the other hand, were supposed to tease, yell, and pester each other, not wonder if the last time they saw each other would be the last.

"Don't ever scare me like that again," Lorenza said.

"I'll try not to," Bria replied.

"You have to do more than try!" Lorenza yelled and turned to face Fabrice, who was right behind her. "Tell her, Fabrice! Tell her she can't scare me ever again!"

Fabrice hugged Bria and held her hands tightly. "You have to be careful, Bria Bria. This family needs you."

"This village needs you!"

Annamaria could no longer restrain herself or keep silent. She had allowed the D'Abruzzos their rightful place as Bria's welcoming party, but she was too consumed with emotion to stay seated. She ran to Bria, wrapped her arms around her, and held her tightly. Annamaria smelled like sugar, cinnamon, and a touch of lemon. Bria assumed she had been making a batch of *biscotti alla cannella*. She'd have to remember to ask if she had brought a tray of the cinnamon cookies.

"*Dio mio!*" Annamaria cried. "I thought you were going to be another tragedy."

"Do I look like a tragedy?" Bria asked.

Her question was meant to be rhetorical, so she didn't expect a response. She got one, anyway.

"Kind of."

Leave it to Rosalie to tell the truth. Standing off to the side, holding a plate of shrimp, Rosalie tilted her head toward the mirror that hung on the wall in the dining room. Bria caught her image and saw that her best friend was right. She might be alive, with no lasting injuries, but she still looked like she had barely survived a near-fatal accident.

Her white fencing pants looked acceptable, but her white boots were smudged with dirt from walking outside. The T-shirt, which someone from the Red Cross had given her to replace the one Tobias had ripped, was oversize, and though it had once been white, it was now a dull gray. Peeking out from the T-shirt was the bandage that covered her wound.

On her way to the Red Cross, she had pulled her hair back into a ponytail because she didn't have time to brush it after wearing her fencing mask. Her hair had gotten loose, and now the ponytail was drooping, and strands of hair framed her face like a rowdy group of split ends. Since she hadn't put on any make-up before the match, she now looked blotchy and sweaty. Overall, she looked—and felt—as if she had just woken up in an army barracks.

"Carlo was right," Imperia said, approaching Bria after Annamaria stepped away. "You are a very good fencer."

"*Grazie.*"

"He told me it was why he fell in love with you," Imperia shared. "I assumed he was exaggerating. After seeing you in action, I understand."

Imperia clasped Bria's hand and held it tightly. A moment later she was walking away, heading toward Massimo. Bria was thrown by the gesture and wanted to follow Imperia to talk more about the son she had lost, but Bria had her own son to worry about.

"Where's Marco?" Bria asked.

"Giovanni took him and Bravo out for gelato," Fifetta said.

"That was lucky timing," Bria replied.

"Not lucky at all," Franco said. "Giovanni knew people from the village were going to arrive, and he didn't want Marco to get scared."

"He said he would text you before he headed back home to make sure things were back to normal," Daisy said.

"*Bene*," Bria replied. "I don't want Marco to be worrying about his mamma."

"A lot of people are worrying about his mamma," came a warm male voice from behind Bria.

Luca was still out of uniform and wearing his jeans, but the sleeves on his green oxford were rolled up. It was the first time Bria noticed he was wearing a bracelet on his right wrist. She knew he wore a watch on his left wrist, because she'd seen him look at it before, but she'd never noticed any jewelry on his right one.

Bria grabbed Luca's wrist and raised it closer to her eyes so she could examine the bracelet. "Is this new?"

"No. It was my mother's," Luca replied. "Papa gave it to her as an engagement ring because he didn't have any money. He found the gold bracelet on the street, and later I added the emerald, which was my mother's gift to him on his retirement."

"*Questo è bello*," Bria said.

"*Grazie*. I only wear it on special occasions."

"My release from the Red Cross is a special occasion?"

Luca laughed. "No, your fencing match."

"You were wearing it today?"

"Yes. I thought it might bring us luck, and since you're still in one piece, I guess it has."

For some reason, Bria felt terribly ashamed. Luca had gone out of his way to show his support, to do something different, and Bria had been so wrapped up in preparing for the fencing match, she hadn't noticed. "Luca, I'm sorry."

"There's no need to be sorry." Luca's light brown eyes shimmered, and he blushed a little. "The only thing you need to do is follow doctor's orders and get some rest."

"First, you have to tell us what happened!" Annamaria cried.

"She can explain it all later," Luca said. "After she's had some rest."

"Luca Vivaldi," Annamaria announced, "you may be the chief of police, and you may be used to people following your orders, but in here you have no power."

"That's right," Mimi agreed. "We want to know why Bria's in that getup."

"Bria, were your clothes drenched in blood and the only thing they had for you to wear was a mummy's costume?" Annamaria asked.

"It's a fencing outfit," Bria explained. "I was playing in a match."

"Didn't you say you did that in college?" Enrico asked.

"She was a champion fencer," Fifetta declared.

"One of the best!" Franco added.

"Did you forget how to play?" Mimi asked.

"Is that why you were drenched in blood?" Annamaria added.

Bria couldn't help but laugh. "I wasn't drenched in blood."

"Were you *covered* in blood?" Annamaria asked.

"She wasn't drenched or covered in blood." Tobias's voice was as even and unemotional as Bria imagined an emergency room doctor's was when he or she was trying to turn chaos into order. "There was just a little bleeding from where the fencing sword pierced her flesh right above her heart."

Cries of "*Dio mio*," "*Caro Dio*," "*Oh caro Dio del cielo*," and variations on the theme, filled Bella Bella as Bria tried to calm her guests down and temper Tobias's inadvertently gory detail.

"It was an accident," Bria explained. "Valentina didn't mean to hurt me."

"Then how did she?" Fabrice asked.

"The rubber end on the tip of the fencing sword fell off," Bria said. "Neither of us noticed until—"

"You were almost killed!" Annamaria cried, interrupting her.

This time, cries of "*Cieli no*," "*Incredibile*," and "*Non posso crederci*" filled the room, so loud Bria almost didn't hear her cell phone ping. She looked at the text she had just received, and it was from Vanni, asking if it was safe for him to bring Marco home. She quickly typed yes and then began the process of kicking everyone out of her house.

"*Grazie molte*," Bria said. "Now you all need to leave, because Marco is on his way home."

Annamaria, Mimi, and Enrico kissed and hugged Bria and told her to call on them at any time of day or night if she needed their help. Imperia and Massimo left next, and while there was no kissing, Imperia did clasp Bria's hands and tell her to be careful. Fifetta and Franco wanted to stay, but Fifetta knew she wouldn't be able to prevent herself from crying in front of Marco, so they embraced their daughter quickly and left along with Lorenza and Fabrice.

"Do you want me to stay?" Rosalie asked.

"No, you go home. I'll be fine," Bria replied. "Luca can walk you home."

"Is that your subtle way of kicking me out?" Luca asked.

"*Perdonami*," Bria replied. "I wasn't trying to be subtle."

Rosalie hugged Bria tightly, and Bria could feel her friend's body shaking. Rosalie bent her head so her lips touched Bria's ear. Her whisper was barely audible but roaring with emotion. "Don't you ever do anything like that to me again, *capisci*?"

Bria did understand. She couldn't imagine a world without Rosalie in it, either. Bria hugged her back with the same intensity. "I won't, *lo prometto*."

After Rosalie and Luca left, the only ones remaining in the house were Tobias and Daisy. How odd that after such an eventful evening, Bria would find comfort and relief in being in the company of virtual strangers. It was just what she needed to take a moment and prepare for Marco to come home. She needed to compose herself and make sure she looked like Marco's mother and not the Red Cross's latest patient.

"You may want to change," Daisy suggested.

Bria looked down at herself and was reminded, once again, that she didn't look presentable. "Oh yes, *grazie*."

She ran into her bedroom and changed into a shirt that covered her bandage and pants and shoes that looked more like loungewear than sports gear. She yanked the rubber band that was barely holding her hair together and let it fall naturally. She brushed it and then looked at herself in the mirror. She looked like she did every other night, like she wasn't almost in a fatal accident.

"Mamma, we're home!" Marco cried.

Hearing her son's voice felt like another sword had been jabbed into her heart. The thought of what had almost happened a few hours ago overtook her mind, and Bria found it so difficult to breathe that she had to physically shake her head to release the gruesome thoughts. She was fine, nothing devastating had happened, and her son's life would not be affected.

She walked into the front room and saw Marco licking a pistachio gelato, his mouth covered in green, and it was as if God had sent her a vision of love. She howled with laughter and was truly grateful to have such a diversion. Otherwise she might have spent all night trying to figure out if the person who had killed Chef Lugo had also tried to kill her. Or if someone else had tried to kill her, someone who had nothing to do with Chef

Lugo's murder. She would have also obsessed over trying to deduce if the fencing incident had anything to do with her fall on the Path of the Gods. Or if they both had been unfortunate, but separate, accidents.

She had no way of proving any of those scenarios, so she did the only thing she could do: she pushed thoughts of homicide from her mind so she could spend quality time with her son.

"Marco, *mi piccolino*," Bria said. "You have a green moustache."

"Of course I do," Marco replied. "I'm eating green gelato."

"Marco, remember what you promised," Vanni said.

"That I'd wash my face once I finished," Marco replied.

"What else?"

"*Ah giusto*," Marco said. "That I'd share my gelato with Bravo."

Marco knelt by Bravo's food dish and turned the cone upside down, causing the rest of the gelato to spill out. It stayed in the dish for only about twenty seconds before Bravo lapped it all up.

"Mamma, why don't you ever tell Bravo to eat slower?" Marco asked.

"Because he'd never listen to me," Bria said. "Do like Vanni said, and go wash up."

"Yes, Mamma."

When Marco was out of earshot, Giovanni turned to Bria. "Are you okay?"

"I'm fine," Bria assured him. "Thanks to Tobias."

"I didn't do anything," Tobias said. "It isn't a very serious wound."

"This means you must be getter closer to the truth," Vanni said.

"If I am, that's news to me," Bria replied. "I still have no idea who killed Chef Lugo or why."

"Someone must not agree with you," Vanni said.

"You really think the person who killed this chef tried to do the same thing to Bria?" Tobias asked.

"No, Vanni's just letting his imagination get the best of him," Bria said.

"Still, I think I'll put a chair in front of our bedroom door tonight," Daisy informed, heading upstairs. *"Buona notte."*

"That won't be necessary," Bria told her.

"She won't sleep a wink if I don't barricade the door," Tobias said.

Bria didn't argue with her guests, because she knew she'd be doing the same thing.

Tobias started up the stairs after his wife, but abruptly turned around. "Excuse me, I almost forgot my book." He went into the living room and grabbed the book that was lying on the coffee table—*Weißer Oleander*—then started back up the stairs calling *"Gute Nacht"* to everyone.

When Tobias walked past Pippa's bedroom, it reminded Bria that she hadn't seen the girl all day. "Is Pippa upstairs?"

"I don't think so," Vanni replied.

"Tobias," Bria called out. "Do you know if Pippa's in her room?"

"One way to find out," Tobias replied.

He knocked on the door to Pippa's room and waited. He knocked again, and this time called out to her. There was no answer. He leaned over the banister on the landing and shared his finding with the group downstairs. "She must be out. There are a lot of bars on the beach that the young people enjoy."

Bria ignored the heat in her stomach and nodded. "That must be it."

Tobias nodded and disappeared down the hallway and then inside his room. Bria felt her stomach tighten even further when she heard a chair being dragged across the floor in that room and jammed underneath the doorknob. Her guests were afraid, and she couldn't blame them. She was, too. Which was why she jumped when someone knocked on the front door.

Giovanni reached the front door before she did, and he looked out through the peephole. He turned to Bria with a furrowed brow. "It's Michele."

"At this time of night?"

Once Giovanni opened the door to reveal Michele, Bria understood why he had come.

"My Vespa! *Grazie!*" Bria raced toward the door. "Is she all fixed?"

"Like brand new." Michele stepped out of the way so Bria could inspect her cycle. "I drove it over here, and the brakes work perfectly."

"*Grazie mille,*" Bria said. "You didn't have to drive it over here. I could've picked it up in the morning."

"After what happened to you, I wasn't sure you'd be able to drive," Michele said.

"That was very nice of you, but as you can see, I'm fine," Bria said.

"I'm glad to hear it," Michele replied. "There's been enough tragedy in the village, what with Louis's death."

Bria couldn't believe she didn't gasp out loud. She held her breath and waited for Michele to continue speaking. She wanted to see if he was going to backtrack on what he said or if he didn't even realize that he had called Chef Lugo by his real name. Bria glanced over at Giovanni, who was playing with Bravo, and assumed from his lack of reaction that he didn't hear what Michele had just said. It was the perfect opportunity for Bria to see what else she could get the mechanic to say.

"Thanks again, Michele," Bria said. "Let me walk you to the curb."

Bria closed the door behind her so they could talk in private. The stars were out, the sky was a gorgeous shade of deep purple, and in the distance the melodic sounds from Music on the Rocks, the most popular nightclub on the beach, could be heard. The night was calm and peaceful, despite Bria's growing sense of foreboding.

Michele stared at Bria but didn't say a word. It was as if he was waiting to be interrogated.

"Did you know who Chef Lugo was before you arrived in Positano or only when you saw him?"

"I suspected it was him from the photos and things that I read about him online, but I didn't know he was coming to Positano," Michele replied. "I was already here when I heard the news."

"You must hate him for what he did to Mamma Rita," Bria said.

"He killed her, just as surely as if he plunged a knife in her heart."

Like someone almost did to me, Bria thought.

"Were you hiding in Annamaria's café to get revenge?"

"Not like you're thinking," Michele replied. "I didn't know what I was going to say to him, but I wanted him to see me. I wanted him to know that someone knew who he really was."

"Why are you telling me this?" Bria asked. "And not Rosalie?"

"I guess I'm testing the waters."

"What does that mean?"

"I wanted to see if you'd believe me or if you'd just assume I tried to kill Louis."

"Because you have feelings for Rosalie and care about what she thinks of you," Bria replied.

"I've made many mistakes, *molti*, but murder is not one of them," Michele said. "I know what people think of me, and it can't be worse than what I think of myself sometimes. But if I'm going to have any kind of chance with Rosalie or any kind of life here in this village, I need to tell the truth. Paolo and En-rico speak so highly of you, so I thought I'd start here."

Despite the misgivings Bria had about Michele, his humility touched her. He sounded very much like his uncle when Paolo admitted to being ashamed of how he had acted as a younger man. Bria didn't know for certain if Michele was telling the truth, but she knew what she had to do with this information.

"You know I can't keep this from Rosalie or Luca," Bria stated.

"I know," Michele said. "*Va bene*, because I have nothing to hide."

Bria sat on the front step for a few minutes after Michele left. His confession had been surprising, and if taken at face value, it took him out of the running as a suspect. Bria knew nothing was that easy, and he could have shared facts he knew the police would eventually uncover. The fact that Michele knew Chef Lugo's identity before his death meant that he had not only means and opportunity but motive, as well. It did not look good for the mechanic.

She was about to get up to back inside when she heard a muffled cry. She waited a moment and heard it again. It was coming from behind the house.

As quietly as she could, she walked around the side of the house, following the narrow path until she got to the top of the stairs that led down to the beach. Immediately, she stepped back into the shadows so she couldn't be seen by the couple halfway down the stairs. She recognized Massimo from his out-fit and his thick mane of jet-black hair, but she didn't immedi-ately recognize the woman, because he was blocking her face. From the way Massimo swayed back and forth, it was clear that they were kissing.

Bria recoiled farther back into the shadows because she had no desire to see Massimo making out with Imperia. That was a sight she could live very happily without ever seeing. She didn't have to worry about having such a memory seared into her brain, because Massimo wasn't kissing Imperia. He was kissing a blonde.

Massimo pulled back and wrapped his arms around the woman's waist. Her face was finally in full view. Bria was right. Valentina really did look better when bathed in moonlight.

CHAPTER 20

Massimo is cheating on my mother-in-law!

Bria crept backward, stepping carefully so as not to make a sound, until she reached the fence. She climbed over it and onto her balcony. As she opened the sliding glass door, she once again thanked God for Giovanni's presence in her life, because just last week he had fixed the loud squeak the door made every time it was opened. Thanks to Vanni, Massimo and Valentina had no idea Bria was lurking close by. And with a plan.

She grabbed the Polaroid camera from her nightstand and made sure it was loaded with film. Experience had taught her that even though the Polaroid was a relic, it took better pictures in the dark than her cell phone did. So much for advancements in technology.

Back on the balcony, Bria leaned over and had a perfect view of Massimo and Valentina, who were still kissing in the moonlight. Their bodies were close together, and they were kissing softly, with passion but not frenzy. This wasn't a first-time rendezvous; this was an ongoing affair.

If Massimo and Valentina had just met and had wanted to have sex with each other, they would have gone to Valentina's house. For whatever reason, they didn't want to be seen together in such an obvious setting tonight. How would Massimo explain being in Valentina's home if he was caught? Better to meet in the shadows, so they could say they had accidentally bumped into each other or, more likely, so they wouldn't have to say anything at all, since people would either look away or not even notice them.

Bria knew that she had only one opportunity to capture the unlikely pair in flagrante delicto. Once she took the picture, there would be a loud click and then the processing of the film, which they would undoubtedly hear. It was a chance she was going to have to take in order to get proof that Massimo and Valentina were liars.

She positioned herself as low as possible, while still keeping her subjects in view. They were wrapped in an even tighter embrace, and Massimo was kissing Valentina's bare shoulder. It was the perfect angle because both their faces were in view: Valentina was looking right in the direction of the camera and Massimo was in profile. Bria clicked the camera's shutter button at the same time that Bravo decided to join her on the balcony and announce his presence with a loud bark, camouflaging the camera's sound.

Bria jumped back from the edge of the balcony as Bravo continued to bark. She couldn't see the clandestine couple any longer, but she presumed the sound of the barking had had the same effect as a bucket of cold water thrown on them would. Bria was able to get her evidence without being caught thanks to Bravo.

"My good little boy," Bria whispered in Bravo's ear. "You're Mamma's little helper."

Bravo barked again and immediately rolled onto his back, expecting to get a belly rub. That would have to wait because Bria's hands were full. One was holding the camera; the other, the developing photo.

It was a full moon, so the glow was bright enough for her to see that Carlo's old Polaroid had once again proved its worth. She grinned when she saw the fully processed photo. It was unmistakable proof that Chef Lugo's producer and his wife were romantically involved.

The first thing Bria did when she woke up the next morning was stand on a chair and take the photo from the top of the bookshelf, where she had placed it the night before. She hadn't wanted to leave it on top of her vanity for fear that Bravo might reach it and chew it to bits in the middle of the night. Every once in a while, his destructible side emerged, and he chewed something to pieces. Luckily, he hadn't destroyed the property of any of Bria's guests. At least not yet.

She looked at the photograph and knew that she had to show it to Luca. This was evidence that could be helpful to the murder investigation. First, she needed to show it to someone else. Someone who definitely would not be proud of Bria's sleuthing.

Bria quickly showered and examined herself in the mirror. The wound was healing nicely, but she made sure to follow the doctor's orders and apply the antibacterial cream he pre-scribed. Even though she thought a small Band-Aid would be sufficient to cover up the wound, she used one of the bandages a nurse had given her to keep it covered and avoid getting an infection.

Once that was taken care of, she put on black leggings, black espadrilles, and a white T-shirt she had borrowed from Rosalie but had never returned. It had a black-and-white photo of Paul Newman leaning against a Lancia Stratos, the vintage racing car the actor allegedly drove after the brand be-came famous for winning the World Rally Championship in 1974. Bria had a busy day ahead of her, and she needed all the help she could find to get through it.

Although she was pressed for time, she made sure she applied some lipstick, mascara, and blush and pulled her thick hair back into a tight ponytail, secured by the lemon-yellow barrettes Marco had bought for her at one of the stores in the village. She didn't expect to have to make another trip to the Red Cross, but if she did, she wasn't going to wind up looking as bad as she had the last time.

She emerged from her bedroom, expecting to be greeted by a houseful of people, but the only person at the dining room table was Daisy.

"*Buongiorno*, Daisy."

"*Buongiorno*, Bria."

"Where is everyone?"

"Tobias is sleeping in, and Giovanni, Marco, and Bravo went out to play soccer," Daisy reported. "It seems your son has a very big match coming up in a few weeks."

"Yes, he does," Bria confirmed. "Did Pippa head out early?"

Daisy hesitated and concentrated on nibbling a piece of chocolate biscotto she had just dunked in her coffee. "I know that young women these days are much more . . . independent than they were in my generation, but I don't think Pippa came home last night."

"I see."

"Or she may have brought someone home with her," Daisy suggested. "And she's too embarrassed for them to leave until the place is empty."

Bria didn't believe in forcing her morals on anyone else; however, she did believe in following directions. Since Bella Bella was also Marco's home, Bria had some ground rules for her guests, which were posted on the website www.Bella-BellaBnB.it and in the brochure she gave each guest. Since Pippa hadn't checked in under normal circumstances, Bria had verbally advised her of the few rules she expected every guest to follow: no drugs or smoking of any kind were allowed on the premises, no loud noise was tolerated after 10:00 p.m., and no visitors were permitted in the house at any time.

If Pippa had brought a tourist or one of the locals up to her room, she had violated one of the basic rules of the house. Regardless of her situation—being unable to leave the village due to the ongoing investigation—Bria would have no choice but to ask her to leave. Playing disciplinarian and engaging in confrontation were Bria's least favorite parts of being a business owner, but the rules had been set up primarily for her son's safety, and there wasn't anything she wouldn't do for Marco. Which was why she was knocking on Pippa's door, with Daisy, who was now biting into her third biscotto, by her side.

"Pippa," Bria called "Could you please open the door?"

When there was no response, Bria turned her ear toward the door to try to hear any sounds on the other side. All she heard was Daisy's munching. "*Scusa*, but I really need to make sure everything is all right."

More silence and then more munching.

"*Bene*, Pippa. I'm using my key to open this door." Bria waited a moment, in case Pippa was inside the room and this final comment spurred her to action. If it did, Pippa was the quietest person Bria had ever met.

"Pippa's left you no choice," Daisy said.

Bria used her master key to unlock the door, but when she pushed it open, the only thing revealed was an empty room. The bed was made and didn't look like it had been slept in. Her suitcase was open on the luggage rack—there was one in a corner of every guest room—and a duffel bag overflowing with clothes was peeking out of the closet.

"Wait here," Bria said.

Daisy watched as Bria went into the room and knocked on the adjoining bathroom door that was slightly open. Bria pushed open the door and saw that the bathroom was as empty as the main room, except that Pippa's toiletries were strewn across

5

the sink and over the shower. She hadn't skipped town in the middle of the night, or during the day, for that matter, because Bria remembered that she hadn't shown up at the fencing match. Pippa hadn't been seen in over a day.

"Pippa must have spent the night in someone else's bed," Daisy said.

It was possible. She thought she knew someone who might know Pippa's whereabouts. It could prove awkward, but the two people she needed to confront were most likely together. If she was right, Bria would get to kill two birds with one stone. Hopefully, only figuratively.

Rosalie was on the dock when Bria pulled up on her Vespa. She usually walked to the marina, but today she wasn't sure if she was going to have to travel farther to conduct impromptu meetings, and she didn't want to waste time. Her espadrilles allowed her to move quickly, but not Vespa quick.

"Rosalie, I need you!" Bria called out.

"You always need me." Rosalie tugged on some rope to untangle it. "I'm busy."

"That can wait." Bria tied her Vespa around the piling in front of Rosalie's boat. "This is important."

"I have a group of bird-watchers who are going to be here in an hour for a tour to see a hawk's nest," Rosalie said.

"I don't think the hawk is going to want any visitors," Bria said.

Rosalie threw the rope onto the dock and looked to the left. "Must be contagious. Check out those two."

Bria turned and was stunned to see her mother-in-law and the man she had caught on film just last night canoodling in public. This was a disaster. Bria had planned to call Imperia and ask her to join her on Rosalie's boat to discuss an idea for Marco's Communion. It wasn't the most logical plan, but it would have gotten Imperia away from her yacht and, more importantly, from Massimo. From the way they were embracing, Bria would need a crowbar to separate the couple.

"*Dio mio!*" Bria gasped. "Massimo's cheating on Imperia."

"He's what?"

"I saw him kissing Valentina last night."

"The slutty tour guide?"

"She isn't slutty. She's pretty."

"In my book, they're the same thing!"

"Keep your voice down. They'll hear us."

"I see you two over there!" Imperia cried.

"Too late," Rosalie said.

"Come over and join us!" Imperia ordered.

"*Ciao*, Imperia!" Bria replied. "*Va bene*, we'll be right over!"

Rosalie quickly wrapped the rope around a piling. "Let's go bring that gigolo down."

"Let me handle this," Bria pleaded. "I have proof."

"What kind of proof?"

"A photograph," Bria replied, patting the small messenger bag hanging off her shoulder. "Right in here."

No matter how many times Bria was on Imperia's yacht, she couldn't shake the feeling that she was intruding. She didn't feel like someone who belonged on a yacht; she felt like an imposter. Like Massimo.

Sitting across from the man she had seen kissing another woman, who was now absentmindedly caressing the hand of her mother-in-law, made Bria want to throw her iced cappuccino in Massimo's face. If the drink wasn't so delicious, she might follow through, but what good would that do? It would only make her appear impulsive and out of control, and it would be a waste of an artisanal beverage.

"Thank you both again for coming to the match yesterday," Bria said.

"I was the host of the event," Imperia said. "Where else would I be?"

"And where else would I be than with my Imperia?" Massimo questioned.

Not only had Bria never imagined any man *owning* her mother-in-law, but she had never imagined that her mother-in-law would allow any man to make such a comment. Yet, in response, Imperia smiled and playfully slapped Massimo's hand. Bria's heart sank because she could see that Imperia was falling in love with this charlatan, that it wasn't infatuation, and that she was going to be the one to destroy her mother-in-law's happiness. Imperia was going to blame Bria for ruining her life, and their relationship was going to be more strained than ever before. Marco's Holy Communion party was going to be more of a disaster than it was already destined to be.

Bria couldn't expose Massimo. She couldn't break Imperia's heart now that it was starting to thaw. She had to keep quiet. Unfortunately, Rosalie couldn't.

"Where'd you get to last night, Mass?" Rosalie asked, looking Massimo in the eye.

"*Scusa*?" he replied.

"After all the fencing and bleeding, where'd you get to?"

"I'm not sure what you mean," he said. "I was at Bria's with Imperia."

"Only briefly," Rosalie noted. "You left early."

"We left together," Imperia said.

"When you got back to the yacht, did you remain together for the rest of the night?" Rosalie asked.

Bria closed her eyes and wondered if there was a patron saint of invisibility.

"That is none of your business," Imperia said, clearly irritated.

"That's all right," Massimo said. "We have nothing to hide. We did spend the evening together."

Imperia didn't move, but her violet eyes peered at Massimo. "Most of the evening."

Bria's stomach felt like an inferno. "Did you leave at some point, Massimo?"

He somehow managed to keep smiling while speaking through gritted teeth. "I had to take an emergency phone call to deal with the impact that Chef Lugo's death is having on the television show."

"Did you take the call here on the yacht?" Bria asked.

"Why would you ask that?" Massimo questioned.

"The reception out here isn't the best," she replied. "I'm always dropping calls."

"The yacht has its own satellite. Calls are never missed," Imperia said. "How else do you think I could stay here and run Bartolucci Enterprises?"

"Funny you should mention that, because I've been wondering the same thing," Bria said. "You've been spending much more time in the village than you normally do. *Perché*?"

Imperia glanced at Massimo, then turned back to Bria. "There's never been anyone in Positano worth staying for besides my Marco, of course."

"Until me," Massimo said, flashing a devilish smile.

Now that Bria knew what kind of man Massimo was, she found his very presence to be grotesque. He disgusted her. She needed to leave; she needed to make an excuse to extricate herself from this exceedingly uncomfortable situation. Rosalie had other ideas.

"Proof," she said as she coughed into her hand.

"What did you say?" Imperia asked.

Once again, Rosalie covered her mouth, turned toward Bria, and coughed while whispering roughly, "Proof."

"I think she's saying, 'Poof,'" Massimo offered.

"Poof?" Imperia repeated. "Why in the world would she say, 'Poof'?"

"Is that what you said, Rosalie?" Massimo asked. "Poof?"

"Are you working on a magic act to entertain the guests on your little boat?" Imperia asked.

Bria knew Rosalie was going to reach for her inhaler before she did. She recognized the signs, the wide eyes, the reddened cheeks, the inability to speak. Rosalie reached into the pocket of her pants and pulled out the inhaler, which rarely left her side. Without an exit strategy, Bria was forced to take a similar action. She reached into her bag and pulled out the Polaroid photo.

"She said, 'Proof.'"

Bria handed the photo to Imperia, but before she let the woman look at the image, she looked her straight in the eye. "I'm sorry, Imperia. I did not want to tell you like this."

Massimo couldn't possibly know what the image was of, but he looked frightened. He masked his fear quickly, but Bria noticed the shift. He was a man used to getting caught, so he was a man who knew how to talk his way out of a problem. Regrettably for him, he'd never tried to do that with Imperia.

"What in the world is she talking about?" Massimo asked.

Imperia didn't answer; she simply stared at the photograph. Bria couldn't tell what she was thinking, because Imperia was no longer the hopeless romantic, she had morphed back into the woman Bria knew so well, the steely businesswoman. Despite how angry Imperia was going to be with her, Bria knew she had done the right thing.

"Get out."

Imperia spoke the words so softly, they almost went unheard. So she repeated them, louder and more distinctly. "Get. Out."

"Ladies, you heard Imperia," Massimo said. "You should leave."

"*Per l'amor di Dio!*" Imperia cried. "I'm talking to you, Massimo!"

"*Me*? Why do you want me to leave?"

Imperia held up the photo for Massimo to see. Bria was once again impressed, because Imperia didn't let go of the evidence. She didn't hand it to Massimo, because she knew he might rip it up into little pieces. Maybe Imperia should be the one to play amateur detective.

Massimo's tanned complexion drained of color. He smiled, laughed, started to speak, stuttered, and finally fell silent. It took him a few moments to recapture the power of speech. "I can explain."

"No you can't," Imperia snarled "This is a photo of you and Signora Travanti kissing under last night's full moon."

"It isn't last night's moon!" Massimo protested. "No, it is from a long time ago."

"Then why is there a date at the bottom of the photo?" Imperia asked.

Bria almost shrieked out loud. She had forgotten that the camera had a time-stamp setting. She didn't know how to use all the camera's mechanisms, so she must have unintentionally hit a button. It was a lucky accident, because now there was no disputing when Massimo cheated on Imperia. Things got luckier when Massimo understood he wasn't going to be able to argue his way out of this situation.

"If you ladies will excuse me," he said. "I need to pack my bags."

Bria watched him disappear belowdecks and waited for Imperia to start screaming at her. She prepared herself for vitriol. She did not expect gratitude.

"*Grazie*, Bria."

"*Scusa?*"

"Please don't make me repeat it," Imperia said. "I appreciate what you've done for me, but I still feel like a *stolta*."

"Imperia, you are hardly a fool," Bria said. "You're the smartest, shrewdest woman I know."

"Who's spent the last week making goo-goo eyes at an old flame," Imperia said. "Massimo was never like my Guillermo, which is why I chose my husband. Massimo wasn't worthy of being my husband, but I thought now he could be a little bit more than a friend. He proved me wrong, and he proved that I'm a fool."

"Listen up, Imperia!" Rosalie shouted. "Nobody's more of a fool than me. When it comes to romance and boyfriends, I'm the queen of the fools!"

"That really is true," Bria said.

"You don't need to agree so quickly, Bri," Rosalie remarked. "But you, Imperia, are not a fool. You are a woman who trusted a man, and he betrayed you. *Capisci*?"

Imperia stared at Rosalie, but in a different way than before. With respect. *"Capisco."*

Bria smiled at Imperia. "I guess this isn't the end of our relationship, like I thought it would be."

"*Caro Dio*! Don't get carried away, Bria," Imperia said. "We are related, but I wouldn't go so far as to say we have a relationship."

Imperia looked around and threw her hands up. Bria thought she was still annoyed with her, but, in fact, Imperia had shifted her focus to Massimo. "Where the hell is that man? He had one suitcase, and it's taking him this long to leave?"

The chair made an earsplitting sound when Imperia pushed herself away from the table. Bria looked at Rosalie, and they both looked like they had once again gotten caught trespassing on the boys' side of the gym at St. Maximus High School by Father Nicolosi. They did now just as they had done then: they scurried to the nearest exit and followed Imperia belowdecks.

"Massimo!" Imperia banged on a door. "I want you off my yacht now!"

When there was no immediate response, she burst open the door, and the scene mimicked the one that had played out earlier at Bella Bella, when Bria was searching for Pippa. This cabin was empty. First, Pippa went missing, and now Massimo. Was he hiding somewhere on the yacht? Was his gallant response about leaving a ruse? Was he joining Pippa wherever she was camping out? None of those questions really made sense, because his suitcase and duffel bag were next to the door. Wherever he went, he didn't take his luggage.

They heard a door slam from below, which made even less sense to Bria because she thought she was on the bottom level of the yacht. She was wrong.

"What is Massimo doing in the engine room?" Imperia said.

"There's an engine room?" Rosalie asked.

"Of course there's an engine room. Every vessel has one," Imperia replied.

"Mine doesn't," Rosalie protested.

"*Tesoro*, you don't have a vessel," Imperia purred. "You have a boat."

Bria and Rosalie followed Imperia as she turned around and walked to the far end of the passageway, to a door that looked like it belonged to a closet. When Imperia opened it, they saw that it was the entrance to a ladder. They followed Imperia down the stairs until they were in the bowels of the yacht. There they saw boilers, other machinery, and Massimo coming out of a compartment then closing the door behind him.

"What the hell are you doing down here?" Imperia asked.

"Nothing. I was just gathering my things," he replied.

"Your things are upstairs," Bria said. "We just saw them."

"You love to ask questions, don't you, Bria?" Massimo grumbled. "Stick your nose where it doesn't belong."

Bria had no desire to hide from the truth. She marched past him and entered the compartment, but it was empty.

"What were you doing in there?" Imperia said. "Are you *pazzo*? There's a lock on that door on the outside. You could've been trapped in there."

Bria saw something in a corner of the compartment, underneath a dust ball, that proved that this had just happened. Maybe not to Massimo, but to someone else. As Imperia interrogated Massimo, Bria bent down out of their lines of vision and grabbed the barrette that was hidden in the dust and shoved it in her pocket. It was an inexpensive accessory, like the ones she had in her hair, but this one wasn't yellow and in the shape of a lemon. This one was pink and in the shape of a butterfly. It was the same barrette Pippa had worn when they'd gone on the tour of the Path of the Gods.

Bria didn't know if Massimo was a murderer, but she was certain that he was a kidnapper.

CHAPTER 21

Rosalie grabbed the pitcher and poured more limoncello into her glass. She raised it toward Bria and Imperia, who were sitting across from her at the table on the deck of Imperia's yacht, and took a long swallow. She placed her glass on the table and stared at Bria. "You think Massimo is a what?"

"I think he's a kidnapper," Bria stated.

"That's what I thought you said," Rosalie replied. "Are you *pazza*?"

"I, for one, wouldn't put anything past that man," Imperia said.

"Bria, I know that you have wonderful instincts. You've always been able to tell when we are about to get into trouble, going all the way back to high school," Rosalie said.

"Bria was a troublemaker in high school?" Imperia asked.

"I was more of the hellion and the one who got us into trouble back then, if you can believe that," Rosalie replied.

Imperia eyed Rosalie and took a long sip of her limoncello spritz. "I can."

"The tides have shifted, and now Bria is the one leading me into the danger zone," Rosalie said.

"I am trying to get at the truth," Bria said.

"You think the truth is that Massimo is a kidnapper?" Rosalie asked.

"Yes," Bria said. She then added with less conviction, "At least I think so."

"Do you have proof that he's a kidnapper, like you had proof that he's a philanderer?" Imperia questioned.

Bria placed the pink barrette on the table. "I found this under some dust in the compartment we saw Massimo coming out of."

"The one where he had no business being?" Rosalie questioned.

"The same one," Bria said. "It's Pippa's."

Imperia eyed the barrette while taking a bite of a biscotto. "How can you be sure that it's hers?"

"Because I saw her wearing it."

"I've seen some of my staff wearing decorations in their hair, but they know I feel they degrade the Bartolucci uniform," Imperia said. "Maybe one of them saw me coming and tossed it away so I wouldn't chastise them."

"There's a very slim possibility that explains how it got there," Bria said. "The logical explanation is that Massimo held Pippa captive in that compartment."

Rosalie almost choked on her drink. "*That's* the logical explanation?"

"No one has seen Pippa for over twenty-four hours, she hasn't been in her room at Bella Bella, and no one has heard from her," Bria explained.

"Not highly unusual for a young woman," Imperia replied. "Of a certain breed."

"If Pippa were a tourist, absolutely not," Bria said. "But she's part of a murder investigation, and Luca specifically told her and the TV crew to stay put and not leave the village."

"You really think her possible disappearance is courtesy of Massimo?" Rosalie asked.

"Yes," Bria replied.

"I need more facts, Bria," Imperia said. "Support your statement."

"*Dio mio*! You sound just like my brother!" Rosalie cried.

"I think it's more like your brother sounds like me," Imperia said. "Bria, spell out your case."

Bria was used to being challenged by Imperia, but this time was different. She got the impression that Imperia actually wanted Bria to win the argument. She wasn't speaking to her in a harsh tone to put Bria in her place. It gave Bria renewed confidence.

"Massimo and Pippa's relationship has been volatile since the moment we met them both. Pippa was scared of him, and he yelled at her and treated her terribly in public," Bria said. "The yacht is the last place anyone can trace Pippa's whereabouts. She was working with Massimo to find a new series to replace Chef Lugo's cooking show."

Bria took a breath and tried to gauge Imperia's reaction, but her mother-in-law was wearing her best poker face. She needed to wrap up her summation quickly.

"Massimo had no business being in that compartment in the engine room, and Pippa's barrette had no reason being there, unless Pippa had been in that compartment," Bria said. "All of this makes me convinced that Massimo kidnapped Pippa and kept her prisoner on your yacht."

Bria had to wait a few moments before someone spoke.

"You had me at pink barrette," Rosalie said. "You know I believe you and anything you say, no matter how unbelievable."

"I believe you, too."

Bria had to hold on to the table so she didn't fall over. Her mother-in-law actually believed her. "Really?"

"Yes," Imperia said. "You laid out your case, your evidence is strong, and I know what Massimo is capable of."

"Has Massimo exhibited this kind of behavior in the past?" Bria asked.

"Has he ever kidnapped anyone before? No," Imperia affirmed. "Has he delved into that murky pond of unscrupulous business behavior that, let's say, Franco D'Abruzzo would not approve? Yes."

Hearing her father's name, Bria knew Imperia agreed with her profile of Massimo. Although her father didn't agree with how Imperia conducted her business, and felt she had often dipped more than a toe into a murky pond, Imperia, on the other hand, respected Franco completely. If Bria's father wouldn't approve of Massimo's business tactics, Bria knew Massimo was someone who couldn't be trusted. But not trusting that a man would play fair and adhere to the law in a business transaction was not the same thing as believing a man could be a kidnapper.

"Imperia, has Massimo done something in his past that you disapprove of?"

Bria watched Imperia take another long sip of her spritz, the limoncello disappearing at a very unladylike rate. She placed the glass on the table and gazed out at the sea, looking like a socialite contemplating her day from the deck of her yacht. Bria saw more. She saw a woman remembering the moment when the man she loved lost her respect.

"When he was younger, Massimo was what we used to call a *mascalzone*," Imperia said. "His cavalier behavior toward women would never be accepted by the younger generation of today, but back then, it was lauded and revered by both sexes."

"Women back then may have tolerated a man's reputation," Rosalie claimed. "I don't think you can say they accepted it."

A roar of laughter erupted from Imperia's unlined throat. Her violet eyes twinkled in the fading sunlight, and her crow's-feet crinkled at the corners of her smiling eyes.

"*Oh mia cara*! Women, despite their public protestations, have loved and always will love a bad boy," Imperia stated. "Isn't that what's drawn you to the mechanic?"

Rosalie almost choked on her drink. "I'm not *drawn* to Michele."

"Stop acting like a child," Imperia commanded. "When I was half your age, I had already learned that what women desire and what they settle for are two vastly different things."

Bria wasn't sure how their conversation had veered into a discussion of unspoken female mores and how the passage of time had not altered what many would consider a primitive analysis, but she found it a fascinating glimpse into Imperia's mind. She knew very little of Imperia's inner thoughts, only how they were manifested as part of Imperia's public behavior. It was very interesting to hear her speak about her personal beliefs, and while Bria didn't agree with them, she longed to hear more. But she didn't have the time. The possibility still existed that a young woman was being held against her will somewhere in the village. She needed to find out from Imperia if she could be right about that before she made her thoughts public.

"If Massimo could be classified as a bad boy and fall into the category of the type of man women desire," Bria stated, "would he also fall into the category of the kind of man women should be afraid of?"

Once again, the sea held Imperia's gaze; something out there beyond the horizon or locked away in her mind held more interest to Imperia than Bria's question. All three women at the table knew someone's life might be in danger, so it was a question that had to be answered. Imperia turned to face Bria, and her eyes, while not moist with memory, were open and honest.

"You push people, Bria, do you know that?" Before Bria could respond, Imperia continued. "You don't judge, but you have a way of making people tell the truth. No . . . of understanding that they *must* tell the truth."

Bria was stunned, because she felt Imperia did the same thing.

"I didn't mean to make you feel uncomfortable, Imperia," Bria said.

"Yes you did, and it's an admirable trait, one that you should acknowledge is part of your arsenal," Imperia replied. "It's a good tool for an amateur detective."

"Finally, you and I agree on something," Rosalie said. "Bria's a very good detective."

"*Amateur*," Imperia repeated.

"*Grazie*," Bria said. "I have one simple question for you, Imperia. Based on how Massimo has treated women in the past, do you feel that he's capable of kidnapping Pippa?"

Imperia's answer was immediate and unwavering. "Yes."

"Bria, have you lost your mind?"

"Luca, is that any way to talk to your girlfriend?"

"Rosalie! *Basta!*"

Bria stood in between the Vivaldi siblings in Luca's office at the police station and threw her hands up. She looked across the room at Nunzi and raised her eyebrows and shook her head. Nunzi, as expected, didn't change her expression.

"Don't look at me," Nunzi said. "I just work here."

When Imperia had confirmed that Bria's instincts could be accurate, Bria and Rosalie had finished their drinks and made their way to the police station on Bria's Vespa to have an official meeting with Luca before he left for the day. Bria wanted to share her speculation with the chief of police that they might need to add kidnapping to the list of the latest crimes to befall Positano. The only way to prove her assumption wrong—or possibly right— was with police intervention. Neither of them expected Luca to wholeheartedly believe their hypothesis, but they didn't expect him to disregard it completely.

"Do you have any idea how powerful a man Massimo is?" Luca said.

"Are you trying to say a powerful man has never committed a crime?" Bria asked.

"Powerful men don't become powerful by kidnapping people," Luca replied.

"Yes they do!" Rosalie retorted. "That's why Bria and I have a safeword. Mussolini!"

"Now you sound like my grandfather," Nunzi remarked.

"He hated him, too?" Bria said.

"Yes, but I was talking about Giuseppe Mussolini, my grandmother's first fiancé, who died in the war and was the real love of her life," Nunzi replied. "I'm not sure if he was related to the fascist, but my grandmother could never stop talking about him, even after she married my grandfather."

Luca stared at Nunzi the same way he had just been staring at Bria, as if his head was about to explode. "Nunzi! You are forbidden to spend any more time with Bria and my sister. You're starting to talk like them."

"With all due respect, Chief, you can't tell me how to spend my personal time," Nunzi replied. "Plus, these two seem to like visiting your office."

Bria wasn't sure if Nunzi was making a subtle reference to her relationship with Luca, but she wanted to set clear boundaries, nonetheless. "I am here on official police business."

"Me too," Rosalie added.

"Neither of you is part of the police force," Luca said. "How many times do I have to say that?"

"You can say it all you want, but you need to listen to me," Bria declared. "Pippa has gone missing, and we think Massimo kidnapped her."

"Where's your proof?" Luca asked.

Bria placed the pink butterfly barrette on Luca's desk, and it elicited the same skeptical response it had when she first showed it to Rosalie and Imperia.

"I don't think pink is Massimo's best color," Luca said. "But the man's free to put whatever he wants in his hair."

"*Oh andiamo*! It isn't Massimo's barrette. It's Pippa's!" Bria cried. "I found it in a compartment in the engine room on Imperia's yacht."

"How does a barrette found on Imperia's yacht prove Massimo kidnapped Pippa?" Luca asked.

"Massimo was living on the yacht, but in a cabin on the main deck," Bria explained. "When Imperia kicked him out, we found him coming out of a room on the subbasement floor."

"Why did Imperia kick him off her yacht?" Nunzi asked. "I thought she was sweet on him."

"She was," Bria said. "Until I showed her this."

Bria rummaged through her bag and pulled out the Polaroid photo of Massimo kissing Valentina and placed it on Luca's desk. This piece of evidence generated a much stronger reaction from Luca and Nunzi.

"When were you going to tell me about this?" Luca said.

"We're telling you now!" Rosalie exclaimed.

"I had to tell Imperia first," Bria said. "It's what a woman does for another woman, the same way Nunzi told me about Michele so I could tell Rosalie."

"When did you take this photo?" Luca asked.

"Last night," Bria said. "I saw them kissing on the stairs behind Bella Bella."

"That's risky," Nunzi commented. "Not even trying to hide their affair."

"I thought so, too," Bria said. "Between that and kidnapping Pippa, Massimo may be coming apart at the seams."

"Don't you see, Bria, the barrette could be anyone's?" Luca said. "You have one in your hair right now."

"Marco gave it to me. I love it," Bria gushed. "Pippa was wearing this one when we went to the Path of the Gods. I commented on it because I thought it was pretty, and the next time I saw it was in the compartment on Imperia's yacht."

"Which had been locked from the outside," Rosalie added.

Luca paused, and Bria gave him a few moments to think her theory through. "You're sure no one has seen or heard from Pippa in over twenty-four hours?"

Bria exhaled. Luca believed her. He wouldn't be asking such a question if he didn't. "Correct. She's vanished."

Luca walked out from behind his desk and started to pace the room. "Why would Massimo do such a thing? What could Pippa know that would lead him to take such drastic action?"

"She may know that he's the one who killed Chef Lugo," Bria said.

"She could also know that he's having an affair with Lugo's widow," Rosalie added.

"Nunzi, get Matteo and look into Pippa's disappearance," Luca said. "Do it quietly, *per favore*. No need to add to the village gossip. Annamaria has enough on her plate as it is."

Annamaria wasn't the only one.

Bria looked at her phone and saw that she had missed three texts from Sister Benedicta.

"*Madonna mia*!" Bria cried. "I forgot that I promised Sister B that I'd take her to Ravello."

"Why does a nun have to go to Ravello?" Luca asked.

"I volunteered to drive her there to pick up the ceramic angels they're giving to the children as their Holy Communion gifts," Bria said.

"It's a bit late for a drive to Ravello, isn't it?" Luca asked.

"Maybe, but I promised," Bria replied. "I don't think God looks too kindly on those who make promises to Sisters and break them."

"Remember that, Luca," Rosalie said. "God is watching how you treat your sister."

Bria braced herself, expecting Luca and Nunzi to yell at Rosalie for comparing herself to a nun. There was no yelling, only laughing.

"I don't like you, Rosalie," Nunzi said. "But I have to admit, that was funny."

* * *

Bria zipped home on her Vespa, parked it on the side of the house, and got into her Fiat. She drove to pick up Sister B, thinking the nun would finally be ready to test-drive the car she so admired. When she pulled up to St. Cecilia's Grammar School and beeped the horn to greet Sister Benedicta, she learned the nun had other ideas.

"Get out and follow me."

Without commenting on the clandestine and completely out-of-character comment, Bria did what she was told and followed Sister Benedicta into St. Cecilia's, the entire time filled with a mixture of curiosity and awe. The more Bria got to know Marco's teacher, the more she realized she didn't know her very well at all. She was not like the Sisters who had taught her; she was more like a friend who simply had a very limited wardrobe.

Sister B opened a door, which creaked loudly and led down a flight of stairs. Bria had a moment of déjà vu as they walked down into the basement. But the sub-quarters at the school were not nearly as clean and brightly lit as the engine room on Imperia's yacht. The school's basement, however, held one thing Imperia's engine room did not: Pippa.

CHAPTER 22

Pippa was different.

Physically, she was unchanged, but emotionally, a shift had taken place within the young woman. Something had happened to Pippa since the last time Bria saw her, and it obviously had to do with Massimo. Her reappearance now had something to do with Bria.

"Sister Benedicta said I could trust you," Pippa said.

Bria felt a stirring in her throat. She glanced at Sister B, who merely nodded, validating Pippa's comment. "She's right. You can trust me. Anything you say to me stays right here in the church."

"I told you, Pippa," Sister B added. "St. Cecilia's is your sanctuary."

Sanctuary? Bria thought. *Isn't that for fairy-tale characters and defectors seeking political asylum? What exactly is Pippa running from?*

"*Grazie, Suora*, for taking me in," Pippa replied. "I didn't know where else to turn."

"Like I tell my students," Sister B said, "when you don't know where else to turn, turn to God."

"*Buon consiglio*," Bria said. "You can also turn to a friend."

For a moment Bria thought Pippa was going to cry. She took

a deep breath, threw her shoulders back, and looked Bria straight in the eye. "Then that's what I'll do."

"Would you like some espresso?" Sister B asked. "We don't have a dishwasher, and we dry our vestments on the line in the garden, but Mother Superior insists on having the latest model of espresso machine. We have a new Victoria Arduino machine, which Father Vincenzo personally brought to us from Florence just a few weeks ago."

"*Uffa!*" Bria cried. "I tried to get one for Bella Bella, but I was told they were out of stock."

"*Scusa.* Father Vincenzo got the last one," Sister B confessed. "I'll go make some espressos and give you two a chance to catch up."

After the Sister closed the door behind her, there was a long moment of silence. Bria wanted to bombard Pippa with questions, but she was aware that she had been traumatized and needed to feel that she was in control of the situation. Bria didn't have any formal training as a counselor or a nurse, but she was a mother. Now that Marco was getting older, she had learned that if he was upset, she sometimes needed to wait for him to decide when to share his thoughts. Gone were the days when his fears and concerns would tumble out of his mouth with little to no prodding. More often than not, her patience was rewarded.

"I told Massimo that I was going to go to the police," Pippa professed. "I was going to tell them everything I knew and that I believe he killed Chef Lugo."

Bria forced herself to remain calm, because she sensed Pippa had much more to say.

"Massimo wasn't just Lugo's producer. He was also his business partner," Pippa said. "He told me that he was the one who discovered Lugo and turned him into a celebrity. Massimo orchestrated this whole media blitz with one goal in mind, to make Lugo an international star."

So far Pippa hadn't told Bria anything she didn't already know. And nothing she had told her gave Massimo a motive to kill Lugo. "Why would Massimo kill Lugo? He would be sabotaging his own career, right?"

"Because Massimo knew that Lugo was on the verge of ruining everything."

Sister Benedicta knocked on the door and entered the room. She wasn't holding a tray filled with demitasse cups of espresso. She had a suggestion to offer instead. "This room can get so depressing without any windows, so I set up a table in the garden. Don't worry. Sister Louisa has already brought in the laundry."

A change of venue was just what Pippa needed to gather the strength to share the rest of her story. Impossibly smooth espressos with lemon wedges and an assortment of pastries from Caffè Positano helped. Pippa took a bite of the *babà al rum*, and some wayward raisins fell onto her plate. Before she swallowed, she took another bite of the Neapolitan dessert and closed her eyes, clearly savoring the taste of the rum-soaked sponge cake. While Pippa was eating, Bria thought it time to reignite the conversation.

"Do you know how Lugo was going to ruin everything for Massimo?" Bria asked.

Pippa took one last bite of the *babà al rum* and a long sip of espresso. She placed the cup back onto its plate and was finally ready to continue her confession.

"The two men were very close, almost like father and son, but lately they'd been arguing much more than usual," Pippa explained. "At first, I thought it was the stress of putting together a book tour and a new show, but then I realized it was much more than that."

"How did you come to this conclusion?"

"I was working in the recording studio late one night, editing an online trailer, and I overheard them talking in the other room," Pippa revealed. "The intercom was on, so I could hear every word they said. Massimo had found out that Lugo wanted to make some kind of announcement during the live telecast, and he confronted him about it. Lugo tried to avoid answering but finally told Massimo that it was what he had to do."

"I mentioned this to Massimo, but he acted like he had no idea what I was talking about."

"He lied."

"Did Lugo get any more specific with Massimo?" Bria asked. "Did he tell him what he wanted to say?"

"No," Pippa replied. "Only that he had lived with the lie long enough and he had to make things right."

"But he never said what that lie was?" Sister B asked.

"No," Pippa said. "Massimo must have known what he was talking about, because he didn't ask for specifics. He got livid and started screaming. I was convinced it was going to get violent."

"Did it?" Bria asked. "Did Massimo punch Lugo or assault him in any way?"

"No," Pippa replied. "It was just a verbal fight."

"How can you be so sure if you were hiding in another room?" Sister Benedicta asked.

"I crouched down behind the editing table, and the lights were off . . . Only the TV screen was lit, which is how I like to work when I'm editing, so I'm not distracted," Pippa explained. "They didn't see me, but I saw them."

"If Massimo didn't attack Lugo, why do you think he killed him?" Bria asked.

"Because he said he was going to," Pippa replied. "Massimo told Lugo that if he went through with his announcement, he'd kill him."

Sister B gasped and made the sign of the cross.

"Those were his exact words?" Bria asked.

"Yes," Pippa replied. "I can hear his voice as clearly as if he was at this table. He said, 'If you say one word, I will kill you. I will not let some phony chef destroy everything that I've spent years trying to build.'"

"Why would he call Lugo a phony?" Sister B asked. "I thought he was an excellent chef."

"It's because he isn't Italian," Bria said.

"He isn't?" Pippa cried.

"No, he's American," Bria said.

"I had no idea," Pippa admitted. "He did a great job of fooling everyone."

"Everyone except Massimo," Bria noted.

"Pippa, do you really believe Massimo would have killed Chef Lugo simply because he had lied about his heritage?" Sister B asked.

"That might be part of it, but there was something deeper, something that enraged Massimo," Pippa shared. "Whatever Lugo wanted to announce on live TV threatened to destroy not just Lugo's career but Massimo's reputation, as well. If you haven't noticed, Massimo has a huge ego and likes to live a certain upscale lifestyle. There's no way he would risk his entire world tumbling down like a house of cards."

"Even if that meant killing his meal ticket," Bria pondered.

"Yes, I believe so," Pippa agreed. "Massimo would rather find another person to put in front of the camera than have Lugo demolish the life he's built for himself."

"Which is why he kidnapped you," Bria stated. "To shut you up."

Pippa nodded. "He told me that he wasn't going to let some *idiota* working for an hourly wage ruin his life."

"He thought you knew Lugo wasn't Italian?" Bria asked.

"I guess that's what he meant," Pippa replied. "He did say to me, 'I know you know the truth.'"

"Did he hurt you in any way?" Bria asked. "I mean, physically."

Pippa shook her head.

Sister Benedicta didn't make the sign of the cross, but she bowed her head and closed her eyes. Bria knew she was saying a prayer of thanks.

"How did you get out of that compartment Massimo locked you in?" Bria asked.

"You know about that?" Pippa replied.

"I do," Bria told her. "Thanks to your barrette."

"Her barrette?" Sister B asked.

"My pink butterfly barrette!" Pippa exclaimed. "I used it to pick the lock and escape the compartment on Imperia's yacht that Massimo was holding me in. I wasn't sure I'd find a safe place to hide before Massimo caught up with me, so I threw it into a corner as a clue that I had been there."

"That was very smart thinking," Bria said. "But, Pippa, why didn't you go straight to the police?"

Although the sunset had created a purple glow, it seemed that a dark cloud hovered over Pippa. She lowered her eyes, not in prayer but in another form of contemplation. A remembrance.

"I've learned that the police can't always be trusted," Pippa admitted. "Massimo is a very powerful man, and the police usually take the side of powerful men."

"Luca doesn't," Bria affirmed. "And Massimo isn't as powerful as you think he is."

"That's because you don't know him like I do," Pippa said.

"That's because I know Imperia," Bria retorted. "She threw him off her yacht when she found out he's been having an affair with Valentina."

Sister Benedicta and Pippa replied in unison, "The tour guide?"

"One and the same," Bria said. "I saw them kissing, took a photo, and showed Imperia. She immediately told Massimo to leave, and that's how we found the compartment he hid you in. He was searching it before he left . . . maybe to release you."

"Or kill me," Pippa said. "I know that sounds outrageous, but he's really starting to lose it."

"You don't have to worry about that any longer," Bria said. "If you trust me, you can trust Luca and the police force in Positano. They're good people, and they'll help you. If you help them."

"I will," Pippa declared. "I'll tell them everything I overheard about Lugo's announcement, Massimo's threat, the money."

"What about the money?" Bria asked.

"Besides that last confrontation I witnessed, they were always arguing about money," Pippa explained. "Massimo made a bunch of new deals for Lugo that he wasn't happy about, even though Massimo told him that their lawyer approved of them all."

"Do you know who the lawyer is?" Sister B asked.

"No, but it's someone in Positano, because right before the party, Massimo told Lugo he had met with the lawyer earlier in the day," Pippa said. "I know Massimo didn't leave the village, because I'm the one who kept his calendar."

"If you kept his calendar, you must know who the lawyer is," Bria said.

"I only know that they called him the mayor," Pippa replied.

"Dante! I'm so glad you could make time in your busy schedule to meet with me."

Bria smiled at Dante, who stood in the doorway of his office, looking every inch like the dubious mayor he was. Slicked-back hair dyed black; smooth, unlined skin, the result of chemical injections and not hereditary; and thin lips spread out into a sly, somewhat sinister smile. Despite the warm weather that made Positano an idyllic paradise almost year-round, Dante wore a three-piece navy pin-striped suit, a white shirt starched to perfection, and a kelly-green tie.

"Bria Bartolucci," Dante whispered. "You know I would cancel an appointment with the president to meet with you."

"Sometimes, Dante, your importance in this community shocks me," Bria said. "I mean, you have so many duties and responsibilities."

Dante blushed and lowered his eyes. The reaction was so perfectly executed Bria couldn't tell if it was natural or staged. Either way, it was entertaining.

"Many fall victim to the false conclusion that being the mayor of Positano is nothing more than a glamour role," Dante demured. "I am more than capable of filling such a glamorous role, as my couture suggests. And I am more than capable of fulfilling the myriad of duties that come my way, such as meeting with a local businesswoman in my exquisitely decorated office."

Dante opened the door farther and stepped back into the room. He took his hand out of his pants pocket and extended it to officially allow Bria entrance into his office. The scent of vanilla and burnt umber wafted in the air from Dante's wrist, but Bria didn't step into the office until she heard the footsteps coming up the stairs.

"It looks like you're even more important than either one of us pretended," Bria said as she looked around the office.

"I think the word you're looking for is *imagined*," Dante corrected.

"You say *patata*," she replied. "As Chef Lugo might say."

"Must you bring up a dead man's name and ruin all the ambiance?" Dante whined.

"That's harsh talk from the dead man's attorney."

Dante spun around dramatically and screeched to a halt when he saw Luca standing in his doorway. He flinched when Luca slammed the door shut behind him. He began to sweat when Luca started walking toward him.

"Why haven't you told me that you're Lugo's lawyer?" Luca asked. "You know that we've been trying to get in touch with him to find out the contents of Lugo's will."

Instead of answering Luca, Dante turned on the heels of his Ferragamo gold-buckle black-leather loafers and faced Bria. "You ambushed me."

"I made an appointment," Bria protested. "I can't help it if your assistant didn't hear me when I said I was bringing a companion."

"More like a reinforcement," Dante said. "I must ask you both to leave. I've just remembered I have another, much more important engagement."

"Another Botox injection?" Bria joked. "Does Dr. Frangi make house calls now?"

Dante pointed a finger to the ceiling. "Do not malign the name of the best plastic surgeon in all of Italy!"

"Don't malign the name of law enforcement by concealing information," Luca stated. "As the murder victim's lawyer, you have a responsibility to cooperate with the police."

"I have no such responsibility, because I am not Chef Lugo's lawyer," Dante declared.

"*Madonna mia*!" Bria cried. "Dante, stop lying! We know you're a lawyer, because Annamaria had to get you to notarize documents to allow the filming to take place in her café."

"And we know that you're Chef Lugo's lawyer, because Pippa overheard him talking about you with Massimo," Luca added.

"That *idiota* heard wrong!" Dante cried. "I'm not Lugo's lawyer. I'm Massimo's attorney!"

Bria and Luca looked at each other, not even trying to conceal their surprise.

"You're Massimo's attorney," Luca said.

"That makes more sense," Bria said.

"It does," Luca replied.

"Yes," Bria said. "Dante and Imperia are friends, and Imperia has known Massimo for years. There's a connection between the two men."

"Well done, Bria," Dante said, smiling, despite his obvious annoyance at being questioned by the police. "I met Massimo years ago, when he was filming corporate videos for Bartolucci Enterprises."

"Then you must know all about the business relationship between Massimo and Lugo," Luca said.

"And if Massimo had any reason to kill Lugo," Bria added.

"Must I remind you two of attorney-client privilege?" Dante asked rhetorically.

"Must I remind you of the mayoral oath you took to protect this village?" Luca said. "We are in the middle of a murder investigation in which your client is one of the prime suspects."

"We know that you and Massimo have met while he's been here in Positano," Bria said.

"Either talk to me now," Luca demanded, "or I will get a subpoena to force you to reveal all the dirty little secrets you keep."

"How dare you suggest my secrets are dirty!" Dante shrieked.

"I'll call Bombalino and tell him all about your clandestine connection to the dead chef," Bria said. "You'll be front-page news."

"I know how much you enjoy being in the headlines," Luca taunted. "But I doubt even you want this kind of publicity."

"*Basta! Bene!*" Dante cried. "Massimo demanded to meet with me to discuss the will!"

That was not what Bria was expecting to hear. Maybe Massimo had had death on his mind before there was any death to think about. It could be a coincidence, or it could be that Massimo had known death was going to visit Positano all along.

"Why would he want to speak with you about his will?" Bria asked.

"Not *his* will. Lugo's."

"Why would he want to speak with you about *Lugo's* will?" Luca asked.

Dante ran his hand through his well-oiled hair and grabbed a clump in his fist. He muttered to himself, and although Bria couldn't hear all the words he was saying, the ones she picked up were enough to make her blush. She hadn't heard a string of obscenities like that since Carlo stubbed his toe in the middle of the night when they first moved to Positano and he was unfamiliar with the layout of their bedroom.

"Because Massimo wanted to change the contents of Lugo's will so that he would be the sole beneficiary and everything would be left to him."

"Massimo can't make changes to Lugo's will," Bria said.

"Yes he can," Luca replied. "Isn't that right, Dante?"

Dante took three giant steps to his front door, and Bria thought he was going to continue walking right out into the hallway, down the stairs, and escape into the village, but he didn't. He opened the door, and as grandly as he had allowed her entrance, he now bid them both adieu.

"I will say nothing more on the matter," Dante declared. "Now leave."

"Not until you confirm what we already know," Luca said.

Bria leaned in close to Luca and whispered, "What is it that we're supposed to know?"

"*Ah per l'amor di Dio*!" Dante cried. "Do I have to spell it out for you?"

"Yes!" Bria snapped. "Obviously, you do!"

"Massimo had power of attorney over all of Lugo's documents!" Dante cried. "He had the power to change Lugo's will without the dumb chef ever knowing it!"

"*Uffa*! If that's not a reason to kill a man," Bria said, "I don't know what is."

CHAPTER 23

"Valentina!"

Bria heard the sound of her own voice, and it made her cringe. Her normally low, almost husky register had completely disappeared. In its place was a voice she hardly recognized. She knew why it sounded different: Valentina made her nervous.

Signorina Travanti or Signora Gordonato, or whatever her name really was, had power. She was like the girls Bria remembered from high school, the ones who possessed poise and guile beyond their years. From afar, she and Rosalie were fascinated by them, but whenever they were in their company, they were intimidated. Because they knew those girls would use everything they had—their physical beauty and their mental cunning—to get what they wanted. They had no problem destroying anyone or anything that threatened their path toward victory.

Bria might be older and more confident now, but whenever a woman like Valentina looked at a woman like Bria, the way Valentina was doing now, the insecure girl Bria once was, who cowered in the presence of the school bully, was reawakened. Bria needed to tell that girl to go back to sleep, or else her plan would fail. The only reason she had invited Valentina to Bella

Bella was to be able to question her, in hopes of finding out if Massimo really was capable of killing Chef Lugo.

"*Ciao*. I'm so glad you could come," Bria called out as she walked into the sitting room. Valentina was standing and looking at a painting done by Antonio de Leito, one of the local artists who sold his art down by the beach. "I thought you were bringing Genie so she and Bravo could have a play-date?"

"They're already playing," Valentina replied. "Outside with Marco."

"*Bene*. Those two have a thing for each other," Bria said. "Hopefully, with Marco as their chaperone, they won't get into any trouble."

"Don't count on it. Genie takes after her mamma." Valentina turned to face Bria. "I think you've already figured out that her mamma can be trouble."

Valentina threw her head back and laughed. She ran her hand through her blond hair, extending her neck, and placed her other hand on her hip. Bria thought she was watching a scene play out from one of the old *teleromanzi* her *nonna* Josefina would watch. Bria was familiar with them, and she remembered the dialogue was typically shocking in order to keep viewers tuned in. If Valentina was going to act like she was a soap opera vixen, Bria thought it was time to be a worthy scene partner.

Bria took a step forward and folded her arms. "Is that why you were kissing Massimo on the stairs outside my balcony?"

To her credit, Valentina stopped laughing, but the smile on her face didn't disappear. "Did you enjoy spying on us?"

"You can't spy on people who don't care if anyone is watching."

Valentina's smile grew bigger. "I really do like you, Bria. You're a very complicated woman. Just like me."

"There was nothing complicated about what you were doing with Massimo the other night right outside my window."

"You make it sound like we were doing something wrong," Valentina said.

"You were!"

"I know you haven't been single for very long, Bria, but since when is it a crime for a single woman to kiss a single man?"

"It isn't a crime," Bria replied. "Not in the legal definition of the word."

"*Oh andiamo*!" Valentina cried. "Don't tell me you think it's immoral for a woman to kiss a man."

"*Ovviamente no*," Bria said. "You're not a woman, Valentina. You're a widow."

The smallest shadow of anger flared up on Valentina's face. It stayed there for only a few seconds, but Bria saw it. She saw the real Valentina, the bully, rear her very ugly head. "That makes two of us."

Fury rose from Bria's belly, its speed surprising her, and she had to corral her energy so it didn't take control of her. The women might have both lost husbands, but they were far from the same. Bria's husband had been dead for almost a year, and only recently had she felt a stirring in her heart to experience romantic love once again. Valentina's husband had been dead for less than a week, and already she had had a rendezvous with another man.

"Unlike you, Valentina, I didn't kiss another man while my husband was waiting to be buried."

"Would you like a medal?" Valentina sneered. "I'm sure there's someone in the village who could whip one up."

This was a different Valentina than the one Bria had previously encountered. Before, she could have been described as mysterious and carefree, but now Bria saw an edge to her, a hostility, that she hadn't seen before. It made Bria think that Massimo might not be the only one capable of murder. Before she could think of the ramifications of that concept, Bria needed to make sure she had her facts straight.

"You don't deny it, then, that you are Signora Valentina Gordonato?" Bria asked.

Valentina walked into the dining room and poured herself a cup of coffee from the ceramic carafe on the sideboard. "Officially, that's my name, but I've always used my maiden name, Travanti. Guess I'm just a modern gal."

"Were you also a bitter bride?" Bria asked.

"Why would you ask that?" Valentina replied.

"I saw you push Lugo away when he kissed you the night of his party," Bria said. "You practically recoiled from his touch."

Valentina raised her cup to Bria. "You're quite the Peeping Tom, aren't you? Or would that be Peeping Thomasina?"

"Make jokes if you want," Bria said. "The fact remains that you're a liar."

"Oh no! I am many things, but I am not a liar."

"*Oh davvero*? You kept it a secret that you came to Positano to follow your husband, and said that you wanted to experience living in the country where your father was born," Bria said. "I call that lying."

"You can call it whatever you want, Bria, but you're wrong," Valentina said. "I was just as surprised to see Louis here as he was to see me."

"Yet you lied about knowing him, and I'm sure you lied about loving him, too!"

Valentina's blue eyes seemed to darken a few shades as she glowered at Bria. "I did not take you for one of those self-righteous women who think *their* definition of love is the only one that counts. I loved my husband, maybe not in the way that you loved yours, but I loved him all the same."

"Then why didn't you come forward after he died? Why did you deny knowing Chef Lugo when Pippa mentioned him on our tour? And why were you kissing Massimo when you should have been grieving your husband?"

Bria's voice was no longer high pitched. It was her usual alto, but it wasn't her own. She had given in to her emotions. She had wanted to interrogate Valentina to get her to reveal the truth about her relationship with Chef Lugo, and instead, Bria had revealed her own self. She did not judge others, but she was disgusted by Valentina's actions. To Bria, Valentina had dishonored her dead husband, and that was one of the worst crimes a wife could commit.

The argument had escalated to such a frenzied state that neither woman noticed Tobias and Daisy emerge from their room and come down the stairs. It was only when Tobias cleared his throat that either woman noticed them. Valentina turned away and drank her coffee, while Bria apologized.

"*Mi dispiace tanto*," Bria said. "I didn't realize you were here."

"That's quite all right," Tobias said. "Even in paradise there are arguments."

"I can't believe Chef Lugo was married," Daisy commented.

Valentina whipped around and looked directly at Daisy. "Why would you say that?"

"Because other than Bria and the police, it doesn't seem like anyone cares that the poor man died."

Valentina continued to stare at Daisy, but her sneer faded. Her blue eyes softened. There were no tears, but it was obvious that she was stung by the comment. "I was married to a lovely young man named Louis Gordon, and our marriage was perfect. Eventually, he grew up and became someone named Luigi Gordonato, Chef Lugo to his fans. When his star began to rise, our marriage began to end."

"Some marriages are like that." Tobias took the book he was holding and placed it on the side table in the sitting room. "They separate when one person can't see that what they have is enough, because they have a hunger for just a little bit more."

"Sounds like you knew Louis very well," Valentina observed.

"No, not at all. I'm just an old man who's always known that everything I have is right here." Tobias reached out to clutch Daisy's hand, and she willingly took it. The wrinkles around her lips and eyes crinkling with a sweet smile. "Daisy is all I will ever need, but not every man thinks like me."

"Once upon a time, Louis thought that way," Valentina said. "Until he and Massimo hatched this plot to take him to the next level. That's when everything was ruined."

Tobias cleared his throat again. "We should go. We don't want to miss the ferry."

"I'll say a prayer for your late husband," Daisy said. "We're going to the Duomo di Ravello. It was my favorite church when I was a little girl, and I want to share it with Tobias."

"The Duomo is beautiful," Bria said. "Take a moment to sit in the square, and if you go into the gift shop, say hello to Angelina. She's been working there for as long as I can remember."

"We will," Daisy said. *"Addio."*

After Daisy and Tobias left, Valentina turned to Bria, looking more like the fun, happy-go-lucky woman Bria had first assumed she was. "I didn't mean to shock your guests."

"I don't think you shocked them," Bria said. "They're older and not used to women acting in a certain way."

"I will not be shamed by you, Bria. I can kiss any man I want to."

"Then why do it in the shadows?" Bria asked. "Why do it with a man who was your husband's business partner?"

"You've seen Massimo. He can very persuasive."

"You did not look like you needed to be persuaded to be in his arms," Bria said. "You were exactly where you wanted to be."

Valentina put down her coffee cup and picked up her bag, which was hanging off the back of one of the chairs. "Some men you kiss because you want them to know what's in your heart, and other men you kiss so they never find out." Valentina turned and walked toward the front door. "*Ciao*, Bria. I'm taking Genie, and we're leaving."

"*Aspetta!*" Bria cried. "Tell me what you don't want Massimo to know."

"*Cin cin*, Bria. *Buona giornata!*"

No! I will not have a nice day! Bria thought.

The front door slammed behind Valentina, and Bria wanted to scream. She had failed. She had gotten confirmation about Valentina's relationship with Chef Lugo, but she hadn't gotten any facts that pointed to Massimo being a murderer. When she got a text from Luca telling her to meet him at Casa Violetta, she realized that this information wasn't necessary for the village to see some justice.

Nestled into a curve in Viale Positano, about two levels higher than Bella Bella, was Casa Violetta, another one of the village's many bed-and-breakfasts. It was where Massimo had moved after Imperia threw him out and where he planned on staying until he and the rest of his production crew were given the okay to leave town. He was stunned when he found out he was getting to leave early.

"What the hell is going on?" Massimo bellowed. "Don't you know who I am?"

"We know exactly who you are," Luca replied. "Which is why we're putting you under arrest."

"I didn't kill Lugo!" Massimo cried.

"But you did kidnap me!"

Luca stepped out of the way to reveal Pippa standing in the doorway of the B and B. Massimo tried to conceal his shock and fear as the woman approached him, but the left side of his face trembled slightly. The woman he had kidnapped, bullied, and berated might just be his downfall.

Bria stood in the doorway, having brought Pippa to the Casa Violetta after Luca had told her he and Nunzi were on their way to arrest Massimo. Luca had asked Bria to escort Pippa, unsure how she would handle the situation. When Pippa slapped Massimo hard across his cheek, Luca realized he had been right. He never expected that, and neither did Massimo.

"How dare you!" Massimo seethed. "Did you tell them? I'll kill you if you opened your stupid little mouth!"

Enraged, Massimo raised his right arm, his open palm eager to make contact with Pippa's face. He would have succeeded if Nunzi didn't have such quick reflexes. She grabbed Massimo's wrist, wrenched it behind him, and snapped on a handcuff. Then she yanked his other arm behind his back and joined his wrists together with another click of the metal bracelet. Even a man as tall and as powerfully built as Massimo was no match for Officer Della Monica.

"*Buon lavaro*, Nunzi," Luca said. "Now we can arrest you for attempted assault in addition to kidnapping."

"Would you like to confess to Chef Lugo's murder and make it a trifecta?" Nunzi asked.

"Don't say a word, Massimo."

Bria knew the voice and wasn't surprised to find Dante standing behind her when she turned around. She knew Luca hadn't forewarned Dante that he was going to arrest Massimo, but the village was small, and rumors spread easily. She couldn't fully blame Dante, though. He might be shady, but he was only doing his job.

"I'm innocent!" Massimo cried. "That *piccola stronza* can't prove anything!"

"This little bitch is going to make you pay for everything you've done!" Pippa screeched.

She brought her arm back and was prepared to strike Massimo once more, but she was stopped by Nunzi's quick action. "Twice would be overkill, Pippa. It's also not fair to hit a man when he's handcuffed."

"You think you've won, Pippa?" Massimo reeled. "Think again! The second I get out of these things, you'll pay!"

"Massimo! *Stai zitto!*" Dante shouted, as he marched up to Massimo. "From here on in, *I'll* do all the talking."

Dante followed Nunzi as she ushered Massimo out of the B and B while reading him his rights. Bria almost felt sorry for him. She knew Dante had agreed to be Massimo's lawyer and had probably helped him straddle some questionable legal lines, not to mention moral ones, by attempting to adjust Lugo's will, but representing a kidnapper, a potential murderer, and an all-around *scocciatoreo* was not what Dante had expected when he took on Massimo as a client. If you lay down with dogs, your suit, no matter if it was expensive and bespoke, got covered with fleas.

"*Scusate*, Violetta, for the interruption," Luca said. "We'll be leaving now."

"Not a worry, Luca," Violetta replied. "I would never have let this criminal stay here had I known what he was."

"Pippa," Luca said, "I'll need you to come with me to the station to make an official statement."

"That would be my pleasure," Pippa replied.

"Bria," Luca said, "are you coming with us?"

Bria was about to say yes, but she saw Violetta with her hand pressed against her heart. She didn't think the woman was in any medical distress, but she did look like she could use a friend. "I'll catch up with you in a bit."

"*Bene*," Luca said before leaving behind Pippa.

"Are you all right, Violetta?" Bria asked.

"*Sì, sì, sto bene*," she replied. "To think I had a murderer in my home . . ."

"That hasn't been proven yet," Bria insisted. "You did rent a room to a kidnapper."

Startled, Violetta realized Bria had made a joke, and quickly joined in the laughter.

"At this time of year, I'm normally fully booked, but since September, I've had more cancellations than usual," Violetta explained. "When Massimo inquired about a room, he had several to choose from."

Bria didn't know why this information made her gut tingle, but it did. She thought about it and realized she had been in the same boat. The only reason Pippa, Tobias, and Daisy were staying at Bella Bella was because she, too, had had cancellations. The travel and hospitality business was not as easy to predict as some imagined.

"I think Annamaria has some leftover sage from when she cleansed her café after Chef Lugo died there," Bria said. "It might make you feel better if you did the same."

"What a wonderful idea!" Violetta said. "Annamaria was right about you, Bria. You really are a wonderful addition to the village."

On her walk to the police station, Bria was still reeling from Violetta's comment. Positano was her home; the people who lived here had quickly become her friends. She saw two of them through the window of A Word from Positano and was compelled to say hello. She knew that Mimi was still upset that the book tour had been canceled. Although her bookstore was always filled with customers, Mimi was a true entrepreneur and was always conjuring up new ways to increase her sales. Not all those ideas were successful.

"Bria!" Mimi shouted when she saw her walk through the door. "You're just the person I was looking for."

"What have I done now?" Bria joked.

"Nothing except help the police arrest Chef Lugo's murderer and Pippa's kidnapper," Annamaria announced.

"We still don't know if Massimo killed Lugo," Bria corrected. "Wait a second! That just happened a few minutes ago. How did you already find out about it?"

Annamaria shrugged her shoulders, and her heavy bosom rose a few inches. "People tell me things."

"Aldo's always trying to get her to write for his paper," Enrico said.

"I prefer to give my knowledge away for free," Annamaria said.

"Which means she likes to gossip," Enrico retorted.

Annamaria playfully slapped Enrico on the shoulder and howled with laughter. It was wonderful to see the woman back to her old self after being traumatized by the events that had played out in her café. Mimi, however, was taking longer to recover.

"Massimo should be arrested for refusing to take me up on my brilliant idea," Mimi said.

"Which brilliant idea was that?" Enrico asked. "You have so many on a daily basis."

Ignoring the good-natured jab, Mimi pulled out a rolling pin from behind the counter, where she was standing. "This idea."

It took a moment, but Bria remembered. Mimi had wanted Chef Lugo to use a rolling pin with her bookstore's logo on it during the filming. The prop would serve to publicize the upcoming book tour to a much larger audience than a TV show could reach. Massimo had flatly turned down Mimi's idea and had made her leave with her rolling pin. If that was the case, why wasn't the bookstore's logo on the rolling pin that Mimi was now holding?

"I must have taken the wrong rolling pin back with me," Mimi announced. "I thought you should give it to Luca, in case he could use it as evidence."

"Why can't you just bring it to Luca yourself?" Annamaria asked.

"No one sees Luca more than Bria," Mimi replied. "I thought she'd be the best courier."

Bria watched as Mimi, Annamaria, and even Enrico exchanged smiling glances. It was obvious that they were trying to do some matchmaking, which was ironic, because Bria was always trying to find ways to turn Enrico and Mimi into a couple. Could these three see the same thing when they observed Bria and Luca together? Bria couldn't ponder that now; she had a delivery to make.

"*Grazie*, Mimi." Bria grabbed the rolling pin. "I'll put this right in Luca's hands."

Bria waved a little flirtatiously as she left the bookstore and was delighted to see that her three friends enjoyed the show.

What Bria didn't always enjoy was the traffic on the streets of Positano. Especially the speeding Vespa coming right toward her. As the scooter swerved inches before hitting Bria, she saw the face of the driver. It was Michele.

Bria leapt onto the sidewalk, which luckily wasn't concrete but a soft patch of dirt that cushioned her fall. Michele wasn't as lucky and landed in the middle of the street. His Vespa was on top of him, and the bag of groceries he was carrying had burst, its contents now spread out around him. Bria noticed that among the oranges, lemons, and bread were two shattered bottles of wine, their contents staining the street and flowing in several streams toward her. Had Michele been drinking while driving? Was that why he had almost rammed into her? Or had his action been deliberate?

"*Per l'amor di Dio!*" Bria said. "Were you driving drunk?"

"No!" Michele protested. "I would never do that."

"Then why were you driving like you were drunk!"

"*Mi scusi*! I should've put the bag in the storage compartment, but I was just heading to the garage and I was already late, and then I saw you and got startled."

"I startled *you*?" Bria cried. "You almost ran me over."

"I'm so sorry. Please forgive me," Michele said.

Bria wasn't sure what to think. The adrenaline racing through her veins was making it difficult to think at all. She didn't know if she should trust Michele or add this to the growing list of reasons why she needed to convince Rosalie never to speak to him again. For a moment, she heard her the voice of her mother, who always said, "You never kick a man when he's down."

"I do," Bria said.

"*Grazie mille.*"

"Let me help you clean things up," Bria said. "I hope the wine wasn't expensive."

"No, Zio Paolo likes the cheap stuff," Michele joked. "Oh no! You're rolling pin broke in half. Please, let me replace it."

Bria was about to inform Michele that this wouldn't be necessary. She was sure neither Massimo nor Pippa was going to need the prop, and she doubted it was going to be useful to the police, since so many hands had touched it already. When Michele screamed, Bria had no idea how wrong she was.

Bria didn't know why Michele had mentioned his former guardian's name or why he was bent over the rolling pin and holding several pieces of paper. She bent down right next to him to look closer and saw that the rolling pin was hollow and papers had fallen out of it when it broke on the ground. She stifled her own scream when she saw the name scribbled at the bottom of one of the pages: *Mamma Rita*.

"What are these?" Bria asked.

"They're Mamma Rita's original recipes," Michele replied. "They were hidden in this rolling pin."

"*Dio mio!*" Bria cried. "Lugo didn't just run away from Mamma Rita. He ran away with all her recipes, too."

Chapter 24

Evening boat parties in Positano were not unusual; they were one of the reasons people flocked to the Amalfi Coast. Being rocked gently by the sea as the sun disappeared behind the horizon, creating an almost dreamlike backdrop to the festivities. Idolizing the pastel building blocks stacked on top of each other in a random, chaotic design that formed the façade of Positano. Gazing at it all from behind dark sunglasses, while wearing an outfit made of linen, and sipping a sweet, intoxicating cocktail were all part of the experience. This was not that kind of party.

Knowing another trip to the police station might make Michele regress and become uncooperative, Bria had taken Michele straight to Rosalie's boat. Michele's Vespa had survived the spill, with only one dent to its frame and a few scratches on its body, which could be fixed with some red paint. They had gathered up the fallen groceries, cleaned up the wine spill, put the rolling pin and the recipes in a storage compartment, and driven to the marina.

Once on Rosalie's boat, Bria called Luca and Michele called Paolo to ask them to join them. Even though Rosalie cut up a stick of pepperoni and placed the pieces on a charcuterie board, surrounded by chunks of cheese and an assortment of olives, and added a bottle of orange limoncello to the tableau on the table on her deck, the atmosphere was far from festive.

Bria updated Rosalie on Massimo's recent arrest and the unexpected discovery of Mamma Rita's recipes. Had they been alone when Bria shared the news, Rosalie would have gasped loudly, gestured dramatically, and pestered Bria frantically to get her to share every morsel of the titillating story. Michele's presence caused Rosalie to act differently.

While Bria whispered details to Rosalie, Michele stood at the railing and stared out at the sea. Bria was moved to see her friend quell her natural inquisitiveness in consideration of this man whom she hardly knew but whom she obviously wanted to know better.

Once Bria had shared the news, Rosalie rose from her seat and headed to the starboard side of the houseboat and stood by Michele at the railing. Unable to suppress her own protective nature, Bria got up and positioned herself close to Rosalie in case her friend needed her support. Bria had nothing to worry about, Rosalie didn't need support, she was giving it.

Rosalie turned to face Michele, but he was peering out at the evening sky. "How are you feeling?"

"Angry, shocked, numb," Michele replied, not turning to face Rosalie. "It keeps changing moment by moment."

"We're going to figure this out," Rosalie said. "Well, at least Bria will. I'll tag along for the ride."

Michele's laugh was shy at first, as if the sound of it didn't deserve to be heard. Bria wondered if Michele felt his voice shouldn't be heard, either. She had no idea what it was like to be raised by strangers, good people but still not his own parents. Then to be blindsided by Lugo's departure and, worst of all, Mamma Rita's suicide. That kind of damage was hard to heal. But not impossible.

"*Grazie*, Rosalie," Michele said, finally turning to face her. "You, too, Bria."

"For what?" Bria asked.

"For making me forget that I wished I had killed a man."

By the time Luca and Paolo arrived, the wishes to commit homicide had been forgotten and the focus was on trying to figure out if the recipes dislodged from the prop rolling pin really had at one time belonged to Mamma Rita. First, Paolo had to admit to sharing Michele's backstory with Bria, and she, in turn, had to admit to visiting Teresina in Frosinone. Michele's response was as surprising as always. He didn't get angry; he was concerned.

"How is Teresina?" he asked.

"*Bene*," Bria replied. "She thought at first that something had happened to you."

"I'm sure she thought I was in some kind of trouble," Michele replied. "Of my own doing."

"That's exactly what she thought," Rosalie told him.

"She was always very smart," Michele replied.

"Teresina was just as concerned about you, Paolo," Bria added.

"She and I have had many differences over the years," Paolo said, "but she's a good woman."

"It ran in their family," Michele replied. "Mamma Rita was the kindest woman I've ever known."

The mention of the woman's name did the opposite of what was necessary. Instead of launching them into a discussion, it drew everyone into silence. But silence wasn't going to get to the bottom of this mystery.

Bria held up one of the recipes. "*Scusa*, but are you certain these are Mamma Rita's?"

"Absolutely," Michele replied.

"It isn't that I don't believe you," Luca said. "But how can you be sure?"

"I understand," Michele said. "It's in a cop's nature not to believe things someone says. Especially someone like me."

"It's in a cop's nature to want to uncover the truth," Paolo corrected, his voice soft but stern.

Michele tilted his head in Luca's direction and raised his hands, palms facing forward, in a show of atonement. *"Sì, scusami."*

In response, Luca held up his hand, palm forward, and waved it to the side. An apology was unnecessary but was accepted. "Can you prove these recipes are Mamma Rita's?"

Michele nodded. "Yes."

"How?" Luca asked.

"They have her name on them."

"They could have been forged," Bria said.

Michele reached forward and pushed the charcuterie board out of the way. A few olives rolled to the side and would have fallen to the deck if Rosalie hadn't quickly extended a hand to catch them. The mechanic picked up the papers and started rifling through them, searching for a clue that would back up his conviction.

"Qui!" Michele exclaimed, pointing to a recipe. "Look at the ingredients!"

They all leaned forward to read the ingredients for zeppole, a favorite Italian pastry.

"Mamma Rita is the only person I know who uses anchovy butter in her zeppole," Michele stated.

"Margherita did love her anchovies," Paolo commented, remembering that fact.

"And this," Michele said, pointing to another recipe. "Who adds mushrooms to *bussolai*?"

"That is odd," Bria said. "*Bussolai* are just twisted bread dough."

"Mamma Rita's were savory," Michele said. "She would put some in my lunch bag so I could snack on them after school."

Bria smiled. "I do the same kind of thing for Marco."

"I think you mean Giovanni does the same kind of thing," Rosalie joked.

"I'm sure it doesn't matter to Marco," Michele said. "All that matters is that someone remembered."

Another silence. Followed by another outburst when Michele grabbed another recipe.

"That's it!" Michele cried. "That's all the proof you need to know that these are Mamma Rita's recipes."

Everyone looked at the piece of paper Michele was pointing at. It was a recipe for chocolate chip cookies made with olive oil and a touch of cinnamon. Different than the norm, but hardly extraordinary. What made it a smoking gun was its name.

"Giancarlo's Favorite," Luca read.

"Mamma Rita's son," Bria gasped.

"The son who died of a drug overdose," Paolo said.

"The first son to break her heart," Michele claimed. "The second was the American."

"Louis Gordon," Paolo said. "May he rot in hell."

"He may be," Bria said.

"*Che cosa*?" Paolo said. "Do you know where that *bastardo* is?"

"He's in the morgue, Zio," Michele answered. "Louis Gordon grew up to be Chef Lugo."

"*Dio mio*," Paolo whispered. "Well, may God rest his soul, anyway."

"You hadn't made the connection?" Luca said.

"No," Paolo replied. "After Rita died, I lost touch with Michele and Teresina, and I did what most old men do when faced with painful memories, I blocked them out. I rarely thought about them or Louis again." Paolo didn't look at Michele, but he placed a hand on his. "I'm not proud of how I acted, but I'd like to think I've been given the chance to make up for my past."

Michele placed his hand over Paolo's and looked straight ahead at Luca. "It's what every man deserves, Zio."

"I'll need both of you to come to the station to give statements about these recipes," Luca said.

"*Certo*," Paolo said. "But why?"

"These are very important clues, Paolo," Bria told him.

"Why were they in Annamaria's rolling pin?" Michele asked.

"It isn't Annamaria's rolling pin," Bria corrected. "It's a prop that Lugo was using in his show. Mimi wanted Lugo to use a different one, they got mixed up, and she's had Lugo's all this time. She gave it to me to bring to Luca, and if you hadn't run me off the road, we might never have known what it concealed."

"You almost ran Bria off the road!" Paolo yelled. "What are you? *Pazzo*?"

"It was an accident," Bria said. "Michele swerved so he wouldn't hit me, and he could've hurt himself badly."

"Is that why there are no wine bottles with the rest of the groceries?" Paolo asked.

"*Scusi*," Michele said. "I'll buy you another bottle."

"I gave you money for two!" Paolo cried.

"*Bene*, I'll buy you two more bottles," Michele assured him.

"I have some bottles of wine," Rosalie interjected. "Take some of mine."

Michele shook his head. "They're probably too good for Zio."

"Michele!" Rosalie gasped.

"No, he's right," Paolo told her. "I only drink cheap wine."

As they were laughing, Bria could see Michele's brow furrow. Something wasn't adding up for him.

"Do you know if anyone gave Lugo the prop rolling pin?" Michele asked.

"No one handed it to him," Bria said. "I was in the back room with Lugo when Mimi came in, and she and Massimo argued about which rolling pin to use."

"Then she left with what she thought was her rolling pin, but it was really the prop with the recipes hidden inside," Michele said.

"Exactly," Luca told him. "I'm surprised Lugo wasn't holding the rolling pin at all times or keeping it close to him. Those recipes could literally prove that he was a fraud."

"*Uffa*!" Bria exclaimed. "That's why Massimo called Lugo a phony chef!"

"When did he say that?" Luca asked.

"Pippa told me that Massimo and Lugo had been arguing and Massimo called him a phony chef," Bria explained. "I thought it was because Lugo was masquerading as a native-born Italian, but I was wrong. It was because Lugo stole all his recipes from Mamma Rita before he ran away from her home."

"I cannot believe he betrayed her like that," Michele said. "She loved him like a mother, like he was her biological son."

"Not all people are good," Paolo stated. "No matter how they're raised."

"I suspected Chef Lugo was Louis, but I was hoping I was wrong," Michele said. "Even when I was hiding in the closet, I was praying it was all a mistake."

"It's hard to imagine that someone could do such a terrible thing," Rosalie sighed.

"Lugo may have done some terrible things," Bria said, "but I think he wanted to change."

"How could you know that?" Paolo asked.

"Lugo was going to make an announcement on live television, something, he said, that was going to change everything," Bria stated. "Until now, we couldn't imagine what he wanted to say. All we knew was that it would somehow upset Massimo."

"Because Massimo already knew the truth," Michele said. "He knew what Louis or Chef Lugo, or whatever he called himself, had been hiding all these years."

"Yes," Bria said. "Massimo knew that if Lugo went through with his announcement, it would destroy not only Lugo's career but his, as well."

"Now we know what Lugo was going to confess," Luca added.

"He was going to tell the world that he was a liar, a fraud, and that none of the recipes that had made him famous were his," Bria said. "He was going to confess to stealing them from Mamma Rita."

"You think that's why Massimo killed him?" Rosalie said.

"It's a solid motive," Bria answered.

"You sound more like a cop every day," Rosalie told her. "What about you, *fratello*? Does the real cop agree?"

"I do," Luca replied. "This revelation proves that Massimo had a motive to keep Lugo silent. If he had told the truth, it would have been the end of his career, and once word got out that Massimo knew about the scam and even participated in it, his career would be over, too."

"Massimo also had the means and the opportunity to poison Lugo's espresso before he went on the air," Bria added. "He knew that the poison would work quickly and would prevent Lugo from sharing their secret. It was the only way Massimo could stop him."

"We should have the toxicology report back in a day or so to corroborate that," Luca said. "Add to that Massimo kidnapping Pippa to keep her quiet, and it paints the picture of a powerful man desperate to keep his world from imploding."

Michele jumped up from the table, hurried over to the starboard gunwale, and held on to the railing. There was music in the distance from one of the clubs and some muted laughter, but they could still hear him sobbing. Rosalie was the first to go over and stand next to Michele and place her hand on his back. She didn't say anything, but at least he knew he wasn't alone.

"I still can't believe it was really him," Michele stammered. "How I would have loved to confront him and make him pay for what he did to Mamma Rita."

"Michele!" Paolo scolded. "Haven't you learned violence isn't the solution?"

"You weren't there!" Michele turned around and pointed his finger at Paolo. "You stayed in your garage here in this perfect little village, while I was in Frosinone with Mamma Rita."

"I'm sorry, Michele."

"I saw how devastated she was when Louis ran away. She was heartbroken. I think we all knew what she was going to do, but we prayed she would find her way out of the darkness." Michele slammed his palms down onto the railing. "She didn't, and it was all his fault!"

Mamma Rita wasn't the only who had her heart broken. When she died, she took a piece of Michele with her. His pain, though understandable, was difficult to watch. But not for Rosalie. The tears in her eyes undoubtedly blurred her vision, but she didn't turn away like the others did. Bria was convinced that if Michele gave Rosalie the chance, she could help him heal.

A good night's sleep healed most everything. When Bria woke up the next morning, she felt energized. It had been a difficult night filled with revelations, pain, and tears, but now when she looked out her window and saw two green-bellied sparrows on the branches of the lemon tree on her balcony and heard the sweet melody of their chirping, she couldn't dwell on the ache of the previous evening. She needed to embrace the splendor of the morning.

There was also something about her routine that was filled with splendor. Getting dressed, waking Marco, drinking her Arabica Robusta coffee as she watched him eat his Vitabella cereal and give some pieces to Bravo, who sat patiently at his side—these were all small gifts that she cherished. Without them, she knew her world would be empty.

They walked to school, and Marco explained what was going to happen at his Holy Communion ceremony, how they were going to receive the body of Christ and pledge their allegiance to God. She got the sense that he was doing more than reciting words that he had been taught in school, that he truly understood what the service meant. Her son was growing up right before her eyes.

Their morning ritual continued as they greeted Sister Benedicta at the gates to St. Cecilia's.

"*Ciao*, Sister B!" Marco exclaimed.

"*Ciao*, Marco," she replied. "*Buongiorno*, Bravo."

Like he did every morning, Bravo pranced up to the Sister and took the treat she surreptitiously held by her side. Marco giggled, as he always did, and then ran to meet Tomaso and the rest of his classmates. Bria was waiting for Sister Benedicta to tell the students to line up and get ready to go inside, but Sister Carolina, an older nun who, she recalled, was a distant relative of Annamaria's, assembled the students instead. What was going on? Why wasn't Bria's routine being more routine?

"Today's the day, Bria," Sister Benedicta said.

"The day for what?"

"For me to finally get to drive your Fiat!" Sister B positively beamed, and then her skin went gray. "If you're free. Are you?"

"I don't have any plans for the rest of the day," Bria exclaimed.

Even if she did have plans, she would have canceled them all. There was no way Bria could disappoint a nun who wanted nothing more than to go for a drive on a beautiful day.

"Wonderful!" Bria cried. "I guess Mother Superior said it's time to go to Ravello to pick up the ceramic angels for the children."

For a moment, Sister B looked like she didn't know what Bria was saying. "Oh yes, Ravello, for the angels. Yes, of course. That's the only reason we're going for a drive."

Bria hooked her arm around Sister B's. Sometimes it was good to break a routine.

Fifteen minutes later Bria was in the passenger seat of her Fiat convertible as Sister Benedicta sat behind the wheel. The top was down, and they were bathed in the glorious sunshine that drenched the Amalfi Coast. Bria rarely got to ride in the Fiat without being the one driving, so the trip was as much of a thrill for her as it was for Sister Benedicta.

Watching the Sister's smile and seeing her habit flap in the wind was the perfect tonic Bria needed. It was better than her *nonno*'s homemade limoncello, even better than Annamaria's espresso. It was reassurance that the world was getting back to normal. She could focus on the new guests who would soon come to Bella Bella and her son's upcoming Holy Communion.

Bria and Sister B squealed with delight as the nun met the twisting turns of the road to Ravello with a teenager's joy. It was obvious by how expertly Sister B handled the vintage car that she came from a mechanic's family. She was familiar with how a car felt and maneuvered on the road. She seemed as comfortable in the driver's seat as she did in a church pew.

Even after they arrived in Ravello, had met with the manager of the ceramic factory, and were almost finished with their errand, Sister B was still beaming. "*Grazie mille*," Sister B said. "This will be a day to remember."

"For both of us," Bria replied.

Bria placed the final box of ceramic angels in the trunk of the Fiat and slammed the lid shut. She looked around at the square in the town where she had grown up, and was filled with nostalgia. How many hours had she spent as a child playing just a few feet away? How many hours had she spent kneeling in the church across the courtyard?

"Would you mind if we lit a candle in the Duomo before heading back?" Bria asked.

Sister B roared with laughter. "That's like asking if the Pope's Catholic!"

"*Grazie*," Bria said. "My father recently mentioned the Duomo and guests of mine were here just the other day, which made me realize I haven't visited in quite a while."

The Duomo di Ravello was an imposing, majestic structure made out of white marble. Built in the ninth century, it was a testament to skilled craftsmanship and a little luck, as it had stood the test of time. Inside were several small chapels, designed in a minimalist style, which made the Duomo a popular wedding venue. An intimate setting wrapped in a magnificent outer shell. Looking at the Duomo from the outside, it was impossible to tell what lay waiting inside.

As Sister Benedicta knelt in the back pew, her head bowed and her eyes focused on the rose-scented rosary beads that she always carried with her, Bria walked toward the front of the chapel to light a candle. She hardly had a chance to take in the scenery when she saw a woman placing flowers at the feet of a statue. A woman she had been talking about just the other night.

"Teresina," Bria said. "How nice to see you again."

It took the woman a moment to remember the first time she had met Bria, but when she did, her eyes widened, and she placed a hand over her heart. "It's no surprise that I should see you here."

"Why would you say that?"

"Ever since you came to visit, I haven't stopped thinking about my sister," Teresina shared. "Don't get me wrong. I think of her every day, but since I met you, she's been on my mind all the time. Sometimes . . . I know it sounds foolish . . . but I can feel her presence next to me."

"I hope that's been a comforting feeling."

"It has been, but I felt the need to honor *mia sorella*."

"*Che bello*," Bria said. "A sister should be honored."

"I don't have a gravesite to visit, so I come here." Teresina looked around the church. "This was her favorite, so this is where I come."

"I'm sure she can feel your presence, too," Bria said.

Tears filled Teresina's eyes. Again, there was no embarrassment for the display of emotion; for women like Teresina, tears were part of life. After a moment, she shook her head and wiped her tears with a tissue. "*Perdonami*, but I have a long drive back home, and I need to leave, but it was so good to see you again."

"Likewise," Bria said, hugging the woman.

She watched Teresina leave the church and felt guilty for not having told her everything she knew about Lugo and how he had returned. But what would she have said? She hadn't wanted to spring it on the woman and then leave her to drive for a few hours alone. One day soon—once Massimo was put away in jail—Bria would visit her again and tell her the whole story.

When she reached for a candle, she realized that the story would need to be revised. The puzzle she had thought they put together had just been thrown into the air, all the pieces breaking apart and separating, destroying the picture she had thought was final.

Bria looked at the flowers Teresina had placed at the feet

of the statute of Saint Margherita. How stupid had she been? A major clue had been living right under her roof this entire time, from the very start, and Bria hadn't even noticed.

How in the world had Bria not remembered that the Italian word for "daisy" was *margherita*? Mamma Rita hadn't killed herself. She had run off and married a German doctor. At some point along the way, she had rechristened herself Daisy.

CHAPTER 25

Back at Bella Bella, Bria sat at the dining room table and wondered what the best way was to reveal the truth that Mamma Rita was actually alive and well and sitting across from her, eating a late lunch. Daisy was picking at the mushroom and parmesan frittata Giovanni had made earlier in the day, too busy reading the lead article in the day's issue of *La Vita Positano* to concentrate fully on her food. The headline—TV PRODUCER CHARGED WITH MURDER OF CELEBRITY CHEF—was hard to resist. Everyone who had been in the village the past week had been anxiously waiting to find out how Luigi Gordonato had died. Especially those who knew him as Louis Gordon.

Bria unfolded her copy of the paper and quickly scanned the article to see if Aldo had uncovered Lugo's real identity. Although Bria was mentioned twice as the cohost of the ill-fated cooking show and the person who found Pippa Del Baglivio when she went missing, there was no mention of Louis. The article didn't even contain the fact that Lugo wasn't Italian but American and had a widow named Valentina, who was Positano's latest tour guide. Either Aldo Bombalino had lost his investigative edge or Luca had convinced him to keep their names out of the paper.

She read the rest of the article, which was more about the

rise and fall of Massimo Angelini than the demise of Chef Lugo, and felt a burning in her stomach. Bria wanted to be relieved that Lugo's murderer was being brought to justice, and yet she still had a nagging doubt that the case was not truly closed. There was more to this story.

It could simply be that Bria didn't understand Valentina's role in all of this. If she was Lugo's widow, why wouldn't she immediately come forward and announce it to the public? At that point, Valentina might not have been a real wife to Lugo in the traditional sense of the word, but what was she trying to hide? There were two answers Bria had come up with, neither of which made Valentina appear like the innocent victim she claimed to be.

If Valentina disclosed that she was Chef Lugo's widow, it would have an immediate impact on her career. Who would want to book a tour of a romantic paradise with a grieving widow? Even if that grief-stricken woman was as attractive as Valentina. As a professional strategy, it made perfect sense to keep her true relationship with Lugo a secret.

There was a second, more duplicitous, reason why Valentina had not tarnished her "single lady" brand. If she knew that the contents of her dead husband's will were somehow subject to the whim of his former business partner, her silence gave her the opportunity to cozy up to Massimo and make sure that she wasn't forgotten financially. It was a morally ambiguous route but a smart road to travel if Valentina needed the money.

Luca believed it was an open-and-shut case. Massimo killed Lugo to keep him from telling the world that he was a fraud and that he had become famous only by stealing a dead woman's recipes. That confession would expose Massimo as part of the plot to deceive the public and would irreversibly damage his career. Maybe Massimo didn't mean to kill Lugo but wanted only to warn him that announcing the truth was a foolish thing to do, and thus he poisoned Lugo so he would pass out before he could utter a word about Mamma Rita. The intent might not have been to murder, but that was what Massimo did.

If the theory fit, why was Bria still bothered? It could be because she was sitting across from a woman who had allegedly faked her own suicide and had been mourned for almost the past two decades. Or—because of that revelation—she had learned not to always believe what you had seen.

Bria had witnessed Massimo's violent nature and his proficiency at emotional manipulation firsthand. He was the classic bully, physically and psychologically, who thought he was untouchable, who thought that he could commit whatever crimes he wanted—harassment, kidnapping, even murder—and never get caught. She wanted to believe, unconditionally, that the case was solved and that Lugo's murderer was going to live out the rest of his life behind bars, never to destroy another life again. She wanted to believe that Positano could go back to being the paradise it was, and that she could move on to happier thoughts, like Marco's Communion. She wanted the seaside village she called home to go back to normal. All of that could have happened had Bria not decided to go to church the other day.

When she saw the bouquet of daisies Teresina had laid at the foot of the statue of Saint Margherita, Bria's first instinct was to call Rosalie to tell her what she had just realized. Her second was to race over to the police station, burst into Luca's office, and claim that she had found a woman who had allegedly died decades ago. But she knew she needed proof. More than that, she wanted it.

It was a startling admission, almost as great as realizing Mamma Rita hadn't died. Bria wouldn't admit it to anyone, maybe not even to Rosalie, which was a shocking admission on an even grander level, but Bria didn't want Luca to think she was rash and reckless. She wanted to earn his respect. She flinched when she saw that she was turning her wedding band around and around on her finger, like it was an endless loop with no beginning and no end.

Basta! she silently cried. *One way or another, I'm going to put an end to this!*

The problem was that Bria wasn't entirely sure if she was talking about the investigation, the truth about Mamma Rita, or Luca.

Daisy's gold-framed reading glasses were perched on the edge of her nose, and the left side of her silver bob fell forward while the right was tucked behind her ear, as she continued to read the paper and munch on her frittata. Her ensemble was crisp and tourist ready: sleeveless lilac linen blouse over white cotton cropped pants. She even wore the espadrilles Bria had advised she get at one of the cobblers in the village, since these were, as she told anyone who would listen, the best shoes for walking around town.

To anyone else, Daisy Kruger looked like an ordinary tourist, but Bria knew better. At least she thought she did. She was suddenly overcome with the dreadful suspicion that maybe she was succumbing to fanciful imaginings, something Luca had accused her of doing. Maybe she was turning a coincidence into a fact. Or she could have stumbled upon a truth that would make Luca rethink the entire case.

There was only one way to find out if the woman who was posing as the wife of a German doctor and one of Bella Bella's most recent guests was really Margherita Parisi. The woman everyone, including Positano's most recent fatality, called Mamma Rita.

Initially, when Daisy had said her given name was Daisetta, Bria had thought it was odd. She had never heard the name before, and while made-up names were common with the younger generations, women of Daisy's age were typically given more traditional monikers. There had been no reason to question her comment, especially since Pippa had said her real name was Papina. It wasn't until she'd remembered that *margherita* was the Italian word for "daisy," thanks to Teresina's offering, that she had had reason to consider Daisy to be a liar of epic proportions.

If Bria was going to find the proof she needed to expose the truth without anyone questioning its validity, she needed to act quickly. Tobias and Daisy were leaving Sunday morning, the day after tomorrow. She had to find the proof that Mamma Rita had faked her own death and had returned to her home country to come face-to-face with the man who destroyed her life. To do that, Bria couldn't worry about the consequences.

Bria quickly typed a text message on her cell phone, reread it twice, and pressed the SEND button. She prayed she wasn't making a mistake, because the ramifications could be tumultuous. Fallout be damned. The clock was ticking.

"Sunday is your last day in Positano, isn't it?" Bria asked.

Daisy jumped in her chair and almost spilled the contents of her glass. "*Scusa.* I was so engrossed in this article, you startled me."

"Aldo does know how to report a story."

"He most certainly does," Daisy agreed. "The whole thing is heartbreaking. I can't believe someone tried to poison that poor man."

"*Atroce*," Bria replied. "An absolute shame."

Daisy put down the paper. "I'm sorry. I know you were there when it happened. It must be impossible not to replay the moment when he died whenever anyone talks about it."

"It is difficult not to relive it," Bria confirmed. "I didn't realize he had been murdered at the time, of course, but I was standing right beside him when he died."

Daisy looked away and made the sign of the cross. She tried to conceal the tears that sprung from her eyes, but they fell too freely to hide them. "*Perdonami*. I've been living in Germany for years, but I'm still an old Italian woman."

Mamma Rita is no different than Mamma Fifetta, Bria thought.

Her heart ached for the woman sitting at her table, even if she thought that woman might be Chef Lugo's real killer. But could such a soft-spoken, dainty woman be a killer? It didn't require any physical strength to poison someone, just access to the right toxin and a strong enough conviction. Daisy was the wife of a retired doctor, so she could very easily have a familiarity with chemicals, and as Mamma Rita, she definitely had motive.

If Daisy had found out that Lugo was using her recipes to acquire fame and fortune, she might very easily have snapped. Despite the fact that she considered him a son, Lugo had betrayed her by running away without notice or explanation and then had compounded that betrayal by taking her recipes and exploiting them to fuel his own ambition. Those were heartless, cold-blooded acts of cruelty, especially toward a woman who had offered him a loving home when he had none.

Bria would never truly uncover what kind of man Lugo had been—a sociopath, an opportunist, a lost soul?—but she did have the opportunity to find out what kind of woman Daisy was and if she was capable of premeditated murder. Giovanni was in the kitchen, Pippa was at the police station finalizing some paperwork, and Tobias and Marco were walking Bravo, which meant Daisy and Bria were alone. It was an opportunity to question the potential murderess that Bria couldn't let pass. Unfortunately, she also couldn't prevent it from being interrupted.

"Mamma!" Marco shouted as he threw open the screen door and ran into the house. "Bravo almost died, but I saved him!"

"What?" Bria cried. "*Mio angelo* saved *mio angelo*?"

"That's right." Tobias was grinning from ear to ear as he placed a hand on Marco's shoulder. "You should be very proud of your son."

"Tobias, what happened?" Daisy asked.

"I hope you'll forgive me, Bria, but on our walk, we passed the candy store," Tobias said.

"Sogni di Cioccolato," Marco clarified.

"That's Gianna's old store, which she sold to a couple from Belluno," Bria said. "Let me guess. You couldn't resist having some chocolate for breakfast."

"Close," Tobias replied. "We couldn't resist some gelato."

"Tobias!" Daisy cried. "You know you shouldn't have so much sugar."

"Our time in paradise is winding down, *meine Liebe*," Tobias responded. "Today sugar, but when we're home, it's back to my regular bland diet."

"I didn't know they started selling gelato," Bria said. "Gianna always said she'd add on refrigeration, but she never got around to it."

"They sell gelato now!" Marco exclaimed. "Twenty-seven different flavors."

"Please tell me you didn't try them all," Bria replied.

"*Non essere sciocca, Mamma*," Marco giggled.

"Oh, I'm the silly one?" Bria asked. "Said the boy with the chocolate moustache."

"Tobias, will you take me tomorrow to try the *fragola*?" Marco asked.

"Marco, *basta*!" Bria cried. "Tobias may be busy on his last day on vacation."

"We can squeeze in another trip," Tobias said. "I love strawberry almost as much as chocolate."

"I think we'll sample one gelato per week," Bria said. "Too much of a good thing isn't always good, *mi bambino*."

"Listen to your mamma, Marco. She's right," Tobias stated.

"Tobias should know. He's a doctor," Marco said. "He said I did the right thing by not letting Bravo have any gelato."

"*Ora capisco*," Bria said. "That's why I should be proud of you."

"Yes," Tobias replied. "Bravo tried his best to eat the gelato, but Marco wouldn't let him."

"*Buono*," Bria said. "You remembered I told you that little boys love chocolate, but it could make dogs very sick."

"Like poison," Marco replied.

Bria flinched, and she wondered if Marco noticed. *"Esatta-mente."*

"He sniffed it and smelled the chocolate, but I wouldn't let him taste it," Marco said.

The fire in Bria's stomach exploded. She maintained the smile on her face and hoped she didn't give away the fact that inside she was screaming like the crazy woman her father used to tell her about who lived in his building while he was growing up. Pazza Luci had iron lungs and would sometimes walk the halls of their tenement and scream for hours. Bria didn't know how much longer she could keep her inner Luci quiet. A change of subject was needed.

"Marco, go get cleaned up so Vanni can take you to soccer practice," Bria said.

"Yes, Mamma," Marco replied. "See you later, Tobias."

"*Wiedersehen*," Tobias replied.

"Tobias, I hope you and Daisy don't have any plans tomorrow morning," Bria said. "I'd like to take you both out for your last day in Positano."

Out of the corner of her eye, Bria saw Daisy's expression change. She didn't appear thrilled at the prospect of spending time with Bria. Her husband thought otherwise.

"What a splendid way to end our trip," Tobias announced.

"*Perfetto*!" Bria cried. "I know just where I'd like to take you."

"Tobias, didn't you say you wanted to see the Grotta Azzurra in Capri?" Daisy asked.

"Our tickets are good for any time of day," Tobias replied. "We could go in the afternoon."

"You'll have more than enough time," Bria said. "What I have planned won't take very long at all, but I do want to give you a special send-off."

Bria watched Daisy literally force herself to smile. "That would be lovely, Bria. *Grazie.*"

"Come, Daisy." Tobias extended his hand to his wife. "Let's go for a walk down to the beach and catch the sunset."

"The sun is different here on the Mediterranean than it is in the Rhine region," Bria remarked. *"Divertitevi!"*

From Daisy's expression as she left Bella Bella, Bria wasn't convinced she would have fun, but at least she had agreed to an early morning excursion. That was when Bria would confront her with the truth about Mamma Rita and her belief that she was Chef Lugo's real killer. She wanted to tell Luca everything, but for some reason, she hesitated. When her cell phone rand and she saw that Luca was calling her, she realized the time had come for her to make a decision.

"Ciao, Luca."

"Ciao, Bria. I wanted to tell you that the toxicology report just came in."

"The medical examiner wasn't wrong, was she?" Bria asked. "Lugo was poisoned."

"Yes, he did die from poisoning," Luca confirmed. "The report states that traces of oleander were found on his lips, tongue, and in his lungs."

"Nothing in his bloodstream?"

"Not that they could find, but Carlotta, the examiner, said that isn't as unusual as it sounds," Luca explained. "She did order a second report just to confirm the findings."

Bria was so deep in thought, she didn't respond.

"Bria, are you still there?"

"Yes. *Scusa.*"

"This is good news," Luca said. "We now have confirmation that Lugo was murdered and how Massimo did it."

"I don't know how to tell you this, Luca."

"Tell me what?"

"I can't tell you everything, not just yet."

"Bria, what are you talking about?"

"I'll explain it all tomorrow. Promise me you'll give me until then."

"Give you until then to explain what?"

"That Lugo was definitely poisoned, but Massimo wasn't the murderer."

"What do you mean, it wasn't Massimo?"

"It wasn't, and I can prove it, but I need you to trust me," Bria said.

This time it was Luca who remained silent.

"Do you trust me, Luca?"

"Yes, Bria, I do."

"*Buono*! Here's what I want you to do."

CHAPTER 26

The courtyard outside the Church of Santa Maria Assunta was crowded, as it usually was on a Saturday afternoon. It was a must-see tourist attraction not just for the religious and spiritual, but for anyone who appreciated architectural beauty and was interested in history. The gold-domed church had been an iconic structure of Positano's coastline since it was originally built in the tenth century to house a Byzantine statue of the Virgin Mary. Since then the Church of Santa Maria Assunta had been home to Benedictine monks, nuns, worshippers, and tourists. Today it would welcome a murderer.

Bria felt her heart race a bit as she sat in a pew next to Daisy and Tobias, not because she allowed sacrilege to tarnish the church's walls, but because she wondered if she had made a mistake. She could have called Luca and told him to come to Bella Bella to make an arrest, but instead, she had taken matters into her own hands. What was she trying to prove? That she didn't need Luca? Was she allowing the confusion she was dealing with in her personal life to infringe upon her semiprofessional endeavors? Was she trying to show Luca and the rest of the village that she didn't need to be involved with a man to be successful?

She looked around the church in awe. Even with her chosen

companions by her side and her mission weighing heavily on her mind, it was impossible for her not to be humbled by the glorious interior design. The church was truly built to be a gift to the woman who was arguably the most important maternal figure in the history of mankind—Jesus's mother.

The inside of the dome was white marble, accented by gold so bright that it seemed to be polished daily. A twelve-foot-high Byzantine painting of the Holy Mother seemed to float above the altar in the church's central nave. All around the church's interior were panels of gold seven feet high, so regardless of where you looked, it appeared that you were housed in a gilded cage, protected from the realities of the outside world by a woman who loved unconditionally. A woman like Mamma Rita.

It was clear that Daisy, although having spent years in Germany, had not strayed from her devout Catholic upbringing. She knelt next to Bria, her knees on the cushioned stool, back straight, a rosary in between her clasped wrinkled hands, looking straight at the altar. She was silent, but her lips were moving as she recited the prayer that Bria assumed she had recited every day of her life. That was what Italian women of her age did. Even if they were married to German men who sat dutifully next to them in a church pew but wore the same apathetic look on their faces that they'd have if they were sitting on a chair, waiting for their wives to pick out a dress.

Bria said a silent prayer of thanks that the men in her life—her father, Carlo, Luca, Fabrice, Giovanni, even her brother, Gabrielo—were different. They understood the importance of believing in a higher power, no matter what that power might be. Despite what Bria perceived as a clear lack of religious background, Tobias believed in his wife.

"I used to come here as a child," Daisy whispered. "It's still the same, and yet so much has changed."

Daisy sat back and exhaled deeply. Tobias put his hand over

hers. Curiously, they both stared ahead and didn't look at each other. They might appear to be a devoted couple, but Bria sensed there was something that separated them. A secret perhaps? An unforgivable act? Bria wasn't sure if they were separated by a thin line or an abyss. It was time she found out.

"Let's go outside," Bria suggested. "I'm sure you remember how beautiful the view is."

Daisy smiled knowingly. "There isn't a thing I have forgotten about this village."

Bria held on to her smile, although she felt a decided chill descend upon her, making it difficult to breathe. She wasn't sure if the oppression was from Daisy or was coming from within herself. Only a little bit longer, she reminded herself, and then the whole charade would be over, and Lugo's real killer would be arrested.

Or I'll have made the biggest mistake of my life, Bria thought.

As she exited the church behind Tobias and Daisy, Bria genuflected once more and made the sign of the cross. "Forgive me, Mother," Bria whispered, "for I may just be about to sin." But if a sin was made with the best of intentions, was it still a sin? Bria couldn't worry about such existential notions; she needed to finish what she had started. She needed to expose a killer.

The view from the courtyard was breathtaking. The deep blue Tyrrhenian Sea; the softer blue of the sky, cloudless and unmarred; the sun blazing almost as brightly as the gold inside the church. The ancient statues of the Sirens jutting out from the water, rocky, jagged, and primitive, were juxtaposed with the colorful homes built into the mountain that could be seen on the curve of the land to create a one-of-a-kind vista. Like Daisy had created a one-of-a-kind persona.

"I know that your real name isn't Daisy."

Bria made that announcement just as she joined Daisy and

Tobias at the stone railing at the edge of the courtyard. The church loomed comfortingly yet ominously behind them; in front of them was nothing but sea and a 140-foot drop to the seashore below. Daisy didn't reply; she merely gripped the railing harder, until the thin skin over her knuckles turned white.

"I know that you're Mamma Rita."

Daisy kept her eyes on the horizon as Tobias turned to face Bria. He looked confused, though not at all nervous, and was smiling in a way Bria imagined he had smiled at many scared patients he met in the ER. They didn't have anything to worry about as long as Dr. Kruger was around. He would take care of everything.

"I think you've mistaken my wife for someone else," Tobias said. "Her name is Daisy. Daisetta is on her birth certificate, but she's Daisy to anyone who knows her."

"I don't believe I've mistaken your wife for anyone but who she is," Bria replied. "Margherita Parisi, or Mamma Rita to anyone who knows her."

Tobias's smile grew even wider. "You're serious, aren't you?"

"Very," Bria replied.

"What proof do you have that Daisy is this . . . Mamma Rita?" he asked.

"When you first came to Bella Bella, you told me there had been a mix-up with your reservation at Casa Violetta and there were no more rooms there," Bria began. "I spoke with the owner, and she told me she's had rooms available since September. Why did you lie about that?"

"Lie?" Tobias turned to Daisy, who continued to gaze out at the sea. "I'm sure the owner was trying to cover for the fact that they had mishandled the booking."

"I think your whole second honeymoon was a cover-up and you didn't want anyone to know the real reason you came to Positano," Bria said.

Tobias was rapidly beginning to lose any trace of his smile. "What exactly would that real reason be?"

"Daisy, do you want to explain it, or shall I?" Bria asked.

Tobias opened his mouth to speak, but Daisy silenced him by placing her hand over his. "We found out that Louis was going to film his new television series here the day before it was supposed to begin. We didn't want it to appear that we arrived just for the filming."

"The story about having your reservations canceled and needing a place to stay was all a fabrication," Bria concluded.

"I had to see with my own eyes if it was true," Daisy said. "If this Chef Lugo was really my Louis."

"But you didn't come here just to see him," Bria said. "You came here to kill him."

"Kill him?" Daisy gasped and looked at Bria with confusion, even horror. "That's absurd."

Bria swallowed hard. The next thing she was going to say was very difficult, but she couldn't back down now, not if she wanted the truth exposed.

"You hated him enough to fake killing yourself. Why is it so hard to believe that you hated Louis so much that you'd want to see him dead, too?"

"Because I loved him like my own son," Daisy said. "Even more than my Giancarlo, God forgive me, because I felt that Louis was a gift from heaven. A chance for salvation."

"You felt that Louis needed salvation?" Bria asked.

"Yes." Daisy turned back to the sea and started to cry. "I did."

Tobias put his arm around his wife and whispered in her ear, "It's time we left."

Daisy shrugged her shoulders to free herself from her husband's touch. "No, I'm tired of running, Tobias. I've spent too many years running away from my sins. I need to stop and accept my punishment."

"What sins have you committed?" Bria asked.

"I betrayed my family!" Daisy shrieked. "I let them believe that I had committed the worst sin of all, that I had taken my own life. *Oh caro Dio!* I ran from them just as Louis ran from me, without explanation, without compassion, and without mercy."

Daisy shook her head, a look of disgust etched onto her face. "I knew my sister would be devastated. She suffered right alongside me when my Giancarlo died. But that didn't stop me. I knew that Michele would be crushed . . . another mother abandoning him, and I knew that he still needed me, but that didn't stop me. I left a suicide note and ran."

Bria lowered her eyes; she couldn't look directly at the woman. "I can't imagine how desperate you must have felt to take such drastic action."

"After my Giancarlo died, I didn't think I could take another heartache, and when Louis ran away, I knew I was right," Daisy said. "I know I was *crudele*, so cruel to Michele, but, *Dio mi perdoni*, Michele wasn't a good boy. He was always getting into trouble. I knew he'd do something that would break my heart, and I couldn't bear to lose another son, I just couldn't."

"So you let him believe you were dead," Bria said.

Daisy grimaced at the comment, but she couldn't run away from it. It was the truth. "I wanted to reach out to him . . . I wanted to reach out to Teresina so many times, but how could I? What would I say to them? How could I explain the horrible thing I had done? I stayed away from everyone and kept to myself. I didn't allow anyone else into my life."

"Until Tobias found you," Bria said.

"Somehow I made it to Trebbin, the town outside Berlin where Tobias was working," Daisy explained. "I was living on the streets and had fallen ill . . . an infection. Tobias found me collapsed in a park, so close to death, so close to getting what I deserved. But he intervened and saved my life."

"You were my salvation." Tobias looked deep into Daisy's eyes, and for the first time, they looked the same. They were both brimming with tears. "Before I met you, I was merely existing. I didn't understand a thing about life or about living, despite being a doctor and literally saving lives on a daily basis. The moment I saw you, that simple, exquisite moment, I understood love."

"And there isn't anything you wouldn't do to protect that love," Bria said.

"Not a thing," Tobias replied.

"Including murder."

Finally, Daisy turned to face Bria. Her words had snapped the woman back to reality. They were more interesting to her than her own thoughts and memories. They were also more confusing.

"What are you talking about?" Daisy asked. "Tobias is a doctor. He saves lives. He doesn't take them."

"Unless he needs to avenge the woman he loves," Bria stated.

Slowly, fear crept into Daisy's face, and Bria fought the urge to turn away, because it was frightening to watch. She was bearing witness to a woman as she took the journey from thinking her husband was a good man to believing he was capable of performing the worst evil of all. To understanding that he would kill for her.

"No," Daisy whispered. "Tobias, tell her she's wrong."

When Tobias remained silent, Daisy grew more frantic. "Tobias, please! Tell Bria she's wrong, that you could never do such a thing."

"I did what any husband would do." Tobias's voice was steady and clear. "I protected my wife from experiencing the kind of pain that would destroy her."

"*Dio mio, no*," Daisy muttered. "This can't be true. Please, God, tell me this isn't true."

Tobias tried to grab hold of Daisy, but she pushed his hand away. She was seeing his true light for the first time.

"You killed my son!" Daisy cried, her voice filled with revulsion. "You killed Louis!"

"I couldn't risk him breaking your heart again," Tobias

replied. "I knew that you wouldn't be able to survive. I knew that this time your suicide wouldn't be a fake, and I could not let that happen."

"I can't believe this," Daisy said. "I can't believe you would do such a thing."

Daisy looked toward the sea, then back at the church. She gripped the railing even tighter in an attempt to steady herself from the onslaught of emotions she was feeling. "We came here so I could see him again. So I could see his face."

"That would never have been enough, and you know it," Tobias said.

"How interesting that you'd know that, Tobias, since you said you don't have children," Bria said. "Which I thought was odd, because Daisy inferred that she did."

"She never forgot that no-good excuse for a son," Tobias said.

"Don't speak about him like that," Daisy seethed.

"You would never have been able to look at him from afar. You'd want to look into his eyes, and you'd want to hold him, feel his ungrateful flesh against yours," Tobias ranted. "You'd want to tell him that you forgive him for shattering your life!"

"Because I do!"

"I know you do! That's why I did what I did!" Tobias banged his fist on the railing and slowly fought to control the powerful emotions that had been released. "I knew from the first day you found his book filled with all your recipes that you wouldn't rest until you saw him again."

"That's how you stumbled upon the fact that Louis had reinvented himself as Chef Lugo," Bria said.

"We were at a bookstore, and I saw all the blood drain from Daisy's face when she saw his photo on the cover," Tobias explained. "She almost fainted right there, and I had to hold her up. She didn't offer an explanation. She just bought the book, and we went home. Later she told me who he was, and we discovered that all the recipes he claimed were his own were actually Daisy's."

"You mean Mamma Rita's," Bria clarified.

"Yes." Tobias nodded. "Not only had this despicable human being betrayed the woman who saved him, but he also got rich off stealing from her! I've saved many criminals in the emergency room, and I've gotten to be a good judge of who should live and who should die."

"You played God with Chef Lugo's life and decided he needed to be executed for his deeds," Bria stated.

Tobias took a moment to ponder Bria's comment before answering. "Yes."

"No," Daisy corrected. "We didn't come here to kill Louis. I wanted to speak with him. That's why I put the note in the fake croissant Pippa made."

"Which is when Tobias knew he had to do something drastic," Bria said.

"I wasn't sure if a coward like Louis would actually meet with Daisy, but if he did, I knew it wouldn't end well," Tobias said. "I had to prevent the meeting from ever happening."

"How?" Daisy asked. "How did you do it?"

"By putting poison on the lavender-scented towels," Bria explained.

"What?" Daisy cried.

"Pippa told us that Chef Lugo put the towels on his face and breathed in the scent to calm him down before making a television appearance," Bria explained. "Tobias made sure that when he took a sniff of one of the towels, it would be his last."

"That's a very clever way to kill someone, Bria," Tobias said. "But a hard one to prove."

"Not if you put all the clues together," Bria asserted. "Luca didn't make it publicly known, but the poison found on the towels was oleander."

"How could that clue link Tobias to the murder?" Daisy asked.

"It's the name of the book Tobias was reading. *White Oleander*," Bria said. "Marco thought the towels smelled like candy, and oleander has a sweet vanilla scent. When you told Marco the other day that he saved Bravo's life, because chocolate could be poisonous to a dog, things started to click."

"Purely circumstantial," Tobias said.

"On its own, yes," Bria said. "But you had access to the towels. And you were the one who pointed out to Pippa that she had forgotten the box they were in, perhaps because you had brought them to your room to lace them with poison? You're a doctor, so I'm sure it wasn't hard for you to get the poison. I don't know where you got the oleander, but that should be easy for the police to find out. It should also be easy for them to find your fingerprints on the towels."

"Too bad you didn't use one of the towels to calm yourself down before you went live on TV," Tobias growled. "You would have died along with that bastard."

"Tobias!" Daisy cried.

"You don't know how close you were to getting that wish fulfilled," Bria said. "Lugo offered me one of the towels, but we were interrupted by Massimo. I guess I owe the kidnapper my thanks."

"Tobias, this isn't true. It can't be," Daisy pleaded. "You aren't a vengeful man."

"He is, Daisy," Bria said. "He also tried to kill me twice."

"That isn't true!" Daisy protested.

"Tobias was with me on the Path of the Gods when I tripped and fell, and Tobias was the one who arrived right before I was hurt during my fencing match with Valentina," Bria said. "He took the rubber tips off the blades, hoping Valentina would kill me."

"It was your own fault, Bria," Tobias said. "You're relentless, and you were getting too close to the truth."

"You were going to kill Bria, too?" Daisy gasped.

"I had to! If she discovered I was the one who killed Lugo, who would protect you?" Tobias asked.

"The sad truth is that it was all for nothing," Bria said.

"No it wasn't," Tobias protested. "That man is out of Daisy's life for good, and his lies will be exposed."

"Had you let things alone, you would have witnessed Lugo expose his lies all on his own," Bria said.

"What are you talking about?" Tobias asked.

"Lugo was going to confess to the world that he was a fraud," Bria explained. "Mamma Rita would have been vindicated, and maybe she and Lugo would have rebuilt their relationship. Instead, your wife gets to mourn the death of another son, thanks to you."

"That's impossible!" Tobias cried.

No one noticed that Luca and Nunzi had walked up behind them until Luca spoke. "It's all true. Tobias Kruger, I'm placing you under arrest for the murder of Louis Gordon."

"No!" Daisy cried.

"Forgive me, *meine Geliebte*." Tobias kissed Daisy on the lips passionately and then placed his palms on the railing. He started to hoist himself over the railing, and Daisy screamed. On the other side of the railing was nothing but certain death.

Luca and Nunzi lunged toward Tobias, and even though the man was quite athletic for someone his age and determined to avoid capture, Luca and Nunzi were able to subdue him. Luca grabbed Tobias underneath his arms and Nunzi grabbed his legs just before they swung over the railing. Together, they pulled him back and didn't let go of him until he was safely on the ground and in handcuffs.

"Why, Tobias?" Daisy asked. "You wanted to protect me, and now you've made it so I'm entirely alone."

"That isn't true."

Daisy thought she recognized the voice, but no, it couldn't possibly be who she thought it was. When she turned around she knew her instinct was right. She saw her sister standing in front of her, the sister she had abandoned, along with her entire family so many years ago, and although she never thought Teresina looked more beautiful, the sight was too much for Daisy to bear. She had just learned her husband, her savior, had murdered the man she considered a son, and now the sister she had thought she'd never see again was standing in front of her. She let out a cry filled with deep shame, covered her face in her hands, and fell to her knees.

Bria resisted the urge to help Daisy to her feet, because she knew that job belonged to Teresina. When Bria figured out Tobias, and not Massimo, was the one who had killed Lugo and that Daisy was Mamma Rita, she knew she had to inform Teresina. She sent her a text telling her to meet her here. She knew it was a gamble, but Bria also understood that the bond between two sisters was unbreakable. She wanted to make sure Teresina saw Daisy before she left the village. If she was wrong about Daisy's true identity, Teresina would have made a wasted trip. If she was right—which she was—it meant the estranged sisters could finally be reunited.

"*La mia sorellina*," Teresina said, tears streaming down her face.

Teresina closed her eyes and made the sign of the cross to thank God for bringing her sister home to her. She then knelt down and took Daisy's hands away from her face so she could look at her. She wanted Daisy to know that her sister had returned to her, as well.

"Rita, I can't believe it's you," Teresina said.

"*Dio mi perdoni per quello che ho fatto*," Daisy begged.

Teresina looked her sister in the eye. Her voice and her gaze were unflinching when she said, "God has already forgiven you, or he would never have brought you back to me."

Daisy wrapped her arms around her sister with such love that it brought tears to Bria's eyes, and she had to look away. She had done more than she had set out to do, and she was filled with gratitude and pride. All she had wanted to do was bring Chef Lugo's real killer to justice. She had never thought she'd bring a family back together.

She wasn't the only one feeling overwhelmed. When she wiped her eyes, she turned back and saw Luca staring at her. He was looking at her the same way Carlo did the first time they met. Bria knew what Luca was feeling, because she was feeling it, too.

She was falling in love.

EPILOGUE

When Bria heard Father Pasquale recite the Eucharistic prayer, she felt as if her heart was going to burst. It wasn't the first time she had heard the words, but it was the first time she had heard them as a mother. That made all the difference in the world. She watched Marco, wearing the same navy blue suit his father had worn when he received his Holy Communion, and the priest's words, the prayer, and the entire service took on a whole new meaning. Accepting the body and blood of Christ for the first time was a heady concept for anyone to grasp, especially a child, but Bria realized the ceremony meant so much more. It wasn't merely about the transformative experience of the individual. It was also about that of the community.

She looked around St. Cecilia's Church, at the faces of her friends and family who had come to bear witness to Marco's participation in this ancient ritual, and was filled with gratitude. Raising a son as a single parent wasn't easy, but Bria wasn't alone. She and Marco were part of an entire community. It appeared that almost the whole village of Positano had come out to support Marco as he took his first baby step toward adulthood.

After the Communion service, the Bartolucci and D'Abruzzo

families and their many friends gathered on Imperia's yacht to celebrate. After much debate, and with negotiating skills that would have served Churchill well, Bria had convinced her mother that the yacht was the most sensible place to hold the party due to its size and location. Just as deftly, Bria then had persuaded her mother-in-law to let her parents cater the event, since they were well adept at such a task as the owners of one of the most successful wedding banquet halls on the Amalfi Coast. Both Fifetta and Imperia had agreed, and most importantly, they had both felt as if they had triumphed.

Bria was feeling just as successful as she and Rosalie were sipping Aperol spritzes on the dock. It was a feeling that didn't last very long.

"Bria!" Imperia walked directly toward Bria, holding a rolled-up newspaper in her hand. "You are a terrible mother!"

"I thought you said Madame Iceberg was starting to thaw when it came to you?" Rosalie asked.

Bria shrugged her shoulders. "We must have gotten our signals crossed."

"I can't believe you would do this to your own son on his special day," Imperia said.

Before Bria could defend herself, her mother did it for her. "Imperia Stalazito Bartolucci! You take back what you said."

Bria's mother and mother-in-law stood face-to-face, and Bria thought she was going to have to ask Nunzi to break out the handcuffs. Imperia opened up the newspaper she was holding and showed Fifetta the front page.

Fifetta turned to Bria and looked as smug and haughty as Imperia. "Bria, what's that thing you always say?"

"What thing?"

"That thing you say when you get to the market and can't believe you left your wallet at home," Fifetta replied.

Bria thought for a moment. *"Uffa?"*

"That's it!" Fifetta cried. *"Uffa, Bria!"*

"*Uffa* what, Mamma?" Bria asked.

"Imperia's right!" Fifetta cried. "You're trying to upstage your own son."

Fifetta turned the paper around so Bria could read the headline, and she finally understood what they were yelling about. Aldo Bombalino had run a special Sunday edition of *La Vita Positano* with Bria's face on the cover, under the headline BRIA BARTOLUCCI IS TWO FOR TWO. The message referenced an earlier murder that Bria had helped solve. Even though there was truth in Aldo's reporting, Bria hadn't asked for any publicity.

"That's okay, Mamma," Marco said, sharing his *pizzella* with Bravo. "I don't mind sharing the spotlight with you."

It didn't matter that Bria was wearing high heels and a yellow silk dress. She bent down and scooped her son up in her arms. She swung him around and delighted in Marco's laughter. He was her joy, her reason for living, and no matter who else came into her life, Marco would always remain her number one priority.

She took a bite of his *pizzella*, and while she had loved the sweet vanilla taste since childhood, it now reminded her of the scent of Chef Lugo's deadly perfumed towels. It would take a while for that smell and the image of Lugo dying to fade from her memory, but she knew she'd have plenty of memories to take their place. Like watching Marco run toward Fabrice and Giovanni. Bria forgot about Lugo and was delighted that Marco had good, strong men in his life to use as examples of what it was like to be a man, now that Carlo was no longer around. It was important, because otherwise he could wind up like Massimo or Tobias and make disastrous choices that were hard to forgive. Both men were on their way to stand trial, and Tobias at least would be spending the rest of his life in a prison cell. Some men, however, could turn their lives around.

Michele was talking with his *zio* Paolo and Enrico on the other side of the yacht. Bria assumed he was filling them in on his meeting with Daisy, his Mamma Rita. After Tobias was taken into custody, she and Michele had met privately. Bria imagined it had not been easy for either of them to see each other after all this time, but it had been necessary. She didn't know if the meeting had ignited the healing process or if it had simply been a farewell, but she was happy they both had agreed to meet.

"Will you be seeing Michele again?" Bria asked.

"Yes, but I have decided for once in my life to take things slow," Rosalie replied. "Now that I know for certain he isn't a cold-blooded murderer, I'd like to get to know him better before getting involved with him."

"Mussolini!" Bria cried.

Heads turned, but the women ignored them and laughed like the little girls they were when they first met.

"You don't need our safeword," Rosalie said.

"Are you sure?" Bria asked. "Because I think someone snatched your body and replaced it with an imposter. You don't sound anything like my Rosalie."

"I've decided to give being an adult a try," Rosalie replied. "At least for the next six months. After that, who knows?"

"*Salute!*" they both said as they clinked their glasses, and then they took sips of their drinks.

"What about you?" Rosalie asked.

"What do you mean?"

"Are you going to meet with my brother again to discuss things other than dead bodies and toxicology reports?"

Bria turned to the left to avoid Rosalie's stare and found herself directly in Luca's line of vision. The man got better looking every time Bria laid eyes on him. Luca wore a sky-blue sports jacket, a white shirt, and navy blue pants paired with his favorite loafers. Casual, relaxed, and very handsome. Luca raised his glass and smiled, and Bria did the same. She suddenly felt self-conscious, that all eyes were on her, and she

344 / MICHAEL FALCO

wasn't entirely wrong. She glanced to the side and caught her sister watching her. Lorenza proved that she could be less subtle than Rosalie at her most outspoken and ran over to her sister faster than anyone wearing three-inch Ferragamo heels should be able to do.

"Bria, is there something you want to tell me?" Lorenza asked.

"No," Bria replied.

"I'll tell you," Rosalie offered.

"Rosalie!"

"Luca's my brother."

"What's that got to do with anything?" Bria asked.

"If you're in a relationship with my brother, that makes me involved."

"You're really in a relationship with Luca?" Lorenza squealed.

Bria replied, "No," as Rosalie shouted, "Yes."

"I believe Rosalie," Lorenza said.

"Renza!" Bria cried. "I'm your sister."

"Which means you won't tell me the truth," Lorenza replied. "Rosalie, I can trust."

"*Grazie!*" Rosalie said.

"*Prego*," Lorenza replied.

"*Basta!*" Bria exclaimed. "We women have to stick together when it comes to men."

"What about when it comes to other women?" Rosalie asked.

"What do you mean?" Bria replied.

Rosalie tilted her head toward the sea. "Don't look now, but the wicked witch of Positano is speeding this way."

They heard the roar and then saw the speedboat. Valentina was at the wheel, dressed like a movie star, wearing oversize white sunglasses, a white bikini top, and an orange and pink floral sarong tied around her waist that flowed in the wind.

Her perfect accessory—a Speedo-wearing Adonis who looked like he was fifth generation Sicilian—was lounging in the chair behind her, next to Genie, who looked more interested in the Adonis than she had Bravo.

Even without binoculars, Bria could tell the man had less body fat and more muscle mass than Giovanni. Bria wasn't surprised by Valentina's choice in companion, but she was surprised by her choice to stay in town.

When Dante finally read Lugo's will, which Massimo had not been able to revise, it was revealed that Valentina was the sole beneficiary. Luca advised her that she would probably have to settle with Daisy to compensate her for the theft and the use of her recipes. Despite having to share the wealth, Valentina would still become a multimillionaire. Bria, like most everyone else in the village, assumed—or maybe *hoped* was the more accurate word—that Valentina would flee Positano to live the life of a jet-setting socialite. Valentina had other plans.

Valentina expertly guided the speedboat next to the yacht and let it idle as she greeted the partygoers.

"Imperia!" Valentina cried. "You must tell me where you got your yacht. I may be in the market for my own."

"Please tell us it's so you can sail around the world!" Rosalie shouted.

"Why would I leave?" Valentina yelled. "Positano is the most glorious place on earth. I'm not going anywhere!"

"*Dio mio*," Bria sighed.

"My gut instinct isn't as good as yours, Bria," Lorenza said, "but even I can tell that one's gonna be trouble."

"*Cin cin!*" Valentina cheered, before gunning the engine and speeding her boat up the coast.

When Bria saw the stern of the boat, she cracked up laughing. Valentina had named her boat *The Merry Widow*, proving that she at least had a sense of humor about herself.

The rest of the party went off without a hitch. They ate, they drank, Annamaria pushed Mimi and Enrico together to dance a slow version of "That's Amore," and Pippa and Nunzi took turns beating Matteo at bocce. The sun began to set, and when the sky shifted from blue to orange, the lights from the village came on to cast a soft, radiant glow that reached all the way to Luca as he stood next to Bria.

"You look beautiful."

"*Grazie*," Bria replied. "You look very handsome yourself."

"Thank you."

"I . . . ," they said in unison.

When they realized they had both spoken at the same time, they laughed. Happy, unrestricted laughter. There was an undeniable attraction. Where it would lead, Bria had no idea, but she was ready to find out. "Would you like to have dinner?"

Luca caught his breath and wasn't sure he had heard correctly, so Bria repeated her question.

"Would you like to have dinner . . . with me?" Bria asked.

This time, Luca was prepared and answered quickly and decisively.

"Yes, I would love to have dinner with you, Bria."

Bria couldn't think of anything else to say, so she smiled.

"Bria Bria!" Fabrice cried. "We need Luca to play a game of soccer with Marco."

Men in suits playing soccer on a yacht was not the smartest thing to do, but it was Marco's party, so he called the shots. She watched Luca join the game, and every once in a while, she caught him looking over at her. She turned away to face the sea and immediately felt the presence of another man. Carlo. Bria smiled when she heard Carlo's voice—reminding her as he had so many times when he was alive—that the sea was like life: you could never see where it ended, but you never wanted it to end.

"Oh, my Carlo," Bria whispered. "I will always carry you in my heart, but it's time to see what else life has in store for me."

This time the wedding band slid off her finger easily. She brought it to her lips and kissed it, then tucked it away in the pocket of her dress. Her left hand, bare for the first time in a decade, didn't look lonely or wrong. It looked like a blank canvas filled with possibilities.

Bria was surrounded by magic. The setting sun, the looming mountains, the dazzling village of Positano, which she now called home. The laughter, the shouting, the beautifully familiar voices of her family and friends. And the memories, the ones that she treasured and the ones that she couldn't wait to make. It was as if her past, present, and future melded together to fill Bria with a calm joy.

This was one of those moments that Bria would remember forever. It was one of the moments that would change her life. Because it was the moment that Bria Bartolucci knew anything was possible.

A little bit more about Positano Cafés.

Without any murder!

There are tons of cafés dotted all throughout Positano as well as the entire Amalfi Coast. I visited many when I was in Italy and they were all welcoming and tourist-friendly. In the ones that I encountered I found that the staff spoke several languages and always English, the menus were wide-ranging and offered all the typical baked goods you'd expect—plus many you didn't even know existed—along with pizza, salads, and sometimes burgers and pasta dishes.

Of course a café wouldn't be a café if it didn't serve coffee. I was not surprised to discover that Italy has some of the finest coffee I'd ever tasted. What was eye-opening for me, however, was that every single café I went to offered non-dairy milk as well. I was truly stunned by that. When I'm in Pennsylvania I have to carry my own almond milk with me because I don't like to drink coffee black and for some reason restaurants in Pennsylvania don't believe in lactose intolerance. The Keystone State could learn something from the country shaped like a boot.

There's a very simple reason why cafés are so popular in Italy. Think about it. Running a café is something the Italians do very well because it comprises all the things Italians are known for—good food, good drink, and good hospitality. No matter which café you pop into, you're guaranteed to have an experience you'll remember for years to come.

When I first arrived in Positano, I was jet-lagged, sweaty, and couldn't check into my hotel for another three hours, but I was determined to behave like a true tourist and drink before noon! It was Pupetto Café to the rescue and it turned out to be the ideal entrée to the Positano lifestyle.

Located right on Fornillo Beach, Pupetto Café is the perfect place to have a cappuccino or an Aperol spritz while taking in the breathtaking views of the Tyrrhenian Sea. It's part of the Hotel Pupetto Positano, so it's well-maintained and managed. But you don't have to book a room to enjoy the café, just meander over, sit in a chair underneath the orange and white striped awning, and bask in the glory that is the Amalfi Coast.

Pupetto Café offers a relaxed atmosphere, stunning views, and a delicious menu so there's absolutely nothing not to like about it. My first meal was a limoncello spritz and a Caponata salad, which is tuna, tomato, olives, and mozzarella. Like every single meal I had in Italy, this one was incredibly fresh and tasty. The most unexpected part of my dining experience was the price. It was cheap! Under 25 euros for a filling, tasted-like-homemade lunch. Needless to say I went back to Pupetto Café several times during my stay.

https://www.pupettobeachclub.it/

Another must-visit café I popped into often was Collina Bakery, which is located in the heart of Positano in Piazza dei Mulini. This is a more traditional café nestled in the village that has an infectious Italian energy. It also has a very modern vibe because its menu is vegetarian friendly and even includes several vegan options among its long list of pastries.

I would often drop in while I was shopping or heading down to the marina to catch a ferry to get an iced cappuccino with almond milk, a croissant, and whatever kind of pastry that had chocolate in it whether it was vegan or not. Yes, I know that chocolate has dairy in it, but that's why I always carry my Lactaid pills with me. I take one before consuming most dairy products and I usually don't have an issue. For whatever reason the pills don't work for me if I drink milk or very creamy cheeses like ricotta or burrata, which is why I simply stay away from them. But enough about me, more about the café!

In the evening Collina Bakery is still the place to go mainly because of its ice cream selection. I had the best gelato I've ever had in my life thanks to their chocolate vegan flavor. Super creamy and dairylicious—even though it's dairy-adjacent—and definitely worth the calories!

https://www.collinabakery.com/

If you want to bring a little bit of an Italian café into your own home, it's not as hard as you might think. I've learned that baking is not part of my skill set, so I'm not going to share any recipes with you. My tip: If you aren't a skilled baker like Fifetta or Annamaria, go to a real bakery and buy *sfogliatella*, *bombolone*, *mustacciuoli*, or whatever Italian pastry your stomach is craving.

Here's an extra trip: If you live in an area where you can't find any good Italian bakeries, just go online! SupermarketItaly.com is an online grocery store that sells every kind of Italian food you can imagine. Meats, pastas, desserts—you'll find it all.

If you *are* feeling adventurous and want to try and make your own pastries, they even sell Italian flour. What's the difference between regular flour and Italian flour, you ask? Well, I've already told you that baking isn't my forte, which means I have no idea either! If you find out, please let me know!

https://supermarketitaly.com/

Although I'm not a baker, I'm not a bad bartender. In the first book in the Bria Bartolucci series, *Murder in an Italian Vil-*

lage, I mentioned in the back section that a friend, who's a tour guide, took me on an excursion throughout Capri. One of the many highlights of that day was having a Hugo spritz at Hotel Quisisana.

The experience was extra special for me because my father's middle name was Hugo. I never found out why my grandmother chose the name Hugo, but it's always stuck out as odd to me and not particularly Italian even though it is a very Italian name. When I got back home from my trip and was going through Positano withdrawal, I was able to quell some of the heartache by making my own Hugo spritz. Trust me, the recipe is much easier than the one for *sfogliatella*, and the finished product is arguably more satisfying.

To make your own Hugo spritz, you'll need the following:

- 1.5 ounces of elderflower liqueur (I don't know what that is either, but it's yummy!)
- 8-12 mint leaves, making sure to leave some for garnish
- 2 ounces of Prosecco
- 2 ounces of sparkling water
- Lime wheels for garnish (If you don't know how to make a lime wheel—or even what one is for that matter—do what I did and go to YouTube for a video instruction!)

Esoteric ingredients like elderflower liqueur and mint leaves might lead you to believe that you need a PhD in mixology to create a Hugo spritz, but the recipe is astonishingly simple. Here's all you need to do:

- Fill a wineglass with ice
- Add the elderflower liqueur and mint leaves
- Stir to combine, gently smashing the mint leaves as you stir

- Add the Prosecco and sparkling water to the top, but don't stir them in
- Top it off with some mint sprigs and lime wheels

And voila! Or actually *ecco*! Because *ecco* is Italian for voila! No matter what language you like to shout in, you won't be shouting for long because once you taste how delicious and decadent your Hugo spritz is, you'll feel a sense of calm wash over you. And you'll feel just as peaceful—and Italian—as Bria does at the end of the book.

Ci vediamo al terzo libro! That means 'see you in book three,' which incidentally will be titled *Murder in an Italian Piazza*. But that's all I'm going to tell you about it now. You—and Bria—will just have to wait until murder strikes Positano for the third time. Until then . . .

Ciao,
Michael Falco